Memoirs of Franz Schreiber

Berlin between the Wars

Charles P. Sharkey

Ringwood Publishing

Glasgow

Copyright © Charles P. Sharkey 2018

All rights reserved

The moral right of the author has been asserted

First Published in Scotland in 2018 by

Ringwood Publishing, Glasgow

www.ringwoodpublishing.com

mail@ringwoodpublishing.com

ISBN 978-1-901514-64-3

British Library Cataloguing-in Publication Data

A catalogue record for this book is available from the British Library

Printed and bound in the UK by

Lonsdale Direct Solutions

Acknowledgements

As with my two previous novels, I am grateful for the help and encouragement of family and friends, in particular, my partner, Lesley Walker, for her continued support in what is a very demanding and selfish occupation.

I also grateful to my friends, James Blake and John McDonnell for their proof reading and valued constructive criticism. I also wish to thank my editor at Ringwood Publishing, Eleni Mina, and all those interns who proofread the final draft before publication.

I am grateful to Henri Guéguen for agreeing to contribute original artwork for the front cover of the book.

About the Author

Charles Sharkey previously worked for 25 years as a criminal lawyer in Glasgow, before retiring in 2015 to pursue other interests.

He now runs his own garden design and landscaping business, while continuing his career as a novelist.

Memoirs of Franz Schreiber is his third novel following *Dark Loch* (2014) and *The Volunteer* (2016), both of which were published by Ringwood Publishing.

He has spent time living and working in Germany. He is also a singer-songwriter who has had a number of songs recorded by other artists. His first studio album *Strange Hotel* was well-received and he is working on a follow up CD.

Chapter 1

Berlin 1916

I have only one memory of my father which has not faded with time. Dressed in his uniform, he is standing with my mother in the hallway, her eyes wet with tears. The morning light was shining through the door's stained-glass panels as they held each other in silence. Being five years old at the time, I also cried, and the more they ignored me, the louder I cried. They only broke off their embrace and turned to me when my tears lapsed into a fit of coughing. Father kneeled before me and smiled. No longer ignored, I stopped crying and Mother wiped my cheeks as Father spoke to me, but what he said I do not recall. He then kissed my forehead and looked at me with his sad eyes, that I did not know at the time were saying goodbye forever.

Over the next few days, Mother cried often and spent much of the time in her room. When she was less upset, she would sometimes read Father's letters to me as though I understood what the futility of war meant, or who the Kaiser was. I found out later Father was stationed on the Western Front at Verdun, some 140 miles from Paris, where the German and French armies had fought each other to a standstill.

To help with the war effort, Mother took on voluntary work, knitting socks and gloves for the soldiers at the front, often leaving the housekeeper, Gretchen, to look after me and keep me out of mischief. Gretchen was in her early twenties; pretty, with blonde hair which she wore in braids. She lived in the servants' quarters at the top of the stairs with the cook, Frau Schwartz, and the cook's son Günter, who was almost two years older than me. Although he was very thin, Günter was tall for his age, distinctive, having been born with a squint in his left eye and two exceptionally big ears that stuck out from his blond hair like jug handles.

One day, when Gretchen was too busy with her housework, she left me in the basement nursery with Günter, who was instructed to look after me. He put me on my rocking horse before looking through my toy box and taking out my tin soldiers. He then lined them up ready for battle. I demanded he take me down from the rocking horse, but he ignored my pleas as he exploded imaginary shells onto the battlefield. The bombardment did not last very long, and the tin soldiers were soon scattered about the floor in the rout. Once he had defeated my defenceless toys, he took me off the rocking horse, and climbed on to show me how a Hussar would charge into battle with his sabre cutting down the enemy. After numerous engagements with his imaginary foe, he dismounted and began rummaging through my box of toys again for something else to play with.

Eventually he took my favourite toy, a teddy bear Father had given me, and threw it across the room to see if it could fly. Even I knew Teddy could not fly, and it landed on the polished wooden floor, before skidding all the way up to the skirting board. Throwing the glass ball that snowed was not one of my better ideas, and Günter's attempt to stop me was too late. The ball left my hand and crashed on the floor. Glass scattered in every direction and a pool of water spread the speckles of fake snow across the parquet floorboards. We heard Mother calling for someone to see what had happened. Günter grabbed my hand and we hid in the corner behind a chest of drawers. The door opened, and Frau Schwartz came in, her face still flushed with the heat of the kitchen.

'Günter, come out at once!' she shouted, her voice reverberating around the nursery. We both cowered with fright. Günter looked at me pleadingly, lifting a finger to his lips, but instead of saving him from his mother's wrath, I selfishly stood up and pointed at him. He looked at me as though I had stabbed him in the back with his Hussar's sabre. While the cook gave her son a verbal thrashing, she patted me on the head with her heavy hand, which was more used to kneading dough than showing affection. The unhappy Hussar was led away by the scruff of the neck, while I gathered up my tin soldiers and put them back into my toy box to fight another day.

I was alone with my toys for a while before Gretchen came in to clean up the mess. I tried to help and began to pick up the pieces of glass. Gretchen slapped me hard on the hand and shouted at me to leave the glass alone. I knew it was time to scream, but only a whimpering sound came from my throat as the tears welled in my eyes. Gretchen was too kind to see me in such a state and whispered in my ear as she knelt to cuddle my quivering body.

'Poor Günter was beaten by his mama and only told her it was you who threw the glass ball when she took the belt to him. Poor Günter ... Bad Franz.'

'Poor Günter ... Bad Franz,' I sobbed.

I soon forgot about Günter now Gretchen had become my friend again, letting me hold the tin bucket while she emptied the dustpan of broken glass. With the floor mopped clean, and the evidence of my fit of madness expunged from the nursery, Gretchen took me by the hand into the kitchen where Frau Schwartz was busy making lunch.

Despite of the austerity caused by the war, Frau Schwartz did her best to make pickled cabbage and cold potato salad edible, and we ate what Mother said others in the city would be glad of. At least Frau Schwartz's strudel, dripping with warm custard, was always tasty and I licked the plate clean. Günter, according to his mother, was still in the doghouse, and had his lunch in his room.

Afterwards Mother played the piano for a while, but

soon complained of being tired and went to her room to read Father's letters. With no music to listen to I was bored and went to the pantry, where Gretchen was taking stock of what little stores we had left. She smiled at me when I asked if Günter was still in the doghouse. 'No, my Liebchen,' she said, which she always called me when I was not being bad. 'He is in his room learning his alphabet.'

'What is an alphabet?'

'It's ... ' she hesitated, having to think for a moment. 'It's what we use to make words.'

While Gretchen went back to organising the ladder, I began to imagine Günter dressed as a wizard, wearing a pointed black hat with the crest of the moon on the front, waving a magic wand, while stirring a pot filled with the alphabet. I left the pantry and made my way to the stairs, wondering if Günter was busy with the toads and bats my story books insisted made a good magic brew.

I began to climb the stairs, but the light from below did not want to follow me and the way ahead became quite dark. I tried to reach the light-switch on the landing, but it was out of reach. A little frightened, I crawled up the last flight of narrow stairs and along the corridor. I listened for a moment outside one of the rooms and heard Günter making words. 'A ... B ... C ... D ... E ... ' Still on my knees, I knocked on the door, calling his name in a whisper. The door opened and Günter stood there in his underpants, looking nothing like the wizard I had imagined. He did not have a pointy hat, and instead of a wand he had a half-chewed pencil in his hand. He helped me to my feet and took me into the room. I could not see the mysterious alphabet anywhere. Günter sat on his bed and opened a large book and began to read from it. 'A ... B ... C ... ' I sat on the floor and listened. I asked him where he kept the alphabet, but he ignored me, continuing to read. When nothing magical happened, I became bored and left him to make his words in peace.

With the winter over, Gretchen took me to the local park for the first time, where I noticed two soldiers walking around with the aid of crutches. I asked Gretchen what had happened to their missing legs. 'The war,' she sighed, pointing to a building at the far end of the park which had a red cross painted on the sloping roof and where she said the wounded soldiers lived until they got better. I could not understand how they would get better if they only had one leg. Would they grow new ones?

While I was feeding the ducks and thinking about the soldiers' missing legs, an old man pushed an ancient contraption up the path near to where we were sitting. He began to turn a handle, making music ring out across the park. A crowd gathered, and I pulled at Gretchen's hand to come with me and stand in front of the man, who was smiling through a wispy grey beard, showing an unsightly ruin of discoloured teeth.

After a few more turns of the handle, the music stopped, and the man removed his cap from his bald head, holding it out with pleading eyes. Gretchen gave me a few pfennigs and I threw them, half frightened, into the man's dirty cap.

The summer days passed with more walks in the park, until one day there was an air of excitement about the house. I thought Father had decided to come home, but it was not my father, but Günter's father, a war hero, who was returning after spending nearly a year in a military hospital recovering from the British shell Günter said blew up his trench. Mother told me to stay out of the kitchen as it might upset me. Despite her warning, I was determined to see the returning hero, and when no one was paying me any attention, I ventured along to the anteroom next to the kitchen, where I sat quietly to wait for Günter's father to arrive.

From my hiding place, I could see most of the kitchen through the half-open serving hatch and noticed Mother was sitting beside Frau Schwartz, holding her hand as they stared at the side door. Günter sat opposite, his arms folded, anxiously swinging his legs under his chair. Gretchen was also there; busy peeling potatoes at the sink and humming a tune I had heard the organ grinder playing in the park the other day.

The vigil continued for some time, and I was beginning to feel sleepy when I heard the gravel path outside crunch under heavy boots. At least it sounded as though he had both his legs, I thought, as Frau Schwartz wiped her hands on her apron and got up to open the door.

Nothing in Gretchen's stories of ogres, witches and warlocks could have prepared me for the unfortunate man who entered the kitchen. Herr Schwartz had a face so disfigured my hands instinctively covered my eyes and I stared in horror at him through the gaps between my fingers. He had only one eye; the other empty socket was covered with skin stretched over it like pigskin on a drum. The whole left side of his face was twisted into fleshy folds, making it look as if it had simply melted in some great heat. When he removed his cap, out of politeness to Mother, his head was covered with gaps of raw baldness, which made him look like a badly plucked chicken. Unable to look at his father any longer, Günter got up and ran out of the kitchen in tears.

For the next few nights I had nightmares and asked Mother if she could tell Herr Schwartz to leave. Of course, she looked at me as though I was very heartless, but, for a while I was too scared to go anywhere near the kitchen in case I came across Günter's father.

While he was in the house, Herr Schwartz remained in the servants' quarters, never venturing downstairs. Mother said the poor man could no longer eat solid food and Frau Schwartz had to spoon-feed him like a baby. When I told her he was ugly, she scolded me and said he was a war hero and must be respected. I told her I hoped Father did not come back a war hero, which only made her cry.

I had all but forgotten about Günter's father, until one afternoon the quiet of the house was shattered with Gretchen's screams. I was in the nursery with Günter and we rushed into the hall where Mother was trying to make sense of Gretchen's hysterical behaviour. It came to pass that Herr Schwartz could no longer bear the pain and hanged himself with his army belt from the upstairs banister.

The next morning, Günter looked relieved when we watched the coffin being taken out to the hearse. With her husband gone, Frau Schwartz became very bitter about the war, especially the Kaiser, whom she blamed for starting it. 'The Kaiser is a pig,' she declared after the funeral, wiping tears from her face and lamenting her unfortunate husband's sacrifice.

It was not long before the war cast a shadow on our home for a second time. I was still in bed when the doorbell's persistent ringing woke me. A panic ran through my body when I heard an anguished shriek, followed by a dull thud on the hall floor. Still in my pyjamas, I rushed into the hall to see Mother lying on the floor with the postman kneeling at her side. Frau Schwartz and the postman helped Mother to her feet. She was clutching a brown envelope in her hand and wailing, making her sound in great pain. When I started crying, Gretchen took me by the hand into the kitchen, where she wiped my tears and gave me a sweet. 'There, there, my Liebchen, don't cry,' she said, as Günter stared at me, no doubt, with more understanding of what had happened than I had at the time.

Mother was taken to her room and spent the next few days in bed, while I tried to learn the alphabet with Günter. It was not until later I learned Father had been killed on the same day he penned his last letter to Mother.

Chapter 2

The war ended almost a whole year after Father was killed. Food was even more scarce with all the returning soldiers to feed, and we all lost weight. I was not sure if Günter's ears were getting bigger or his head was getting smaller, and according to Gretchen, he had to be careful in a strong wind in case he took off.

One morning Mother called on me to get dressed. Gretchen had already left to take Günter to school, so Frau Schwartz had to tie my shoelaces and comb my hair. I put on my warm winter coat, while Mother checked she had enough money in her purse before we left to look for bread.

We joined a long queue outside a baker's. I watched with envious eyes as those at the counter were being served with warm loaves and bagels. The nearer we got to the front of the queue the more anxious Mother became. I could hear her mumbling a 'Hail Mary,' as though the mother of Jesus was going to stop the loaves from disappearing off the shelves.

Soon, the last customer to be served pushed her way out into the street carrying her precious loaf tucked under her fur coat. The shop owner held up his hands and shook his head. Angry customers shouted abuse at him. I wondered what the word Jew meant, and why one man was blaming the baker for the country losing the war. Mother said nothing, but I could feel the despair in her cold hand as she clasped mine. We went back into the street with nothing to show for our patience.

Cold and hungry, we walked in silence until we eventually found another shop still selling bread. We waited for almost twenty minutes before Mother was able to exchange her ration coupons for two loaves and a piece of cheese. I now realised why Mother looked so exhausted every day.

Things only got worse, and during the next couple of years the country was on the verge of famine. On good days there would be food in the shops, on bad days there would be none. The poverty following the war resulted in riots in the streets against a government unable to feed its own people. Mother blamed the communists for all the trouble, but when I asked her who the communists were, she didn't seem to know. Still, at times like this, the best person to be around was Frau Schwartz, who always seemed to find something to cook for us.

'Your father was a good man,' she said one day, placing two pork sausages on the sizzling frying pan. 'If it wasn't for him we'd all have starved a long time ago.' This surprised me as much as seeing the thick sausages. Frau Schwartz had not spoken to me like this before, and I could not understand how my father managed to get us sausages from beyond the grave. My mouth salivated when she turned the pork meat in the hot fat and continued to talk of him as though he was still alive. I found out more about my father that day than I had ever learned from my mother, who rarely spoke of him after she fell and hit her head.

*

By the time I was nine years old, I had grown as tall as Günter, who seemed to slow down to let me catch up. At school I had top marks in most subjects, while Günter failed his exams so badly his mother was beside herself and could not understand why her son, who had done so well in previous years, had become a dunce overnight. It was not long before I discovered what had distracted Günter from his studies.

One day, when Mother was playing her piano in the parlour and Frau Schwartz was busy in the kitchen, I went up to Günter's room to help him with his homework. Günter was soon bored with the logic of arithmetic and seemed to have too much on his mind to concentrate on the simplest of sums.

After closing his exercise book in frustration, Günter smiled when we heard Gretchen singing in the next room. He led me out of his bedroom, putting his finger to his thin lips to hush me as we approached Gretchen's door. To my surprise, he stooped down to look through the keyhole. With a smile on his face, he eventually beckoned me to have a look. Even though I knew what we were doing was wrong, I was compelled to see what made him so excited. Lowering my head towards the keyhole, I immediately pulled away when I saw Gretchen standing naked in her bathtub. When he was sure I was over my initial shock, Günter nodded for me to take another look. Unable to resist the temptation, my heart was thumping while I watched Gretchen sponge the soapy water on her porcelain white skin as the sun from the window created a nimbus of light around her. She stopped singing and turned towards the door. I pulled away from the keyhole again, thinking she could see me spying on her. Günter grinned at the look on my face but decided I had seen enough. We returned to his room as Frau Schwartz called on Gretchen to come down and help her in the kitchen.

Günter never looked so happy, laughing with excitement at what we had just seen. I was still rather confused with the fact Gretchen had hair where her thing should have been and thought her more to be pitied than made fun of. Günter was beginning to doubt his wisdom in letting me look through the keyhole and took a penknife from his chest of drawers, cutting his thumb until it bled. 'We must become blood brothers, Franz,' he said, grabbing my wrist tightly. I tried to pull away when he nicked the top of my thumb and rubbed our blood together. He then made me promise never to mention what we had seen to anyone on pain of death. When I asked again about her missing thing, he assured me he had once seen his mother bathing when he was little, and she had none either. He told me all women and girls had none, which I found hard to believe. 'How did they pee?' Günter had still not worked out the answer to that question and shrugged his shoulders.

The next morning when we left for school, I refused to take Gretchen's outstretched hand. Günter was holding her other hand and grinning like an idiot.

Chapter 3

The years of austerity continued, and we became accustomed to the queuing, the rationing and even the hunger. When I complained about the meagre meals one day, Frau Schwartz told me we had a lot to be thankful for. At least we were better off than the poor unfortunates who had to scavenge in refuge bins to find something to eat. 'There for the Grace of God … ' she lamented, scraping the last of the jam from the bottom of one of her precious jars. I could not understand why being better off than someone who was starving would make me feel less hungry.

Günter must have been thirteen or fourteen years old when his face became plagued with spots. He squeezed them as soon as they became ripe, which only made them pop up somewhere else. He also took great care of his hair, which he combed in a middle parting whenever he was anywhere near a mirror, the symmetry of his hair only making his eyes look less aligned and his ears bigger than they already were. It was clear to me he was infatuated with Gretchen, and he became pitifully jealous when he discovered she had a boyfriend. I only found out later his name was Aaron, and that he worked at our local post office. Günter would go into a sulk whenever Aaron called to take Gretchen out for the evening, hiding himself in his room with only his spots for company. At first his mother teased him at his foolishness, but that was soon to change.

One morning I awoke to hear Mother trying to resolve a heated argument between Gretchen and Frau Schwartz in the kitchen. I got dressed and went into the hall to listen to the commotion. It was soon obvious to me Günter was the subject of the row. Gretchen was crying and complaining to Mother, how she caught Günter spying on her when she was in the bathtub. My knees began to feel weak, recalling the day when I spied on her with Günter, who had obviously made a habit of it.

'Lies, lies … My son is a good boy! You dirty Jew lover!' shouted Frau Schwartz, as Mother tried to keep her from hitting Gretchen.

'Your son had his hand down his trousers when I opened the door!'

'Never! This is not true, Frau Schreiber. My Günter would never do such a thing!'

'Your son is a monster!' shouted Gretchen.

Afraid Günter might try to incriminate me in his debauchery, I went upstairs to find out what he had been up to. His door was ajar, and he was lying on top of his bed with his pillow over his face. He looked as though he was trying to suffocate himself as he listened to the furore going on downstairs. He took the pillow away as soon as he heard the door creak open but said nothing. His face was drained of blood, except his spots, which made him look as if he had a touch of the measles. He was close to tears, and I knew for certain Gretchen had been telling the truth. I asked him why he had his hand down his trousers, but he stared at me as though I had poked him with a sharp stick. I sat on the end of his bed for a few minutes, watching him rock his head back and forward in obvious distress at the memory of his discovery.

'Günter, are you all right?'

He did not answer or even look at me but continued to rock his head back and forward like a demented sinner in deep contrition for his disgrace. Unable to offer him any solace, I left him to his torment.

With Gretchen downstairs and her room empty, I had a powerful urge to take another look through the keyhole into her bedroom. Her scent, which had obviously beguiled Günter, hung in the air around the door with the allure of a spell. I listened to the voices still arguing downstairs for a moment, then, with my heart beating fast, I leaned down to the keyhole. After a few seconds my eye adjusted to the light from the window, until I noticed the watering jug lying on its side on the dresser. The tin basin was on the floor, but thankfully Günter's Bathsheba was no longer in it to tempt my soul to lewdness. My fading memory refreshed, I descended the stairs in a state of grace.

Slightly flushed, I went into the kitchen, causing the quarrelling women to stop. Gretchen's eyes were red and puffy, but she had stopped crying. Frau Schwartz face was so red I could feel the heat from across the kitchen table. Mother was pale and smoking again.

Trying to remain calm, I greeted all in the room with a nonchalant, 'Good morning,' even though I knew it was far from being a good morning. I whistled nervously, while looking through the cupboards for something to eat. Gretchen responded to another slur from Frau Schwartz, by rushing from the kitchen in tears. We listened in silence as the front door opened and closed with a bang. Mother held up her hands in despair and went back to the sanctuary of her bedroom.

That evening, Mother, still looking pale, chain-smoked and drank glass after glass of sherry. Her voice was slurred, and I tried to get her to stop drinking, but she ignored my pleas, pouring herself another sherry. I became even more concerned when she started randomly talking to God, before staggering to her bed. Troubled with her behaviour, I was sure she was worried about something more serious than Günter putting his hand down his trousers outside Gretchen's bedroom.

The next morning the house was unusually quiet. Hungry, I went to the kitchen to see what Frau Schwartz was making for breakfast, but she was not there, and the stove was stone cold. Puzzled, I walked along the hall to Mother's room and knocked. She did not respond. I opened the door to speak to her, but she was not in her room. Feeling a little concerned, I ran upstairs to look for Günter. When I got to the upper floor his door was lying wide open. The bed was stripped of its bedding. I looked through his chest of drawers, which were empty of his things. I sat at the top of the stairs.

'What's the matter, Liebchen?' asked Gretchen, opening her door to find me crying, as much from hunger as anything else.

'You came back,' I said, wiping my face with the sleeve of my pullover. 'Where has everyone gone?'

'Frau Schwartz and Günter have gone to another house. Your mother can no longer afford to pay her,' she said, smothering me in her embrace the way she often did when I was little.

'Where has Mother gone?'

'She had to go to the market, she'll be back soon.'

For the first time ever, Gretchen took me into her room and let me sit on the end of her bed. I watched her in the mirror while she combed and plaited her hair. The watering jug was lying inside the tin basin in the corner and I blushed when she caught me looking at them.

Once she had finished weaving the strands of her hair, Gretchen put on her apron and we went down to the kitchen, where she made a breakfast of bread, cheese and pickles. It was strange not having Frau Schwartz in the kitchen, but I was glad it was her who left and not Gretchen.

Although I missed both Günter and his mother, life went on much as before. There was now more food to go around and Gretchen spent most of her time in the kitchen making the best of what we had. I even began to put on weight.

Just when things were getting better, I arrived home from school one day to find Mother and Gretchen in the front room. The atmosphere was one of despair. I noticed Mother had a roll of new banknotes in her hand. 'It won't even buy a loaf of bread,' she bemoaned, throwing the money onto the dining table and lighting a cigarette. 'We're ruined!'

'It can't be true,' exclaimed Gretchen.

'It's true all right. The country is bankrupt,' insisted Mother, pouring herself a large brandy.

'I can't believe all this is worthless,' lamented Gretchen, lifting a bundle of notes and staring at them.

'The mark has completely collapsed … I tried to buy coal, but this whole bag of money wasn't enough.'

'They can't be worthless,' I said, looking at the crisp new Reichsmarks lying on the table.

'Look,' snapped Mother, taking a handful of notes and throwing them into the fire. 'That's how worthless they are!'

A strange feeling came over me as I watched them burn. Even though she insisted they were useless pieces of paper, I was still consumed with an almost irresistible urge to stick my hand into the flames and rescue them. I turned to Gretchen and could see in her eyes she was thinking the same thing, but we were both paralysed by Mother's presence. We watched them burn in stunned disbelief.

While Mother poured herself another brandy, I walked over to the table and began to examine the rest of the banknotes; picking up what was left and putting them back into her handbag before she threw anymore into the fire. Clearly distressed, Mother took the bottle of brandy and went to her room for the rest of the day.

Over the next few days the morning papers reported the sudden, catastrophic collapse of the economy. Inflation, which had been bad enough since the end of the war, had got completely out of control. Money was being printed by the government at such a rate, what cost a mark one day, cost a thousand the next, and a hundred thousand the following day, until the currency was virtually meaningless. Father's careful investments were completely worthless, thwarted by the one variable he did not take into account; Germany losing the war.

Soon the country's ability to produce or import enough food had collapsed alongside the Reichsmark. Everything was scarce again, and Gretchen had to use all the skills she had learned from Frau Schwartz to make at least one hot meal a day. The rest of the time we went hungry.

Gretchen tried her best, but the daily rations she served were not enough to keep the pangs of hunger from gnawing at me all day. Mother would often say if we got through the next few days, things would get better. But things only got worse.

The city was in complete chaos, and bread riots returned to the streets. There was sporadic gunfire during some of these riots. The communists' calls for revolution could be heard on every street corner and the country was in danger of slipping into civil war. Going out, even during daylight hours, was fraught with danger and I was even forbidden from playing in the back garden in case I got hit by a stray bullet from one or other of the feuding factions. The government looked like it was about to topple at any minute.

In the desperate struggle for survival, life had become cheap and we read stories of whole families starving to death, while others with food to spare ignored their plight. Eating horsemeat had become commonplace, and there were even rumours of cannibalism, which I heard Gretchen speaking to a neighbour about. Mother said God had forsaken us for our sins and Germany had gone to Hell. Surely Hell wasn't this bad, I thought, as I got to my knees and prayed for God to do something.

Since the morning of the economy's devastating collapse, I had not returned to school but continued my studies at home while my stomach rumbled, and my fingers turned blue. During this desperate time, I kept myself busy in Father's library, which had become a place of refuge for me as the world outside slipped into the abyss. I continued my studies during the daytime and would read novels at night while Gretchen darned socks and Mother went through her depleted bag of jewellery, trying to decide which precious stone she was prepared to sacrifice to put bread on the table. She had become shrewd with her jewels after her initial naivety saw some of her more expensive pieces leave her hands for next to nothing.

The anarchy in the country culminated in a failed attempt by the Nazi Party to seize power in Munich. Mother, who had shown no interest in politics in the past, had become strangely fascinated with Adolf Hitler, who was languishing in Landsberg Prison awaiting trial for high treason. When I saw pictures of him in the newspapers, I was amused at his funny appearance and wondered how such a ridiculous little man could even think he could overthrow the government.

With the approaching winter, the house was cold, and most nights we sat together in the front room with our coats on, burning the last of the coal. One night, while I was reading my school books, all the lights in the house went out; from then on we lived by candlelight. The house became an eerie place of creaking floorboards and long shadows.

When the coal was gone we had to start breaking up furniture for the fire. I felt sad when I took a hammer to Günter's chest of drawers and his mother's old wardrobe. It would not be long before we had no furniture left, while the fire continued to devour everything we put into it in return for little heat. Thankfully, Mother managed to secure a couple of bags of coal in exchange for one of her fur coats, which saved the more valuable pieces of furniture. Food was the main problem; meat was impossible to find and even potatoes were hard to come by in the markets. We ate an inordinate amount of turnips, which Mother called swine food as she forced herself to keep it down.

The chaos in the country subsided a little when the government finally dealt with the madness of hyperinflation, which in the end had reached the farcical scenario that the Reichsmark was being printed in trillion-mark banknotes. This insanity only stopped when the government created a completely new currency, which they called the Rentenmark. To everyone's surprise, the change of banknotes stopped hyperinflation in its tracks. Mother could now sell her jewellery for the new mark, which would be accepted anywhere and not just on the black market, but her savings and Father's investments were lost forever.

The strain had taken its toll on Mother, who fell ill a few days before Christmas. She was confined to bed on her doctor's orders. Gretchen did the best she could for both of us. When our food and coal supplies began to run low, Mother took apart a brooch and gave Gretchen five diamonds to sell so we could have at least something decent to eat on Christmas Day.

I followed Gretchen into the hall as she put the diamonds into her purse. 'I will be back in an hour or so,' she said, fetching her coat from behind the door.

'I will come with you.'

'No, Liebchen, you stay here and look after your mother.'

'Mother is asleep, and we'll not be away long.'

'But Liebchen, what if she wakes up and there's no one in the house?'

'I'm not a child,' I said, with a tinge of anger in my voice. 'I'm going with you and stop calling me Liebchen.'

'Well, if you are going to get all upset … '

'I'm not upset. I just want to go with you.'

'Very well, Franz, if you insist.'

The tramcar was crowded, and I stood beside Gretchen as it screeched along the tracks into the city centre before turning east. I looked out at the city's grand buildings for a short while before the steam rising from everyone's damp clothes began to cloud the windows and the last of the daylight faded from the evening sky.

Eventually the tram stopped, and some of the passengers got off, allowing Gretchen to find a seat. Now forced back with the crush of new passengers, I was almost sitting on Gretchen's lap. The tram set off again and I had to hold on tight to the seat in front to keep my balance. With the shuffling movement of the carriage, the back of my legs began rubbing against her knees. I began to feel a rapid movement in my trousers, which every jolt of the tram exacerbated. Mortified, I could feel my face redden as I tried desperately to keep my trousers under control, but the crush only got worse when more passengers got on at the next stop. I moved forward again, only to be pushed back onto her legs. I began reading the notice of prohibitions above my head, anything to blank out the memory of Gretchen bathing, which had decided to occupy my mind at that moment. I did not realise there were so many things you were not allowed to do when riding a tramcar. Although having an erection was not one of the prohibitions mentioned, I was sure it was frowned upon.

Thankfully, when I ran out of tedious regulations to read, the tram stopped again, and Gretchen nudged me to get off.

Once in the street, the yellow glow from the gas-lamps and the constant drizzle of rain created a haze, making it difficult to see more than a few yards ahead. Gretchen studied a scrap of paper on which Mother had scribbled down the dealer's address and pointed across the road. I did not like the look of the place, and with some hesitation followed her along the rows of gloomy tenements.

We must have walked for over twenty minutes until I was sure we were lost. Eventually, we crossed another road towards a building which looked as though it was leaning on the one next to it. 'I think it's this one,' she said, looking at the piece of paper again. I followed her up to the second landing, until we stood in front of a door which had the name Kaufmann on it. She knocked, anxiously turning to me as though she was going to a dental appointment. We waited and listened in the semi-darkness, with only the faint light from one of the other apartments making it possible to see anything. Gretchen knocked again, and we heard someone walk slowly towards the door. There was a clatter of heavy metal locks and chains before the door finally opened.

'What do you want?' grunted an old man, with a thick Polish accent.

'We're looking for Herr Kaufmann,' said Gretchen.

'And who might I ask are you?'

'I'm here on behalf of Frau Schreiber, my name is Fräulein Gerber, and this is her son, Franz.'

'Frau Schreiber!' His wrinkled face cracked open with a smile, 'Well come in, have you something for me?'

'Yes,' said Gretchen, holding onto my arm as we followed him along a narrow hall into a room cluttered with junk, and lit with a couple of oil lamps. There was a birdcage hanging in front of the window and a parrot that squawked until the old man soothed it with words of comfort and a piece of mouldy cheese. A fusty smell of mothballs and stale beer hung in the air. We waited for Herr Kaufmann to stop feeding the parrot. 'Take a seat,' he said, putting a piece of cheese in through his beard to wherever his mouth was. 'Why is Frau Schreiber not here herself?'

'She is unwell,' said Gretchen as she sat down on a shabby looking sofa while I remained standing.

'Oh, that's unfortunate. Not too bad, I hope?'

'No,' I said. 'She will be fine in a few days.'

'Good, good ... What is it you have for me, already?'

Gretchen took out her purse and placed the five diamonds on the palm of her hand. Herr Kaufmann's eyes lit up and he produced a loupe eyeglass from his waistcoat, motioning for me to sit down. I sat next to Gretchen and watched the old man pick up one of the diamonds and scrutinize it for purity. With the oil lamp glowing on his head I noticed for the first time he was wearing a rather ill-fitting wig, which was so thick it must have been made of horsehair. It was combed to the side with a razor-sharp parting and I could see the empty holes where hair had once been. It must have vexed him, I thought, to have to go through the process of losing his hair for a second time. When he moved his head, the wig remained in the same position as though it floated on a thin layer of lubricant. While I investigated the flaws in his wig, he continued to examine each diamond in turn before putting away his eyeglass and taking a roll of banknotes from a well-worn leather wallet. After a few grunts he placed twenty crisp Rentenmarks on the sofa next to Gretchen, patting the money with the palm of his hand. 'For all five stones,' he said, with a tone of generosity which was seemingly causing him pain.

'No, that's nowhere near enough!'

'Oh, not so hasty, Fräulein Gerber,' said the cagey dealer. 'Thirty,' he offered, putting a further ten notes down one at a time, his face expressing increasing pain with each mark he parted with.

'You are trying to rob us,' I said, getting up. 'Let's go, we'll get a fairer price elsewhere.'

'What's your hurry, young man?' demanded Herr Kaufmann. 'How much are you expecting for these flawed stones?'

'They're not flawed, you're a crook ... Let's go Gretchen.'

'Who is it I'm doing business with, already?' asked the jewel dealer, looking over his spectacles at Gretchen and ignoring me. 'Is it you or the boy? Here, look for yourself,' he said, handing her the loupe. 'Remember the best stones must be of the highest clarity and cut. These are not.'

'Make us a fair offer,' said Gretchen, after a cursory look at one of the diamonds through the eyeglass. 'Frau Schreiber has told me what to accept.'

'Well, tell me how much you expect, and I'll tell you if I'm willing to pay. Remember these are hard times and things do not have the value they once had.'

'Twenty marks for each stone,' insisted Gretchen, the shrill in her voice giving the old man another reason to spread his wrinkled face with a smile, as his watery eyes floated in their sockets with the joy of having to barter with such a pretty adversary.

'Twenty marks,' repeated Kaufmann. 'And you're calling me a crook,' he laughed, turning to me. 'Let's not fall out, business is business. Even Frau Schreiber would not be expecting so much for such inferior stones. Let's say ten marks for each.'

'Eighteen,' said Gretchen, before I could speak.

'Fourteen.'

'Sixteen,' she responded, a little too quickly for my liking.

'Let's split the difference my dear,' said the old man, placing more marks on the sofa and giving them another pat with the palm of his thin-skinned hand, which was criss-crossed with protruding purple veins resembling a rail terminal. 'It's my final offer!'

'All right,' agreed Gretchen, handing him the five diamonds. She quickly gathered up the money and put it into her purse, causing the old man's face to crack with another smile. 'You see, young fellow, this is how business is done. Would you both like something to drink? I have some nice lemonade.'

'No, thank you, we have to get back to Mother,' I said coldly.

'Ah, your mother, please give her my regards and I hope she is feeling better soon.'

'I will.'

With the oil lamps casting long shadows down the narrow hall, we followed Herr Kaufmann to the front door. Gretchen said goodbye, but I said nothing, still convinced he was a crook. When we got back into the street Gretchen smiled, pleased with her negotiation skills, and said Mother was only expecting fifty to sixty marks and not the seventy-five Kaufmann paid. She told me Herr Kaufmann was a Jew and a shrewd man when it came to money matters. Perhaps I had misjudged the old man.

The rain had stopped and I followed Gretchen, a little frightened, back along the narrow lanes. The glow from the streetlights aided our escape from the maze of sidestreets, and I was relieved when we reached the tram-stop. Mother was feeling a little better when we got back, and was pleased with what we got for the sale of the diamonds. With seventy-five new Rentenmarks to spend, Gretchen was able to restock the larder and buy enough coal to see us through the winter. Mother finally recovered from her illness in time for Christmas.

On New Year's Eve, I was treated to an afternoon with Mother and Gretchen at the cinema on Bahnhofstrasse. It was the first time I had been to a picture house and it was the most I had ever laughed. Even mother laughed when the Keystone Kops chased Charlie Chaplin in and out of buildings, and up and down busy roads, until he finally escaped on the back of a very fast-moving tramcar. On the way home, we scurried along the pavements, battered by a strong, icy wind. My face was almost numb by the time we got indoors. The winter still had a long way to go.

After a lunch, Mother retired to her room with a bottle of sherry, leaving me to entertain Gretchen with my impersonation of Charlie Chaplin. As I instructed, she drew a small moustache on my upper lip with a piece of coal. After a satisfied look in the mirror, I took one of Father's old walking-sticks and pretended to walk like Chaplin up and down the hall, while Gretchen began to play a funny tune on the piano. Even Mother came back out of her room for a while to join in the fun.

It's easy to laugh when you do not know what's around the corner.

Chapter 4

Some days stay in your mind forever, leaving an indelible mark on your memory that no amount of time can erase. The first Monday of February 1924 was one of those days, and it still causes me pain to recall what fate had in store for me. I had no idea things had become so bad, and I naively thought Mother's bag of jewellery would last forever. The reality was only a knock on the door away, which woke me from a pleasant dream of summer days in the park with the organ-grinder playing polkas. The first thing I remember about that day was Mother standing grim-faced in the hall as Gretchen opened the front door to an elderly man in a grey suit.

The man handed Mother a document as four other men in overalls came into the house and began removing furniture from the living room. For a moment, I thought Mother had sold everything we had. However, she had sold nothing. The man in the grey suit had served Mother a court order which confirmed the extent of our debt. Initially I protested as each item was taken away with such indifference to our feelings, until Mother shouted at me to stop my nonsense. Gretchen put her arm around me as the piano was taken out, while Mother stood in the middle of the room with a cigarette never far from her lips and a sherry glass in her hand.

The front room was soon bare as the walls were stripped of the paintings I had for so long taken for granted, but now grieved, while looking forlornly at the outline their removal left on the wallpaper. The loss of our precious things was difficult enough for me to take, however that was only the beginning of the morning's revelations.

My heart quickened when Mother told me to go to my room and pack my suitcase. It was only then I noticed her trunk lying in the hallway, alongside Gretchen's suitcase. I watched my bed being removed as Gretchen helped me pack my things, squeezing what we could into my suitcase. In spite of my protests, I was not allowed to take any toys. They were packed into a large chest to be auctioned with the rest of our things. I began to feel unwell.

Unaware at the time Mother had been preparing for this event for some months, her stoic manner surprised me. The house, which I assumed belonged to her, was in fact mortgaged. It now belonged to the bank; the same bank which had so negligently allowed all Father's investments to become worthless.

Just as we were leaving, the postman arrived with a handful of brown envelopes. Mother simply dropped the envelopes in the rubbish bin without opening them. I looked at Gretchen for some understanding, but she was on the verge of tears.

The cold greeted us when we left the house to the removal men and the court officer, who carried Mother's heavy trunk down the steps to the pavement. A cab was waiting in the street and Mother gave Gretchen a long hug and whispered words of gratitude to her. It was at that moment I realised Gretchen was not coming with us. She turned to me with tears running down her face and said, 'Now, my Liebchen, you must promise me you'll look after your mother.'

'Why can't you come with us?' I pleaded.

'It's not possible … it's not possible.'

From the back window of the cab I watched Gretchen wave goodbye before she turned and walked in the opposite direction. Tears began to run down my face as everything which had been familiar to me began to disappear in the cold fog that clung to the streets that morning. Mother sat impassive, the shame of our eviction making her withdraw further into herself.

Once out of the quiet, suburban streets of our

neighbourhood, the roads became busy with tramcars, automobiles and the occasional horse-drawn cart as we passed through the chaos of Potsdamer Platz. Soon we were alongside the Tiergarten, passing under the giant shadow of the neo-Grecian edifice of the Brandenburger Tor, with its Doric columns and the triumphant Quadriga looking out over our once imperial city, now broken by the shame of defeat. The car turned east along the broad, tree-lined boulevard of Unter den Linden.

We sat in a queue of traffic for a while, watching the comings and goings of the citizens of the new Republic. Everyone in the centre of the city wore a hat; men wore trilbies, bowlers, fedoras, and top hats; while the women covered their heads with hats in all shapes and colours. Mother took my hand as the cab crossed the river near the cathedral, eventually passing the railway station at Alexanderplatz. We turned north, and my anxiety grew the further from the city centre we went. I soon noticed the people appeared less affluent and there were fewer varieties of hats to be seen. Men for the most part wore flat-caps, while the women wore scarves, shawls or nothing at all on their heads. I stared up at Mother for reassurance when we turned another corner to see a queue of people, their clothes no more than rags, waiting outside a soup kitchen. This was a part of Berlin I had not seen before. Where in the name of God were we going?

After another five minutes or so, my feeling of dread decreased a little, when the cab turned into a more pleasant neighbourhood and pulled up outside a rather ordinary apartment block.

Mother paid the driver, and I followed her up the stairwell to the second floor. There was an odious stench of pickled eels coming from one of the apartments, but I said nothing. Mother's breathing was laboured as she struggled with the heavy trunk onto the second landing where she let it rest.

There were two doors facing each other, one painted black and the other burgundy. The latter had a rectangular mark where the nameplate used to be, the other a crude metal plate with the name Kessler embossed on it. Mother produced a set of keys and opened the locks of the burgundy door and I followed her, with some apprehension, into the apartment.

There was a strong smell of dampness, and the dust rose from the hall floor when she banged the storm doors closed. We left our luggage in the hall and entered what was the main living quarters. The room was sparsely furnished with an uncomfortable looking sofa, a couple of chairs and a dining table, but it was not as bad as I first feared. I noticed Mother's gramophone in the corner and a half-dozen bottles of sherry she had saved from her creditors' clutches. There was also a kitchen recess with a gas cooker, a large white-enamelled sink and a few cupboards on the walls.

Off the hall there were two good-size bedrooms, both with beds, wardrobes and drawers. I was surprised to see the beds were already made with bedclothes I recognised as our own. In the corner of the smaller room, stacked up neatly, were around a dozen or so of my books. Mother had obviously paid several visits to the apartment without my knowing and the kitchen was well stocked with food. My initial dread subsided.

Once the suitcase was unpacked and my clothes put away in a chest of drawers, I sat down on the bed to have a better look at my new surroundings. The bedroom was half the size of my old one, and not unlike Günter's sparsely furnished attic room. The back of the building looked over a train station, and I could see people standing on the platform opposite as the stationmaster walked up and down with two red flags in his hand. The waiting passengers began to move towards the front of the platform, and I could feel the floor vibrate as the window rattled in its frame. There was a train arriving, heralded with the horrendous screech of metal on metal. The station quickly filled with grey clouds of steam, smoke, and noise, as the train came to a shuddering halt. The doors on the carriages began to open and close with a repetition of bangs, followed by a series of whistles. After a few minutes the train pulled away with more steam and noise, leaving the stationmaster alone on the platform with his whistle still in his mouth.

While the train headed off to its destination, I noticed a large advertisement poster on a gable end to the left of the station, with an enormous smiling face of a clown under the banner: The Berlin Metropolitan Circus. I could not make out the detail, but it looked like an old poster that had been put up some time ago and forgotten about. Back at the platform the stationmaster was smoking a cigarette and looking at his watch, before going into the ticket office at the side of the waiting room.

In the kitchen, Mother was already making lunch, and the smell of poached herring soon reached my bedroom. After putting my books on top of the chest of drawers, I went to join Mother for lunch.

On closing the bedroom door, I heard a noise that sounded like meowing on the outside landing. Curious, I opened the front door to find a black cat, purring and rubbing itself against the door frame. On bending down to pat its head, the cat rushed passed me into the hall.

'Franz, your lunch's ready,' Mother called, as I closed the door and followed the cheeky cat into the living room.

'What's that doing in here?' scolded Mother as the intruder sat staring up at her, sniffing and purring at the prospect of some freshly poached fish.

'It was on the landing, maybe it used to live here.'

'Why did you let it in? Take it back out or we'll never get rid of it.'

'But Mother, can't we keep it?'

'No, we don't know where it's been, the damn thing will

probably have fleas. Take it out.'

'But Mother, it's hungry.'

'Franz, don't argue with me, I don't have time. Take it out this minute!'

Reluctantly I lifted the cat and carried it, despite its protests, back out to the cold landing. As I was putting it down, the neighbour's door opened and an elderly lady, with a kindly face, appeared with a saucer of milk, which she placed on her door mat. The cat quickly lost interest in me and went straight over to the saucer of milk. 'Is it your cat?' I asked.

'No, it was left behind by the family who lived in your apartment. I feed it now and again, that's all. Do you like cats?'

'Yes, but my mother doesn't like them, she thinks they smell and have all got fleas.'

'Franz, where are you?' shouted Mother from the kitchen.

'I better go,' I said, closing the door on my new neighbour, who was pouring some more milk onto the saucer for the hungry cat.

Mother was in one of her moods, and I knew there was not much point in mentioning the cat's plight.

'Wash your hands and sit down.'

'Where's the bathroom?'

'There's no bathroom, use the sink, here,' she said, handing me a thick block of soap.

'No bathroom?'

'No, there is a toilet downstairs and we'll just have to get used to using a tub.'

'Why is the toilet downstairs?'

'Why do you ask so many questions, Franz? Here, eat your food before it gets cold.'

'Is this our house?'

'No, we rent it from the landlord, and it's not a house, it's an apartment.'

'Is the furniture ours?'

'No, it comes with the flat. Please stop asking so many questions,' she said, and began to cry.

'I'm sorry, Mother. I'll not ask any more questions. Don't cry.'

'It's all right. I'm just tired. Eat your food and we'll go for a long walk,' she smiled, drying her eyes, before tucking the handkerchief up her sleeve.

We sat eating our lunch by the window, looking out at the unfamiliar street, which still had old-fashioned gas lamps, and not the new electric ones which illuminate so much of West Berlin. Two old men in long black coats and trilby hats crossed the road. They reminded me of Herr Kaufman and I wondered if they were also Jews. I turned to see Mother nervously puffing on a cigarette. She hardly touched her food.

'Did you find your books?'

'Yes, Mother.'

'You'll have to keep up your studies until I can arrange for you to go back to school.'

'To my old school?'

'No, we'll have to find you a new school that's not so far away. Eat up and we'll go for a walk.'

On the way downstairs, I searched for the cat, but it was nowhere to be seen. Once out in the streets we took a walk around the neighbourhood. The cold wind had died down and Mother bought two hot bagels from the bakery on the corner, which we ate while sitting on a bench watching the birds fight over the titbits we threw them. She began to hum a tune she often sang with Gretchen.

'What's it called?' I asked when she stopped singing and began mumbling something to herself about the baby Jesus. 'The song, Mother, what's it called?' I repeated.

'Oh, it's called *Die Lorelei*; it's an old poem I learned at school. Oh! I wish I had still had my piano.'

'Maybe we can get a new one.'

'Yes, maybe one day.'

'Where did Gretchen go?' I asked, now Mother was in the mood for talking.

'Gretchen has found a new position in the Hotel Adlon. We couldn't keep her any longer after we lost all our savings. Banks! Never trust them, they're all crooks.'

'Could she not have stayed with us?'

'Gretchen hadn't been paid for months. She was willing to stay for board and lodgings, but even that became impossible when we had to give up the house.'

'Will we see her again?'

'Maybe someday, who knows? Maybe someday ... Let's go home. It's getting too cold sitting here.'

That was my first real conversation with Mother; short, granted, but she was talking to me the way she once talked to Gretchen and Frau Schwartz. At that moment, I was glad we had moved to an apartment on our own. Now if she wanted me to do anything she would have to speak to me herself.

As the days passed, the conversations became more frequent and more interesting and she told me all about her own childhood. She grew up in a village, somewhere between Berlin and Hanover, and she often talked about how she missed the countryside and the smell of the fields at harvest time. It was there she met my father at a dance in the local church hall. Father had been there for a short holiday away from the smoke and greyness of Berlin. They married the following year. 'That was all a long, long, time ago,' she sighed, with a mixture of sadness and bitterness in her voice, 'before the war.'

At first, I rarely ventured outside the apartment unless with Mother, and it would usually only be to go to the shops at the top of the street or to Mass on Sunday. Some days the cat would be sitting on the stairs meowing, as though demanding to get back into what was once its home; other days it was nowhere to be seen. Whenever Mother saw the poor thing, she would shoo it away before I got a chance to even pat it. The cat, which I decided to call Harvey, seemed destined to remain destitute.

Stephanuskirche was only a few blocks away from the apartment. Mother was becoming more and more devoted to the smell of frankincense and burning candles, and we were always in the chapel a good fifteen minutes before the Mass started. Each Sunday we would light a candle for Father, before taking our pew and getting to our knees; Mother, no doubt, praying for the restoration of the life she had before the war, while I was praying for her to let me keep Harvey.

Mass was a bore to me, with its dreary litany celebrating Christ's suffering for the sins of the world. The chapel was not as grand as the one I had been baptised in, but still managed to conjure enough solemnity that I was sure God was watching me every time I yawned or nodded off. In pride of place, above the altar was a large cross with the crucified Jesus hanging forlornly from its oak beams. It was much more grotesque than the one in our old parish. This Jesus, unlike the other, looked like he was suffering the pain of the nails hammered into his hands and feet, not to mention the crown of bloody thorns and the painful looking gash in his side made by Longinus's spear. His lips looked thin and parched as though the taste of vinegar was still on them, while his tormented face did not look up to the heavens in triumph but down to the ground in utter wretchedness and despair. The other Jesus seemed to have a more pleasant time on the cross than this one. As with most things to do with God, it did not make sense to me. Had there been two crucifixions?

Some Sundays, after Mass, we would take the tramcar into the city centre to Mother's favourite part of Berlin, the busy Unter den Linden, with its fashionable shops and cafes. We would sit at the same corner café, watching the well-dressed citizens walking by, while we sipped our coffee and ate pretzels. It was almost worth suffering the cold to spend an afternoon watching the world go by and to see Mother looking more like her old self as she smiled and acknowledged acquaintances from our more affluent past. I was rather surprised no one ever stopped to speak with her other than to say, 'Good day, Frau Schreiber', before walking on. I guess at the time, I did not understand the social stigma of bankruptcy and the extent of our fall from grace. Poor Mother must have often blamed herself for her lack of understanding of the stock markets and her naive belief in the banks until it was too late. It was clear to me; even then, Mother's jewellery had been Father's only wise investment; although I am sure he did not think so at the time.

*

One day, Mother took me to the Hackescher market, so she could buy something cheap for our evening meal. It was late in the afternoon and the market was quiet. Everyone was dressed in black, even the younger men wore beards, and many had curls of dark ringlets hanging down from under their broad, brimmed hats. 'Jews,' was all Mother said, when I asked about their strange appearance.

Most of the stalls were already closing and Mother had to settle for a bag of eels, which were more like dead snakes to me than fish. She was not even sure how to cook them and I listened without enthusiasm as the fishmonger explained the process to make these unpleasant things edible.

As we walked back home, Mother stopped at a jeweller's shop window. I watched her look with anger at a large brooch, like the one I had often seen her wearing when she still had her jewellery. Her voice was hoarse, and the words she uttered had the haunting tone of a curse. 'Two hundred marks … God damn you, Kaufmann, you profiteering swine!'

So, this was Herr Kaufmann's shop and where most of

Mother's things ended up, to be sold for a handsome profit. I was about to ask Mother how much he had paid her for the brooch but thought better of it. After another forlorn look at what was once just another piece in her large jewellery collection, we walked the rest of the way in silence, the smell of the eels destroying my hunger.

By the time we got home, Mother had also lost her desire for the slimy beasts and she threw them in the refuse bin. She would not let me give them to Harvey, afraid he might become dependent on us. We ate some bread and cheese and went to bed early to save what was left of the coal for the morning.

Chapter 5

Mother's fascination with the Charlie Chaplin look-alike continued, and she was engrossed in the would-be usurper's trial in Munich. She would often follow the daily reports of the case, reading to me the harangues of Herr Hitler. *'I want to fulfil the vow which I made to myself five years ago when I was blind and crippled in the military hospital: to know neither rest nor peace until the November criminals have been overthrown, until on the ruins of the wretched Germany of today, there should arise once more a Germany of power and greatness, of freedom and splendour ... The first thing we must do is rescue Germany from the Jew who is ruining our country. We want to stir up a storm. We want to prevent Germany from suffering as another did, death upon the cross.'*

'Whose death upon the cross?' I asked to make some conversation, knowing fine well who he was referring to.

'Jesus Christ, the son of God,' she said, blessing herself to acknowledge the fact. 'And it was those filthy Jews who did it, like that swine Kaufmann,' she growled in a way I had never heard her speak before.

'Was Jesus not a Jew?' I asked, feeling confused at the blame Herr Kaufman and the Jews were getting.

'Jesus!' said Mother, looking at me as if I had just blasphemed the man who died for my sins. 'Go to your room and don't be asking silly questions,' she snapped.

I retired to my room where I lay on top of my bed. I did not think my question about Jesus was silly, sure someone had told me he was a Jew, although, the more I thought about it at the time, the more I began to think I just made it up.

The room was cold, and I wrapped the top blanket around

me to keep warm, lying there, thinking about Jesus on the cross and wondering why he was not able to make a miracle and save himself. It was then I heard it for the first time, the haunting sound of a violin. The music was pleasing, and I went over to the window to listen, wondering where it was coming from. I went back to the living room to ask Mother.

Now she had drunk all the sherry, Mother was already asleep in front of the fire, so I decided to take the opportunity to explore the source of the music. I opened the front door and could hear the violin was coming from one of the apartments on the top landing. The music, like a strange charm, compelled me to climb the stairs to the next landing and to a door with the name Kolinski on it. I sat on the top step and listened to the meandering melody, enchanted with the beauty and mystery of it.

While I sat there, the cat, which I had not seen around for days, appeared beside me playfully purring and rubbing its head against my leg. Eventually the music stopped, and I went back downstairs with Harvey following behind. The front door was still ajar, and Mother was in the hall, combing her hair in the mirror. She did not notice the cat, which was wise enough to slip past her into the warmth of the living room.

'Where have you been?'

'I was just sitting on the landing,' I said, watching Harvey curling up beside the fire.

'Why would you want to sit out in the cold when you have a perfectly good room?'

'I was bored in my room.'

'Bored, you have your books … anyway, I have to go out tonight and I've left your dinner on the table.'

'Where're you going?'

'I've got a job waiting tables in a bar in town.'

'Waiting on tables?'

'Yes, I will not be back until late, so make sure you get to your bed before nine o'clock and say your prayers.'

'Why are you working in a bar?'

'Because we have no money and it's the only work I can find to pay the rent and put food on the table. Go and eat your supper. I'll have to leave soon. Remember, Franz, don't open the front door to anyone once I've gone out. Do you hear me?'

'Yes, Mother, but I need to go to the toilet first.'

'Hurry up for God's sake!'

On my return from the unpleasant experience that was the outside toilet, Mother had obviously discovered the cat, which was back on the landing. All I could do was shrug my shoulders at Harvey's pleading eyes and close the door over to drown out his unhappy meowing. Mother was wearing her coat and fussing with her hair. She was wearing bright red lipstick and her face was covered in much more makeup than she usually wore. She looked like a different person.

Dinner was ham and potato salad again. I poured a glass of lemonade and pushed the food around with my fork, listening to Mother getting ready to go out. The front door opened, and she called out to remind me to be in bed by nine o'clock before closing the door with a bang.

Not feeling hungry, I eventually got up from the table and walked disconsolately into the hall. The silence was overwhelming as I waited there in the dark, realising for the first time in my life I was alone, no Gretchen, Günter, Frau Schwartz or Mother to speak to. There were only empty, strange rooms to wander through without purpose.

Not wishing to upset Mother, I returned to the dining table to eat my supper. The streets outside were being lit by the gasman, who was walking from one lamp to another, lighting each one in turn as the evening sky turned black despite his best efforts. The room was gloomy, lit with only one oil lamp, which I brought over to the dining table to finish my food. Mother must have been playing solitaire again and had left the game unfinished; bored I shuffled the pack a couple of times, before dealing the cards out to test my own patience. The clock in the hall ticked away incessantly, making the apartment feel all the quieter, while the light from the lamp cast creepy shadows across the room. For the first time in my life I felt utterly abandoned.

I don't remember going to bed that night, but the room was in darkness when I woke to hear keys rattling at the front door. There were whispers and giggles. I heard Mother telling whoever was with her to be quiet, as the floor boards creaked along the hall into the living room.

I got up and sat on the edge of the bed, listening over the noise of a train passing. Mother was doing all the talking. It was hard to hear anyone else over her incessant chatter. When sober, she would speak very little, but drunk all the words she had neglected came in a torrent. I opened my bedroom door to listen, but Mother had stopped talking. Holding my breath, I crept along the noisy floorboards on my tiptoes to listen at the living room door. I gently turned the door knob and slowly opened the door to see Mother on the sofa with a man on top of her, kissing her neck and touching her exposed breast. Horrified, I pulled the door closed with a bang and ran back into my room. Mother came after me in a temper.

'What are you doing spying on me like a communist?'
'I wasn't spying on you!'
'Get to sleep and don't get back up until the morning.'
'I'm hungry.'
'Did you not eat your dinner?'
'I'm still hungry.'
'You'll just have to wait until the morning.'
'Lilly! Come back here!'
'Who is he, and why is he calling you Lilly?'
'He's a gentleman friend … Now get to sleep,' she said, closing the door and ignoring the second part of my question.

How could I sleep? The darkness of the room was all consuming as I lay there abandoned by my mother, who preferred Lilly to her own name and being with a stranger, to playing solitaire. In my desperation I contemplated running away and finding Gretchen. She would look after me and not treat me like Mother.

A train passed outside without stopping at the station, causing the window to rattle and the metal bed to shake. It was the express mail train from Dresden, which every night at midnight made the same journey into Berlin's Hauptbahnhof. I listened, in silent misery, until it faded away into the distance.

Unable to get back to sleep, I pulled the covers over my head and began to run through my times-tables, but it was impossible. By the time I was half way through the three times table I could hear the sound of music and more drunken laughter coming from the living room. Mother was playing her gramophone and I recognised the tune immediately, *The Whispering*, which I quickly grew to hate as she replayed it time and time again to more drunken laughter.

The following day Mother did not get up until the afternoon. Her new friend was already gone, and she was back to her laconic self. She sat at the dining table and smoked one cigarette after another. I made her a cup of coffee, but there was nothing in the cupboard to eat. The *ersatz* coffee got her out of her trance. She told me to get dressed. We were going out.

The shops were busy, and I assumed Mother must have sold more jewellery, which was surprising since the bag where she kept them had been empty for some time. After a walk around the clothes shops, where she looked forlornly at the dresses, we went to the local grocers where she bought the necessities, as she called them; coffee, milk, bread, sugar, butter, potatoes, sausages and cigarettes. To my dismay, she also bought two bottles of cheap sherry and a bottle of cognac. We walked home with the heavy shopping bags with Mother in a better mood. She did not seem to mind one bit when Harvey followed us into the apartment.

Chapter 6

The city began to look less grey as the winter gave way to spring. The daffodils were already pushing their way through the grass in the local park, and after a few more weeks the delicate pink blossom was soon on the trees. The change in the weather made Mother less miserable, and she stopped throwing Harvey out on the landing. He became part of the Schreiber family, now that she had decided we needed a cat to catch the mice we could hear scratching behind the skirting boards at night.

Indolent by nature, Harvey was not interested in catching mice; oily sardines were his preferred meal, and, he did not have to chase them. He was company for me when Mother went to work, although he would sometimes insist in going out late at night and staying away until lunchtime. Mother called him an alley cat, and said he was only interested in us when he was looking for food, but even she had grown used to him getting under her feet.

Like Harvey, Mother went out most nights but, unlike Harvey, she seldom came home alone. When she was entertaining, I found it was impossible to get to sleep and often lay awake as the night trains rattled past my bedroom window, casting flickering, ethereal light from their ghostly carriages onto the ceiling. Sometimes I would kneel on my bed to look out the window, wishing to be on one of those trains.

When the gramophone eventually stopped playing and Mother's bedroom door opened, I would curl up in bed with the blankets over my head, blocking out the moans and groans, until the sudden silence that followed left me in a state of grief for my poor, dead father.

In the mornings, when the stranger was gone, there would often be money lying on the dresser, which Mother said were tips from the bar. She must be a very good waitress, I thought, when counting over twenty marks one morning while she was still sleeping.

Although Mother told me she worked in the Kurt's Bar on Friedrichstrasse, I often found booklets of matches with different bars and clubs advertised on them. Before going out at night, Mother spent most of the time sitting by the window, drinking coffee and chain-smoking. After she left for work, and Harvey had headed for the alleys, I would often go upstairs and sit on the top step, reading one of my books, hoping to hear the violin, sometimes falling asleep during these rare moments of inner peace.

While there were others, Mother had two regular visitors. There was Otto, our landlord, the fat man, whom I had previously seen on top of her in the living room and who kept me up most Friday nights with his singing and boisterous dancing. The other, whom I heard Mother call Karl one night, spent every other Thursday at the apartment, but unlike Otto, he was not the type to sing or dance.

Sometimes I wasn't even sure Karl had been in the apartment the previous night, until Mother's sadness gave it away as she sat smoking and drinking coffee, while staring out the window. When Otto stayed overnight, she was always much more cheerful when he left in the morning, and while most of our neighbours went to the local synagogue, we would go shopping for our weekly groceries.

One morning, while lying awake, I heard Mother's door creak open, followed by the slow, deliberate steps of someone creeping along the hall. I got up to investigate. The man was about to leave when he turned and stared at me. He wore a dark brown cap and spectacles, and had a serious, rather morose face. I can't remember if he had a moustache or a goatee, but his eyes were full of sadness and there was an apologetic smile on his thin lips as he pulled the door close behind him. I ran through the hall and into the living room and watched him cross the road from the window. He stopped on the other side of the road for a moment and lit a cigarette, turning back to look up at Mother's bedroom window, before walking towards the main road. Mother was miserable all that day and she sat for hours looking out at the lamppost where the man had stood that morning. It was then I was sure the stranger was Karl, and Mother was in love with him.

Even after all this time, I had only seen Herr Kolinski a couple of times from our front window. Mother told me that was the name of the man who played the violin and that he was a widower, who had lost his two sons in the war. She warned me not to go near him as he did not like children.

'How can he not like children, if he had two sons?'

'Just stay away from him, Franz. Old people don't like other people's children annoying them, especially when they have lost their own.'

Even though I was forbidden to disturb Herr Kolinski, I still sat outside his door in the evenings and listened to the violin when Mother left for work. I had also met his next-door neighbours, Herr and Frau Wassermann, who would often pass me on the stairs. Frau Wassermann was a kind old woman, who would sometimes give me a boiled sweet while praising Herr Kolinski's beautiful music. One day her husband took an unwelcome interest in my welfare as I played on the stairwell with Harvey.

'You don't go to school?'

'No, Mother took me out last year.'

'Why would your mother do such a thing?'

'We had no money.'

'No money, you don't need money to go to school. You can go to the state school, it's free. Why does … '

'I don't know.'

'It's not right; you should be going to school. How will you ever get work when you're older and have to fend for yourself?'

'I will become an actuary, like my father.'

'An actuary, what's an actuary?'

'If you don't know, maybe you should go to school.'

'You should not be so cheeky to your elders.'

'Herbert, let the boy alone. It's none of our business,' said Frau Wassermann as she pulled her husband away and gave me another boiled sweet.

My long absence from school came to an end when Mother received an unexpected visit in the autumn from two rather severe looking men from the local school board. They threatened Mother with criminal proceedings for failing in her duty to have me educated. She was obliged to send me to the local school the following week, which once bore the exiled Kaiser's name, but was renamed the Weimar State Elementary School. The only uniform I had to wear was my old one.

When I got there, it did not matter what uniform I wore; none of the other children even wore one, never mind a smart blazer with a badge bearing a Latin motto on it. The chaos in the playground on my first morning made me yearn for my old school. When the bell began to ring, I reluctantly followed behind the other pupils into the austere building.

Unfortunately, my uniform and privileged upbringing made me something of a loner, and I did not see anyone in my class I could bring myself to be friends with. My ability to answer most of Frau Grossmann's questions did not endear me to the more aggressive types in class, and their initial jealousy and name calling turned to violence on more than one occasion. Needless to say, I was always the one who ended up with the bloody nose. Even my old school badge did not last long, and both it and the pocket were ripped from my blazer during a fight, that to my surprise at the time, I almost won. I was soon as scruffy as everyone else, and careful not to answer too many questions in class. The bullies eventually gave up on me and found someone else to pick on.

One night, I woke up when the bed shook violently because of a passing express train which must have been travelling very fast. Save for the light coming up from the train station, it was quite dark. I got up and ventured into the hall, shivering from the cold. I lit the oil lamp in the living room and checked the time. It was after midnight and Mother was still at work. I heard the violin from the flat above. I put my boots and coat on and went upstairs to listen. Before I got a chance to sit down the music stopped and I heard sobbing coming from behind Herr Kolinski's door. This made me feel uneasy, and I hurried back downstairs to my bedroom. I imagined he must be crying for his wife and two sons, and pictured him all alone in his apartment, which made me sorry for him.

The next morning, while mother was still in bed, I dressed and was about to leave for school, when I heard a door opening and closing upstairs. I stood behind the front door in the hall and waited to see who was making their way downstairs. Through the spy-hole I watched Herr Kolinski, wearing a trilby and a long grey coat, going quietly down the stairs. Despite Mother's warning not to go near him, I put on my coat and followed him into the street.

The morning air was crisp, and the sky was bright overhead. I hurried after him. He was soon at the busy junction on the next corner. He waited for a tram to pass before crossing. I followed discreetly, intrigued as to where he was going. We passed the synagogue on Oranienburgerstrasse, its gilded ribbed dome catching the morning light. As I marvelled at this imposing structure, Herr Kolinski turned up the next street. I ran to catch up.

A short time later he crossed a large, open square where

market stalls were being erected by men and women in traditional peasant clothes. He walked briskly through the organised chaos, where some farmers obviously believed in keeping their produce as fresh as possible: there were crates and pens full of bleating lambs and bewildered looking poultry, waiting to be sold to anyone who could afford them.

We were soon in the maze of streets and I watched Herr Kolinski stop for a moment to buy matches from a blind man standing beside a plaque which stated he had lost his sight in the war. While Herr Kolinski put some coins into the blind man's tin, I was distracted by the smell of fresh rolls and bagels coming from a Jewish bakery on the corner. I had sacrificed my breakfast to follow Herr Kolinski and now felt hungry. When I turned back from the baker's shop window, he was gone. Not sure which way he went, I crossed the square and turned down the next street.

Although I had become accustomed to seeing Jewish people, I was surprised to see so many in orthodox clothes coming and going from shops on either side of the road. The shops were mainly jewellers, watchmakers and tailors, all open for business, while the rest of the city was still half asleep. No one seemed to notice me as I walked along, looking in through the windows to see if I could catch a glimpse of Herr Kolinski.

Just when I was beginning to give up, I heard someone call my name. I turned to see him standing outside a tailor's shop, with his black trilby hat in his outstretched hand. 'Franz Schreiber,' he said with a smile. 'Are you looking to buy a jacket or perhaps a nice shirt? It doesn't cost anything to have a look.'

'How do you know my name?' I asked, feeling nervous at being discovered. Did he know I was following him? Was he mocking me?

'Oh, that was not too difficult to find out, since we live in the same apartment block. I've seen you with your mother coming and going, and Frau Wasserman told me how she often finds you sitting on the steps outside my door listening to the violin ... You like the violin?'

'Yes.'

'Come into the shop and take some tea with us. The shop will not get busy for a while, yet.'

'No thank you, I need to go school,' I rattled nervously, remembering Mother's warning not to go near him. I stepped back, fearing he would grab me and pull me into the shop.

'Ah, school, the best years of your life ... You're not afraid of me?' he asked, the tone in his voice quickly changing.

'No,' I said defiantly, while preparing to take to my heels.

'Here, take this with you,' he said, stepping forward, as though trying to placate a nervous puppy, and handing me a paper bag with a warm bagel in it. 'And the next time you want to listen to the violin just knock on the door. I will be happy to have your company.'

'Thank you, Herr Kolinski,' I said, stepping back awkwardly as soon as I had the warm bag in my hands.

'Goodbye Franz, enjoy school. I'm sure it's much better than having to work all day.' He smiled at me, before putting his hat on and going back into the shop.

With my stomach still rumbling, I sat on a bench near the market and began to devour the bagel. Before I had finished eating, a clock on a tower opposite the market began to chime and I realised I was going to be late for school. Not too concerned, I pulled up my socks and sauntered off, my curiosity about Herr Kolinski greater than ever.

Chapter 7

We had been in the new apartment for almost a year when Mother decided it was time I had some new clothes. She took me to one of the large department stores on Friedrichstrasse and bought me two pair of trousers, two shirts, two pullovers, a blazer with shiny buttons, and a pair of shoes. She also bought herself a new dress and another phonograph record, which she played as soon as we got home. I sat at the window and ate a bowl of rice pudding, while she danced the Charleston all around the house. It had been a long time since I had seen her look so happy. The crazy dance soon made her exhausted and she eventually sat down to twirl her fake pearls and smoke a cigarette.

'Franz!'

'Yes, Mother?'

'Why don't you go and put your new clothes on?'

'But I thought they were for school.'

'Yes, they are, but you can wear them today. I have someone coming around for dinner and I think it's time you met him.'

'Who, Mother?'

'He is the owner of the new nightclub I've been working at and we are going to be married.'

'Married,' I repeated, the word sticking in my throat.

'Yes, Franz. You'll not cause me any problems and speak to him with respect. Without him we would be on the street long ago and begging for scraps of food like the people you see at the poorhouse.'

'Why do you have to marry him? What about Father?'

'He's dead … These are hard times and we have to live as best we can without your father.'

'Is he going to live here?'

'No, we'll move to his beautiful house after the wedding. He will make sure we are never hungry again and you'll be able to go to a better school and perhaps university. Promise me, Franz, you'll not say or do anything that will make me angry with you!'

'Yes, Mother, I promise. When will you marry him?'

'Not for a while yet, he only proposed to me last night.'

While Mother prepared dinner I went into my room to get changed. There were fewer trains running at the weekend. When I looked out at the empty station platform it began to rain. The clown on the gable end looked miserable and the grey skies closed in overhead. I went back into the living room where Mother was waiting anxiously for her guest to arrive. She was dressed in modest clothes and not the flamboyant outfits she wore to the nightclubs and bars.

A cloud of steam floated over the room, causing the windows to mist up as pots of potatoes and carrots boiled away on the stove. In the oven a chicken was roasting, and I watched her basting it with the hot fat from the baking tray, the way Frau Schwartz used to do. It was the first time I had seen Mother cook anything that was not in a pot of water.

With dinner under control, she turned her attention to the dining table, which was already overdressed with a white tablecloth, linen napkins, and our best cutlery and wine glasses. She walked around the table a couple of times, moving forks and knives until she had the settings aligned to her liking. I sat on the sofa watching her antics as she turned to wipe the condensation from the widows before giving the chicken another basting.

A sudden knock at the front door made her panic. She quickly took off her apron and positioned me beside the fireplace, rearranging my hair and brushing imaginary dandruff from my shoulders before going to answer the door.

Still standing to attention I waited while Mother's voice

took on a different tone as she greeted her future husband. I nervously unbuttoned my jacket and listened as they spoke in whispers to each other. It seemed to take forever for them to walk the short distance from the front door to the living room. My apprehension grew until the living room door finally opened. She entered, arm in arm with a man old enough to be her father. 'Franz,' she said in a formal manner, 'this is Count Boris Alexander Romanoff.'

'You embarrass me, Anna, I'm no longer a Count,' he said in a thick Russian accent. 'Call me Boris,' he said, shaking my hand vigorously.

'Hello.'

'Ah, a man of few words and a handshake of few fingers,' he said, with a hearty laugh as he opened his large hand and saw my clenched fist. Mother stared at me as if I had committed high treason, before turning back to smile at the Russian as though he was our ally, instead of our enemy, during the war. No wonder she did not tell me about him and made me promise not to say or do anything that would embarrass her.

Unwilling to engage in conversation with him, I studied my future stepfather in silence. He wore an expensive black suit with a stiff white collar, and a purple cravat, studded with a diamond pin. What was left of his hair was combed across his head in a vain attempt to cover his obvious baldness. He had grey-blue eyes, nestled like sparrow eggs, under his bushy eyebrows.

Mother brought over a large tureen of lentil soup to the dining table as though she was expecting the rest of the Russian royal family to join us for dinner. The Russian helped her place it in the middle of the table before tucking a napkin under his double chin. I wondered how it was possible for my father's enemy to come to Berlin, marry his widow and adopt his son, without there being a national outcry. Is this what my dear father fought and died for in those rat-infested trenches in France? I felt a defiant cry rise inside, but I let it out through my nostrils in a silent scream as Mother handed me a bowl of soup and admonished my sulk with another stern look.

'Franz, has your mother told you the good news?'

'No.'

'Anna?'

'I've told him, Boris, he's maybe not sure what good news you're talking about.'

'The wedding, Franz,' said the Russian, taking my mother's hand as she took her seat at the table.

'Yes,' I nodded, with a sudden desire to throw my knife at the bushy-eyed Count as Mother smiled inanely at him.

'You must be a poker player,' he said, 'keeping your cards close to your chest, young man.'

'He's a quiet boy at the best of times,' said Mother, trying to excuse my reticence.

'We'll soon be the best of friends once you get to know me. It can't be easy meeting your future stepfather for the first time. Once your mother and I are married we'll make a happy family,' he continued, again putting his massive hand on my mother's, who had to stop eating to look at him.

After soup, Mother cleared away the bowls and went back to basting the chicken. The Count soon gave up any further attempt at polite conversation with me and occupied himself by humming what I assumed was a Russian tune until Mother brought over the chicken. Unable to stop my mouth salivating, I watched the Russian take the carving knife from my mother's hand and slice through the crisp skin. I had not tasted chicken for so long I was happy to hand the Count my plate.

'You like chicken?' he asked, hesitating with another piece above my plate as though a bribe was being offered in exchange for a conversation in words of more than one syllable.

'Yes, please,' was as much as I could muster.

True to form, with the smell food wafting in the air, Harvey began crying at the front door and I got up to let him in to join the feast. He had been missing for a few days and was quite shabby looking, which obviously embarrassed Mother. She made it clear to the Count that Harvey was only a stray we fed now and again, although Harvey's familiarity with the rug in front of the fire belied her story. I said nothing, still trying to maintain my hate for the Count.

After dinner Mother and the Russian played cards and spoke in whispers, leaving me to excuse myself and retire to my room. Harvey declined to join me and curled up at the Count's feet. Even he was a traitor.

In time, and despite my initial hostility, I grew fond of the Count, who, unlike some of Mother's previous lovers, showed her nothing but respect. She no longer had to work in the bars at night, and he lavished her with beautiful gifts and money.

Boris, as he insisted I referred to him, called at the apartment two or three times a week with gifts for Mother and a bar of chocolate for me. His oily hair seemed to smell less of olives, and those bushy draped eyes became familiar to me. The chocolate, I accept, had something to do with my change of attitude, and we were soon on friendly terms as he told me all about the life he once had in the imperial court before the Russian Revolution swept the communists into power. 'Were you not able to stop the revolution?' I asked him, when Mother went to her room to get changed.

'The Tsar was a weak man. He ruled a vast empire, but he was ruled in turn by his domineering Austrian wife and her mad priest, Rasputin,' he said with a mock spit. 'He should have never gone to war in the first place and there would have been no revolution in Russia.'

'Who was Rasputin?'

'He was a charlatan priest, who bewitched the Tsarina.

Through her he pulled the wool over the Tsar's eyes, interfering in the government of the country and the conduct of the war. He was eventually murdered and thrown in the Neva River, but too late to save the Tsar and Russia.'

'What happened to the Tsarina?'

'Alexandra was murdered with the rest of the family. The children ... I loved them all. How could they have killed those beautiful princesses and poor Prince Alexei?' he said, blessing himself.

After a few moments of silent reflection, he began to tell me how he had returned home from the war to find his palace in Saint Petersburg ransacked and his parents and brothers murdered. Everything of value had been taken, except for a strong-box hidden in the family crypt, which the communists failed to find. Inside the box were the family jewels and he managed to escape to Stockholm with them. After the war was over in Europe, he moved to Berlin and bought his first nightclub for a fraction of its original value when the Reichsmark collapsed. He now owned three nightclubs and a casino and was a rich man once again. How rich he did not say. As I listened to him, I began to wonder if I would become a Count when he died and would be able to reclaim the palace in Saint Petersburg once the communists were finished with it. He smiled at me and for a moment I wondered if he could read my mind.

Mother eventually made her grand entrance. She was dressed for a night on the town. Boris got up to greet her as she twirled to show off her new silk dress while stroking the fox-stole draped around her neck. I noticed she was wearing an emerald and sapphire brooch, not unlike the one she had sold to Herr Kaufmann in our time of need.

Mother had already told me they were going out for dinner and onto the opera house. I, of course, was not invited, but my disappointment was eased with the ten marks the generous Count tucked into my shirt pocket before leaving.

I watched from the window as Mother got into his chauffeur driven car. If I could not get the palace, at least I would get his car when he died.

It was still light outside, and I realised I had not heard Herr Kolinski's violin for over two weeks. The silence in the apartment was becoming unbearable and so I turned on Mother's gramophone for company and listened to her new American jazz record. After a few plays I became bored of the frantic music. I took the spare keys from the back of the door and ventured on to the landing, determined to pay Herr Kolinski a visit. There was no sign of Harvey, who was probably enjoying a night on the town himself.

Hesitating for a moment, I listened at Herr Kolinski's door but heard nothing. I took a deep breath before rattling the brass letterbox. My heart began to beat fast on hearing the lock being opened.

'Ah, Franz, you have come to visit me at last. Come in and I'll put the kettle on. Has your mother gone out already?'

'Yes, she has gone to the opera,' I said, following Herr Kolinski through the hall and into the living room.

'The opera, how marvellous and what opera is she going to?'

'Das Rheingold.'

'Ah, Wagner, that will be a long night. Take a seat, young man. Do you like tea?'

'Yes,' I replied, taking a chair next to the window as he lit the stove. The room was like the living room in our apartment, but it was impossible to see the walls, which were covered from floor to ceiling with a chaos of books of every colour and size. The violin, which I had heard so often, was lying on top of a black upright piano, which was covered in sheets of music.

'I'm afraid I have no milk or sugar left,' he said, handing me a delicate-looking cup covered with roses.

'That's all right.'

'Would you like some biscuits?'

'Yes,' I nodded, sipping the black tea and taking a chocolate biscuit from the plate he put in the middle of the table; at least the biscuits were sweet and took away the bitterness of the tea.

'How is school?'

'It's all right, but you have more books than they have.'

'They're not all mine, most of them were my sons' books. Well, I guess they're all mine now,' he said, saddened by the thought. 'I'll never read them all, but I can't part with them either.'

I wanted to ask him about his sons, but how could I, knowing they were both killed in the war? I could see some framed pictures on the mantelpiece and recognised the same uniform I remembered Father wearing on the morning he left to fight in the trenches. He must have noticed me looking at them. He got up and picked up two of the photographs and brought them over to the table. 'This is my oldest boy, Jacob,' he said. Jacob was wearing an officer's uniform, with the iron cross, first class, pinned to his chest. 'He was a captain and killed in the war fighting the Russians. Why they were fighting the Russians I don't know. This is Isaac; he was killed only a few weeks before the war ended in the west ... only weeks,' he sighed. 'Jacob is buried somewhere in Poland and Isaac in France, God knows where! And for what?'

'My father is buried in France,' I said, as though it would cheer him up.

'Your poor father and a million other fathers and sons ... madness, nothing but madness,' he said, putting the two frames back on the mantelpiece on either side of a silver menorah. 'Thank God I have still a daughter,' he said, taking another picture frame to the table. 'Rebecca ... Isn't she beautiful?'

'Yes,' I said, still sipping the bitter tea.

'She's at boarding school, and when she's not, she lives with my sister, Sarah, who has raised her since my wife passed away. I was not in any state to look after her at the time, but it's all for the best. She has her cousins there who are young like her, and I have my memories.'

'Do you never see her?'

'Of course, she comes here to stay every so often, and I spend a few weeks at my sister's home every year ... Would you like to hear some music before it gets too late and the neighbours begin to complain?' he offered, lifting the instrument to his shoulder before I could answer.

For the next hour or so, I sat and listened to the enchanting sound of the violin while the notes danced around my head in a way Mother's jazz music could not. Each time, before he played, he would introduce the piece by its title and name of the composer. I would try and retain this knowledge but forgot what he said as soon as he began playing. Eventually he played my favourite piece and its mystery was revealed: Mendelssohn's *Violin Concerto in E minor*. When he stopped, I asked him if he would play it again, which brought a smile to his face. 'This was my wife's favourite also.'

At some stage I must have fallen asleep and felt a little embarrassed when Herr Kolinski gently shook me awake. It was dark outside, and my first thought was Mother might already be home from the opera and be wondering where I got to. I thanked Herr Kolinski and apologised for falling asleep, but he didn't mind and smiled. 'If someone falls asleep when I'm playing, I must be playing well. You can't fall asleep listening to badly played music, especially on the violin.'

The gas lamps were lit, and the yellow flames cast shadows on the walls of the stairs as I went back down to my own landing. Startled, I noticed someone sitting on the steps outside the apartment with his head in his hands as though in some distress. There was a strong smell of beer from the stranger and I could hear him moaning to himself. With my heart beating fast, I fumbled with the keys, determined to get into the apartment as quickly as possible. Turning to close the door behind me, I stole another look at the man. It was Karl, with his dark, sad eyes looking up at me as I slammed the door closed and put on the security chain. Engulfed in darkness, I rushed into the living room to light the oil lamp.

I stood quietly in the hall as a freight train passed outside, shaking the building for what seemed like an eternity. Mother would be home soon, and I wondered if she was mad enough to arrange for Karl to wait for her. Her behaviour in recent months made me think she was capable of any folly. Would this be the night the Count came back to find one of Mother's other lovers sitting on the stairs? Would there be murder? I began to imagine a bizarre crime of passion under the flickering gas light: Karl's knife plunging in the Count's heart, then to add to the tragedy, Otto would appear from the shadows with a pistol, disposing of Karl.

After a few deep breaths, and keeping the security chain in place, I turned back the locks and carefully opened the door. Karl just sat and stared at me for a moment until he finally asked where Mother had gone.

'To stay with her sister in Leipzig,' I lied, quickly closing the door with a bang. For a moment I stood and listened, hoping to hear his footsteps descending the stairs. I jumped with fright when the door was suddenly knocked.

'Open the door, Franz,' he said.

'Go away,' I said, surprised he even knew my name.

'I just want to wait for your mother. I have a letter for her. I know she's with the Count. Please open the door, Franz.'

'No, put it through the letterbox and I will give it to her.'

He did not reply, and I could hear his heavy breath against the door as I prayed for him to go away. Suddenly the letterbox opened, and an envelope was pushed through into my hand. After a few desperate moments of anxiety, I heard his footsteps descending into the street. I rushed to the living room window and watched him under the glow of the streetlight as he wandered across the road and into the darkness. He was gone. I looked at the crumpled letter in my hand and put it in my pocket.

I sat by the living room window until the Count's car finally pulled up outside. It was raining, and I watched him kiss Mother on the cheek before getting back into the car behind his chauffeur. Just as the Count's car drove off, my heart nearly stopped when Karl appeared from the darkness and stood in the middle of the road with his hands outstretched towards Mother. I could hear him pleading with her as she shouted something abruptly at him, before turning away and running into the shadows of the building. I watched Karl, afraid he would follow her, but he just stood there like an abandoned child in the rain.

The following morning as I prepared to leave for school, Mother was back sitting at the living room window smoking and drinking coffee, looking unhappily out into the rain-drenched street. I still had Karl's letter in my bedroom and decided it was not a good time to give it to her. So, I said nothing, hoping her mood would change by the time I returned from school.

*

One sunny afternoon Mother and I sat at our usual table at the Café Kranzler when we were joined by one of her friends from her time in the bars and nightclubs. This beautiful-looking lady was dressed in a double-breasted pinstriped suit and wore a fedora hat with a pink carnation in the ribbon. After kissing Mother, rather strangely on the lips, she sat down and removed her hat to unleash a bouquet of golden curls. Mother introduced her friend to me as Maria, and I, realising my manners, immediately stood up and shook her slim, manicured hand. It was then I noticed the small white dog at her feet, which wore a sparkling collar attached to a slender lead that Maria held in her other hand. 'Maria is now an actress,' said Mother. 'We used to work together at the Kasbah.'

'Not much of an actress, but someday, perhaps I will be ... Oh, this is Lulu,' she smiled, lifting the poodle on to her lap. I patted the dog's soft curly coat, but she was not interested in my attention or the biscuit I offered her, and simply turned around on Maria's lap to find a comfortable resting place. Maria ordered a coffee and a bowl of water for Lulu, who was panting and looking up at her mistress with adoration.

Mother and her friend began to chat in giggles. Maria took out a cigarette and fluttered her eyes at the waiter. He immediately came to our table and lit her cigarette. He took a step back and she smiled at him through a cloud of smoke. That seemed to put him in a trance.

While Maria fed Lulu pieces of chicken, I noticed she was wearing a boutonnière of violet flowers, which were wilting in the hot sunshine. Her heady scent of perfume and tobacco smoke created an opiate of elegance, making me a little giddy as I sipped my coffee and watched the looks of longing from men passing by our table. Indifferent to her admirers, Maria began talking about her recent film, her hands animated as Mother laughed at her friend's theatrical antics. The beguiled waiter reappeared, this time with a tray of cakes, which Maria had ordered. I was asked to choose one, which I did. Mother then went into her handbag and brought out her purse, handing me her door keys and a couple of marks.

'When you've finished your coffee, take the tram home. I'll be home in a few hours.'

'Where are you going?'

'To get my hair set.'

They left the table arm in arm, with Lulu scurrying along at their feet. I watched them walk down the sunny side of the street like a courting couple as Mother put up her parasol. The waiter stood with his silver tray under his arm and shook his head, looking as bemused as I felt.

Once back at the apartment block, I paid Herr Kolinski a visit. He was pleased to see me as he welcomed me into his living room, where he had been eating his lunch. I declined his offer to share his meal and settled for a glass of lemonade. I told him all about Maria and he laughed and slapped his leg, even though I was not trying to be funny. After his lunch he asked me if I wanted to learn to play the violin. I nodded as he produced a smaller version of his own violin. 'This belonged to Jacob when he was learning to play around your age,' he said, gently tuning the strings. 'I would like you to have it and I will be happy to teach you.'

'Thank you, Herr Kolinski, I would love to learn.'

'Maybe not at first you won't, it's not an easy instrument to endure when played badly and every violinist must first play badly before they play well,' he said, handing me the violin.

My lessons began immediately, and he showed me how to hold the instrument, demonstrating with his own violin, before tucking it under his chin. I followed each thing he did, but the bow was unforgiving of my inexperience and rasped across the strings as I produced my first few tortured notes. 'Practice makes perfect,' he repeated time and time again as I grimaced at the screeching each movement of the bow made.

After half an hour or so, he must have suffered enough and concluded the lesson with another flawless rendition of Mendelssohn's masterpiece. It seemed to me I would have to live a very long time and practice every day if I were ever to play like him.

'What age are you, Franz?'

'I will be fourteen on my next birthday.'

'Don't be so eager to grow old. You're still only thirteen,

are you not?'

'Yes.'

'Remember, Franz, only violins age for the better,' he said, lifting his instrument and looking at it with affection. 'No, Franz, you should never be in a rush to grow old ... unless you're a violin.'

Chapter 8

It was already the middle of summer and there was still no mention of any date for Mother's wedding to the Count. Whenever I asked her about it, she always managed to avoid telling me anything. Then, out of the blue, she decided to throw a party.

Maria arrived in a suit, wearing a monocle and handing Mother a posy of violets. The Count arrived shortly after with a bouquet which required three vases to accommodate. He kissed Mother on the cheek and patted me on the head, before taking Maria's hand and kissing it as if she were some exotic Russian princess. Maria, of course, indulged the Count, producing a cigarette for him to light with his gold lighter. More guests arrived, mostly Mother's friends from the nightclubs, in their flamboyant dress and exaggerated manner that only got more theatrical as the champagne and caviar were passed around.

Mother began talking loudly and spilling her champagne, before putting on one of her jazz records and began pestering everyone to dance. Glad to get out of the noisy, smoke-filled room, I excused myself and went to my room. Harvey ignored my overtures to join me, preferring the attention he was getting from Mother's lady friends. He was such a tease. Once the party was in full swing and my absence of no consequence, I slipped out the front door and spent the evening in Herr Kolinski's company. He taught me more notes on the violin and afterwards made pancakes and tea. It was after midnight before I made my way back downstairs and went to bed, falling asleep without difficulty despite the noise in the living room.

The next morning, I got up to find the living room

cluttered with dirty plates, overflowing ashtrays and empty glasses lying in every corner. The smell of tobacco smoke, perfume and alcohol was overpowering. Maria, still in her doubled breasted suit, was asleep on the sofa. Everyone else had gone. Mother, I assumed was in her room. I lit the stove to make a pot of coffee, which woke Maria. 'Good morning, Franz, you're up early.'

'Would you like a coffee?'

'That would be wonderful, darling, and see if you can find my cigarettes.'

While Maria groaned and moaned about her sore head, I looked for and eventually found her cigarettes under the sofa. She gave a dramatic yawn and got up to sit at the dining table as I poured out her coffee and lit her cigarette. She smiled as she sipped the coffee. Her lipstick was smudged, and her tired-looking eyes blinked thick lacquered eyelashes at me.

'Has your mother finally gone to bed?' she asked, blowing a cloud of smoke up to the ceiling as though trying to get rid of it.

'Are you making another movie?'

'Oh, I'm in a silly little thing at the minute, but one day I will go to America and become a star,' she said, without a hint of modesty. 'You and I will go to the cinema someday and have a great time together watching one of my movies,' she added, framing her face in her hands as though she was about to be photographed. Then, as if she had just received an urgent telephone call from Hollywood, she stubbed out her cigarette and exhaled a spiral of smoke. 'I better get going.'

'Can't you stay for breakfast?' I asked, enjoying her company so much I did not want her to leave so soon.

'I would love to, Franz, but I have to go home and change, I've agreed to have lunch with my new director today.' She took another sip of coffee, before fixing her lipstick, and considering herself in her compact. 'I look terrible,' she sighed, before clicking the mirror over. She looked anything but terrible and I wanted to tell her how beautiful she looked but was too embarrassed. She left, leaving only the scent of her perfume behind. I watched her from the window. She looked every bit the movie star as she flagged down a taxi with a wave of her hand.

Not long after the party I awoke one morning to hear Mother sobbing uncontrollably. She was in her bedroom and I gently knocked on the door, but she told me, through heaving sobs, to go away. Undeterred, I turned the door handle, but it was locked. I pleaded with her to open the door, but she continued to cry and call out laments of remorse, begging God to forgive her. A sudden fear gripped me, and I could feel the hairs rising on my arms as I stepped away from the door. Something terrible has happened. I knocked at the door once more, but the only response was more sobs. I left her in peace and went to the living room to ponder what might have put her in such a state.

On the dining table I found a cigarette still burning in the ashtray beside a half-finished cup of coffee. I put the cigarette out and looked at the morning newspaper that was lying open. My heart almost stopped as I read what had clearly distressed her. The body of Karl Barber, the Berlin expressionist artist was recovered from the River Spree yesterday and formally identified by his heartbroken mother … There was a photograph of Karl, smiling as though he had not a care in the world alongside a canvas of his work, *The Harlequin*. I closed the paper. I could not look at it anymore. The letter, which I had conveniently forgotten about now screamed at me from my sock drawer.

I could no longer hear Mother and went back along the hall to listen at her door.

'Mother, are you all right?' I pleaded. 'Will I get someone?'

'No ... I'll be all right ... I just need some sleep,' she moaned.

I went into my room and pulled open the bottom drawer and stared at the envelope. My heart began to thump in my chest as I peeled it open and took out the letter. I was fearful of what might be in it but was still determined to know as I unfolded the pages. The handwriting was staccato and difficult to decipher, but I slowly read the woes of the late Karl Barber.

Dear Anna,

I know you no longer wish me in your life now you have found someone who can give you and your son the things in life which I cannot. This letter is to say goodbye and to promise you I will not come to you again; I know that to see you again would only make me want you more - if that were possible. I still remember the first time you were in my studio; I was overwhelmed by your naked beauty and could not at first find the paint or colours on my palette to do you justice. Now you are the only one I want to paint, and I struggle from memory to capture your skin, your hair, your mouth and most of all your eyes, the window to your soul. The artist without his muse is blind to beauty and I can no longer suffer in this darkness.

Yours forever, Karl.

My hand trembled as I read the letter for a second time. Do I give it to Mother? Would she thank me or hate me forever for not giving it to her when he was still alive? Should I destroy it, accepting the letter would only give her more pain and achieve nothing more? I began to think of its contents again. Mother was an artist's model and posed naked for him! There would be paintings of her in the nude; my thoughts changed from worrying about her heartache and more about her reputation. Dead artists had a habit of becoming fashionable.

Unable to control my imagination, I had visions of Karl's obsession producing ten, maybe twenty, naked portraits of my mother. Now he was dead, would they be displayed to the world in some kind of retrospective of the late artist's work? His suicide would surely add more value and mystique to the paintings and they may even end up in Le Louvre, alongside the enigmatic smile of the Mona Lisa, who at least had the decency to keep her clothes on.

What would the Count think of his future wife naked before the world? What would they say at school if it ever got out that my mother's naked portrait could be seen on a day trip to Paris? Why even Paris, no doubt those who would inherit the artist's work would probably display it in the National Gallery for all in Berlin to see. I was having cold sweats as I began to think of school trips to the gallery just for the depraved male teachers to gawp at my mother.

While I was pondering this nonsense, I heard Mother's door open and put the letter back in the drawer, before going into the hall to see if she needed anything.

'Are you all right?' I asked, following her into the living room.

'I'm fine, I just need a cigarette,' she said, looking desperately into the empty packet she had left on the table with her cold cup of coffee.

'I will go to the shop and get you some,' I said, taking my jacket from behind the door.

She smiled as she rummaged through her purse, but I rushed out, desperate to pay for them myself as some form of recompense for not giving her the letter.

Hurrying home with the cigarettes, I climbed the stairs three at a time and was struggling for breath by the time I reached the second landing.

Mother was still sitting at the dining-table, sipping cold coffee and staring out the window. I gave her the cigarettes as though they were a panacea for her heartbreak.

Mother never confided in me whether she loved Karl or not, but I was sure she did as much as he did her. The melancholy in her eyes that morning never left them; even if she laughed at something funny, the sadness was always there. I am sure she blamed herself for Karl's suicide, but unlike Father's death, when she found solace in going to Mass and lighting candles, she stopped going to chapel altogether.

I do not know if the Count ever found out about Karl, or whether Mother could no longer go through with it, but the wedding was called off shortly after Karl's funeral and I never saw the Count again.

After only a few weeks the food began to run out and Mother went back to working in the bars and nightclubs. Otto resumed his weekly visits to the flat, while Mother's drinking became a serious problem.

Chapter 9

It was in the autumn when I met Rebecca for the first time. Herr Kolinski had already told me she was arriving that morning. Keen to meet her, I sat at the living room window patiently waiting for her to arrive. Eventually a taxi pulled up and she got out wearing a blue coat and carrying a small suitcase. I went into the hall and heard her climbing the stairs, passing our front door, before rushing up the last flight to her waiting father. I listened to Herr Kolinski greet her in Yiddish.

'What are you up to?' asked Mother, having observed my dash from the window to the front door.

'Nothing … That was Herr Kolinski's daughter, she's staying with him for a few weeks.'

'Daughter, I never knew he had a daughter?'

'She boards at school and only comes home a couple of times a year.'

'Well, don't be going up to his apartment and annoying him, he'll want to spend as much time with her without you hanging around.'

'No, Mother, but I have my violin lesson tomorrow.'

'You don't have to go. One lesson won't make any difference.'

'But mother … '

'Don't argue. I already have a headache, don't make it any worse.'

Mother's dismissive tone annoyed me. Herr Kolinski was not just a neighbour, but my only real friend. I went to my room and stayed there until Mother began to get ready to go out. When she was gone I went into the living room; as usual my dinner was plated and waiting for me on the dining table.

It was pickled herring and cold potato. I pushed it away and sat in the dark for a while. There was the sound of muffled voices from Herr Kolinski's apartment and I wondered what he and Rebecca were talking about.

After another late night, Mother remained in bed while I got dressed and made breakfast; a little piece of pickled herring for Harvey and a boiled egg for me. Later, while sitting at the window, I watched some Orthodox Jews on their way to the synagogue, wearing their sombre black clothes and hats. These were the Hasidic Jews who mainly lived in the Jewish Quarter, but occasionally came into our neighbourhood to protest against the local rabbi, who they saw as corrupting the Torah with his liberal interpretation of its tenets.

Once they had disappeared around the corner, I went into my bedroom to collect some of the books Herr Kolinski had given me over the months, and went upstairs to his apartment, convincing myself there was an urgent need to return them.

'Good morning, Franz,' he said, opening the door to find me standing there with the books piled high in my arms. 'You've read them all already?'

'Yes,' I lied, having only looked at a few of them.

'Here, let me take some before you drop them. Come in, there's someone I would like you to meet.'

I followed him into the living room, feeling a little nervous at the prospect of meeting Rebecca. The room was bright in morning sunshine and she was sitting at the piano tidying up the sheets of music. 'This is Franz,' said Herr Kolinski, putting the books he was carrying on the floor.

'Good morning, Franz,' said Rebecca, taking the other books from me. 'Mathematics and physics,' she said, looking at the covers for a moment, before putting them on top of the piano. 'Papa said you were something of a genius.'

I was unable to find my voice or wit to say anything; her

vivacious, dark eyes and smile left me dumb. I had never seen anyone so beautiful before. Thankfully, she turned back to the piano and began to play as Herr Kolinski beckoned me to sit with him at the dining table.

The room soon filled with music. Herr Kolinski beamed with pride at the flawless recital as he whispered, 'Chopin,' to me. As I listened to the intensity of Rebecca's performance, the prospect of playing the violin in front of her made me feel sick, but I need not have worried.

'That's our taxi,' said Herr Kolinski, as a cab sounded its horn outside. 'I'm sorry, Franz, we will have to go now. We are going to the circus today.'

'The circus!' I said, rather more excitedly than I had intended.

'Why don't you come along with us?' suggested Rebecca, getting up from the piano and putting on her coat.

'Why not?' said Herr Kolinski.

'I would love to, but I'll have to ask my mother?'

'We'll get the taxi driver to hold on for a few minutes,' he said, putting on his coat and hat and smiling reassuringly at me.

It was with excitement, and a little hesitation, I went back downstairs. Mother's headaches were becoming more frequent, making her short-tempered, so I wasn't sure what kind of mood she would be in when opening the door to her bedroom. She was sleeping, so I decided not to bother her and went into my own room to get my coat. Taking some money from my sock drawer I rushed downstairs to the waiting taxi.

The traffic became chaotic and noisy by the time we reached Potsdamer Platz. Rebecca pointed out the big-top in the distance, and we laughed with excitement. The taxi forced its way through the crowds of people who were heading in the same direction. Eventually the driver gave up and dropped us off within walking distance. We followed the crowds towards the massive tent, the excitement growing with every step.

Herr Kolinski paid for the three tickets, and we took our seats as the ringmaster emerged from a cloud of smoke in the centre of the ring. He strutted around the ring, boasting about the unique nature of each act, which he assured would enthral and entertain us like nothing had ever done before. Everyone cheered when six beautiful white horses, carrying female riders in shimmering costumes, circled the ring to the sound of the ringmaster's whip. Soon we were being entertained with dancing elephants: ferocious-looking lions, and death defying trapeze artists. Each time an act finished their routine, the clowns would come out in their baggy clothes and painted faces, knocking each other over and throwing buckets of water at the harlequin who was trying to control them. It was during these moments of general mayhem the audience laughed the loudest, myself and Rebecca included; although at times I only laughed because I saw her laughing. Herr Kolinski was happy eating his bagels and slapping his leg with his other hand whenever he was amused. I was having the best day of my life.

All too soon the show was over, and we were on our way back home. Herr Kolinski bought three toffee apples and we ate them as we walked in the late afternoon sun for a while, before getting the tramcar to Alexanderplatz. Everywhere there were posters of the grinning clown, entreating those who had not yet had the pleasure to join him at the famous Berlin Metropolitan Circus before they missed the experience of a lifetime.

While on the tram I learned from Rebecca that she and her father were going to Krakow in the morning to spend the rest of her two-week vacation with her grandparents. As she spoke my mouth became dry and I could not think of anything to say. I wanted to go with them, but knew it was impossible.

*

It rained relentlessly for the next two weeks, making the days exceptionally long and dreary. To pass the time, I tried to make friends with some of the local children, who regularly played in the back courtyard, but quickly found we had nothing in common. I retreated into my room and my perpetual loneliness. I spent most of my time listening to passing trains and reading novels. Mother was now drinking more than ever, and she and Otto were having furious rows most nights, until they tired themselves out and went to bed, often leaving the gramophone screeching on the last few grooves until I got up and took it off. No wonder Mother suffered from so many headaches and was sick most mornings. How I wished for the Count to come back and restore me to the future I had planned for myself as his stepson and heir. Then, I would marry Rebecca and she would become a Countess.

One day Mother did not emerge from her bedroom until late in the afternoon. She had been drinking again and looked awful. Her eyes were tired, and I noticed for the first time the black circles, giving her a haunted look. In spite of eating very little, she was at least putting on some weight.

When the winter began to take hold, Otto stopped coming to the flat. Mother began to spend more and more time in her bedroom only emerging for the occasional cup of coffee and cigarette. Her once beautiful face was showing signs of age and neglect. If only she would stop drinking.

When eating supper one evening, I asked her if she had seen my school clothes as they were not in my room. She looked at me long and hard and said, 'I'm sorry, Franz, I had to sell them with most of my own clothes to get money to pay the rent and buy food … you've still got your old clothes. They'll have to do for now.' The piece of sausage meat I was about to swallow almost stuck in my throat, but before I could protest, Mother got up abruptly and went back to her bedroom with a bottle of sherry.

That night I lay on my bed listening to her crying and cursing herself. I lit a candle and watched the shadows it made on the walls. Herr Kolinski began playing his violin, drowning out Mother's moans and groans of self-pity. The sound of the music made me think of Rebecca, who had gone straight back to boarding school from Krakow. I wondered if she ever thought about our day at the circus. It was my fourteenth birthday in the morning, but I did not expect any gifts. Even if she remembered, Mother had nothing to give.

Chapter 10

Lying in bed one morning, I heard Mother getting up early despite being out most of the night. Hoping she had something to make for breakfast, I went into the living room where she was crouching over a bucket at her feet. I then noticed some small, wet balls of hair lying nearby on a newspaper. The blood began to drain from me when I realised the balls of hair were six tiny kittens. Before I could say anything, Mother took another one from the bucket and placed it with the rest of the drowned litter. Harvey, who was meowing in distress from behind the kitchenette door, had miraculously given birth.

'Why are you drowning the kittens?' I shouted at her.

'Go back to your bed … we can't feed one cat, never mind a litter of them!' she said coldly, while wrapping the kittens up in the damp newspaper.

I stared at her in disbelief as she turned to throw the evidence of her slaughter into the bin. Unable to look at her any longer, I ran from the apartment, slamming the door behind me.

Not sure where I was going and blinded with tears, I ran across the main road with little regard to my safety. It was bitter cold, and my coat, which had only one button left and was far too small for me, gave little protection. Holding it tight to my chest, as the wind conspired to blow it open. Shivering, I hurried along the icy pavements. It was so cold that I took shelter in the Alexanderplatz station, determined never to go back to the apartment. With the trains endlessly coming and going, the big railway clock gradually exchanged minutes for hours. Eventually one of the guards, who had been watching me for a while, came over and asked me what

I was doing there.

'I'm waiting for a friend.'

'And who is your friend?'

'Maria Bernhardt, the actress, if you must know.'

'And what train is Fräulein Bernhardt on?' he asked doubtfully.

'The one thirty from Dresden.'

'There's no train arriving from Dresden. What are you doing here and why are you not at school?'

'I have TB,' I said, feigning a cough, making him take a step back and put his hand to his mouth.

'You can't stay here! Get out of here before I call the police.'

With the shelter of the station deprived to me, I went back out to the bitter wind that was howling around the buildings. With nowhere else to go I walked up one street and down another. The roads became busier nearer the city centre, and I stopped only for a moment on reaching the Café Kranzler. With no money for coffee or cakes, I crossed the busy road and walked up the middle of the wide thoroughfare of the Linden, towards the Brandenburger Tor.

Eventually I reached the Hotel Adlon and promptly walked passed the doorman only to find the collar of my coat being pulled from behind. He dragged me back out into the street before my feet touched the expensive foyer carpet.

'And where do you think you are going, young man?'

'I want to see my friend; her name is Gretchen.'

'And what does Gretchen do here? Is she a guest?' he enquired with a sarcastic tone.

'No, she is a waitress.'

'A waitress is she, and you think you can march right in and demand to see her. Now get out of here before I get the police to you,' he barked, giving me a hard push, nearly knocking me off my feet. Humiliated, I walked away as he rushed to open the door of a large black Daimler that had just pulled up.

Determined not to give up so easy, I went around the back of the hotel to see if there was another way in. I walked down an alley where there was a coal wagon being unloaded next to an open door. One of the chefs came out to speak to the two men who were emptying bags of coal down a large chute. The chef noticed me standing nearby.

'What do you want … ? We don't have anything to give you.'

'I don't want anything … I just want to speak to Gretchen.'

'Gretchen? And what is she to you?'

'She worked for my mother.'

'Your mother,' he laughed, looking at me and shaking his head.

'Please, I only want to speak to her for a moment … my mother's not well … my name is Franz Schreiber.'

'Wait here,' said the chef, before going back into the hotel and closing the door behind him.

The two men continued to unload the wagon until the last bag was emptied down the chute. They looked totally exhausted. One began coughing, spitting phlegm and coal dust from his mouth. Once he had recovered he turned to me. 'I don't think he's coming back, son.'

'But he must.'

'Give the door a knock, Hans,' he said to the other man, who began pounding the door with his fist.

'All right, all right,' complained the chef as he opened the door. 'She's coming, she's coming.'

It began to rain, and I tried to keep my coat closed, afraid of what she might think of my shabby clothes. The two coalmen were now throwing the empty coal sacks onto the back of the wagon but did not look like they were in a hurry to leave.

'Franz … Franz, it's really you,' exclaimed Gretchen as she pushed past the chef, who was still standing in the doorway smoking. She ran to me and gave me a hug. I began to cry, relived that she still cared about me. 'What's wrong with your mother, Franz?'

'She drinks too much and cries all the time. Can you help her?'

'Of course, Franz, but first you look like you could do with something to eat. Have you eaten today?'

'No, there's no food left.'

'My God, what happened to your poor mother?'

'I don't know, but she hates me.'

'She doesn't hate you, Franz. She must be very ill. We'll have to get her a doctor.'

Gretchen took me into the kitchen and I told her what had become of us, which made her cry. The chef ordered one of the cooks to make me something to eat as he dried my coat over a stove. The more I told Gretchen, the more she cried. Devouring everything the cook put before me, I was feeling the best I had felt for months,

'Tell your mother I'll come over after work,' she said, noting down the address and handing me ten marks. I'm sure Aaron will be able to give me another ten marks for your mother. I will bring some food with me tonight. Now don't walk all the way back in the rain, take the tram.'

After another tearful hug, I left the hotel kitchen filled with hope that Gretchen would put an end to Mother's drinking and to my misery.

It took me over an hour to walk home, saving the ten marks for food. When I climbed the stairs to the apartment, Mother was sitting on the landing, her hair hanging over her face and our suitcases sitting beside her. 'Where the hell have you been?' she said, her breath smelling of sherry. 'Get your suitcase!'

'What's happened?'

'We've been evicted; we'll have to find somewhere else to stay before it gets dark.'

'But Mother, I saw Gretchen today … '

'Gretchen, we don't need Gretchen. What can she do for us!' she hissed at me as though she had lost her mind completely. 'Now hurry up or we will be sleeping on the streets.'

'What about Harvey?'

'The cat is with Frau Kessler.'

'Can we not take it with us?'

'No, she's too weak, and we don't even have anywhere to stay ourselves, she'll be better off here with Frau Kessler. Now let's get going before it starts to get dark.'

'Can I at least say goodbye to Herr Kolinski … '

'No … No … We haven't got time!'

I followed Mother back into the bitter wind, my stomach in knots with dread. There was no taxi waiting outside this time. Mother walked ahead, talking to herself. I ran to keep up with her. Where she got the strength, God only knows. On Friedrichstrasse, she took some addresses down advertised in a shop window and we made our way to the public phone outside the post office, where she made a number of phone calls. She turned dejectedly to me. 'We don't have enough for a deposit,' she said, counting the coins in her purse.

'Here, Gretchen gave me this,' I said, showing the ten marks, which she snatched from my hand without a hint of gratitude. She began phoning again until she finally secured an apartment we could now apparently afford.

The last of the daylight was fading from the sky, and after walking for miles we eventually arrived outside a block of apartments that looked like they grew organically from the ground like some misshaped fungi. The street was filthy, and the smell of raw sewage made me feel sick. I reluctantly followed Mother up the stairs to the top landing, where an old man was waiting impatiently.

'Five o'clock, you said … I was about to leave.'

'I'm sorry,' said Mother, struggling to get her case on to

the landing as I pushed her from behind to stop her falling back downstairs on top of me. 'We had to walk a very long way to get here.'

'Have you got the deposit?'

'Yes,' replied Mother handing the landlord the money. 'It's all there.'

'You don't mind if I count it,' said the unpleasant man, thumbing through the money with his dirty fingers.

Once the landlord was satisfied Mother was not lying, he opened the door and led us into a bleak hall. He lit an oil lamp and showed us into what he called the living room. The smell was awful and stank of stale urine and beer, but as Mother turned to complain the landlord was already on his way downstairs. Even if Mother got her deposit back, it was now too late to find anywhere else. Exhausted, I let my suitcase fall to the floor.

Mother, knowing we had nowhere else to go, began to take some carefully wrapped sausages from her suitcase, before searching the cupboards for a pan to cook them in. I helped her unpack the other bits and pieces she had salvaged from our former apartment, including packets of tea, coffee and sugar. 'See if there's any coal in the bunker and try to put a fire on,' she said.

Mother found a pot and frying pan, which she scrubbed under the cold tap, before putting on some supper. She was continually talking to herself as she opened and closed cupboards, looking for cutlery and plates that were not broken or filthy.

'That's the fire on,' I said as the flames took hold and the wood kindling crackled violently.

'Good, at least that's something. Here take this, it's the best I can do; we'll get something decent to eat tomorrow.'

The sausages tasted off, but I ate them anyway. Mother did not look in the mood for complaints. She did not make any for herself, content with a coffee and a cigarette. At least she did not have one of her headaches. I hoped she would stay sober for a while until we got the filthy apartment cleaned up. The thought depressed me.

Then it struck me that there was only one bedroom and I was going to have to sleep on the settee. The smell of urine in the room was overpowering and the sausages wanted to come back up. Mother threw me some bed clothes and got ready to go out, I did not ask her where she was going, and she left without even saying goodnight. I sat in the dark trying to make sense of our descent into poverty. Not being able to say goodbye to Herr Kolinski also troubled me, as much as not being there for Gretchen when she must have arrived to find no one to help. Even worse was the realisation I would never see Rebecca again.

Chapter 11

My body racked with pain, I awoke the next morning after the most uncomfortable sleep possible. To add to my misery, the apartment was freezing cold. Having slept in my clothes, they now smelt as bad the settee. I began to scratch myself wondering if fleas would be hard up enough to live in such a place. With some effort I got up to take a better look at the hovel we were living in. Apart from the settee, there were a couple of chairs and a small dining table, but not much else. The damp-stained wallpaper looked like it was clinging to the walls with nothing more than willpower. How could we ever make this our home? The windows were filthy, and I wiped one with my sleeve to look out into the grey morning. Over the noise of the passing trams, the street echoed with the shouts of street traders. I had no idea where in Berlin we had ended up, but it was the most miserable looking place I had ever seen.

I had no choice but to make the most of it, and shivered uncontrollably, while putting on a fire to heat the place up before making a pot of coffee. The smell of coffee must have stirred Mother from her sleep. She was standing at the living room door in her dressing gown and with a cigarette in her mouth. 'This place is a dump,' she moaned, lighting up and staggering towards the table and the pot of coffee. 'We'll have to find somewhere else,' she slurred. She was still drunk.

'Is there any money to buy food?'

'Yes, I'll go out later and get what we need.'

'Do you want me to go now and buy some groceries?'

'No, I have to go out later, anyway. There are some sausages in the cupboard ... you can have them for your breakfast. I'm going back to bed after this,' she said, pouring a cup of black coffee and taking a long draw from her cigarette.

After another cup of coffee and a few more cigarettes, Mother went to her room. I lit the stove and put the frying pan on to heat, but when I removed the sausages from their wrapping paper, there were teeth marks on some of them, making me fear we were sharing the apartment with rats. I threw them into the rubbish bin and turned the gas off. With nothing to eat and unable to stomach being in the apartment much longer, I decided to go out and get some fresh air and find out what kind of neighbourhood we lived in. I left without telling mother, no longer feeling the need to get her permission.

One street was as rundown as the next, and the blocks of slums seemed to lean against one another as much for comfort as support. It was cold, and a soup kitchen at the top of one of the streets was already busy with hungry, dirty faces clutching tins and pots in the hope of something warm to eat. For a moment I was tempted to join them; however, my pride was stronger than my hunger, but only just. Across the road a man was sitting on a wooden box with two war medals on his coat lapel, his hands shaking violently as he begged for a few pfennigs from passers-by. I continued to walk away from the apartment in the hope of finding some familiar streets.

After an hour or so I came across a street market selling all kinds of second-hand things, much of which was old junk to me. I wandered aimlessly around the stalls just glad to be out of the apartment for a while. I then walked further along the main street and looked in the shop windows to pass the time. One of the larger stores had a Christmas tree outside and its windows were full of toys and decorations. The thought of Christmas made me feel even more miserable. My melancholy did not last long when the smell of bread, coming from a bakery on the next corner, distracted me. I crossed the road and stood at the shop window, which was full of freshly baked bread, cakes and pastries, making my mouth salivate and my stomach rumble.

Hoping she had been to the grocers and bought something decent to eat, I turned to go back to the apartment. Before getting very far it began to rain, quickly turning to sleet in the bitter wind. I hurried along, half blinded by the icy sleet which was now tearing at my face and hands like tiny needles. Unable to see much ahead, I crossed roads taking little notice of the car horns honking at my apparent indifference to my own safety.

On reaching the doss-house, the wind had died down and the sleet had turned to snow. There was a queue forming at the soup kitchen as the steam from the large pots of soup mingled with the falling snow. I tried to walk past the cold hungry faces, but found myself in the queue, shuffling my feet to stop them freezing to the pavement. A nun poured me a bowl of peas and barley soup and indicated for me to take a piece of rye bread. I followed those at the front of the queue into a hall of tables and chairs, where homeless men, women and children were already devouring their soup. I sat at the edge of a table, glad to be able to put my bowl down before it slipped out of my unfeeling hands. There was a clatter of noise as the famished faces scraped the bottoms of their bowls, while the nuns walked around picking up the empty dishes. Despite a revolting smell of urine and body odour from some at my table, I continued to eat, wondering how I managed to become destitute without doing much wrong in my life to anger God. I ate the rye bread, dunking it into what was left in the bowl to soften the hard edges.

Ashamed of my own wretchedness, I managed to leave the soup kitchen without speaking to anyone. Outside I struggled to keep my feet in what was fast becoming a blizzard.

Eventually I reached our tenement block. It did not look so awful now its ugliness was covered in snow. After kicking the lack of feeling out of my feet on the first few steps, I hurried upstairs into the apartment hoping Mother was well enough to have kept the fire going at least. She wasn't. The apartment was cold, and she was still in her bedroom. I gently opened her door to see if she needed anything, but she screamed at me with such ferocity to get out, I almost fell back into the hall.

Once I had regained my composure, I took the bucket and filled it with coal to put a fire on. My hands were still numb as I placed each piece of coal on the grate around crushed sheets of old newspapers and the last of the kindling. The fire was slow to come to life, but once it did, I put my hands over the flames to get some feeling back in my fingers. I then heard Mother moaning in her bedroom. I got up from my knees, determined to get her to leave her room and have something to eat. I looked in the cupboards, but there was nothing there. I banged the doors closed in anger. She had not even bothered to go out and buy the groceries.

Venturing back into her room, Mother did not shout this time. She did not even seem to notice me standing at the foot of her bed, even though she was sitting up and staring at me. She began moaning as if in great pain, which frightened me. 'Mother, what's wrong? Will I get a doctor?'

'No, Franz! No … They'll send me to prison,' she pleaded.

It was then I noticed the blood stains on the bed clothes. 'What in the name of God have you done?' I demanded, pulling back the bedding, terrified she had cut her wrists. Never in my wildest nightmares did I expect to see the scene which now dumbfounded me as I stared in horror at the smallest baby I had ever seen, lying twisted like a broken doll between her blood smeared legs. 'Franz, take it away! Please! I don't want to look at it. God forgive me … God forgive me ... '

Stupefied by the gruesomeness of what lay before me, I took a deep breath to regain my balance, before stripping a pillow that was lying on the floor. With the peas and barley soup churning in my stomach and my hands shaking, I lifted the dead baby to put into the pillow case, only to find it was still attached to Mother. There was now warm, sticky blood on my hands. I dropped it back onto the bed and stared at Mother's pleading eyes. 'Cut it!' she screamed. 'Franz, for the love of God cut it! They'll send me to prison!'

Terrified Mother would end up in prison, I rushed into the kitchen and pulled the cutlery drawer open so hard its contents scattered on the floor. I began to fear the neighbours would think there was a murder in progress, although I was not sure if there had not already been one. After finding a pair of scissors under the sink, I became too frightened to go back into the room to use them. There was a noise from the hall that distracted me, and for a moment it sounded as if there was someone at the front door. I stood motionless for a few minutes but heard nothing more. I took a deep breath and went back into Mother's room to get the ghastly ordeal over as quickly as possible.

Mother was still sitting up, unable to look at the unholy carnage lying between her legs. Frozen with fear, I stared at the twisted umbilical cord, afraid, either the dead baby or Mother would scream when I cut it. With my hands trembling and eyes half closed, somehow, I managed to separate Mother from her mortal sin. There were no screams, just Mother sobbing with relief.

Exhausted, she lay back on the bed, while I, still trembling from head to toe, lifted the source of her torment and put it into the pillowcase. The tiny body was still warm. I took it into the living-room and put it on the table, unable, in my confused state, to decide what to do with it. To my alarm, there was a hard knock at the front door causing me to drop the scissors, which stuck in the floor only inches from my left foot. I walked back and forward, not sure what to do with the blood-stained pillow case or what was inside it. For a moment I thought of throwing it out the kitchen window, but a semblance of sanity prevailed, and I put it in a bucket under the sink. There was another knock at the door, this time more demanding. Breathing heavily, but slightly reassured Mother was now quiet. I washed my hands in the sink, wiping them dry on my trousers, before going to the front door.

'What's going on in there?' demanded a stout middle-aged woman as she tried to look over my shoulder into the hall.

'Nothing, my mother's been ill, and I dropped a drawer on to the floor when I was looking for her medicine.'

'What's wrong with her to be making so much noise?'

'She's got stomach pains. She's sleeping now.'

'Well, try and keep the noise down,' she said, still lifting her eyes over my shoulder and looking into the dimly lit hall. 'Is your father not at home?'

'No, he's dead ... He was killed in the war,' I added quickly, as though the nature of his death would make a difference.

'Oh ... Well, keep the noise down.'

With her questions satisfied, the neighbour turned and went back downstairs muttering to herself as I closed over the door and locked it. I looked in on Mother, who was quietly crying, the bloody bedclothes now strewn across the floor. I went back into the living room, frantically pacing the room and wondering what to do. The whole thing was like some grotesque, demonic dream. The fact she was pregnant would have been a shock, but to find out in this hideous way left me horrified. With all the blood and my understandable panic, I had not even noticed if the dead baby was a boy or a girl. Although, oddly curious, I was not brave enough to find out now the body was wrapped in its bloody shroud. It would take more than morbid curiosity to make me look upon such a gruesome sight again.

The snow was still falling outside while the dead baby remained in the bucket under the sink. My cowardice returning, I was now too afraid to go back under the sink but knew the evidence of Mother's promiscuity could not stay there much longer. Still trying to make sense of my own scattered thoughts, I made Mother a cup of coffee and told her there was a packet of cigarettes in the living room, tempting her out of bed so I could at least change the soiled bedding.

With some gentle persuasion, she got up and put her nightgown on. I helped her towards the living room as she muttered confused prayers to herself. She hesitated when we got to the door, no doubt fearing the thing she was so desperate to be separated from would be waiting there for her with an accusing bloody finger. I reassured her everything was all right and guided her to the settee, where she sat in all her misery, still mumbling for God's forgiveness.

Now strangely calm, I went back into the bedroom and took the remaining bedclothes from the bed and gathered them with those she had thrown on the floor. The mattress was also saturated with body fluids and I wiped what I could with one of the sheets, before turning it over.

Taking Mother's suitcase from above the wardrobe, I put the soiled bedding into it. Under the bed I found an empty bottle of sherry and a small bottle which contained some kind of medicine, whatever was in it, smelt unpleasant. I put it and the sherry bottle into the suitcase, before leaving it in the hall.

Feeling much better now the bed had been made, I took the tin bathtub from the kitchen recess and put it into Mother's room, before going back into the living room, where she was sitting with her head in her hands. 'Mother,

I've made the bed for you, but you'll have to get yourself washed,' I said, putting a large pot on the stove to heat some water. She did not answer.

Undeterred and fearful of another knock at the door, I filled the bathtub and pleaded with her to go back to her room and get washed. She nodded weakly and I helped her back to her feet and along the hall to her room. With Mother out of the way, I took the suitcase into the living room and opened it next to the sink cupboard, but quickly lost my nerve. Even in such a short passage of time, my dead sibling had become even more hideous to me and the thought of touching it again turned my stomach. The rights and wrongs were not a consideration, only the dread that I had to force myself to do what my mind refused to do. Smoking one of Mother's cigarettes, I tried to think of what to do with the tiny body once it was secreted in the suitcase.

Somehow emboldened by the rush of nicotine to my brain, and before I had the chance to deter myself, I opened the sink cupboard, shamefully grabbing the pillowcase, and throwing it into the open suitcase, before quickly closing the lid as though I had trapped an evil genie in a bottle.

The cigarette was still burning in the ashtray and I took another long draw in the hope of some more relief from the nervous adrenaline that was making my body feverishly shiver. The smoke filled my lungs, making me light-headed, and instead of relief, it brought up the peas and barley. I managed to get to the sink just in time to see the doss-house soup for the second time that day.

Being sick cleared my head, and I was now determined to get rid of the suitcase and its contents that night. The idea the rats might already be feasting on it made me feel even more anxious. I thought for a moment of burying it, but where? I took another draw from the cigarette; the idea of throwing the suitcase into the river came to me.

Back in her bed, Mother was fast asleep. Determined to

get the ordeal over as soon as possible, I took the bathtub and poured its contents down the sink. I recoiled in fright as the other part of the severed umbilical cord fell into the sink with the bloody bathwater. Was there no end to this nightmare?

I could not face opening the suitcase again, and, so lifted the rubber textured cord and threw it into the fire. The sound of it crackling and hissing in the flames made me feel sick again, but there was nothing to throw up. I curled on the couch.

In spite of the time dragging, it passed all the same, and I eventually decided it was late enough to risk taking the suitcase to the river. I was glad to get past the downstairs neighbour's apartment without incident and was soon walking along the snow-covered pavement in the direction of the nearest bridge. The lateness of the hour and the heavy snowfall gave me some protection from prying eyes, but I was still terrified of being discovered in what had now become the devil's work. The suitcase, although not heavy, was big and awkward and I quickly discovered it glided along much more easily on the thick snow, now crystallised with a glitter of fresh ice.

The river, I knew from my afternoon walk, was not too far away. I struggled on until voices coming along the street made me panic. As they drew near, I picked up the case with both hands and ran along an alley into an adjacent street, all the time expecting a police whistle to follow me.

Eventually, I looked back, but could see no one in the diffused gaslight and falling snow. By chance, this forced change of direction found me in a street leading straight to a pedestrian bridge.

The bridge was deserted as I approached, dragging the suitcase with both hands, which were now turning blue. Once on the bridge, I stared at the large flakes of snow falling into the darkness, quickly melting into the black water below.

After an anxious look back to the road, I lifted the suitcase and pushed it over the railings. There was a splash as it hit the water, but it did not sink. It floated under the bridge, emerging on the other side. The falling snow began to gather on top, and I watched it float down the middle of the river, until it vanished into the vast darkness.

On my way home, I cursed my stupidity for not putting some stones into the suitcase to make it sink. I began to fear it would be fished out in the morning. I tried to reassure myself that even if they found the suitcase and its gory contents, there was no way they could trace it all the way back to Mother.

By the time I got home, she was still asleep, and the fire was almost out. My hands and feet numb, I sat in front of the faltering flames, taking off my wet shoes and socks, and placing them on the hearth to dry out. The room was quiet, except the occasional spark from the dying fire as the coals crumbled into ashes.

Chapter 12

Stumbling over to the sink and washing my face in the ice-cold water, the whole grisliness of the previous night came rushing back to me. I made a pot of coffee and took a cup in to Mother, but she was sound asleep. It was hard to believe what had taken place in that room: everything seemed strangely normal. Picking up Mother's dressing gown from the floor, her purse fell out of one of the pockets. Opening it, I took ten marks and went to the local shops and bought some groceries and a packet of cigarettes. The chemist shop on the corner would not sell me any rat poison because of my age.

When I got back, Mother was sitting in a stupor in the living room. She looked frightened as though she feared what I might say to her, but, I had already decided not to mention what had taken place. I did, however, find it hard to look at her when handing her the packet of cigarettes. 'I took some money from your purse and bought food … Hope that was all right?' I said, while emptying the bags of groceries.

She nodded but did not say anything, nervously lighting a cigarette and turning to look out the window. Even though she insisted she was not hungry, I made breakfast for both of us, deciding not to tell her about the rats in case it put her off eating it.

She ate the breakfast in spite of herself. Considering what she had been through, she seemed to have suffered no physical injury obvious to me from her manner. We sat in silence for a long while until she finally spoke. 'Franz, can you go back to the other flat and get the gramophone, I left it with the Kesslers,' she said, her voice weak, almost inaudible.

'How can you even think about your gramophone after what you've been through? Why do we need it now?'

'I don't want it. You might be able to sell it. We don't have much money left and I don't feel well enough to go to work tonight.'

'I don't know how to get there.'

'You can take a tram from the bottom of the street to Alexanderplatz, you know the way from there,' she explained, handing me some coins from her purse, her voice sounding much stronger already.

'Will you be all right; do you not need to see a doctor?'

'No, I just need some rest … I'm sorry you had to deal with … '

'I don't want to talk about it!' I said, getting up from the table. 'You should go to bed; I'll be back as soon as I can. There's a market in the Scheunenviertel, I can try and sell the gramophone there. How much do you think we will get for it?'

'You might get twenty marks, maybe a little more.'

Once Mother had gone back to bed I took the tram to Alexanderplatz, a place so familiar to me that I was glad to be there. Although most of the snow from the previous night had turned to slush, it was slippery underfoot. By the time I got to my old apartment block, my socks were soaking wet, the holes in both my shoes making them all but useless in such weather.

Herr Kessler, still in his pyjama bottoms and vest, opened the door. He did not look pleased to see me; maybe he thought we would not return for the gramophone and he would get to keep it. After telling him why I was there I asked him about Harvey, but he shrugged his shoulders. 'How would I know where that damn cat is?' He then went back into his apartment where I could hear him speaking with Frau Kessler. He returned with the gramophone, handing it to me without another word before abruptly banging his door closed.

Prior to taking it downstairs, I went up with it to the next landing, hoping to be able to say goodbye to Herr Kolinski, but there was no answer. I assumed he was at his shop, and went back downstairs with the heavy gramophone, calling for Harvey, but she was nowhere to be seen either.

On my way to the market in Scheunenviertel, I hurried across one road after another, trying my best to avoid being knocked down. On reaching the market, I was glad to be able to put the gramophone down and rest my arms, before deciding which stall to take it to.

'What are you doing?' asked a voice I instantly recognised. I turned to see Maria in a long fur coat, standing beside me. A burly looking man in a dark blue uniform and peaked cap stood next to her holding Lulu.

'Fräulein Bernhardt!' I gasped, almost falling to my knees as though I had just had a visitation from an angel.

'Hello Franz, I saw you struggling along the road. Didn't you hear Helmut calling after you?'

'No.'

'Where are you taking your mother's gramophone?'

'I need to sell it. We were evicted from the apartment and we have no money.'

'Helmut, give me Lulu and take the gramophone to the car. Now, Franz, tell me what's been happening. How is your mother? What happened with her and the Count? I heard he got married to some ugly Russian ballerina ... Did your mother get my letters?' she asked in a flurry, not giving me a chance to answer before she smothered me with a hug of fur and perfume. We walked to the car behind Helmut, who carried the gramophone like it was a precious relic.

Feeling as if I had just been woken from a nightmare, I took a seat next to Maria in the back of the car, her perfume helping to mask the smell from the clothes I had not taken off in three days. Maria did not seem to care, pulling me close as she asked what had happened to make Mother have to sell her gramophone in a flea market.

'She became ill and lost her job. The landlord kicked us out,' I said, as though making a formal complaint to a magistrate.

'That swine Otto … I knew he was only after one thing.'

Helmut gave the horn a blast and we drove off into the traffic. The car coughed and spluttered at first, until it picked up speed.

'Where are you living now?' she asked.

'Brunnenstrasse … number thirty-five.'

'Where on earth is Brunnenstrasse? Helmut, do you know where it is?' she shouted over the noise of the engine.

'Yes, Fräulein Bernhardt, it's not far.'

We drove past the soup kitchen and on towards Brunnenstrasse, Maria gripped my hand tightly and was near to tears when Helmut pulled up outside the apartment block. 'My God, Franz, how the hell did you both end up living here?'

I just shrugged my shoulders, what could I say?

Helmut got out of the car first as a group of half-starved children immediately gathered on the pavement, their faces showing signs of malnutrition. When Helmut opened the door for us, the children pushed and shoved each other to get close to Maria, their hands outstretched as they begged for money. Maria followed me, throwing a handful of coins onto the pavement to distract them until we got into the building. I led her passed the stinking communal toilet and up the dirty stairs. When I showed her into the apartment, her breathing became heavy. Mother's bedroom door was lying open, but she was not in her bed. Maria put her gloved hand to her mouth as I opened the living room door. Mother was sitting at the window smoking and drinking coffee as usual. 'Anna,' muttered Maria, her voice breaking as Mother turned towards her, without expression.

'It's me, Maria ... What in the name of God has happened to you?'

They embraced, Maria's beautiful clothes contrasting sharply with Mother's shabby dressing-gown. The tears began to run down my face when I heard Mother sobbing like a child in Maria's arms.

Once they had talked themselves dry of emotion, Maria stood up and looked around the room. 'Anna, pack your things, you and Franz are not staying here a minute longer. You can stay with me until we find you both a decent apartment.'

'We don't have any money,' said Mother, shaking her head in despair.

'Don't worry about money,' said Maria. 'I have enough for both of us. What's the point in having a rich lover if I can't spend his money,' she said, winking at me.

It did not take long to get our belongings together; we had little left worth taking. Maria went downstairs to fetch Helmut to carry our things to the car. I followed with my few possessions in my arms. We then drove through the busy streets until we crossed over the river to the west bank where Helmut turned the car into a parking bay outside a modern block of flats.

Maria's apartment was on the third floor and we took the elevator, which required an elderly man in a uniform to operate. I could see him looking at Mother disapprovingly from the corner of his eye, no doubt wondering what someone so dishevelled looking was doing in the company of Fräulein Bernhardt. He straightened his tie and coughed when he saw Maria staring at him with rebuke in her eyes. The elevator abruptly stopped. 'Third floor, Madam,' he coughed again, doffing his cap to Maria and ignoring Mother as though she was merely a servant and not worthy of his manners. This lack of courtesy to my Mother obviously irked Maria and she turned back to the lift operator. 'This is my dear friend, Frau Schreiber. She will be staying with me for a few days with her son, Franz,' she said, putting her hand on my shoulder. 'I expect you to show them the same respect as any other resident in these apartments. Do you understand?'

'Yes, of course Fräulein Bernhardt.'

'Good, see you do.'

Once she had dismissed the lift operator with a wave of her hand, Maria turned and smiled at Mother. 'He won't recognise you the next time he sees you Anna, you will be looking like your old self in no time.'

I could not believe my eyes when Maria opened her apartment door and led us into a hallway that was bigger than our whole apartment. We followed her to the warm living-room, which had two large bay windows overlooking the river. While she and Mother made coffee and chatted, I wandered around the apartment and marvelled at its modern art deco furniture. I went over to the windows and looked out over the river at the barges and the plethora of boats bobbing on the swell. I thought about the suitcase and its journey towards the sea and wondered where it would be now. It made me shiver to think of its contents again and the horrors of that night. Helmut put his hand on my shoulder. 'Would you like some lunch, young man?' he asked, as I turned to see him standing with a white apron on and a spatula in his hand.

After a lunch, Helmut drove the three of us into the city centre. Maria took Mother to her favourite beautician's, while Helmut and I went to a nearby department store where he insisted I pick out some clothes and a pair of shoes. Once Helmut was satisfied the ones I tried on fitted me, he took my old uniform and asked the shopkeeper to dispose of it. She was reluctant to even take them at first, and Helmut had to thrust them into her arms. She immediately dropped them on a heap behind the counter and called for one of the assistants to take them out to the bins at the back of the shop. When

Helmut paid for the clothes, he made a point of placing the money on the counter and not in her outstretched hand. He winked at me with his big, jovial smile. 'Now, Franz, let's get out of here.'

Helmut bought a bag of boiled sweets from another shop and we went back to the car to wait on Maria and Mother. It was an hour and a dozen boiled sweets later before we saw them, arm in arm, walking towards the car. Helmut had to take a double look at Mother, who was now wearing her hair and make up in a similar fashion to Maria, and could have passed for her older, elegant sister. She was wearing a new expensive looking coat, which had a stylish fur collar and matching cuffs. They were both carrying shopping bags with the most exclusive shop names in Berlin on them. It was obvious to me Maria must have spent a small fortune restoring Mother to life. Helmut could not take the grin from his face when he got out and opened the passenger door for them to squeeze into the back seat beside me. The smell of expensive perfume almost overwhelmed me, but I was so happy for Mother that I breathed it in as though this scent of extravagance was the elixir of life itself.

A few days later, Helmut helped us move what little we had to our new address, which was in Alexanderplatz and not far from our old neighbourhood. The new apartment was wonderful, with a large living room, separate kitchen, two good-sized bedrooms, and to Mother's delight, it also had the luxury of a bathroom. The rooms were also furnished with decent things, making Mother smile as Maria showed her round. Maria then told us the rent had been paid in advance for six months and it would continue to be paid until Mother was well enough to find work and pay it herself. Although not as luxurious as Maria's apartment, it was still a million miles away from the slums in Brunnenstrasse.

*

During the next few weeks, Mother miraculously reverted

to her former role as Frau Schreiber. In time, she became friendly with our next-door neighbour, Georgi Metrov. He was a strange character, with a pale complexion, plucked eyebrows, thin lips and long slender hands he manicured daily. His apartment reflected his gregarious personality, with its gypsy weirdness, smothered in multi-coloured fabrics. The living room was like a grotto from a Bavarian fairy-tale, perfumed with a heady scent of lavender and rosewater.

Nervously tapping his long fingernails on the table, he would tell stories about all the weird and wonderful characters he knew from the nightclubs where he worked as a female impersonator and singer. There was Herr Dünkel, a ventriloquist, whose wooden-headed doll, Kaiser Willy, told such outrageously salacious jokes Georgi said would make the devil blush. Then there were the identical twins, Trudy and Heidi, dancers who revealed more of themselves to the audience than was decent, and according to Georgi would even make Kaiser Willy blush. And, of course, there was Georgi himself, the star-turn, with his flamboyant clothes and outrageous wigs, blessed with the voice of an angel, albeit one who smoked forty cigarettes a day.

After a few weeks convalescence, Mother began working again, this time as a waitress in a restaurant on the Linden. It did not pay much, but with tips and Maria paying the rent, we had more than enough to live on, so long as Mother kept her promise never to drink again.

Chapter 13

1926

Not long after we settled in our new apartment, Mother enrolled me in the local school, determined I finish my education. Although a state elementary, it was much better than the last one and was only a short walk from the apartment. This time there were no bullies to worry about and school became a normal routine to my life again.

The memory of the few days we lived in Brunnenstrasse gradually faded as the months passed from winter, through to spring. To my knowledge, during this time, Mother had not touched any alcohol. Such was the change taking place in her she had even become reconciled with the Catholic Church, attending Mass every Sunday no matter the weather. Accepting my indifference to religion, she did not force me to go with her.

On Easter Sunday, I got up to find her singing to herself in the kitchen. She was dressed in the black dress she usually wore to Mass. Thankfully, she had also stopped wearing the bright makeup she used to wear, when working in the nightclubs. Her hair was now styled in a way more suited to her age.

'Franz, good, you're up. I have boiled you a couple of eggs for breakfast. Can you make your own tea? I have to go to chapel early this morning, Father Witzleben is holding a morning confessional before Mass,' she said, lifting her prayer book and rosary beads from the sideboard. I often wondered if she ever told the priest about the dead baby or the herbal remedy she must have taken to bring her pregnancy to such a macabre end. Would a Catholic priest forgive such a sin ... would God?

Mother had not long returned from Mass when Maria unexpectedly arrived with Lulu and Helmut. Lulu was her usual self and was only pleased when her mistress pampered her. While Mother prepared lunch, Maria began talking about her wardrobe as though it was a burden for her to have so many clothes and shoes. She nodded to Helmut, who got up and went down to the car. He returned a few minutes later with a large box.

'There, Anna, you can have the lot,' said Maria, opening the box and lifting one stunning dress out after another.

'I can't take your beautiful clothes,' said Mother, standing with her hand to her mouth and near to tears.

'I'll take them,' said Georgi, who was at the door with a tea caddy in his hand. 'I hope you don't mind. The door was open ... ran out of tea ... Anna, could you spare a little?'

'Of course, Georgi,' said Mother. 'Now you're here you can join us for lunch. This is my dear friend Maria I told you about.'

'Enchanted,' he said, shaking Maria's hand and giving her an unnecessary bow.

'Ah, Georgi, we've met once before,' said Maria. 'The Mikado ... You won't remember, I was just one of the dancers back then. As I recall you had more make-up on than I did.'

'I know you should never gild the lily, my dear, but unfortunately I have to prune my roses from time to time,' he said, rubbing the stubble on his chin.

We all laughed at Georgi's antics as he lifted one of Maria's dresses and held it to his chest. 'I'm serious, Anna, if you don't want them ... '

'No, of course I want them,' said Mother. 'Thank you, Maria, thank you.'

'Well if any don't fit, I am only next door,' said Georgi, his eyes lighting up when Helmut returned from the car with a box full of shoes, even though he had no chance of getting his large feet into any of them.

Once Mother and Georgi finished gushing over the dresses and shoes, we sat down to lunch. To my utter surprise, Mother began to say grace. Embarrassed by her sudden need to pray before we had lunch, I, like everyone else, bowed my head.

'Anna, you haven't asked me why I'm getting rid of all my dresses,' said Maria, once she was satisfied Mother had finished her discourse with God. 'Well, I'm going to America!'

'America!' Mother echoed.

'Yes, I am going to make movies in Hollywood. Isn't that fantastic?'

'Hollywood!'

'Stop it, Anna. You're beginning to sound like one of those parrots in the zoo.'

'I'm sorry, Maria. It's just a shock.'

'Why? Did you not always say I was going to be a great movie star one day?'

'No, Maria. It was you who said that,' replied Mother, which made us all laugh.

For the next hour we ate and listened to Maria, telling us all about the American producer who wanted her to star in a new film he was planning to make. Georgi was more excited than anyone and repeated, 'That's wonderful', every time Maria finished a sentence. As I listened, I was pleased for Maria, but sorry for Mother, who looked anxious at the thought of losing her friend again.

*

On the day of Maria's departure, Mother and I went with her to Bremerhaven. It was such a long journey we had to change trains in Hamburg, where we had enough time for some lunch. The second train took us all the way to the Bremerhaven where a passenger ship was waiting to set sail for England. Maria was booked on the RSM Olympic, which was due to leave from Southampton in a few days' time. She was then planning to stay in New York for a couple of weeks before travelling to California. It all sounded like a great adventure and I wished I was going with her.

When the time came to say goodbye, Maria kissed me and took a small flower from her hat and pinned it onto my lapel. 'You're a man now, Franz, and you must look after your mother,' she said, reminding me of the day Gretchen said something similar. Maria embraced Mother and they exchanged heartfelt words of farewell.

Mother cried as we watched Maria follow a porter onto the gangway reserved for first class passengers. Maria turned back for a moment and waved to us. We waved back, and I, without thinking, shouted 'I love you, Maria!' which made Mother look at me strangely.

On the train journey home, the grey sky matched our mood and we said very little to each other. Mother sat looking out the window with an envelope on her lap. I only found out later that Maria had given her the envelope at the quayside and it contained four hundred marks.

Berlin was bleak when we arrived in the evening and we took a taxi from the Hauptbahnhof to get home as soon as possible. Mother made us a light supper and went to bed early. I sat up for a while and foolishly daydreamed of going to America and joining Maria in Hollywood.

The next day Mother was in better spirits and we went to the Kranzler to drink coffee and watch the world go by. My initial fear of losing Maria's charity subsided when Mother talked of the future with optimism and hope. She handed me twenty marks from the money Maria had given her and told me to spend it how I pleased.

Only a few weeks after Maria's departure, Mother found a better job in a restaurant near the Opera House. Her wages were much better and the way she talked about it to Georgi, she obviously enjoyed working there. Georgi was still in and out of the apartment every day, borrowing this or returning that. Once in the apartment, he would sit and talk with Mother for hours, both smoking cigarettes as though their lives depended on them. He even managed to prise three of Maria's dresses from Mother, which were too flamboyant for her sober return to modesty and religion.

We all missed Maria, but Georgi kept us informed of her Hollywood career, trawling through newspapers and fashion magazines, and collecting anything about her for his scrapbook. He was becoming slightly obsessed.

One day, while I was sitting with Mother having lunch, he came in wearing one of Maria's flapper dresses, his blonde wig cut and styled to copy the way Maria looked in the latest edition of *Vogue*. He sang a song, and made such a good, comical impersonation of Maria that both Mother and I ended up in fits of laughter. Georgi revelled in the hilarity he was causing but went too far when he tried to do the splits and almost gave himself a hernia. By the time he had finished his antics and calmed down, what was left of my lunch was stone cold.

Maria was still wiring the rent money every month, but we had not heard anything from her until a letter arrived inside a Christmas card. Mother breathlessly read it to me as though I was still a child.

Dear Anna and Franz,

Hope you are well and you both have a lovely Christmas holiday. I would love to be home for the festive season, but I'm due to start filming again in a few weeks with Douglas Fairbanks. My first movie, 'Shipwreck' was a great success here and should be screened in Berlin in a few weeks' time ... at least that's what they tell me. Lillian Gish called to congratulate me after the premiere and we have now become friends. She is very kind and even more beautiful in the flesh.

I think I've fallen in love with her.

Anyway, I better go. I'm playing tennis with Chaplin today; he hates it when you're late. Maybe in the summer you both could come over for a few weeks. Who knows, if you like it, you might even want to stay.

Let me know. Don't worry about the cost; if you want to come I'll send the tickets.

Miss you both. Give my love to Georgi.

Merry Christmas
Your friend always
Maria.

Mother read the letter again, her face bright with joy, promising we would go to Hollywood in the summer. I stared at the three stamps on the front of the airmail envelope: did it really come all the way from America? My heart was pounding with excitement at the thought of meeting Charlie Chaplin, and I had to sit down for a while to take it all in.

Georgi was even more excited when he saw the letter, his eyes lighting up when he read out the names of Chaplin and Gish in a high-pitched voice. Then, he became a little glum. 'It's wonderful, but if you both go you might never come back.'

'Don't be silly, we will only go for a month at most,' said Mother, taking Georgi's hand. 'What would we do in Hollywood?'

'I could become Maria's manager,' I suggested.

'Listen to him,' laughed Mother. 'He's not even finished school yet.'

'Promise you won't leave poor Georgi,' he said, making a sad face. We all laughed.

*

When Maria's movie, *Shipwreck*, finally arrived in Berlin, the three of us went to the local picture house to see it. Georgi was overjoyed and couldn't stop talking about it all the way there. The other passengers on the tram must have thought he was a little simple as he waxed lyrical about Maria, before standing up and declaring, 'Maria Bernhardt is the greatest actress in the world.' Mother was a little embarrassed and tried to get him to sit down. I just laughed at his antics.

After all the months we waited to see Maria's film, it wasn't very good. She played a princess, shipwrecked on an island in the Caribbean, with a band of pirates chasing her over the sand dunes and through the dense jungle. Of course, Maria was beautiful, and lit up the screen every time she appeared, even if it was only to flutter her eyes. With the lack of any real storyline, I couldn't stop myself yawning every so often. Some of the audience had had enough and left before the dashing leading man came to Maria's rescue and killed all the pirates. When it finished we clapped loudly, even if no one else did. Georgi didn't seem too disappointed and Mother was just happy to sit and watch her friend for a while. The American moviegoers must be easily pleased, I thought, as we continued to sit there looking up at the blank screen after everyone else had left.

Chapter 14

One day after school, while knocking repeatedly at the door, Georgi came out to see what all the noise was about. 'Sorry, Georgi, I forgot to take my keys. Do you know where she's gone?'

'No, but she went out quite early. Come in and have tea with me, I'm sure she won't be too long,' he said as I followed him into his apartment. 'Is she working tonight?'

'No, it's her night off.'

'Franz, can you get the kettle, Liebling? I have to try and get this finished,' he said, fluttering around a half-dressed mannequin in the middle of the room in his blue and yellow silk kimono. 'How was school today?'

'It was all right ... Do you want sugar in your tea?'

'Oh, no, Liebling, I'm sweet enough, don't you think; just a little milk.'

'Why do you never drink coffee?'

'It's bad for my complexion,' he said, admiring his pallid reflection in one of the many mirrors in the room.

After sticking a few more pins in the dummy with a flurry of artistic exuberance, he sat down with his legs crossed, lighting a cigarette as though it was a stage prop. He smiled with satisfaction as he looked at his dressmaking, before lifting his delicate teacup with a rattle of silver bangles. 'What do you think?' he asked, his green eyes too fragile to endure criticism.

'It's wonderful ... What is it?'

'It's my new stage costume; isn't it breath-taking? I'll have to stitch it together now I'm happy with it ... Are you all right?'

'Yes, but I'm worried. I think my mother's drinking

again.'

'I haven't seen her drinking.'

'When she came home last night she went straight to her room and I could hear her talking to herself.'

'Well, we all do that sometimes.'

'No, she sounded drunk. The way she used to be. Georgi, if she's started drinking, she will get unwell again ... '

'I'll speak to her,' he said, putting his thin hand on mine and patting it. 'Let's not get upset, she'll think we've been talking about her if she comes back and sees us both with long faces.' Clapping his hands to dispel the gloom, he quickly changed the subject. 'Did I tell you my father was a fisherman back in Bulgaria, and that's what he expected me to be, although my mother thought I would make a fine priest ... A fisherman with these hands ... I ask you,' he laughed, with a display of his extravagantly manicured nails. 'A priest ... with a face like this?' he laughed again, cupping his face and fluttering his eyelashes.

Before he could start another story, we heard Mother on the landing. Overcome with excitement, Georgi rushed out to persuade her to come and see his new costume. My heart sank when she followed him into the living room, dressed as her alter-ego, Lilly. I could smell drink from her as she complimented Georgi so much a blush came to his pale cheeks. Although she tried to pretend otherwise, Mother was drunk. Unable to hide my annoyance, I left her there with Georgi.

Mother had become a drunk again and was rarely sober. When she was not at work she spent all day in her bedroom drinking. I begged her to stop before it killed her, but I don't think she cared anymore. On one occasion, when she ran out of drink, she became hysterical, demanding I borrow money from Georgi to get her a bottle of sherry. Instead of begging money from our neighbour, I asked her to speak to the priest, but she cursed me, her face contorted as though she was possessed.

With summer only around the corner, I checked every morning for a letter and the promised tickets from Maria, but apart from the usual post there was nothing. The constant disappointment was getting me down as much as Mother's alcoholism. I began to think Maria had forgotten all about us now she was friends with Lillian Gish and Charlie Chaplin.

A letter finally arrived in early June. Mother, during one of her lucid intervals, handed the letter to me after reading it to herself in silence. The letter had none of Maria's earlier optimism, expressing fear her Hollywood career might be over after her last performance was ridiculed by the critics. There was no mention of the travel tickets she had promised. Mother wrote back to tell her how much we all enjoyed her last film, and not to worry about a few heartless critics. Georgi was also glum when he read the letter and blamed the director for putting her in bad films and not making more use of her talent.

As the months passed Mother continued to drink, her behaviour became increasing erratic. She was even arrested one night for being drunk and abusive in a public place. Georgi had to go to the police station in Alexanderplatz to vouch for her. The police were good enough to give her a warning before releasing her into Georgi's custody. She was still drunk when he brought her home. For her own safety we locked her in her room, which she wrecked in her delirium, before eventually calming down to a whimpering contrition. The following Sunday she went to Mass for the first time in months, I hoped she would speak to the priest, maybe he could help her with the demons that troubled her.

It all came to a head when I came home from school one day to find Georgi waiting for me at the bottom of the stairs, his face ashen.

'What's wrong? Has she been arrested again?'

'Oh, Franz … Your mother's been taken to hospital …

Poor Anna,' said Georgi in a breathless flutter, clasping his hands together. 'Come upstairs and I'll make a pot of tea.'

'What happened to her?' I asked, following Georgi upstairs and into his apartment.

'She's been taken to the asylum.'

'The asylum!'

'Franz, I tried to stop her. She ran down the stairs in her nightdress before I could do anything. I chased after her, but she was running through the traffic screaming and hollering. She would have been killed only for the policeman who caught her in the middle of the road. He would not let me take her back upstairs. An ambulance came, and she was taken away ... Poor Anna,' he sighed, putting his hands in front of his face and sobbing into them like a child.

'Where's the asylum?'

'The policeman gave me the address, it's just outside Berlin. I think we need to get the tram and then a train. He wrote it all down, here Franz,' he said, handing me the piece of paper with the directions. 'We can go and see her this evening. She'll be expecting you,' he said, pouring the tea, his wrists rattling with bangles and nerves. 'I'll put some of her clothes in a bag in case they let her home.'

After a second cup of tea and half a dozen cigarettes, Georgi turned back into a delicate butterfly, fluttering from one corner of the room to another in his shimmering kimono, always looking for something he was sure he could not live without. 'The hairbrush is on the sideboard,' I said. He stared at it as though it had put itself there just to annoy him.

We took a tram to the city centre where we caught the train just as it was preparing to leave the station. Georgi had mercifully dressed down, and his pale, thin face showed no hint of the riot of colour from the previous night's cabaret, while his plain brown suit and spats made him look more like a Chicago gangster than a female impersonator.

He was unusually quiet during the journey, and I was too

worried about Mother to think of anything to say. Once we left Berlin, the countryside passed-by with little interest to me. It felt like a hundred years had passed since I travelled to Bremerhaven with Mother and Maria.

On reaching the village we walked for about a mile until the walls of the Mental Hospital came into view. At the entrance a sudden fear came over me and I stopped for a moment to stare at the name above the gates 'The State Mental Hospital'. Georgi came back and took my arm, and I reluctantly went with him into the foyer that echoed with hurried footsteps and banging doors. Georgi introduced himself to a severe-looking sister at the reception. ' … and this is Frau Schreiber's son, Franz.'

'Follow me … Smoking in the ward is strictly forbidden,' she warned, pointing to a notice on the wall as we entered the main ward. 'The doctor will be along in a few minutes to speak to you.'

My anxiety turned to despair when I stood before Mother's bed. She was sitting up nursing a pillow like it was a child. She was mumbling incoherently and took no notice of us. I did not need the doctor to tell me my mother had gone completely insane.

Chapter 15

The train pulled into the station with a shudder, shaking me from my stupor. I followed Georgi through the crowded platform. People were rushing up and down the stairs, my mother's madness of no consequence to them. We emerged from the station and crossed the road to the tram terminal. Georgi paid the fare and we sat at the back of the tram in silence. When we passed the Café Kranzler, I recalled the days spent there with Mother when she was at her happiest. I suddenly felt sick. Georgi must have noticed the colour leaving my face and ushered me off the tram at the next stop where I vomited in the gutter. We walked the rest of the way home, the fresh air clearing my head.

Back in the apartment I tried to decide what to do now Mother was not there to make the decisions. I looked through her things to see if she had any money, but I only found five marks in one of her handbags. Finding so little money was bad enough, but I also discovered three letters from the landlord's agents giving Mother notice the rent was overdue. I assumed Maria had not been wiring the rent in time, but suddenly it struck me, maybe she had stopped paying altogether. The most recent letter showed Mother had managed to pay two of the earlier bills, but last month's rent was still outstanding. I took the letter through to Georgi who was getting ready to go to work.

'I know, Franz ... I've known for some time Maria had stopped paying the rent. Poor Maria is probably struggling to pay her own rent. I read MGM let her go after her last film,' he said, combing the knots out one of his wigs.

'Why didn't you tell me? I could have left school and got a job.'

'Your mother told me not to say anything.'

'The last month's rent is still overdue, and I have only five marks.'

'Franz, I can give you some money, but it won't be enough. The little savings I had … Well, I gave to your mother to clear what she owed.'

'I'm sorry, Georgi … '

'Here, Franz,' he said, taking out ten marks from his wallet.

'No, I can't take anymore of your money,' I said, getting up, angry with everything that was happening. 'I will get my own money and pay back what Mother borrowed from you.'

'It doesn't matter Franz, it is only money.'

Georgi followed me to the door, trying to put the ten marks into my hand, but I resisted, pushing him back harder than intended. He looked at me with nothing but kindness. I turned and ran down the stairs, determined I would not be a burden to him or anyone else.

I must have walked for hours, up one street and down another, looking for something which was not there. Somehow, whether consciously or unconsciously, I found myself standing in the open ground where the circus had been. The memory of that day was so strong I could recall it with remarkable vividness; the white horses, the elephants, the clowns, and of course Rebecca in her blue coat.

For the next few days I tried to find work, but was turned down everywhere, until a coal merchant took me on, but only because one of his men was off sick. The work was backbreaking, and I struggled to do anything without someone shouting abuse at me. I lasted two days before I was told not to come back. The owner only paid me one day's wages, saying I was more of a burden than a help to him. I did not argue, what would be the point? I went home in the evening with only three marks to show for my two days of hard labour.

Before I could get into the apartment, Georgi was standing on the landing as though he was waiting for me. He put his hand to his mouth and tried to suppress a laugh when he saw me in my work clothes, covered from head to foot in coal dust.

'Franz, what the hell have you been doing to get in to such a state? You've not joined a minstrel show?'

'That's not funny, Georgi, I've been working …'

'Where, down the mines?'

'No, I was working in a coal merchant's on Klosterstrasse. Well, I was working there, until today. They told me not to come back.'

'Why?'

'Because I was useless, that's why.'

'Franz, I'm sorry, but I have more bad news for you. The landlord was here a couple of hours ago looking for his rent. I paid him half to give you some more time, but it won't be long before he's back. Landlords are like bloodsuckers.'

I sat on the stairs, physically exhausted and emotionally drained. 'I don't know what to do Georgi,' I said, with tears of despair running down my dirty face.

'Don't cry, Franz, life is too short to be miserable. You can move in with me and just give up the apartment. That's not such a bad idea, is it?'

'I can't give up the apartment, what if my mother gets out of hospital, where will … '

'Your mother can come and live with me as well. I have a spare room lying empty. We will manage. Besides, I would love the company. I'm tired of living alone.'

'If I get a decent job maybe I will be able to pay the rent, at least until Mother is well,' I said, ignoring Georgi's kind offer; for the moment anyway.

'All right, if you find work and can at least pay some of the rent, I will have enough to make it up for a few months. You can always pay me back when you have it. Why don't you try one of the department stores, they're always looking for shop assistants? It won't pay very much, but it will be something,' said Georgi, handing me the ten marks I refused to take a few days earlier. This time I thanked him and promised I would pay him back everything.

'You better go and have a bath, you look filthy,' he said, wiping the tears and coal dust from my face with a damp cloth.

That night I fell asleep as soon as my head touched the pillow. The next morning, I was up early and dressed in my best clothes, before taking the tram into the city centre. I got off at a stop on the Kurfürstendamm, where most of the big department stores were within easy walking distance from each other. My first attempt resulted in an apologetic smile from one of the floor managers. 'Sorry, we're not looking for anyone. Come back in a few weeks' time.' I didn't fare any better in the next store and after a few hours of nothing but rejection, I was left feeling more useless than ever.

Then, while in another department store and despondently making my way to the exit, a boy who was not much older looking than me, picked up a bottle of perfume from a nearby display. He then put it inside his coat, before he noticed me staring at him. He quickly left the store. I followed him outside, where he disappeared into the crowds of shoppers with the bottle of perfume. It was at that moment I decided to become a thief.

Thinking about the overdue rent, I entered a department store on the other side of the road and wandered around for a few minutes trying to build up courage, before walking along the perfumery aisle behind a young couple. Although feeling nervous, I did not hesitate, and as the couple distracted the lady at the counter, I lifted a bottle of perfume, putting it in my coat pocket, and then continued down the next aisle and with my other hand lifted a second bottle. I walked out the front door closely behind a lady in a fur coat as though I was with her. The doorman held the door open for both of us and doffed his cap. It was so easy I was annoyed with myself for not doing it sooner.

Using the same tactics, I paid a visit to another two department stores that morning, including one which had turned me down for work only a few hours earlier. In no time, I had six bottles of perfume in the various pockets of my coat. Not wanting to put myself in any unnecessary peril, I decided to find a buyer for the perfume before stealing any more. Unfortunately, not having planned so far ahead, I had no idea where to sell them without being arrested. Then, remembering Herr Kaufmann's jewellery shop, I surmised that diamonds and perfumes were both luxury items which would look well together in his shop window. I took the tram to Alexanderplatz, before walking to the Jewish Quarter.

The shop front had not changed much from the time Mother's brooch was for sale in the window. The doorbell clattered and announced my entrance. Herr Kaufmann looked up from behind the glass counter with his eyepiece lodged firmly in his left eye socket.

'Herr Kaufmann, do you remember me?'

'Close the door,' he said, removing the loupe from his eye and staring at me for a moment.

'Yes, you're the young fellow who called me a crook,' he said with a wry smile. 'How is your mother? I haven't seen her for some time ... is she well?'

'No, not very.'

'Nothing too serious, I hope.'

Not wanting to say she was in the asylum, I blurted out, 'She's in hospital having tests done for something. The doctors don't know what's wrong with her.'

'Oh, that's too bad ... Have you something for me or have you come to buy, perhaps?'

'I may have something, but I'm not sure.'

'Well, come into the back-shop and we'll have some

coffee and talk business.'

I followed him in and opened my coat, taking out a couple of bottles as he put the kettle on the stove. His eyebrows lifted theatrically when he turned to see what I had placed on the table.

'Your poor mother is now selling her perfume?'

'No, they're not my mother's. I have been asked to sell them by an acquaintance. They're not second-hand.'

'My dear boy, everything is second-hand,' he said, putting the ground beans into the coffee pot. 'What makes you think a jeweller would be interested in the perfumery business?'

'Maybe you could diversify and increase your profits.'

'You sound as though you've been to business school since our last meeting.'

'Business is business, I'm learning.'

'I take it your acquaintance has more than just a couple of bottles.'

'I have six with me and can get more if you want them.'

'And how much does your acquaintance want for his bottles of scent?'

'Four marks per bottle. They sell for six marks each in the big stores.'

'Four marks, but I could buy them from any supplier for that price.'

'But you'll make two marks on every bottle.'

'But I can't sell them for what the department stores sell them for and I have to make a profit. I will give you one mark each, and before you call me a crook again, do you have a bill of sale?'

'No.'

'Then, I will be taking a risk they are possibly … how shall I put it … stolen.'

'Three marks each,' I said, putting the rest of the bottles on the table to tease his obvious interest.

'Your name?' he asked as he poured two cups of coffee.

'Franz.'

'Ah, yes I remember. I will be willing to take them for two marks each on a sale and return basis. I'll have to pass them on to one or two of my own acquaintances, who may be able to sell them discreetly for perhaps four marks. I can't take the risk of selling them in the shop, in case the police show an interest, you understand. If I have no paperwork to show who supplied these items I could get into serious trouble.'

'All right, two marks each, it's a deal,' I said, sure it was as good as I would get.

'I'll pay you once I've secured their sale, otherwise I'll have to return them to you unsold.'

'I need the money now,' I pleaded.

'Sale or return was the deal, which means what it means.'

'But Herr Kaufmann, I need the money now!'

'All right, already, what I will do is give you six marks to tide you over and if you come back tomorrow and I've sold them on, you'll have the rest of the money waiting for you … Is it a deal?'

'All right, it's a deal,' I agreed as he took out the six marks and handed each coin to me individually from his purse as though they were precious stones.

'If your acquaintance can be tempted to move into the jewellery business we can start talking in real money,' he said, producing the top of a twenty mark note from his battered leather money bag to emphasise his point. 'Even watches are much more to my taste than perfume.'

'I will ask him,' I said, sure the old man was too wise in the ways of the world to fall for my phantom friend charade.

The following morning, and true to his word, Herr Kaufmann paid me the six marks and took a further three bottles I stole on the way to see him. He again suggested other items that would interest him, and I told him I would speak with my acquaintance that afternoon. He smiled but said nothing more.

The department stores were such easy places to steal from I soon became confident in taking anything I could lay my hands on from their shelves. All the same, some stores were more difficult to steal from than others, but they all had their weak spots, especially when they were busy. I began to carry a satchel to steal as much as possible from each store in one visit. Herr Kaufmann bought virtually everything I brought to him, especially watches, which, although, harder to steal than the perfume, earned me much more. In only a few weeks I was able to pay the outstanding rent, and surprise Georgi.

'I can't take that, what about your rent, you must pay your landlord first. I can wait,' he said, raising the palms of his hands towards me and refusing to take the twenty marks I was offering him.

'It is all right, Georgi, I have paid the rent. Here, take it.'

'You have earned all this in a couple of weeks working in Cohen's department store. What job did you get, general manager?'

'They pay well, and there is plenty of overtime. Here, take it.'

'You must not kill yourself working all the hours God sends,' he said, finally taking the twenty marks and putting his hand on my face. 'You're a good boy, Franz, but have you been up to see your mother lately?'

'Yes, a few days ago,' I lied, a flush coming to my cheeks. I could see in his eyes he did not believe a word I was saying, but he did not challenge me. Instead, he offered to go with me on my next visit.

'It can't be easy to see your mother in such a place, Franz, but you must be brave, she needs you to be there for her.'

Thankfully, someone knocked at his door before he could ask me any more awkward questions. I left as he answered the door to a salesman holding a vacuum cleaner. Georgi was all for new gadgets and immediately invited the young man in to test it out on his threadbare Persian rug, which was the only carpet he had in the apartment.

After a sleepless night, I got dressed with only one intention - to visit Mother and ease my conscience for a while. I decided to go alone and not to disturb Georgi, who needed his rest after another late night working at the cabaret. I bought a box of chocolates and travelled to the asylum with a feeling of dread, not sure what to expect. The journey was awful as my guilt taunted me and my head pounded with the constant rattle of the carriages until I was almost physically sick. When the asylum finally came into view my sense of panic eased a little. Perhaps Mother would be cured of her lunacy and I could take her out of that place. With the money I was making she would not have to work anymore.

Once in the hospital ward, I felt the sickness rise in my stomach again when I saw what was left of my poor mother. Her once beautiful face was emaciated beyond recognition, and her eyes were empty as though her soul had already left her shrivelled body.

'We had to shave her hair off when she started pulling it out,' said the nurse, as she went over to Mother and removed an uneaten bowl of gruel. 'You haven't eaten your lunch again, Anna. Your son is here to see you.'

'Mother,' I pleaded weakly, but she did not stir as I stood at her bedside and offered the box of chocolates. She looked at them as if they were offending her. I put them on the bedside table, before trying to engage her in conversation, but she did not understand anything I said. She began to nurse her pillow, mumbling to herself as if I wasn't there. I became quiet in my own thoughts, trying to remember her before her breakdown.

For over half an hour she continued in her detached melancholy until the bell rang and brought the heart-wrenching visit to an end. While kissing her goodbye, there was a moment when she looked at me with some recognition in her eyes. 'Mother … it's me … Franz, do you remember me?' My words did not seem to mean anything to her and she began to cuddle the pillow again. Unable to deal with her madness any longer, I left the asylum and ran all the way to the railway station without stopping.

*

The following day, I put a pair of silver cuff-links into my pocket and walked briskly to the exit. I must have been careless. Even before I reached the doors, someone shouted the words I feared most – 'Stop, thief!' I turned to see one of the shop assistants hurrying towards me. Heart pounding, my pace quickened, while trying not to run and draw the attention of the doorman, who turned to look at the assistant as I slipped past him.

Once outside, I ran along the crowded pavement with the doorman and the shop assistant shouting after me. Just when I was making good my escape, I foolishly looked back and collided with an old woman, knocking both of us to the ground. A few of the bottles of perfume in my satchel smashed on the pavement and I cut my hand on the glass trying to break my fall. With my eyes stinging from the rising vapour, I got back onto my feet and ran, half blind, in to the fast-moving traffic.

Despite almost being mangled under the wheels of a tram, I made it to the other side of the road in one piece. Unable to run much further, I stopped to catch my breath and wipe the tears from my eyes. On the other side of the road I could see a crowd gathered around the old woman as she was helped back to her feet. The shop assistant was holding my satchel and angrily pointing towards me. It was then I noticed two policemen further along the pavement, waiting for a gap in the traffic to come after me. Still out of breath, I ran as fast as I could, only to see another police officer coming towards me and blocking my escape. I turned in a panic, not knowing which way to run as the other two policemen finally crossed the road behind me. They began blowing their whistles, while running towards me. There was an alley just up ahead and I ran towards it, only to trip, head over heels into some tables and chairs outside one of the cafes. Before I could get to my feet, one of the policemen caught hold of my collar. My struggle to break free stopped when the other officer grabbed me and twisted my arm up my back.

Subdued, I was frogmarched back into the store, where my pleas of innocence were greeted with hostility from the floor manager, who came towards me in a fury with my discarded satchel in his hand. 'You'll go to prison for this,' he shouted.

In his office, the satchel was emptied onto a table. I was surprised just how much I had stolen that morning. Satisfied they had their thief; the police took me back out the front door in handcuffs. My short career as a thief had come to a humiliating end.

After a night in the police station, I was taken to the juvenile court in handcuffs. The remaining bottles of perfume, along with two watches, six ties and the pair of cufflinks that got me caught, were produced as evidence against me. I whispered my guilty pleas as each charge was read out by the clerk of court. The watery-eyed judge referred to me as a delinquent and ordered me to be sent to a reformatory, where, apparently, with the help of God, and some old-fashioned discipline, I would be saved from a life of crime. Before I knew what was happening, two policemen took me out to a prison wagon where I was manacled to another two delinquents.

Chapter 16

The Berlin skyline disappeared in the distance under heavy skies and smog. Apart from the two boys manacled to me, there were three other boys in the wagon, one looking more miserable than the other. The guard who sat in the back with us was an ugly man, with a face that reminded me of a vicious dog I once saw guarding its patch outside a butcher's shop. He made it clear he wanted quiet and threatened one boy with his baton for talking too much. The silence suited me, I was lost in my thoughts about the life I was leaving behind and what waited for me at the end of this journey. Damn, if only I didn't get greedy. I should have stopped when I stole the watch, which was worth twenty pairs of cufflinks. I felt like banging my head on the seat in front for being so stupid.

It took a couple of hours before we finally reached the reformatory, which I found out later was once an army training barracks. Once inside, the wardens, carrying wooden batons, yelled at us as soon as we got out of the wagon still manacled to each other. We were then marched into a dormitory, which smelled of urine and disinfectant, the latter failing miserably to mask the former. Each dormitory housed over twenty detainees from all over Berlin, and from the smell, some of the city's worst recidivist wet-the-beds among them. To further reduce my sense of individuality, my hair was cut short and I was given a pair of overalls to wear, which were too big for me. 'You are here to work, not to enter a beauty contest,' screamed a fat-faced warden, when I complained about the size of my overalls. The warden, I later learned, was Wolfgang Schultz, and it was easy so see why the other detainees called him the Pink Pig. Originally from Danzig, Schultz was a brute of a man, with a bull-like shaved head and bulging eyes, making him look as if he was constantly constipated. 'What's that smell?' he demanded, sniffing me as though he had foraged out a truffle with his pug nose.

'It's perfume.'

'Perfume! Are you some kind of whore?' he shouted in his thick East Prussian accent for everyone to hear.

'I stole them to sell,' I said, trying to sound as tough as the other boys. 'That's why I'm here. The bottles broke when I fell.'

'You smell like a girl and sound too bourgeois to be a thief. What the hell are you?'

'I'm a delinquent,' I said. 'It's what the judge called me.'

'Don't try and be funny with me,' he yelled, slapping me hard across the side of the head and knocking me to the ground before storming off.

One of the boys offered me his hand and helped me get to my feet. 'He's nothing but a bully and a coward. This place is full of them,' he said. 'My name's Dieter.'

'Franz ... Franz Schreiber ... pleased to meet you,' I replied in a hollow sounding voice, the thump on my head making me temporarily deaf in one ear.

'He's right; you do sound too bourgeois to be here, but they'll soon knock that out of you.' Everyone laughed, except me.

It was still dark the next morning when the wardens came in to the dormitory screaming at us to get up. Half asleep, I followed the others to the latrines. Once I had made my toilet, I was pushed by Schultz into the shower-room and forced to get washed in ice cold water, which made me feel as if I was about to have a heart attack as I washed myself quickly with a hard bar of green soap. Shivering violently, I then grabbed a towel from the rail and got dried, only to be pushed back under the freezing shower. 'That will stop you smelling like a whore,' shouted Schultz. He then stood and watched me shower until he was satisfied my skin was beginning to turn blue. 'Get dried and get out of here, you skinny whore.'

Unable to speak for shivering, I rushed past him expecting a thump to the back of the head, but he must have been distracted when some of the other boys came in with two other wardens. I got dressed, without properly drying myself in case Schultz dragged me back into the shower. He was mean enough to do anything to humiliate those he had unbridled power over. My fingers were so numb I could not tie my bootlaces, and I shuffled out to the parade yard frantically blowing into my hands to get the blood circulating.

Before my body had stopped shivering, we were marched to another part of the barracks where we were split up into work groups. Standing like soldiers on parade, we were put into squads of eight; my group included Dieter and the five boys who had arrived with me from court. 'What's happening?' I asked Dieter, who was standing beside me as I knelt down to tie my laces.

'We're going to one of the local farms to be used as slave labour.'

After a few minutes standing in the freezing cold, a horse and cart pulled up at the front gate and we were ordered to get into the back of the filthy, dung-smeared cart. Schultz took a seat next to the farmer, who then gave the horse a taste of the whip without bothering to check we were all onboard. The old nag broke into a half-hearted trot as the last boy was still struggling to get his trailing leg into the cart. Two of the other boys pulled him in and we trundled down the broken-stone road towards a distant, mist-shrouded farmhouse. Dieter was standing next to me, looking indignant as though he was some unfortunate aristocrat being taken to meet his end at the blade of Madame Guillotine.

The farm was only a short journey away and we were

soon standing in a muddy courtyard. The gruff farmer, in his checked shirt and brown corduroys, began handing us various implements from the barn, including shovels, pitchforks and rolls of wire. I was put on possibly the worst job, along with Dieter, and told to clean out the dung from the cowshed.

When the farmer and Schultz took the other boys into the fields to mend fences and repair stone walls, Dieter threw down his shovel and took out a tin of tobacco. We sat down and rolled cigarettes, laughing as we watched the rest of the boys in the field cursing and arguing with each other. When we had finished our smoke, we made a half-hearted attempt to justify our existence, and took turns shovelling the soiled straw into a wheelbarrow, before dumping it in a heap at the back of the yard.

At midday we were called into the farm kitchen by the farmer's daughter and given thick pieces of rye bread with butter and a glass of lukewarm milk that had a sour taste to it. Although half starved, most of us were more interested in the girl than the food. She was called Ingrid, and looked about sixteen years old, slightly plump with long blonde hair, braided in ponytails and with a pretty face. She smiled at us mischievously as she sat by the fire and watched us devour our food. It was with some reluctance I went back out to the cold, miserable cowshed to shovel more dung.

In the evening as the light faded, we were all herded onto the cart and taken back to the reformatory. That night I lay on my bunk bed and thought about Mother all alone in the asylum. I tried to think of what she was like before she lost her mind completely, but all I could see was her in the hospital bed with her head shaven. Then, with the sound of Herr Kolinski's violin playing in my head, I fell into a deep sleep, only to be engulfed by another dream about the suitcase and the dead baby. The nightmare had now become so familiar it no longer frightened me in the way it used to, so long as I was not tempted to open the lid of the suitcase.

Thankfully we were only required to work on the farm three days a week. The rest of the time we attended the schoolhouse, no doubt to obtain the education we were supposed to get in the first place. In class I sat beside Dieter and another boy named Paul Weber who arrived at the reformatory a few days earlier. Paul was a year older than me, although, with his thin, pale face and doe-like brown eyes, he looked much younger. I wasn't surprised when he told me he had been arrested for stealing food from the back of a delivery lorry.

Dieter had a soft spot for Paul and on at least two occasions he had to save him from being bullied by other boys in the dormitory. Paul was soon following Dieter around for his own protection. It was only then I realised I had been doing the same thing.

The masters in the school were evidently teachers who were not good enough to find jobs in the real world, and it showed. I decided not to bring any unnecessary attention to myself and acted as stupid as the rest of the class, deliberately giving wrong answers to questions a child could have answered in kindergarten. Paul was so backward in matters of education he copied my incorrect answers, with a furtive smile. Dieter was one of the few boys with any real education, but even he showed little interest in the classes we attended.

At night, after lights were out, Dieter would often light a candle and demand the attention of the other inmates. He then made speeches about the exploitation of the workers and the need for a communist revolution. Not everyone wanted to listen to his preaching and he had to ignore repeated calls to give it a rest from those more interested in getting to sleep and dreaming about the farmer's daughter.

His main disciple was Paul, who sat at his feet, listening to every word. I often wondered whether he understood a single thing Dieter said in his rants against the evils of capitalism.

Dieter turned to me one night when he caught me yawning, which interrupted his flow on the merits of Marxism. 'Am I boring you, Franz?' he asked. Everyone turned towards me.

'No, Dieter, but it's all a bit pointless when we are all stuck in here.'

'Pointless? We will not be here for ever, and when the revolution comes you'll have to pick which side you're on. You told me yourself, your own father was betrayed by the banks, leaving you and your mother destitute. You, more than most, should see capitalism for what it is, an abomination. The Russians had the right idea; no man should be master over any other man.'

'If no man is master, then will there not be chaos?' I asked rather weakly.

'That's what the capitalists want you to believe. The Russians have set up soviets, and collective farms for the benefit of all, not just for greedy landlords.'

'But they have their leaders.'

'Yes, but leaders who answer to the people … Here, read this,' he added, taking a crumpled pamphlet from under his pillow. 'This was printed in Berlin by Karl Liebknecht, who was murdered by the capitalists for speaking out against injustice. So, don't let the wardens find you with it.'

Dieter then called an end to the meeting and everyone went back to their bunks. In the flickering light coming from the gaslight outside, I looked at the worn pages of the pamphlet, with its hammer and sickle on the front page and bold gothic script. I began to read a quote taken from *The Communist Manifesto*:

The modern bourgeois society that has sprouted from the ruins of feudal society has not done away with class antagonism. It has but established new classes, new conditions of oppression, and new forms of struggle in place of the old ones. Our Epoch, the epoch of the bourgeoisie, possesses, however, this distinctive feature: it has simplified the class antagonisms. Society as a whole is more and more splitting up into two great hostile camps, into two great classes, directly facing each other: Bourgeoisie and Proletariat ...

These words may have been the seeds of revolution in Russia, but they soon had my eyes feeling heavy. I turned on my side, with my back to Dieter so he wouldn't see me drift off to sleep with memories of my bourgeois childhood to comfort me.

Freezing, I woke the next morning with the words from the manifesto somehow imbedded in my head. Knowing Dieter, I was sure he would start quizzing me on the content of the pamphlet, so while he was still sleeping I read the opening few pages again. After much head scratching, all I could determine was, the industrialists and the middle classes were the bourgeois and the workers were the proletariat, and the bourgeois were the exploiters of the proletariat, and if things did not change soon the workers would revolt. I noted the prediction of Engels and Marx had already cost the Count his title and Russian estates. I was beginning to get my head around the basic ideas when Dieter woke through a fit of coughing.

'Are you all right?'

'Aye ... I had TB a few years ago ... my lungs are fucked ... Still reading it?' he finally asked, as he got up to catch his breath and put his overalls on.

'Yes, but it's not clear from what I've read where the millions of unemployed or the idle rich fit into this model of social antagonism,' I replied, trying but failing miserably to hide my privileged accent. 'It only mentions two classes: the bourgeoisie, who are the industrialists and middle classes, and the proletariat, who are the workers.'

Dieter smiled at me. He must have sensed I was trying

my best to impress him. 'The idle rich are clearly part of the bourgeoisie. They use their wealth to make others do their bidding; servants, maids, chauffeurs and the like, while the unemployed are clearly part of the proletariat, because the capitalists have cast them on the scrapheap once they have no more use for them ... Put that away,' he whispered. I almost fell out of my bunk when I turned to see Schultz and two other wardens standing at the opened dormitory doors, their hands on their hips and legs spread apart, looking at the half-dressed boys like hawks stalking frightened rabbits. I put the pamphlet under my pillow and jumped out of bed as Schultz started shouting his orders.

After our usual routine of cold showers and gruel for breakfast, we spent the morning collecting turnips and feeding the pigs buckets of swine food. The smell was repugnant, but it did not put the pigs off, especially a big fat sow we immediately christened Schultz. Some of the boys hated Schultz so much they took out their vengeance on his porky look-alike and threw stones at it to keep it away from the feed so the smaller pigs got their fair share.

It was market day and as soon as the farmer left to sell one of his bulls, Dieter decided he had had enough and downed tools. He was heading back to the city. Only Paul agreed to go with him. The rest, like me, had no intention of giving up three hot meals a day to wander the streets of Berlin in the dead of winter. Dieter tried his best to persuade the doubtful with one of his speeches more suited for the Reichstag than a farmyard. 'We are here as beasts of burden, slaves to the capitalist system which only benefits those in power. Their laws punish the weak, the poor and the dispossessed for trying to survive in this cruel world they created, where only the strong and the rich get the spoils of the workers' labour. The rich get rich, but the poor stay poor, because that's how the capitalist system works ... '

While we listened, Ingrid appeared from the barn where

she had been milking the cows. Even Dieter stopped talking to gather his thoughts. She was carrying two metal buckets, with the froth of the milk spilling over the rims. Singing to herself, she walked down the path on the other side of a stone wall from where we were standing, staring at her. She stopped and looked at us for a moment, before carrying on up to the house with a trail of milk spilling freely in her wake.

Once she was gone, Dieter started preaching to us again about the evils of capitalism, and our duty to escape, but his politics were wasted on us; the farmer's daughter had been too great a distraction for everyone. Hans, a streetwise boy from the slums of North Berlin, suggested someone should ask her if she was up for some fun. 'What for?' asked Dieter, 'are you looking to lose your virginity?' Some of the boys laughed, but the best I could do was force a feeble grin, wondering if I was the only virgin there. Hans, who did not see anything funny to laugh at, grunted a curse at Dieter and raised his fists for a fight. Dieter did not seem too concerned, and nonchalantly rolled up his shirt sleeves, all the while egging Hans on to make the first move. Just when the rest of us were hoping for a scrap, Hans lost his nerve and put down his fists to moans of derision. Dieter smiled in triumph. With no one prepared to do any more work that afternoon, we sat around and smoked, leaving the cows to wander back to their shitty sheds by themselves.

It was getting dark when the farmer returned. He saw that very few of the chores he had left us to do had been done, but he said nothing, and we climbed into the cart to be taken back to the reformatory.

That was the last time Paul came to the farm with us. The following day Schultz kept him back to clean the warden's barracks. When we returned in the evening, Paul's face was bruised. When Dieter demanded to know what happened, Paul just turned away and said nothing.

Over the next few months Schultz continued to keep Paul back whenever we went to the farm. Paul became withdrawn and I often heard him sobbing during the night even when there were no obvious signs of Schultz's temper on his face. We all knew Schultz was doing more than just beating Paul about the head. But if it wasn't Paul that Schultz picked on then it would be someone else. None of us were keen to take his place.

In the spring, just weeks before he was due to finish his sentence, Paul was found behind the latrines, his face purple and his lips badly burned. There was a bottle of weed killer found beside his body. Dieter took Paul's death worse than anyone and with loathing in his voice he promised he would kill Schultz as soon as he got the chance.

A few months later my sentence was over, and I left the reformatory for the streets of Berlin. As the wagon took me through the gates, I heard Schultz shouting and bawling at a handful of new arrivals. I pitied them.

Chapter 17

My return to Berlin was not as wonderful as my longing for freedom had promised. Fearful of being arrested again and sent back to the reformatory, I stayed away from the department stores and the temptation to resume a life of crime. With nowhere else to go, I joined some down-and-outs huddled around a fire under a railway bridge near to the river. Struggling in the cold to get to sleep, I took a mouthful of schnapps one of the homeless men offered me. It made me grimace when the cheap raw alcohol caught the back of my throat. Urged on by the toothless vagrant, I took another swallow, hoping it would be enough to anesthetise my mind. Feeling a little dizzy, I handed the schnapps back to my grinning neighbour, who finished what was left before throwing the empty bottle into the river. With the strong alcohol going straight to my head, I stared at the fire as the flames began to dance around like tiny ballerinas. The schnapps and stench of urine from the men lying close to the fire made me feel nauseous, but I was too tired to find anywhere else to rest for the night. Despite the smell and the cold, I eventfully fell into a deep, dreamless sleep.

It was early spring and still cold, but I had become hardened to such misery. Begging outside the Alexanderplatz Station became my way of earning enough money to buy some food and a bed for the night in the doss house. Most people just walked on without even looking in my direction, a few lingered long enough to part with a few pfennigs before carrying on to the station. One day, someone stood beside me, making me uneasy. Head bowed and wrapped in a blanket, I held out the tin, but no coins were dropped into it. I slowly raised my head to see Herr Kolinski looking down at me.

'Franz, what are you doing?' he asked, as though the evidence of my occupation was beyond his comprehension.

'Herr Kolinski,' was all I could say, lowering my gaze from his shocked eyes.

'Get up,' he insisted; the only time I ever heard anger in his voice. 'My friend, you are not a beggar,' he added, grabbing my arm and pulling me to my feet. 'What in the name of God has happened to you? Where is your mother? Why did you not come to me if things were so bad?' he said, embracing me in the folds of his coat. 'You are coming home with me, my dear Franz.'

To say it felt strange to see my old apartment block is an understatement. In my rags, and hunched like a medieval leper, I followed Herr Kolinski into the building, stopping for a moment outside my old apartment. I imagined Mother behind the storm doors, sitting at the window smoking and drinking coffee, pining for her dead artist. Herr Kolinski took my arm and we went on to the next landing. There was no sign of Harvey anywhere.

I froze when Herr Kolinski opened his door and I heard the piano coming from the living room. I turned back, desperate for the sanctuary and anonymity of the streets. 'What's the matter Franz? It's only Rebecca.'

'I can't.'

'Don't worry, come and sit in my room and we'll get you cleaned up.'

The piano stopped, and he greeted Rebecca with lavish praise about her beautiful playing. I stood in his bedroom, frightened to move as I listened to Rebecca asking her father what he was up to. Answering her inquisition with some Yiddish chants, he came back into the bedroom with a tin tub, some towels and a large bar of carbolic soap. 'Get those things off, and we'll find you some clean clothes to put on.'

It took three large pots before Herr Kolinski was satisfied

there was enough hot water in the tub. I could hear Rebecca in the hall pleading with him to tell her what he was up to as he sternly admonished her not to go into the bedroom. I listened to the living room door close over before getting into the tub. It was then I noticed my filthy, gaunt reflection in the wardrobe mirror.

The hot water made the upper part of my body even colder and I shivered uncontrollably. I quickly washed; still frightened Rebecca would come into the room in defiance of her father and see me looking like a half-drowned rat in a tub of dirty water. I was ashamed of myself and what I had become.

The piano began to play again, and I relaxed a little. For a moment, the pain from the cuts and blisters on my hands and feet became acute, while my body was slowly cleansed from the grime of street life. In a short while, Herr Kolinski came back into the bedroom and placed a pile of clothes on a chair. 'These are some of Jacob's clothes, they'll have to do for now.'

Washed and dried and smelling of soap and rosewater, I dressed. The clothes were far too big for me, and somehow made me feel lighter, as though a weight had been lifted from my being. I rolled up the trousers and sleeves and sat on the bed too afraid to move until Herr Kolinski, ignoring my protests took me with his arm around my shoulders into the living room.

'Franz?' exclaimed Rebecca, getting up from the piano to look at me.

'Hello Rebecca,' I said, sheepishly taking a seat by the window. Rebecca, sensing my discomfort, turned back to the piano and began to play again.

Satisfied I was not going to run out the front door, Herr Kolinski began to cook a meal of lamb's liver, boiled potatoes and cabbage. I had not eaten since the previous afternoon and the smell from the kitchenette made my throat gulp hard. Once the meal was ready, Rebecca sat opposite me and plated the food her father placed on the table.

Then, the questions I had been dreading started. I told them of Mother's misfortune and her eventual mental breakdown. This shocked and infuriated Herr Kolinski, who again berated me for not coming to him for help. 'When did you last see your poor mother?' he asked, overloading my plate with more food despite my feigned protests.

'A long time ago, I can't remember …'

'A long time ago, you can't remember! That will never do!' he said, shaking his head. 'I will take you tomorrow. Once you've had a good night's sleep. Which hospital is she in?'

'It's the asylum.'

'Papa, can I go?' interrupted Rebecca.

'Don't ask me. It's up to Franz.'

'If you want to,' I said, burping loudly with the shock of this unexpected food reaching my stomach. We all laughed.

Later that day, Herr Kolinski went out while I listened to Rebecca playing the piano as she told me about life at university, where she was now studying medicine. She put away her classical music score and played the ragtime and jazz music she had learned from the radio. She was playing *Basin Street Blues*, when her father returned, holding his ears and pleading with her not to traumatise the piano. 'What is this American nonsense you're playing?'

Rebecca went back to playing Chopin to please her father, while he brought out a leather folder from his briefcase, containing barber's scissors and combs. 'Now, Franz, I think it's time we found your head under that mop of hair,' he said, putting down newspapers on the carpet. 'Bring a chair over here.'

Once most of my hair was lying on the newspapers, Rebecca smiled, holding up a mirror to the back of my head, while complimenting her father's skill as a sheepshearer.

Herr Kolinski swept up, throwing fistfuls of hair into the fire, causing the lice and nits to pop like tiny explosions as it went up in a blaze of yellow flames. He then rubbed gasoline into my cropped head to kill what was left.

Trying to come to terms with my new, rather severe look was not helped by the smell of the gasoline, which made me light-headed. There was just enough hair left to comb and Rebecca kindly put it into a side shed, which at least gave my head some shape. She smiled. 'There you are, just as handsome as I remember.'

In the evening, Herr Kolinski produced my old violin. With Rebecca looking on, I felt awkward as he handed it to me, urging me to play a piece we had often played together during my many lessons. But my fingers were strangers to the strings, and the unforgiving bow rasped embarrassingly as Rebecca tried, unsuccessfully, to stifle a fit of giggles. Herr Kolinski, always the optimist, urged me through the first few bars until we were both playing in some kind of harmony. Rebecca began to accompany us on the piano.

What was left of the evening soon came to an end with Rebecca sleeping on my shoulder as her father played Mendelssohn's masterpiece. Having endured hell, I now had a glimpse of what heaven might be like.

Following a deep, deep, sleep, I awoke on the sofa with a start. Disorientated, it took me a moment to adjust to my surroundings. It was not a dream, and the fact I would see Rebecca again made me anxious about my appearance. With the unforgiving daylight showing no mercy, I looked in the mirror above the sofa, trying to make sense of the haunted face staring back at me.

A few minutes later, Herr Kolinski entered the living room carrying a brown parcel. 'Good morning, Franz, you're awake. Here, take these and get changed in my room. You can leave the other clothes on the bed and I'll put them away later.'

'Thank you, Herr Kolinski,' I replied, taking the parcel.

I dressed in the shirt and suit he brought back from his shop, his tailor's eye having calculated my measurements perfectly. I could not remember the last time I wore new clothes and felt awkward when I went back into the living room where he handed me socks and a pair of black shoes. While I put them on, Rebecca appeared from her room. 'You look very handsome,' she said, making my face redden. 'What time is it?' she asked through a tired yawn, kindly ignoring my embarrassment.

'Ten past eight,' said her father, 'hurry up and get ready … the tram leaves in twenty minutes.'

Even with my new clothes, my mind was still uneasy as I sat and waited for Rebecca to get ready. I had a strong desire to escape from this overwhelming charity, which made me feel the full extent of my uselessness, but my longing to be in her company for as long as possible kept me from fleeing. On the half-hour, we left to catch the tram I had avoided taking for so long.

'You're very quiet,' said Rebecca, as her father waved his hat to stop the tram.

'I'm all right, just a bit nervous about seeing my mother again.'

The carriage was crowded, and we stood for most of the journey until we reached the station, where we transferred to the train bound for the hospital. I noticed a few of the passengers staring at me; one was even sniffing the air. Although I had washed most of the gasoline from my cropped hair; it still stank. Rebecca did not seem to mind the smell and smiled at me reassuringly.

The asylum was as bleak as I remembered, and my anxiety grew when we walked with the other visitors to the main entrance. Rebecca was holding my hand as we passed bed after bed of bewildered faces. 'She's not here,' I whispered, on seeing an old man lying in what had been Mother's bed.

'Maybe she got better,' suggested Rebecca.

'Nurse! We're looking for Frau Schreiber. This is her son, Franz,' said Herr Kolinski.

'Her son? Will you wait here a moment,' replied the nurse. 'I'll be back in a moment.'

The sister, whom I had met on my last visit, appeared a few minutes later with the nurse following behind. 'You're Frau Schreiber's son?' she asked, obviously not remembering me.

'Yes.'

'Where have you been, your mother's friend was trying to find you. I'm afraid your mother died a few months ago … I'm sorry, but we couldn't get a hold of you for the funeral.'

'Died?' I mumbled, feeling faint and unable to say anything else.

'She was buried in the hospital grounds … if you follow me.'

'I'm sorry,' whispered Rebecca, holding my hand even tighter.

'My God, this is terrible,' said Herr Kolinski.

We followed the sister out to the back of the hospital where there was a graveyard on a sloping lawn with a couple of dozen wooden crosses. The matron guided us towards the paupers' plot at the back of the cemetery. There was a cross with her name on it but no dates, and a wreath of withered flowers with a card, the writing smudged by the rain, but still legible: *Death comes to us all, but for some far too soon: From your dear friend Georgi Metrov.*

Mother had died of liver failure or, as the sister put it, cirrhosis of the liver. Whatever it was called it meant the same thing, she drank herself into an early grave. Herr Kolinski offered to have her body exhumed and reburied in the city necropolis and have a gravestone made, but I declined his generous offer. 'What does it matter now if she's in a pauper's grave or a golden mausoleum?' I said. 'She's dead.'

Herr Kolinski was rather taken aback at my coldness and insisted the streets had made me hard, but he would respect my decision.

The following week Rebecca returned to live with her aunt in the west of the city, which was only a short tram ride from the university. With Mother dead and Rebecca gone, I fell into a deep depression.

Even though Rebecca's departure meant I could now sleep in her room, I would have preferred to sleep on the couch for ever, knowing she would be there to speak to in the morning. Herr Kolinski was extremely tolerant of my long lies in bed and indolent afternoons sitting around doing nothing. It was only when Rebecca returned to stay over at the weekends that my mood changed. In time, the depression gradually lifted, and I started playing the violin again, desperate to impress her with any new piece learned during the previous week.

My idleness came to an end when Herr Kolinski offered me a position in his shop. I was apprenticed to the master tailor, Leon Levi, a rather grumpy little man, who always had a measuring tape around his neck and a well chewed pencil behind his ear. All day long he measured and cut cloth, pins sticking out of his mouth, mumbling in Yiddish and cursing in German. Every time I thought he had run out of pins, he would somehow manage to produce another one from his lips as though he was regurgitating them when needed. His wife, Hannah, was the seamstress and was much friendlier than her husband, often offering me biscuits from a tin she rarely shared with her husband.

In a short time, I was soon taking the measurements of our many customers in all their shapes and sizes. Having impressed Herr Levi with my accuracy and diligence, I was eventually allowed to cut my first pair of trousers under his twitching eyes and heavy breathing. My hands were shaking, but I was determined to keep to the chalk marks.

After cutting the last piece of cloth he slapped me on the back knocking the pins I had between my lips all over the floor.

Hannah, teased her husband that he was no longer the best tailor in the business as she put the material through her noisy sewing machine, producing a perfect pair of gent's trousers.

Insisting I should become independent again, Herr Kolinski found me a bed-sit near to the market place, which was only a short walk from the shop. I moved out of his apartment the following day. I now lived for Fridays, our busiest day of the week, when Rebecca often helped in the shop after her morning lectures. While she served the customers, I tried to cut expensive cloth in a straight line, painfully distracted by her presence. The rest of the week she was at university. Hannah must have noticed my change of mood on Fridays, and would pick her moments to make silly remarks, which would make me blush and Rebecca angry.

Every Friday afternoon I would plan for the right moment to ask Rebecca if she would like to go to the picture-house some evening, but when the opportunity arose, I could never find the confidence to say what was on my mind. Sometimes I could see Hannah in the corner of my eye, urging me to open my mouth, shaking her head when Rebecca put her coat on to leave: another opportunity gone. Like a lovesick fool, I would spend the next week building up my confidence, only for the same thing to happen again. Hannah was on the verge of giving up on me, until finally one afternoon the words in my head decided to ignore my cowardice.

'Yes, why not, I've not been to the cinema in ages. Which film do you want to see?' she replied to my nervous invite.

'Oh, what one would you like to see?'

'I don't know, what's on?'

'I don't know,' I said, my mind blank, while trying

desperately to remember at least one film I had seen on a poster.

'*A Woman of Affairs*,' suggested Hannah. 'My friend saw it a couple of nights ago, and said it was wonderful. Greta Garbo's in it and she's wonderful. I wouldn't mind going myself.'

'*A Woman of Affairs*, what do you think?' asked Rebecca.

'All right, if that's what you want to see.'

'What time?'

'When ... tonight?'

'Yes, unless you've got something else on.'

'No, I'll come for you at seven.'

'All right, bye everybody,' she said, leaving the shop with its tingling bell drowned out by Leon's sniggers. When he regained his composure, he said it was the most painful few minutes he had suffered since he had a boil on his backside lanced by a short-sighted nurse. Hannah gave me a hug as if I had just achieved some wonderful feat. Feeling elated, I sat back down to cut another pair of trousers.

The movie was boring, but Rebecca was engrossed, and I noticed a tear running down her cheek when the heartbroken Garbo drove her car into a tree at the end. I was just glad there was a tree there.

We went for coffee afterwards.

'Wasn't she wonderful?' Rebecca enthused, her mind still on the film, which I had already forgotten about.

'Yes, she was,' I said, sipping my coffee slowly, trying to prolong our time together if possible.

'It's all right Franz, you don't have to lie. I saw you yawning. You can pick the film next time.'

'Are there any films with Maria Bernhardt that we can go to?'

'Maria Bernhardt?'

'Yes, she was my mother's friend,' I added, which made Rebecca put her cup down and stare at me as though I was telling the biggest lie she ever heard.

'Your mother was a friend of Maria Bernhardt ... Franz?'

'It's true ... Maria, she is also my friend ... in a way.'

'Maria Bernhardt was your friend!'

'Yes, Maria was going to take us out to America before ...'

'Before she killed herself ... '

'What? Before she killed herself? Maria's dead!'

'You didn't know? She committed suicide about a year ago ... Was she really your mother's friend?' asked Rebecca, taking what I had been saying a little more seriously. She reached across the table and put her hand on mine. 'I'm sorry, Franz ... I thought it was just something you were making up.'

'We better go,' I said, abruptly pulling my hand away from hers.

'I'm so sorry, Franz, don't be angry with me.'

'I'm not, I had better walk you home.'

*

The following day I went to see the only person I could speak to about Maria who would not think I was making up stories. I took the tram to Alexanderplatz and walked the rest of the way, past the town hall and Herr Kaufmann's shop. The shop was open and I was tempted to go in and see him, but that part of my life was better left in the past.

Georgi stared at me for a moment, disapprovingly shaking his head. 'Franz,' he rasped, with his hands outstretched and wrists jingling with even more bangles than I remembered. He had lost none of his flamboyance and was still wearing his kimono. 'What happened to you, where have you been all this time? I tried to find you ... your poor mother.'

'I know, I only found out after she was already dead.'

He put the kettle on to make a pot of tea and I took a chair by the window. I thanked him for being at my mother's funeral. He began to cry, insisting it was the least he could do for a dear friend, assuring me she was now in heaven with Maria. 'The world is a sadder place without them,' he declared, drying the tears and mascara from his eyes.

'I didn't know about Maria until last night.'

'Only last night, it was all over the papers, where have been?' he asked again, this time staring at me for an answer. I told him everything that had happened to me over the last year and a half, his mouth getting wider with every new revelation.

'Why did you not come to me when you were released from the reformatory? You know I would have let you stay here. Why did you not come?'

'I wanted to, Georgi, but, how could I? I still owed the money you gave my mother. I could not come and be a burden to you again. Here, that's thirty marks. I will pay you the rest as soon as I have it.'

'Franz, you know I would have been happy not to have this money. You should have come to me and not gone to a doss-house or beg in the streets.'

'What happened to Maria?' I asked as he put the money in a drawer without counting it. 'Franz, if you need the money, it's there for you. Promise no more begging in the streets.'

'I promise, Georgi ... What happened to Maria?'

'She killed herself, how could she do such a thing? Here, read it for yourself,' he said, handing me a newspaper clipping, which had a picture of Maria standing beside Douglas Fairbanks. I read slowly, with my eyes increasingly being blurred with tears.

Yesterday morning, the actress Maria Bernhardt was found unconscious in her Californian home. She died a few hours later in hospital. An empty bottle of sleeping tablets was recovered from her room along with a suicide note addressed to Max Reagan, the director who had discovered her in Berlin and with whom it is believed she was having an affair. This beautiful rising star's career had stalled after her recent performances failed to match her earlier promise. One critic referred to her as a 'remarkable beauty with an unremarkable talent.' Her publicist, Margot Marx, has confirmed she will be laid to rest in the Forest Lawn Memorial Cemetery in Los Angeles.

Georgi put his hand on mine and said, 'Life is so cruel, Franz, but we have to carry on. Don't be sad, make them proud of you. That's the best you can do.'

'Do you really think there's heaven?' I asked, handing him the clipping.

'I don't know, but there must be something or what is the point of life.'

'Does there have to be a point?'

Georgi, who hated to see anyone unhappy, clapped his hands to dispel the gloom and began telling me about his latest act for which he had bought a new wig, costing twenty marks, a sum which could almost pay my rent for the month. Before I could say anything, he put the voluminous blonde curls on and began an impromptu performance of one of his new songs, pretending to smoke a cigarette as he fluttered his eyes at his imaginary audience. I gave an exaggerated applause and he bowed, thanking me for my kindness.

While Georgi was prancing around the room, a strong urge came over me to sit him down and tell him all about Rebecca. Finally, when he was taking a break from his theatrics and enjoying the reward of a real cigarette, I told him about my feelings for her and how I planned to marry her one day. After a few words of premature congratulations, he broke into song, excited about the prospects of a wedding, while contemplating what he might wear. I immediately regretted telling him.

*

For the next couple of months, I went to the cinema with Rebecca, one week she would pick the movie, the next I would get to decide. We always went to the same café for coffee and afterwards I always walked her home to her aunt's and took the tram back. She had become increasingly interested in Maria, and I told her all I knew about her during our long walks across town. When I ran out of things to say about Maria, I began telling her stories about Georgi, who I promised I would take her to meet some day.

One night, after walking her home as usual, the moon must have gone to my head and when I kissed her goodnight, I also told her I loved her. This did not get the reaction I was expecting. The smile she had when I kissed her on the cheek disappeared and she turned and ran upstairs without looking back. I went home feeling rather foolish.

The following Friday while I waited anxiously for Rebecca to come into work, Herr Kolinski came to the shop instead. I listened as he told Leon that Rebecca would not be in that afternoon as she had to study for her exams. He turned to me with an apologetic shrug of his shoulders. 'Rebecca asked me to tell you, Franz, she will not be able to go to the cinema this evening. She has too much studying to do. I'm sure you understand.'

'Yes, of course, Herr Kolinski,' I said, while trying not to look too disappointed, and insisting there was always next week.

Chapter 18

There wasn't a next time, and every time I asked Hannah about Rebecca, the answer was always the same; she was finding her studies so demanding she had little time for anything else. I could not understand why she could not take the occasional evening off to go to the cinema; no one needs to study every night without having some time off. I began to think she was avoiding me because of what I said, using her studies as an excuse.

Fridays became just like any other day, and I stopped asking if she was coming back to work in the shop. The weeks passed into months with little regard to how I was feeling. If time heals, it was not in any hurry to remedy my condition. On my days off I would often walk past the university in the hope of seeing her, but the long hours spent waiting for her were in vain.

*

In October 1929, the economy went into freefall after the catastrophic collapse of the American stock exchange. Berlin was once again in a state of anarchy. A plethora of communist and fascist posters began to appear all over the city: *Down with the bourgeois state; Germany needs a new Beginning; Capitalism has failed the People.* I took little notice of the growing crisis; I had seen it all before.

The economic chaos was not helped by the fact that we had one of our worst winters for years. The winds blowing from the east were relentless and dumped more snow on Berlin in one day than we had the whole of the previous winter. I, like everyone else, was glad when the spring arrived.

On one of my days off, and when the sun was strong enough to make for a pleasant morning, I took a stroll along the Linden. It was while I was watching a troupe of men marching with the banners and emblems of the Red Front League, that I saw Dieter Jäger handing out pamphlets at the corner of Friedrichstrasse. He stopped what he was doing when he saw me standing on the other side of the road.

'Hello, Franz,' he shouted, walking towards me. 'How the hell are you?'

'Hello, Dieter. I'm well.'

'Let's go for a drink,' he suggested, shaking my hand and slapping me on the back.

'What about your leaflets?'

'No one ever reads them anyway,' he said, putting them into his canvas shoulder bag.

We found a nearby tavern where Dieter ordered two beers. He looked much older than his twenty years and still carried himself with the self-confidence that had marked him out from everyone else at the reformatory.

'You're doing well,' he said, looking impressed with my appearance.

'I've got a good job in a tailor's shop not far from Alexanderplatz.'

'I can't imagine you working as a tailor. You didn't learn that in the reformatory.'

'I thought you'd be in uniform by now.'

'No, marching through the streets is not for me. I've more important things to do.'

'Like what?'

'Like planning for the future of this country,' he said without a hint of modesty in his voice. He leaned over. 'Within a few years, this inept capitalist government will fall, and we will have a communist one to take its place.'

I gave a mock laugh, thinking he was joking. He quickly turned serious. 'Franz, this is not a laughing matter. If we do not seize power, the Nazis will take it and ruin this country. That is why you do not see me marching around the streets in a uniform, what I have to do must be done behind the scenes.'

'If what you do is so secret, why are you in the streets handing out leaflets?'

'The leaflets, I've been handing them out for years. If I suddenly stopped the authorities might get suspicious and think I was up to something more radical. The reason I am telling you, is I think you should join us.'

'Why would I want to join the communists?'

'Soon there will be only two choices, the Communist Party or the Nazi Party. Which one of them would you rather have control of the country?'

'I'm not sure Dieter; one is as bad as the other.'

He slammed his beer glass down on the table and stared at me. 'Remember that fat pig Schultz and what he did to Paul?' he said, lighting a cigarette and waiting for a response.

'Yes, how could I forget?'

'Well, he is now one of Goebbels' deputies; is that the kind of low-life you want running the country?'

'No, of course not.'

He grabbed my arm. 'Franz, there will be a time, soon, when you will have to decide which side you are on. I hope we do not end up enemies.'

'Why would we be enemies? I could never be your enemy.'

'Then, be my comrade. You're not like the other boneheads who can't think for themselves; you have a mind of your own. You are educated. You could be another Marx or Engels, someone who people would listen to.'

'I think you are talking about yourself, Dieter … Who would listen to me?'

'I did. That's why I want you to join us. The party needs people like you.'

'Can I think about it?' I said, easily flattered.

'Here,' he said, handing me a piece of paper with an address on it. 'It's a trade union hall in the north side of the city. You can find me there … Join us, Franz, if not for yourself, for Paul. He was your friend as much as mine.'

When we got back into the busy street we shook hands and said goodbye. With little hesitation, he jumped on the back of a moving tram, which was heading towards the Brandenburger Tor. Although I was glad to see him again, I had no intention of joining the communists or any other political party for that matter.

*

By the end of the summer, and despite the fact the economy was getting worse by the day, business had strangely picked up in the shop. We were so busy that we often had to work late into the evening just to keep up with the new orders that were coming in daily. Even after all this time I was still not over Rebecca, who I had not seen for almost a year.

Then, one day while I was taking the measurements of a customer, I overheard Hannah telling Leon that Rebecca had become engaged. Leon quickly changed the subject when I went into the back shop. They both looked at me but said nothing as Hannah went back to her sewing machine and Leon mumbled something in Yiddish.

Over the next few weeks I listened to Hannah's unguarded gossip with customers and heard her boast that Rebecca's fiancé, Benjamin was the eldest son of Hector Cohen, who owned three of the largest department stores in Berlin. It was now obvious to me why we had become so busy lately.

*

I took a tram one evening and travelled to the north of the city. Some men join the Foreign Legion to forget an unrequited love; I decided to join the Communist Party.

I got off in Müllerstrasse, the heart of this soviet enclave.

Across the road, outside a building draped in a very large red flag, a crowd was standing waiting for the doors of the hall to open. I stood at the edge of the group, smoking and listening to one or two conversations before we began to shuffle into the damp-smelling building.

There were rows of chairs laid out all the way up to the podium, where half a dozen men sat stony-faced behind a long table draped in another red flag. The chairs were quickly filled as more and more people entered the hall. I decided to stand at the back. Cigarettes were passed around, and the hall was soon engulfed in a cloud of smoke. There was no sign of Dieter.

There was a rapturous applause when one of the men on the podium, in a rather shabby three-piece suit, got up to speak. 'Thank you, comrades, thank you. I am glad to see so many of you on such a cold night ... ' he coughed, putting his hands in his waistcoat pockets as though looking for something. 'The government, if it deserves such a title, is on the verge of collapse. Within a few short months, you'll see, the German workers will not suffer any more lies and will rise up against this corrupt regime that pedals capitalist tyranny for the benefit of the industrialists and the bourgeoisie. In the meantime, however, we must continue to enhance our right to govern by contesting these elections just as the Nazis are doing ...'

There were howls of abuse at the mere mention of the fascists, and to allow the crowd time to calm down, the little man removed his glasses and wiped his face with a large white handkerchief. He raised his hands to hush the unrest.

'They are our real enemy ... they seek to corrupt the working man into thinking they will look after their interests when it's their own self-interests they will be looking after. We must be as ruthless as our enemies, remember what the nationalists did to Karl Liebknecht and Rosa Luxemburg.'

The mention of these two names was met with

spontaneous applause and calls for revolution, which gave the gifted orator time to clean his spectacles again. He calmed the excited audience with the palms of his hands and they grew quiet again. 'We must be prepared to fight fire with fire!'

There was another thunderous applause when more party activists pushed their way into the packed hall. The smell of stale beer, tobacco and body odour was crushing. I pushed my way through the tightly packed audience to be near to one of the side doors for some fresh air.

In time, I became bored listening to one angry man after another saying virtually the same thing. It seemed they all had to have their few minutes of glory. There was still no sign of Dieter and I began to question why I had made the journey across the city in the first place. Disillusioned, I forced my way out of the hall.

In the lane two men were passionately arguing about something to do with party dues, while exchanging puffs of cigarette smoke. They were both wearing cloth caps and red neckerchiefs. I lit a cigarette, feeling the cold as the wind found its way to the sweat trapped under my shirt. The two men shook hands and went back into the hall.

'Franz?'

It was Dieter, with a grin on his face and his arms around a girl. She was very pretty and wearing a Breton hat and red scarf.

'So, you decided to come, Franz.'

'Yes, I thought about what you said.'

'Good … This is Eva.'

I took her hand, giving a gallant bow of the head, which made her laugh. 'Franz Schreiber. Pleased to meet you.'

'Franz, you're still such a pompous bourgeois,' said Dieter, knocking my hat off.

'Oh, don't be cruel,' said Eva, bending down to pick up my old flat cap, which I thought would look better at a communist meeting than the trilby I usually wore.

'Let's go and have a beer,' said Dieter, walking to the top of the lane.

'What about the meeting?'

'Oh, it's all the same old rubbish every night,' said Dieter, lighting a cigarette and putting his arm around Eva again.

'But this is my first meeting and I haven't joined yet.'

'There'll be plenty more meetings, you can join then,' she said, taking my arm as we crossed over the road to the beer hall.

While Dieter went to the bar, I followed Eva to a table in the corner where I offered her a cigarette. 'Where are you from?' I asked, hearing a slight foreign accent in her voice.

'Berlin, but originally I'm from Poland, a small town near the border. Everyone speaks German there, but we would go to bed at night never quite sure if we'd wake up German, Polish or even Russian the next morning. We moved to Berlin when I was twelve.'

'Are you Polish or German?'

'I am a Jew. In Poland, I was treated as a German and in Germany I'm treated as a Pole, take your pick,' she said, sounding rather annoyed with my questions.

Before I could say anything else, Dieter arrived back with the drinks, spilling beer as he banged the three jugs down on the table. A brass band began to play the *Internationale*. It became rowdy, with foot stamping and beer glasses banging on tables.

'To the revolution,' said Dieter as we clanked our beer jugs together.

'The workers,' said Eva.

'To Paul,' I said, because I could not think of anything revolutionary to say, which would not sound silly.

Dieter looked at me and smiled, 'To Paul.'

With the froth of the beer still on his lips, Dieter began to eulogise passionately about the 1919 uprising as though he had been there, banging the table whenever his own words infuriated him. Ignorant of most of what he said, I felt a fraud; nodding in agreement when he blamed the government for siding with the rich over the workers. This time, he insisted, Stalin would intervene, and the capitalists would be swept aside. We clanked our glasses together again. 'Prost!'

Over the noise, while Eva went back to the bar to get more beers, Dieter changed the subject and told me he had seen Schultz address an SA youth rally a few days earlier. 'Come the revolution,' he said, 'Schultz will get what he deserves.'

'Do you really think there will be a revolution?'

'Of course, like Plato said: first we have monarchy, then democracy, which will lead to political chaos, and ultimately to a strong dictatorship. We are now at the end of this weak democracy and we have our chaos.'

'I thought you wanted a communist state, not a dictatorship.'

'To make communism work, we will need a dictatorship first, and then, we will move the masses towards true communism.'

'Whether they like it or not,' I said.

'The people don't know what they want, but they know what they don't want … this weak republic.'

'What about the Nazis?'

'Fuck the Nazis!'

Eva eventually returned with a tray of beers and I got up to help her, but she told me to sit down and stop being such a bourgeois. They both laughed, and I sat down, my face turning red. The beer was stronger than I was used to and made me a little woozy. I lit another cigarette, watching in quiet envy as comrade Eva snuggled up to comrade Dieter, while he ran his fingers through her short blonde hair and sipped his beer. Eva looked at me for a moment, somewhat surreptitiously, as though teasing my jealous eyes. Embarrassed, I quickly looked away.

I went to the bar to get another round of beers. Already a little drunk, I began singing along with the awful band. The bar was awash with spillage and I had to shout at the bartender to be heard above the barrage of noise.

On my way back to the table someone shouted, 'Nazis!' as a mob of Brownshirts forced their way into the hall with clubs and pickaxe handles. Chaos reigned, and I was pushed to and fro in the heaving crowd, trying desperately to avoid being hit by flying missiles. I struggled to keep my feet, still gripping onto the handles of the beer-jugs, which were now half empty. Beer glasses and bottles rained down, and I tried to get behind a pillar for cover. I suddenly felt a crack on the back of my head. The noise in the room drifted off into the distance. My hands could no longer feel the handles, and the ground seemed to move under my feet.

I must have been unconscious for at least a couple minutes before my senses slowly returned. The fog in my head began to lift, and I realised I was lying in a pool of spilt beer and blood. I then felt someone take my arm.

'Franz, are you all right?' asked Dieter, while trying to get me up from the floor.

'He'll have to go to hospital,' said Eva over his shoulder.

'He'll be arrested if he goes there.'

'It looks bad. Can someone get a doctor?' shouted Eva.

'Franz, can you hear me, it's Dieter. We may have to take you to hospital. Can you hear me?'

The circle of faces gradually came into focus, as the noise in the room rushed back into my ears; shouting, swearing, and the crunch of broken glass underfoot as tables and chairs were being turned back on their legs. I was pulled back onto my feet and held up against a wall, still dazed and feeling sick.

'The cowards have gone,' said Dieter. 'Let's get you out of here before the police come.'

Outside a cold wind blew hard in my face and I tried to stop shivering in case it was perceived as fear. Dieter put a cigarette in my mouth and Eva held her scarf at the back of my head to soak up the blood. Dieter lit my cigarette and called me a working-class hero, wounded while fighting the fascist pigs. Fighting, I was only trying to get back to the table without spilling too much beer, but I said nothing as Eva continued to dab the back of my inflated, heroic head. 'We will take you back to our place, it's not safe to be in the streets tonight,' said Eva. 'The fascists will be back looking for more trouble.'

They lived in a tiny one room apartment with no electricity. Eva lit a few candles and took off her coat, putting it across the unmade bed in the recess. The candles threw flickering shadows around the room and I noticed a poster of Lenin on the wall above the bed, surrounded by small Soviet flags. While Dieter made a pot of coffee, Eva sat beside me and examined the back of my head with the tips of her fingers, gently touching the congealed blood. 'I don't think it's as bad as we thought,' she said, 'it's stopped bleeding.'

'I'll be all right.'

Dieter poured the coffee, and we sat, smoking and talking of revolution all night until I, still a little groggy, fell asleep.

I awoke the next morning on the sofa as the daylight struggled to penetrate the heavy brown curtains. Stiff and sore, I almost had to lift my head with both my hands to sit up. My clothes were crumpled, damp and stank of stale beer. Dieter and Eva were sleeping under Lenin in the bed recess.

Trying not to wake them, I slowly opened the front door, pausing for a moment on seeing Eva staring at me. She smiled but said nothing.

The streets were grim, and I made my way along the unfamiliar pavements until I reached the tram stop on Müllerstrasse. It was bitter cold, and it made my face feel numb. I was glad when the tram arrived.

When the tram turned into Wilhelmplatz, I saw Adolf Hitler for the first time. He was wearing a brown trilby hat and a long trench-coat, which was belted tightly around his waist. He walked purposefully through a line of saluting SA men, outside the Hotel Kaiserhof, before getting into a waiting car. His black shadow, Goebbels, gave the Nazi salute to his master as the car slowly drove off. Not far behind Goebbels I saw Schultz coming down the hotel stairs with other senior party officials, his pink face beaming with self-importance.

Chapter 19

It was after eight when I arrived at the shop. Hannah was busy at her sewing machine while Leon was arranging shirts behind the counter. 'What time do you call this?' he demanded, nodding towards the clock.

'What are you making, Hannah?' I asked, taking off my hat and coat and ignoring Leon.

'We have a new order in from one of the big stores, twenty pair of trousers and a dozen tweed jackets. Herr Kolinski brought the order in this morning. He has a meeting with another store this afternoon to try and drum up some more business.'

'That's great,' I said, with little enthusiasm in my voice.

'You'll find the measurements on your table,' said Leon, strangely sullen.

'What's wrong with you?' I asked, but he went into the back shop without answering.

'He was attacked last night by some thugs. They stole his watch and slapped him about,' whispered Hannah, shaking her head.

'Why?'

'Why? Do you need a why? I told him to stop wearing his kippah when he's in the street, but would he listen? What do I know?'

'Because he's a Jew?'

'No, because he's an old Jew. The cowards wouldn't pick on someone their own age in case they get slapped right back. Don't say anything to him … he's … well, he's not himself this morning.'

'Did he report it to the police?'

'What good would that do? He'd probably get another

slap from one of those swine. They're all the same … Jew haters.'

I went into the back shop and watched Leon measure out the dinner suit he was working on. He turned away when he saw me looking at him, the side of his face was slightly bruised, and his left eye was bloodshot. I pretended not to notice.

My workbench was already stacked with material and using Leon's measurements I began to chalk the cloth for the new order. Still feeling a little light-headed, I thought of Eva lying in bed with Dieter. She was as strange as she was beautiful, alluring as she was foreboding. I did not know what to make of her and Dieter, but I envied their love as much as the commitment they had for what they believed in. They were real communists, committed to the overthrow of the republic and the creation of a workers' state, at any cost. I was still not sure if that was such a great idea; did we really want to end up like the Soviet Union?

'Franz! Watch what you're doing!' Leon shouted abruptly as I cut the cloth over the chalk line. 'I'm sorry Leon, I've got a bit of a headache.'

'A headache at your age?' he said as if he forgot his own pain to criticise mine. 'I told you not to go to that meeting last night. That would give anyone a headache, drinking cheap beer and listening to all that rubbish.'

'I thought you supported the communists?'

'Communists, Nazis! What's the difference?'

'The Nazis are thugs and bullies,' I said, seeing the old sparkle coming to his eyes. He loved an argument.

'They are all thugs and bullies. They all want power to tell everyone else how to live their lives. If I could afford it, I would emigrate to America tomorrow … anyway I'm too old to start a new life. I'll be dead soon enough.'

'Well, make up your mind,' shouted Hannah from the front shop.

'She'd be sorry if I went,' he said, taking another pin from his lip and sticking it in the half-dressed mannequin. 'My life will be over soon enough, and I won't be sad to leave this miserable world. If the Jews are the chosen people then I wish God had chosen someone else ... It makes me wonder sometimes if there is a God ... why create such a miserable place, when he could have created a real paradise, where everyone could have enough to eat and be happy ... If there is a God, he doesn't care much for his own creation.'

'You're only happy when you're miserable,' shouted Hannah.

I had never seen or heard Leon so depressed, and it made me sad. I put on the kettle.

'What happened to your head?' he asked as I turned to light the stove.

'Some Nazi thugs attacked the meeting last night. I was hit over the head with something before we chased them back out into the street. We beat a few of them up and the rest ran off like cowards.'

'You beat a few of them up! Sit down; no wonder you have a headache. Let me make the coffee ... Hannah! Come in and make Franz a cup of coffee,' he shouted as he looked at the cut to my head. 'That's a good old thump you got,' he said, beaming with pride.

When he repeated my half-truths to Hannah, she became over-excited about having a hero in the shop. As though we were now both comrades in the same battle, Leon finally told me what had happened to him, while I pretended not to know anything about it. Hannah smiled at my pitiful acting and poured me a coffee with a wink before opening her precious biscuit tin.

For the rest of the day as I cut the cloth for Hannah to sew, Leon would make random comments about me and my head wound, patting me on the back as he passed in and out of the back shop whistling the *Internationale*.

The next morning, I awoke feeling unwell. The pain in my head became acute and I began to feel sick. I hugged the sink to stop myself falling to my knees and began vomiting so violently it burnt my throat. My gut continued to retch as the blood drained from my face, making me feel faint and utterly wretched. Once the convulsions finally stopped, exhausted, I fell back onto the bed as the room began spinning one way, while the mattress seemed to sink into a vortex going the other way. I had to try and get back on my feet and get to the hospital, but I was so weak I could not even lift myself from the bed. I passed out.

My dreams and nightmares came and went until I regained consciousness to find Rebecca sitting in front of the fire reading a book. The glow from the flames lit up her face, and, for a moment, I thought I was still dreaming. I tried to get up, but my body was so weak and the bed sheets so tight I could not move. I tried to speak, but nothing came from my mouth. I began to roll my head on the pillow to try and attract her attention as the metal framed bed began to creak, she finally turned from what she was doing.

'You're back from the dead,' she said, coming to the bed and gently lifting my head to put a glass of water to my dry lips.

'Thank you,' I croaked, the cold water reviving me a little.

'How do you feel?' she asked, wiping my forehead with a cold, damp cloth.

'What happened?'

'Hannah was worried when you didn't turn up for work the other morning ... '

'The other morning?'

'Yes, you've had a fever for three days. Leon came around to see what was wrong and when he could not get an answer, he decided to force open your door. He found you delirious on the floor and fetched the doctor.

Since then Hannah has taken turns with me to look after you. You've had some awful nightmares. If we were Catholics, you would have been given your last rites now.'

'Thank God you're not.'

'I thought you communists didn't believe in God.'

'I'm not a communist; I just went to find out what they're all about.'

'And did you find out?'

'No, not really.'

'Well at least you didn't go to one of those Nazi meetings.'

'You know I'd never do that.'

Confined to my bed on doctor's orders, I only got up for a few hours a day to sit by the fire whenever Rebecca or Hannah came by to make me something to eat, or just to keep me company for a few hours. By the end of the week, when the infection in the back of my head cleared, my strength gradually returned.

The doctor then assured me I was well enough to return to work. I was in no great hurry to go back to making trousers so long as I knew I could see Rebecca every other day. I feigned sickness as he took my temperature and reconsidered his prognosis. 'Maybe you should stay in bed for another week or so. You can never take chances with a blow to the head.'

Whenever Rebecca was there, we would sit and talk for hours. One evening she told me all about her dead brothers and how much she missed them. With her voice breaking, she raised her hand to stop a tear running down her cheek. I took her other hand to comfort her, which brought a smile to her face. We stared at each other, until she turned away and withdrew her hand from mine. She got up and walked around the room talking about things that did not matter to either of us.

Then the tone in her voice changed as she lifted her coat to leave. 'I won't be able to come back after tonight,' she said. 'I'm going on holiday with some of my friends for a few weeks. Hannah will still come until you're able to look after yourself.'

'Going on holiday … Where are you going?'

'Paris. I will send you a post card.'

'Is Benjamin going with you?' I asked, trying but failing to sound nonchalant. It was the first time her fiancé's name was mentioned.

'No, just a few girlfriends I met at university.'

'Why are you marrying him?' I asked, unable to help myself. 'Is it because he's rich?'

'How dare you! What gives you the right to ask me a question like that?'

'I'm sorry, please sit down, Rebecca,' I pleaded as she put her coat on. 'I'm really sorry. I know it's none of my business. Please don't go … stay for a while.'

'No, I have to go,' she said, staring at me long and hard as she continued to button her coat. I must have looked pathetic to her as I begged her not to leave, but I could not help myself. 'I'm sorry, Franz. It's getting late, I better go. Look after yourself … Hannah will be over tomorrow night … Goodbye.'

Cursing my own stupidity, I stood at the window and watched her cross the road in the torrential rain to wait for her tram. I noticed she had forgotten her umbrella. For a moment I was tempted to run down with the damned thing, but the tramcar pulled up before I could make up my mind what to do. Wiping the condensation from the window, I waited as the conductor rang the bell and the tram slowly moved off. She was gone.

The following evening Hannah arrived and was pleased to see I was up and sitting in front of the fire. She checked my temperature, which she said was still too high, but getting better. She made supper, which I was unable to eat even though I had not eaten all day. I asked if Rebecca had gone to Paris. She looked at me as if she was about to cry. She got up and kissed me on the forehead before putting on her coat to leave. 'Franz, you will have to try and forget about her,' she said in a whisper. 'She will be a married woman soon ... You should not torment yourself, you're young and will soon forget all about her ... Goodnight, Franz, and try and get some rest.'

Despite my desire to run off somewhere and hide from the world, I returned to work the following week to find Leon and Hannah snowed under with more new orders from the department stores.

Eventually, I decided the only way to cope with the void Rebecca had left in my life was to find another passion to take its place. I became determined to learn as much as possible about communism, buying books, reading them every night until I was able to quote long passages from *Das Kapital*, verbatim. I even bought a new Breton cap like the one Dieter wore and began smoking the same brand of French cigarettes as he did.

Then, trying to make myself sound important, I told Leon one morning I was going to another party meeting at the weekend. I did not get the response I was expecting. He was unimpressed and said I should be out enjoying myself and not wasting my time with politics. 'They're all the same ... Find a nice girl to make you happy. What do you want with these communists?'

Resolute, and contrary to Leon's advice, I took the tramcar back to Müllerstrasse, wearing my new Breton cap and red neckerchief, which I tucked under my collar. Outside the hall, a group of men in the uniform of the Red Front League were standing at the door with clubs in their hands. I tried to walk past them but was stopped and asked for my membership card. I told them I was a friend of Dieter Jäger and was intending to join that night. I gave one of the men my name and he went into the hall.

A few minutes later he returned. 'You have to wait here;

Comrade Jäger will be out to speak to you in a moment.'

I waited at the bottom of the steps and lit a cigarette, pulling up my collar to keep warm. It was fifteen minutes before Dieter appeared. The men at the door gave him a clenched fist salute, which he ignored.

'How have you been, comrade?' he asked, shaking my hand and slapping me on the back. 'I see you've got a new hat,' he said, with a hint of mockery in his voice, causing me to remove it from my head and feel a little foolish. 'How's Eva?'

'Eva's fine, she'll meet us later. She's making a speech in a few minutes. Let's get a beer; my throat is as dry as hell.'

'Are we not going to stay and listen to Eva's speech?'

'No, it's just the usual old stuff about women's suffrage in the movement; I've heard it all before.'

The bar was not very busy, and Dieter bought two beers. I told him about my illness, but he didn't seem to be listening, constantly looking around, and not even drinking.

'What's the matter?' I asked, rather annoyed at his indifference to my welfare.

'Franz, do you still want to join the party?'

'Yes, I was going to join tonight.'

'Well don't, not officially anyway.'

'What do you mean?'

'What I have to tell you must go no further,' he said, looking around to make sure no one was listening as he began to whisper close to my face. 'I have been ordered to infiltrate the Nazi Party and find out what they're up to, and, if possible, sabotage their election plans.' He sipped his beer for a moment, looking around the other tables again before continuing. 'The problem is the police have me on their records as a communist provocateur, and we know most police officers are Nazi sympathisers. We are certain they have passed my file to the Nazi Party's intelligence unit at Potsdamer Platz.' He brushed the hair from his forehead.

'We need someone who they have no record of to join their party and gather intelligence ...'

'You mean me!' I said, moving back in my seat as he nodded. 'Absolutely no way ... I'm a tailor for God's sake.'

'Keep your voice down. The Nazi Party is full of disgruntled shopkeepers. Being a tailor is a fairly innocuous occupation and they would not be suspicious of your motives for joining ...'

'But I work for a Jew, and the others in the shop are Jewish. They will check my background and know I am not a Nazi supporter,' I replied, causing Dieter to sit back in his chair and raise his hands in submission. Just then Eva came in and I went to the bar to buy another round of drinks. My hands were shaking as I handed over the money to the bartender. I made some comment about the cold.

Dieter and Eva broke off their conversation when I returned to the table with the jugs of beer.

'How's your head?' she asked, taking off her scarf and gloves, before lighting a cigarette.

'It's fine.'

'Dieter tells me you are afraid to help us,' she said with such frankness I could not find anything to say in response. 'Maybe you think being a revolutionary is all about going to meetings and wearing red bandanas to impress the girls.'

'No,' I said, looking at Dieter, who shrugged his shoulders. 'How can I do it? I've already told Dieter I work for Jews ...'

'Then leave your job. We have plenty of tailors who can give you a position and they'll make it easy for you to take time off when necessary.'

'I can't just leave. Herr Kolinski is like a father to me and it would hurt him if I went off to work for someone else after all he has done for me.'

'You're not a child anymore ... How are you paid?' she asked abruptly, her voice cold. 'Are you registered?'

'What do you mean?'

'Do you pay tax?'

'No ... he just pays me a certain amount in my hand each week.'

'Then you can continue to work where you are and register as unemployed.'

'I can't do it. There must be someone else you can get to do this,' I said, feeling the walls closing in on me.

'Not now we have taken the risk asking you. Dieter was sure you'd help, I wasn't. So, will you do it?'

Dieter had not said anything for some time and I felt he was embarrassed for me. We drank in silence for the next few minutes, as Eva turned away and looked out the window. Their silence made it difficult for me to look at either of them. They wanted an answer and I finally gave an awkward cough. 'All right, I'll do it,' I said, hearing the words coming out of my mouth before having the sense to stop them. The atmosphere immediately changed, and Eva reverted back to her sweet self, while Dieter gave me instruction on how to join the Nazi party and become friendly with those higher up the ladder, Goebbels if possible ... Why not Hitler, I thought sarcastically to myself.

Dieter was talking and talking, but I was only taking in some of what he was saying, even though he kept repeating things, most of what he said was lost in the noise all around us. My mind was elsewhere, questioning my own sanity. This is not what I expected when I spent all those hours reading Marx and Engels to impress them. I began thinking I could just pretend to do what they wanted and never show my face there again. Then, as Dieter continued to tell me things I did not want to hear, Eva smiled at me as she got up to get more beers. It was that smile that told me how naive I had been.

'Here,' said Dieter, handing me a telephone number to use only when I had to contact him or Eva. My alias was to be Kasper, no second name, and he assured me only he and Eva would ever know my real identity. The operator on the end of the line was only there to pass on messages and would not ask me any questions. I was never to use my real name when calling, under any circumstances.

Numb, I took the tram home, with my new cap and neckerchief tucked into my pocket. I got off before my usual stop and walked the last mile to clear my head, still questioning my sanity for getting mixed up in politics in the first place. Eva was right; I was willing to be a revolutionary so long as there was no revolution. But what if I was discovered spying on the Nazi Party? Their thugs would not think twice about beating me to death and dumping my body in the canal. I recalled how Mother once called me a communist spy when I was not even sure at the time what a communist spy was. Now I knew … I was about to become one.

Chapter 20

There was no postcard from Paris. Hannah was right. Rebecca would be married soon and there was nothing I could do about it. I often thought about Benjamin, I knew he came from a wealthy family, but I had no idea what he looked like. Even though I had never met him, I could not help being envious, especially when I heard Hannah telling one of our customers how handsome he was. He was the heir to a fortune and I was a reformed thief who stole from his father's department stores. How could I resent Rebecca for loving him and not me?

At least the fear of what Dieter and Eva were planning for me distracted my melancholy for a while. I was in a constant state of angst until someone left a note for me at the shop to call Dieter. The fact things were coming to a head settled my nerves. I phoned the number Dieter had given me. The person who answered gave me instruction to go to a café on Müllerstrasse at seven o'clock, before hanging up abruptly.

The café was closed when I got there, and I stood outside and waited for about ten minutes. I was about to walk away when Dieter appeared with a grin on his face. 'Don't look so worried, Franz, it belongs to a friend,' he said, taking out a set of keys from his coat pocket and opening the door. It was the type of café that served cheap food and did not bother much about its appearance. The floor was stained in places, and the old tables and chairs had seen better days.

We talked for about half an hour. He wanted me to go to a Nazi Party meeting in two days' time and become a member. I was to listen to what was said and memorise anything of importance. 'Just pretend you're a Nazi from now on,' he said with a smile. 'They just do the same things we do; talk too much, get drunk and start fights.'

'You make it sound as though it's a game.'

'What else is it?'

*

The next day, with the sound of Hannah's sewing machine pounding in my head all morning, I had an overwhelming desire to tell her and Leon what I was planning to do that night, afraid of being wrongly exposed as a Nazi. The more I thought about it, the angrier it made me. I was annoyed with Dieter and Eva for putting me in this situation, but I was more annoyed with myself for letting them.

'Have you got a date with some young woman?' asked Leon as he piled up more material for me to cut. 'The time will only go as fast as time goes.'

I smiled, but said nothing, trying to stop myself from looking back at the clock.

After work I rushed home, changing into some old clothes to keep up the pretence of being unemployed and disgruntled with life. I had collected several Nazi leaflets as Dieter had advised and stuffed my coat pockets with them. I chain-smoked and drank coffee for an hour or more as I waited to leave.

At a kiosk on the corner I bought a copy of *Der Stürmer* and read it on the tram, hiding behind it and its anti-government propaganda. The tram took nearly an hour in the heavy traffic until it pulled up outside a hall, which was similar to the one in Müllerstrasse. Instead of red Soviet flags, the building had a large swastika hanging from a flag pole. SA stormtroopers strutted around the entrance, with their chests sticking out like prize cockerels. I joined a group of men walking towards the front door. When they entered the hall, they gave the Nazi salute. I did likewise. Inside, the men lined up to show their party cards to a thin-faced man sitting behind a desk with two Brownshirts standing behind him. My heart began to pound so hard, I thought the blood vessels in my ears were about to rupture. As the queue moved along, I had a sudden desire to leave, but managed to steady my nerve as the man in front of me eventually showed his card and received a nod to go in.

'I haven't got a card yet,' I said to the clerk, avoiding his cold, piercing stare.

'Wait over there,' he barked, pointing to another desk. I nervously completed a form with my own details, only lying about being unemployed. The clerk briefly considered the form before stamping it and filling out a card, which he handed to me without a word. I was now an official member of the Nazi Party.

The speakers were minor party officials and were merely repeating what they read in the Nazi newspapers that morning. It soon became tedious, and I had to stop myself from yawning on a few occasions. The fascist meetings were not much different from the communist ones. Everything was the government's fault, and the Nazis, like the communists, would put the country back to work and save the economy.

Over the next few weeks I attended several meetings in different parts of the city, reporting back anything that might be of interest to Dieter. He made me feel what I was doing was of great value to the party, although I failed to see why.

At one meeting I became acquainted with a party member called Hugo Nagel, who turned out to be a sergeant in the state police. He was stout man in his early forties, and wore an old-fashioned handlebar moustache, the ends of which he constantly twirled to a waxy point with his fingers. Hugo was less convincing as a Nazi than anyone I had met in the beer halls. He told me one night, over a few beers, that he hated many of our ignorant comrades and felt they only wanted to blame others for their own worthless lives. Hugo wanted the country to go back to the days of the Kaisers and believed Hitler would restore the monarchy. Hugo did not speak with any bitterness about the government, or even the

Jews, and I always felt unsure about him. I resolved never to get too drunk with him in case I let my guard down. He was a policeman after all.

To add credence to my apparent dedication to the Führer, I had read a number of books, including *Mein Kampf*, to give gravitas to my rants on National Socialism. If someone ridiculed my argument, I would quote one of Hitler's diatribes on capitalism or the Jews and that would be enough to get most around the table on my side. *Mein Kampf* was slowly becoming a new bible for the masses; like the bible, most of those who revered it had never read it for themselves, and those who had, could easily exploit their ignorance.

My life had become bizarre, and if Herr Kolinski and the others at the shop could hear half the things I said at these drunken meetings they would be horrified, if not terrified. Even though I had become preoccupied with my role as a spy, I had not freed myself from the spell Rebecca had over me. My feelings for her came back as bad as ever the day her wedding dress arrived in the shop for alterations. It hung up in the back shop to torment me.

When the day of the wedding finally arrived, and despite everything, I still had an overwhelming desire to see Rebecca again, even if it was to watch her marry someone else. I dressed in a black, two-piece suit and put a little oil on my hair, combing it in a side shed. Herr Kolinski had given me a silk kippah to wear in the synagogue. I put it on to see how it looked and was surprised. I could easily pass for being Jewish.

It was a beautiful morning, and I walked along Oranienburgerstrasse to the synagogue in the warm sunshine with the skullcap in my pocket. Leon and Hannah were already standing outside with some of the other guests. Leon was trying to get as much out of his cigar as possible before having to go in.

I lit a cigarette, joining them while we waited for the

bridal party to arrive. Hannah was a bag of nerves and wanted to go in before there were no seats left. Leon puffed on his cigar and ignored her; only nodding to go in when the car carrying the groom finally arrived. I put on my skullcap and followed. The synagogue was already full, and we had to stand at the back. Hannah was furious with Leon, calling him an old fool.

After a few minutes the rabbi appeared, rhythmically chanting prayers while shaking frankincense in every direction. He then beckoned Benjamin to come forward and stand with him under a canopy of white linen, covered in scattered rose petals. Just behind them, under a stained-glass Star of David was a large silver menorah, and what I took to be the Torah Scrolls lying opened on the altar. Suddenly Hannah pulled my sleeve and I turned to see Rebecca, with her face veiled in white silk, holding her father's arm as they walked slowly down the aisle to stand with Benjamin under the wedding canopy.

The marriage ceremony was in Hebrew and seemed to take forever. My thoughts wandered in all directions and I searched longingly for an occasional glimpse of Rebecca. The finality of the marriage was brought home to me when I heard the sacred glass being broken under Benjamin's heel. Leon nudged me, and sniggered, 'That's the last time he'll be allowed to put his foot down.'

After the ceremony I took a taxi with Leon and Hannah to the Hotel Adlon. I was surprised at the number of police officers standing outside the building and began to panic. I scanned their faces, fearful Hugo might be there, and was about to tell the taxi driver to drive on when Leon opened the cab door and got out. With my head down, I hurried past the police officers and went straight into the bar and ordered a double whisky, leaving Leon and Hannah to walk around the hotel foyer like tourists in a museum.

When Rebecca and her new husband arrived, I went back

into the foyer to watch them being showered with rice and rose-petals as they entered the hotel to excited applause and cheers. I watched for a few more minutes while an elderly man set up a tripod for his camera and began to organise the close family members, getting them, with some difficulty, to stand on either side of the marble staircase. He then positioned the bride and groom on the landing before finally taking the first picture. I went back into the bar and ordered another drink. Other guests, not required for the photographs, also spilled over into the bar, where a jazz trio was now playing. The singer, a Negro girl in a sequined black dress, began to sing George Gershwin's *I Got Rhythm*. I lit a cigarette and stared at my face in the smoked mirror behind the bar. I was still wearing the silk skullcap, and took it off, putting it back in my jacket pocket. Leon and Hannah returned from their exploration of the hotel. 'It'll be Herr Cohen who is paying,' she insisted, 'There is no way Herr Kolinski could afford all this expense.'

Leon was more interested in the pictures of past guests, including Charlie Chaplin, Douglas Fairbanks, Mary Pickford, Greta Garbo and Marlene Dietrich. He also took great pleasure in pointing out the more notable guests to me; including most of the owners of the large department stores, some politicians and even Dr Bernard Weiss, the deputy police commissioner. It was then I realised why there were so many police officers outside the hotel. Herr Kolinski had also told Leon that Albert Einstein returned his invitation with sincere apologies due to prior commitments in Vienna. There was no doubt the Cohen family were well connected.

Eventually, the master of ceremonies, dressed in white tie and tails, called on the wedding guests to make their way to the main function room for the reception where champagne and canapés were being served. There must have been around three hundred guests in the grand hall, with its glittering crystal chandeliers and large mirrors reflecting the wealth on show. The tables were decked out in pristine white linen, silver cutlery and hundreds of sparkling wine glasses. There were place names at every setting, and, after studying the table plan, I took my seat beside Leon and Hannah. We were at the back of the hall with several well-dressed ladies and gentlemen, who worked as floorwalkers in the Cohen Brothers' department stores. I ordered another whisky and exchanged meaningless pleasantries for a few minutes, hoping none of them would recognise me.

The bride and groom were introduced into the room by the booming voice of the master of ceremonies. Rebecca was radiant, walking around the hall holding Benjamin's hand, happily accepting small gifts and flowers from many of the smiling guests. The flower girls' arms were soon overflowing with gifts and bouquets as Hannah, in floods of tears, handed Rebecca a white lace shawl.

The bridal party were then enthusiastically clapped towards the top table where they took their seats to more applause.

The meal was smoked salmon and Black Sea caviar, followed by a main course of kosher lamb and vegetables. I declined to take a sweet as Hannah chided me for my lack of appetite, before drowning her own gateau with cream. It was just as the coffee was being served that I noticed Gretchen for the first time serving one of the other tables. She was a little heavier looking, but had not changed very much, her hair was still plaited the same way she always wore it. I tried to catch her eye but she never turned in my direction. I wondered if she would even recognise me after all these years.

The dinner over, the speeches began with Herr Kolinski first to speak, welcoming Benjamin into his family, and thanking all the guests for being there. The best man then told some anecdotes about the groom, and I laughed and clapped with the rest of the guests but was glad when it was finally over. I went back into the piano bar to get another drink as the hall was cleared for the dancing.

'What's the matter with you?' asked Leon, joining me at the bar. 'You've been miserable looking all day.'

'Why, did she have to marry him? Is it his money?' I moaned, the whisky making me forget myself.

'I thought you were over all this ... You're drinking too much ... Come back into the hall and stop this nonsense.'

I ordered another whisky.

'Franz,' said Leon, grabbing my arm. 'You're drunk already; don't make a fool of yourself.'

'I can get drunk if I bloody want to ... Leave me alone.'

Leon left, shaking his head and mumbling to himself.

The girl in the shimmering dress began singing, 'Falling in Love Again ... what am I to do ... can't help it' ... I lit a cigarette and watched her in the mirror opposite. She was very pretty and took my mind off Rebecca for a while as she shimmied in her low-cut dress, exuding sexuality like a scent. Her reflection was staring at me as I stared right back.

'Hello Franz, I haven't had a chance to speak to you this morning,' said Herr Kolinski, putting his hand on my shoulder. 'You should come back into the hall,' he said, taking the glass of whisky from my hand and putting it down on the counter. 'I'll buy you a drink later.'

'I have to go to the ...' I slurred, suddenly feeling sick, and rushing away to the toilet. I only just made it to the wash-hand basin when most of the whisky and much of what I had eaten came back out of me through my mouth and nose in a spate of retching that left me struggling to breathe. Only when I had emptied my stomach did I begin to feel a little better. I stared at myself in the mirror, my face was ashen, and my eyes were watering from the effect of the retching. I washed my face in cold water, and considered leaving the hotel and going home, when Leon came in and stood at the urinal, pretending to be peeing. It was obvious to me Herr Kolinski had sent him in to check on me. 'That's the dancing going to start in a few minutes. There are a couple of good-looking girls in there. I wish I was your age again,' he said, his acting not on the same level as his tailoring. I had another look at myself in the mirror, before going back into the hall.

Throwing up most of what was in my stomach had cleared my head, but the taste of sick was still in my mouth and I drank a glass of water to clear it. I was not sure how much of a fool I had made of myself, but I was feeling sober enough now to at least pretend to be enjoying myself.

The centre of the room was now cleared of tables and a traditional Polish band was in the process of setting up. There were tables and chairs positioned all around the hall and I sat beside Hannah, who looked at me the way a mother looks at a naughty child. 'Franz, please don't drink anymore, it's not good for you to drink so much.' Before I could think of something to say back to her, there was a sudden cheer, followed by loud, rhythmic clapping which quickly spread around the hall. Benjamin and Rebecca took their place in the middle of the room, as the band began to play a Jewish folk tune to start the first dance. Herr Kolinski then invited Benjamin's mother to dance, and other guests gradually joined them. In just a few minutes the dance floor was full.

After a few relative slow dances, the music became louder and the dancing faster, until the floor almost bounced with the thunder of stamping feet. The atmosphere in the hall was one of boundless energy and enjoyment. Feeling much better, I smiled at its madness.

Then, out of the blue and much to Leon's amusement, Hannah grabbed my arm and pulled me onto the dance floor. I was still not fully recovered from being sick and struggled to keep up with the speeding circles of guests, appearing all around me. I was grateful when Hannah finally ran out of breath and had to sit down.

When things finally quietened down, and Hannah was talking to a couple of old friends, I took the opportunity to ask Rebecca to dance. I felt almost possessed as I crossed the floor to where she was standing with her bridesmaids.

'Franz, at last, I was about to break tradition and ask you,' she said, taking my hand.

'You've been dancing all night; I didn't think I'd get the chance,' I said, putting my arms around her and kissing her on the cheek. 'Congratulations on your marriage. You look beautiful.'

'Thank you, Franz,' she said softly in my ear, 'I'm glad you came.'

Before I could say anything else, the band changed tempo again, and Rebecca was taken from my arms as the room erupted into the Charleston. I retreated to my chair beside Leon and Hannah.

Having recovered from what had happened earlier, I felt the need for another drink. I took the opportunity to go back to the piano bar when Hannah dragged her reluctant husband onto the dance floor.

The jazz trio was on its break and standing at the bar. I stood beside them and ordered a drink. They were Americans and I could make out a little of what they were saying. The bass player was boastfully telling a story about meeting Louis Armstrong in New York. I was watching the girl. She was drinking an exotic cocktail and tapping her long fingernails on the glass. She seemed bored with the bass player's story. Her hair was short, and I noticed she was not wearing a bra under her tight-fitting dress. I turned away when she caught me looking at her. She then spoke to me in German.

'The boys are going back to their room afterwards to get drunk. Is there anywhere you could suggest that might be a little more entertaining? It's alright; none of them understand a word of German.'

'There's a few places … if you don't mind cabaret.'

'I love cabaret. Will you wait for me after the show? We've only got another hour to play.'

'Sure. I'd love to show you around.'

'Is there any song you'd like me to sing?'

'Yes ... *Whispering*.'

'I haven't sung that for a while, but I'll give it a try.'

'What's your name?'

'Diana.'

For the next hour I sat and watched the band perform song after song, many of which reminded me of Mother dancing around on the edge of her madness. The hate I had for some of them had passed with her death as though they had now become some form of requiem to her unhappy life. Diana ended her act with a sultry performance of *Whispering*. I wiped a few whisky tears from my eyes.

As the rest of the band packed up for the night, she finally came over and sat beside me. 'Would you like a drink?'

'No, let's go, before you're too drunk to go anywhere,' she said, taking my hand and leading me into the foyer where Hannah and Leon were talking to some of the other guests. I shouted goodbye to them and staggered out the hotel with Diana on my arm. They just looked at each other in utter bewilderment.

That's as much as I remember of that night. I woke up the next morning with my head thumping and my mouth dry. Diana was already dressed and about to leave. She turned to look at me. 'I thought you were just too drunk last night, but that was until I heard you talking in your sleep.'

'I'm sorry. Can I see you again?'

'I don't think so,' she said, opening the door to leave. 'Whoever Rebecca is, she's a lucky girl to have someone love her so much. You should tell her how you feel ... Goodbye, Franz, and try not to drink so much.'

Chapter 21

With Rebecca married and on honeymoon, a kind of peace came to me I had not had for such a long time. I did not have to try and stop thinking about her, it just happened, as though her marriage to Benjamin had cured my obsession. The mood in the shop became better too, no doubt because of the fact I no longer walked around all day with a dark cloud of misery following me about. However, the actual work itself had become tedious, but it was at least better than standing outside the labour exchange on Kundstrasse, which was struggling to deal with the hordes of unemployed men queuing there every day.

With very little to tell him, I only met Dieter occasionally. He no longer bothered to tell me which meetings to go to, letting me make my own decisions. Most of those attending these meetings knew little about the party's politics, other than it promised work and bread. The adrenaline I felt in the boisterous atmosphere of the beer halls, contrasted with the daily boredom of working in the shop. I left work early one evening to attend a meeting at the Rathaus, where Goebbels would be making an important speech about the Nazi Party's election strategy.

I showed my party card at the door and took a seat near to the podium as the hall gradually filled. No one paid me any notice, and I took out a copy of *Der Angriff*, the newspaper Goebbels used to attack the party's rivals, pretending to be engrossed in its pages. The excitement grew as the first few officials took their seats on the podium behind a long trestle table covered in the party's flag. The diminutive orator kept his disciples waiting with his customary late appearance.

While we waited, my focus was on the four men, all

wearing dark sombre suits and swastika armbands, sitting on the rostrum. Two of them were known to me by name, and their details were already with Dieter. The other two were strangers and I studied their faces, hoping to be able to identify them later. The hall suddenly became excited, before erupting in a manic applause when Goebbels appeared from the side of the podium. He was wearing a grey double-breasted suit and trilby hat, smiling and wallowing in the adoration he obviously felt he deserved. I clapped and cheered as hard as the next man, until the euphoria was calmed by Goebbels, once he was satisfied with the hysteria he had created by his mere presence.

Only when there was complete silence did he begin to speak: 'Gentlemen, the German bourgeoisie is coming to an end and a new Germany must be forged. To do this we must continue to challenge the capitalist cancer that is poisoning the world. The republic of traitors has had its day, and those Jews who have helped to destroy our nation for their own gain will pay a heavy price for their treachery.' The hall erupted in spontaneous applause. Goebbels raised his hand to bring the hall back to silence, before resuming his speech. 'Germany will once again be strong, virile and Germanic under the National Socialist Party. The communists are cowards and would betray this country to the Soviet Union and the tyranny of Stalin if they got their way! It's for that reason we must support the Führer in his destiny to make our fatherland great again. We must bring the fight to the communists before they corrupt the minds of the German workers.'

Struck by his charismatic oratory, I watched as he brought himself to a climax, his face red and his fist clenched in the air. 'Our time is near and soon there will be a new government in Germany ... a National Socialist government! *Heil Hitler!*' The room exploded with applause. I was impatient to hear what else he would say to excite his admirers, but like a satisfied hypnotist he gave his spellbound audience the Nazi salute, before limping off the podium.

The rest of my evening was spent in a beer cellar with a few low-ranking Nazis, keen to hear anything they were saying, which might be of interest. The talk was all about Goebbels. The other speakers were more or less ignored when the drinking and arguing started. Everyone had something to say about what the Gauleiter had promised, but what did it mean?

'He was planning another attack on the communists, but this time there would be no mercy,' insisted one man.

'There was going to be another *Putsch*,' said a big man in Lederhosen, sporting a Bavarian hunting hat, who said he was with Hitler in 1923. I did not think he had to dress like a fool to prove it.

'No,' said another man, flushed with beer. 'There is no need for another *Putsch*; the German people will elect us into power.'

'Whatever happens there won't be a republic for very much longer,' said Hugo, winking at me, and dreaming of the Kaiser's return from exile.

*

After the July elections in 1932, I met Dieter a few weeks later in the Tiergarten to give him what little information I had gathered from my last few party meetings, which did not amount to much. He could find out more simply by reading the newspapers. He listened but seemed distracted and made me feel uneasy. When I had finished what I had to say he just nodded, before telling me about a Nazi attack on another party meeting, which left two comrades dead and a dozen seriously wounded. He punched the palm of his left hand in frustration and cursed the Nazis. He told me one of those seriously wounded was his younger brother, Johann. This surprised me; I didn't even know he had a brother. I realised just how little I knew about Dieter and his life. I offered him my sympathy, but he quickly changed the subject and began looking at what he had written in his notebook. I sensed he had something else on his mind. 'Good work, Franz, I'll pass this on to the district committee,' he said, putting the notebook in his jacket pocket. 'Franz,' he said, before continuing in a slow serious voice, 'the work you are doing is important, but most of what you find out we already know about.'

'I'm sorry, but I can only tell you what I hear at these meetings. That's what you asked me to do,' I said, annoyed at with his attitude. 'How can what I do be important, if you think most of what I give you is next to useless?'

'It's important we have someone who has infiltrated their meetings and is seen as a trusted member of their party. But just attending public meetings is a waste of your talents.'

I was not fool enough to fall for his charade; he was buttering me up for something unpleasant. 'If you have something to say, Dieter, say it!'

'Okay,' he replied, hesitating briefly for a young couple to pass. While we waited, he took a packet of cigarettes from his jacket pocket and handed me one. We both sat on a nearby bench and smoked in silence until the couple were out of earshot. I nervously exhaled a lung full of smoke when he turned to me and began speaking. 'Franz, the Nazis are now recruiting a number of administration clerks in preparation for the next round of elections, the district security committee want you to apply for one of these positions in their Potsdamer Platz office.'

'Me!' I almost fell off the edge of the bench. 'Are you mad?' I said, getting to my feet and shaking my head. 'No, get someone else to do it. I've done enough of your dirty work.'

'Franz,' he said, grabbing me by the arm. 'With your help we can be one step ahead of them.'

'As far as I can see they're always ten steps ahead of you

... Go to hell!'

'You are the only one we can trust to do this, who the Nazis won't suspect. If I could I'd do it myself ...'

'Would you?' I shouted, turning to face him.

'You're our best spy,' he said in a strained whisper.

'Is that what I am ... a spy ... a sneak?'

'You're a communist who is trying to save this country from the fascists. You're not a sneak ... Eva thinks you are a hero.'

'Hero, don't give me that shit! She thinks I'm a coward who had to be coerced into doing this. The only thing I am to you and Eva is a pawn in your struggle to gain power. Who's to say if the communists get control of the country they won't be just as bad as the Nazis?'

'You're starting to worry me, Franz. It's not as if I'm asking you to join the Brownshirts. You'll be working in an office as a low-level clerk and getting paid for what you do.'

'By who?'

'The Nazi Party of course.'

'Oh, Dieter, you make me laugh.'

'What have you got to lose?'

'What about my life?'

'Now you're being over-dramatic. The worst they'll do is kick you out.'

'Dieter, if you're trying to get me to put my life at risk, at least treat me with some respect.'

'Remember, Hitler wants to be Chancellor, and they're trying to clean up their act.'

'They'll kill me if I'm caught, and you know it!'

'All right, Franz, if you don't want to do it I can't force you. Eva was right. I should never have got you involved in the first place ... just go back to your tailor's shop. We'll have to find someone else.'

'Hold on, Dieter. Is that it? Go back to your tailor's shop? I thought I was your best spy?'

'You are ... We'll also pay you once a month to make up for any short fall in your wages,' he added, sensing a change in my tone, and slowly turning me to his will.

'What do you mean shortfall?'

'The Nazis won't pay you very much as a junior clerk and you'll have to give up your job as a tailor.'

'Give up my job?'

'Yes ... you can't do both.'

We sat in silence for a while. I had wanted to give up working in the shop for some time and this arrangement meant I would at least be getting paid the same money. My arrogance quite liked the idea that both the Nazis and the communists would be paying for my services; it reflected my growing indifference to both. I had also become used to my undercover role and, unlike the tedium of the tailor's shop; it gave me the same rush of adrenaline I got when stealing from the department stores. It made me feel alive.

'All right, I'll do it. What the hell?' I relented, shaking my head. We sat back down on the park bench as he enthusiastically explained to me where to go and what to say. He seemed certain I would get a job in the Nazi Party's propaganda office and told me to stop working in the shop as soon as possible, emphasising that to continue would put everyone at risk who worked there. Once again Dieter had managed to persuade me to put my life in danger for a cause I was still ambivalent about. I was now sure this was what Dieter and Eva had planned for me all along, becoming a Nazi Party member and attending all those pointless meetings was just to give me a background that would make it easier to get into a position where I could get information not in the public domain.

Despite my undoubted misgivings, a few days later I engineered a furious row with Leon over a pair of trousers I deliberately cut too short, while I angrily blamed him for measuring them wrongly. Leon called me an insolent fool as

I threw my tape-measure at him and walked out. There was a sick feeling in my stomach as the shop door closed behind me for the last time.

For the next few hours I sat in my apartment feeling a profound self-loathing for being so deceitful to my friends, while trying to reason with myself that I could not tell them the truth without putting their lives at risk. There was no other way. Even more upsetting was not being able to tell Herr Kolinski my true reasons for leaving, and I could not bear to think of what he must have thought of me when told of my sudden departure over a cheap pair of trousers. That night I could not sleep, tormented by my guilty conscience.

Over the next few days Herr Kolinski made several visits to my apartment, pleading with me to open the door and talk to him while I lay in silence, with the covers over my head, until he left. On his third visit, he pushed an envelope under the door with fifty marks in it and a letter telling me he understood why I had to leave. It was then I suspected he always knew how I felt about his daughter, and no doubt my behaviour at the wedding only confirmed my foolishness over her. The following week I moved to new rooms. The break with my former life was complete.

It was not long before I received a letter in response to my employment application. The letter, which had an embossed swastika at the top, instructed me to attend an interview the following week, while also requesting extracts of my birth certificate. I stared at the letter for some time, both fascinated and repelled in equal measure, but strangely more afraid of my fascination than my repulsion.

The night before the interview I only managed a few hours' sleep before waking up in a cold sweat, dreading the coming morning. When it was finally time to get up, my body was so exhausted I could have easily fallen into a deep sleep, from which no amount of worry could have stirred me. I forced myself out of bed, my anxiety returning to quell any thoughts of further sleep.

My membership card would be the first thing the SA would ask for and I double-checked it was in my wallet. I also put a few Nazi leaflets in my coat pocket I had collected at the various meetings across the city. If they searched me for any reason, then hopefully they would be impressed with my apparent fanaticism. Looking at myself in the wardrobe mirror, my appearance was suitably serious, with my smart three-piece suit, white shirt and blue and red striped tie. My hair was slightly oiled and combed to the side, and I was pleased with my moustache, which had taken a couple of weeks to grow. Shod in my black brogue shoes, which had been polished to a soldier's shine, I stood to attention before giving myself a Nazi salute, while clicking my heels. I was so impressed, if I saw myself in the street I would walk the other way.

The offices were in a dilapidated building at the back of a warehouse in Potsdamer Platz. I was escorted by an SA officer to the second floor and told to take a seat in the corridor with another four applicants. There was a constant noise of typewriters clattering from a room further down the hall, reminding me of Hannah's sewing machine, only more annoying. A pretty secretary, wearing a white shirt and black skirt, took my certificate and instructed me to sign a mandate authorising the party's right to obtain a medical report from my doctor. 'Herr Becker will see you shortly, Herr Steinberg.'

'Schreiber, my name is Schreiber.'

'Please take a seat.'

I sat opposite a middle-aged man, who, shuffling his hat in his hands, smiled meekly at me when our eyes met. He looked like he was waiting for a dentist's appointment. To calm my own nerves with some frivolous conversation, I introduced myself and he did likewise, telling me he had been selling vacuum cleaners to housewives up and down the country until the company he was working for went bankrupt. He was married with two young children, and I was sure he needed the job more than I did. When his turn came, I wished him luck as he entered the interview room, still shuffling his hat from one hand to the other.

It was another ten minutes before the door opened again, and the redundant salesman left with a strained smile on his face, his hat still in his hand.

'Herr Steinberg, you can go in now,' said the secretary, who I was beginning to think was getting my name wrong on purpose.

Herr Becker, an overweight man with short grey hair and a chubby face, sat behind a large desk under a picture of Adolf Hitler, which looked as if it had been cut out of a magazine and stuck in a cheap frame. Becker was probably in his forties, wearing an SA shirt with the collar open. He lit a cigar, blowing a cloud of thick grey smoke towards the ceiling and nodding for me to take a seat. On the desk there was a small swastika flag surrounded by folders piled up in heaps.

'Franz Schreiber, a tailor by trade, but now unemployed I see.'

'Yes, Herr Becker.'

'You did not finish school or obtain any qualifications,' he said, looking through a buff folder.

'No … no,' I stuttered. 'My mother became ill and there was no one else to look after her.'

'Your mother is now dead?'

'Yes.'

'Your school report states you were excellent at mathematics.'

'It was my favourite subject,' I said, now worrying what else he had in that folder about me. Did he have my record from the reformatory? I could feel the sweat running down the side of my face. I had to hold my nerve.

'Well, that will not be much use to you here. I need someone to keep the filing system in order, not a mathematician.'

'I am good at organising things,' I said, but he ignored me and moved on to other matters.

'I see your father was killed in the war.'

'Yes, when I was about six years old. I don't remember much about him. He's buried somewhere in France.'

'He was in the same regiment as my brother, Wilhelm. He's also buried in France. Maybe they knew each other.'

'I would like to think so.'

'You joined the party at the beginning of the year. What made you join?'

'I read Herr Hitler's book and I believe he ...'

'Have you really read it?'

'Yes, Herr Becker.'

'Cover to cover?'

'Yes, Herr Becker.'

'Did you understand it?'

'Yes, Herr Becker. I found it fascinating.'

'Good for you ... I didn't, but don't tell anyone,' he laughed, through a mouthful of cigar smoke. 'If I offer you the job, when could you start?'

'Straight away.'

'Good, I like you, Franz. The other applicants were just beady eyed, unemployed bank clerks and salesmen. Well, come back tomorrow, you can start in the filing room, it's a bloody mess in there.'

'Yes, Herr Becker ... *Heil Hitler!*'

'*Heil Hitler*,' he retorted with little enthusiasm as I closed the door behind me.

Back in the street the sun was shining, and I could not believe it was so straightforward. I walked along to Pariser Platz and decided to have a drink in the Hotel Adlon, before trying to contact Dieter.

The bar was quiet. Two elderly men sat in the corner

drinking cognacs and reading the morning papers. The waiter was clearing away some coffee cups and I asked him to get me a whisky and ice. I took a table at one of the windows and read a magazine about Roosevelt's bid for the White House, which was predicted to be a landslide. His promise of a new deal for the American people sounded familiar.

After a couple of drinks, I went into the foyer and phoned party headquarters, leaving a message for Dieter. I returned to the bar and ordered another drink to quell the adrenaline that was still running through my body. The bar was now empty, and I sat in the sunlight by the windows, closing my eyes for a moment to try and remember the interview and what was agreed. The sun was warm on my face, making me feel drowsy. My eyes became heavy with lack of sleep. I gave myself a shake and picked up a newspaper that someone had left behind. On the front page there was a picture of Hitler addressing an SA rally in Munich. Standing behind him, with his right arm raised in adulation, was Wolfgang Schultz. The whisky caught my throat and I began coughing violently. The waiter stared at me with some concern as he lifted the empty glass.

'Are you all right, sir?'

'Yes, get me another whisky,' I said, still trying to catch my breath.

The waiter returned with the drink a few minutes later and placed the glass on the table. 'Will there be anything else, sir?'

'Does Gretchen still work here?'

'No, sir, Gretchen left a few months ago. She's had another baby.'

'Another baby?'

'Yes, it was a boy this time. I think she called him Aaron.'

'If you see her, please tell her an old friend was asking after her,' I said, paying for the drinks and giving him a few marks for a tip.

'Who shall I say was asking?'

'Franz Schreiber.'

He smiled and returned to the bar.

The following morning, I took the tram to Potsdamer Platz to start my new job as a filing clerk. I showed my party card to the SA men at the back door before walking to the second floor. Herr Becker was sitting in his office with the door open. Through a cloud of cigar smoke, I could see he was speaking to someone on the phone. He motioned for me to come forward as he continued his telephone conversation. Patiently waiting for him to hang up the receiver, I watched as the ash on his cigar grew, making me strangely concerned about its imminent collapse. He nodded towards a glass ashtray on his desk, which I moved towards him just in time for the law of gravity to assert its certainty.

'Now, Franz Schreiber, you're a punctual young man,' he said, nodding towards the clock and replacing the receiver. 'Do you know who that was? Well, of course you don't. It was Goebbels giving his bloody orders. I hate the little crippled bastard, but don't tell him I said that,' he laughed, putting his cigar into the ashtray and getting to his feet. 'Now, Franz, what am I going to do with you?'

'You said yesterday you had a job for me in the filing room, Herr Becker.'

'Oh, that's right. Follow me, young man.'

Becker pulled up his braces, slapping them over his shoulder, and walked with his short, overburdened legs to another part of the landing. I followed him into a smoky room where there were three women, all wearing swastika armbands, typing ferociously on large, ancient typewriters. I could hear them giggling with each other as I followed Becker into an anteroom which was crammed with battered grey filing cabinets. 'Goebbels wants these files sorted. There are all kinds of unsavoury characters in here; politicians, communists, Jews, and even a few of our own party members he has a grudge against. Start with this cabinet and put them in order. There are cards over there to list the files separately, each has its own number ... Do you understand, young man?'

'Yes, Herr Becker.'

'If you need to know anything, the girls will keep you right.'

With the momentous clatter of the typing pool in the background, I began to sift through the files, many of which had photographs on the front. There was a system already in place and those regarded as communists had the classification A1 next to their names. Once I was sure Becker was safely in his office, I began looking for files on Dieter and Eva, but could not find any under their surnames. I went back to the first filing cabinet and began to organise the paperwork, putting the salient information onto the index cards, while at the same time nervously noting the names and addresses in a notebook to pass on to Dieter at our next meeting.

At the end of my first day, Becker inspected my work and was more than happy with the progress I had made. Over the next few days I continued to bring order to the filing and added name after name to the notebook.

To satisfy Goebbels' appetite for Machiavellian scheming, the office was busy producing new pamphlets and posters on a daily basis, keeping the relentless propaganda machine going. One minute the communists would be the subject of his ridicule, the next, the government, and anyone else he had taken a dislike to over the preceding days. Much to Becker's annoyance, the phone in his room was constantly ringing. He could often be heard banging it down, cursing obscenities about every new demand from Goebbels' office. 'Those bastards just can't make up their mind about anything,' he shouted one day as he strutted about the office in a rage.

The printing press on the ground floor was printing day

and night through the weeks leading up to the November elections. At the end of my first few weeks working in the stuffy filing room, the new system was beginning to take shape. However, just as I finished one cabinet, a new bundle of files would appear from the industrious secretaries to be placed in the index and filed. There seemed no end to the number of people Goebbels saw as a threat to the party.

During coffee breaks I would sit with the secretarial staff in the main office and listen to their chat. The oldest was Helga, a rather fat woman with a caustic tongue. She was always talking about her husband, Kurt, who was in the SA. Helga somehow managed to blame the Jews for Kurt losing his job as a ticket collector on the subway, although she never explained her reasoning any further. She obviously believed the party's propaganda and loved telling stories about how many Jews her husband's SA unit had beaten up. When Becker was not around, she dominated any conversation in the office, often talking crudely about things that made the other two giggle and blush like schoolgirls.

Frieda was the quiet one, in her mid-twenties and rather plain-looking. She said very little as though afraid of saying the wrong thing, wary of Helga's cruel sarcastic wit. It was soon apparent to me she was Becker's favourite and spent much of her time in his office taking shorthand. Helga was clearly jealous. 'There she goes again,' she said one morning as Frieda put the phone down and picked up her notebook. 'I don't know why you're taking that with you. It's not as though you're going to use it.' Frieda blushed, but said nothing. Pretending I did not know what Helga was implying, I retreated to the sanctuary of the filing room, where I could hear Helga taking her bitterness out on her typewriter as she hammered the keys and muttered obscenities.

The other typist, Elise, was around my age and had a pretty face with blonde hair she kept in a braided ponytail. Her boyfriend, Albert, was also in the SA but she rarely spoke about him. She always dressed in a white blouse and a dark skirt and, like the others, wore the swastika armband while in the office. Elise did not have much interest in politics and it was soon clear to me she was there in body, but very rarely in mind. Her conversations with the other girls were more about the latest fashions rather than the state of the economy. Although she did make frequent remarks about her admiration for Hitler and his little cute moustache, she was clearly oblivious to his politics.

When I became more familiar with my surroundings, I would often leave the filing room door ajar to allow me to keep a furtive eye on who might be in the main office at any given time. A further bonus was soon apparent to me as I realised I was able to see Elise's long legs under her desk. I had to force myself not to stare at them, but soon found it impossible. As the weeks passed, her skirt gradually moved further up above her knees until one day I caught sight of her bare thighs above her laced black stocking tops. At first, I wasn't sure if she knew I could see her, but she always gave me a smile when I went in to collect more files. Working for the Nazis was not as bad as I thought it would be.

Chapter 22

In late October Dieter arranged another meeting in the Tiergarten. I was a little late in getting there after making a convoluted journey across the city on the underground and then by tramcar, always fearful I was being followed. Everywhere I went there were Brownshirts standing around, but at least I had my party card to show them if they stopped me for any reason. I reached the Brandenburger Tor just before noon and walked through the park where I saw Dieter standing at our usual meeting place, smoking and nervously looking at his watch. He walked briskly towards me and shook my hand. 'What kept you?'

'What are you talking about? It's only a few minutes past twelve … '

'I'm in a hurry. I've got to get back soon. I'm meeting a delegation from Moscow this afternoon; we need to see if they'll back us if there's a civil war.'

'Civil war! Do you really think it will get that bad?'

'We're on the brink as it is. The government is near collapse and the Nazis will attempt to seize power if they get the chance. We'll have no choice but to do the same. The republic is finished.'

'But is it right getting the Russians involved? Is that not the worst thing that could happen? The people will not accept …'

'We're only looking for money and arms from them. That's all we want. The Nazis have big business and the army backing them, not to mention three hundred thousand stormtroopers. Without outside assistance we are helpless against them.'

'What about the trade unions?'

'Half of their members are bloody Nazis,' he said, the disgust etched on his face. 'Anyway, enough politics, did you manage to get any useful information?'

His eyes opened wide as I passed him the notebook with more than fifty names and addresses in it. He looked through the pages, which contained the details of many of his comrades, some of whom he knew personally. He told me he would need more information on certain individuals, but he would let me know their names, once he had discussed the list with the party's security committee. He was surprised when I told him I could not find a file on him or Eva. He lit a cigarette and said it would only be a matter of time. I described the layout of the office and who worked where, and how Goebbels seemed to run it over the phone from the Kaiserhof Hotel. I told him Herr Becker was just like any other lazy office manager who hated his boss.

'Becker, we know of him. He's one of Gregor Strasser's men. It was Strasser who took Goebbels on as his secretary, one of his greatest mistakes. They now hate each other. The difference is Goebbels has Hitler's ear to whisper into, Strasser has to shout into it to be heard. We've been trying to engineer a split between Strasser and Hitler for years to break up the Nazi vote, but he's still grudgingly toeing the party line, although his brother Otto has already left. Anything you can find out about Gregor Strasser might help that split and would be of great value to us.'

'I'll do what I can ... Becker shouts his mouth off behind Goebbels back all the time, but he still carries out his orders.'

'Goebbels is vermin, and as dangerous as a plague. He knows how to manipulate Hitler and get his own way. He has to be stopped.'

'How?'

'I don't know, but we're waiting for our chance ... and how is your wife?' he suddenly asked.

'Fine,' I replied, sensing the anxiety in his voice. Two

long shadows appeared on the ground beside me. I had the good sense not to turn around and pretended to be engrossed in conversation. The two SA men passed without a word. We watched them stroll along the path, before they turned out of sight. 'Don't worry about them. Half of them are fucking lowlifes who like dressing up in uniforms to feel important,' said Dieter. 'It's those SS bastards you have to worry about. I better be getting back … don't want to keep the Russians waiting.'

I watched Dieter hurry away; I had never seen him nervous before. I knew things were going bad, but after seeing fear in Dieter's eyes for the first time, I was now sure I had backed the wrong horse.

When the November election results were broadcast, the office exploded with cheers and cries of victory. Becker laughed and joked, while making Nazi salutes to Hitler's picture, enthusiastically toasting the new Chancellor with a mug of beer. The excitement only died down when President Hindenburg made it clear in a post-election speech he had no intention of naming Hitler as Chancellor, even if he was the leader of the largest party in the country. Goebbels was soon on the phone ranting and raving at Becker, and the propaganda machine went into overdrive to attack Hindenburg's undermining of the democratic process.

That afternoon, while I was sitting on the floor of the filing room, Becker came in and threw a swastika armband at me. 'Put that on, Goebbels is going to pay us a visit shortly. He's not happy with some of the posters he's seen on the streets. I must go downstairs and see what the problem is before he arrives. Remember to tell him as little as possible and only speak to him if he speaks to you first. He's a sly little bastard.'

'Yes, Herr Becker.'

A sudden panic took hold of me and I felt the notebook in my jacket pocket instantly grow to twice its size. Terrified of being searched, I decided to hide the notebook in a folder in the bottom drawer of one of the filing cabinets. Closing the drawer, my anxiety subsided a little and I went back to looking at Elise's legs. She was wearing white stockings for a change, and as she crossed and uncrossed her legs, she drove me to a pleasant distraction. I was beginning to wonder whether this was pleasure or pain when I was brought back to grim reality with the thunder of stomping boots coming from downstairs. I straightened the swastika on my arm and tried to look busy, nervously fumbling through the index cards. I could hear Becker give a hearty *Heil Hitler*. He must have been practicing it all morning.

Even though they had all met him before, the girls were also on edge as we waited for the lopsided gauleiter to appear. I longed for a cigarette but did not want to be smoking with Goebbels in the building. We could hear a distinctive voice coming through the gaps in the floorboards; Dr Goebbels was making a speech. I could scarcely make out what he was saying, before he suddenly stopped. After a few more *Heil Hitlers*, the deafening march of boots began to ascend the stairs. It sounded as though he had all three hundred thousand stormtroopers with him. Although I had seen Goebbels a few times before and heard him speak at the Rathaus, I had never spoken to him and could feel my mouth drying up when he entered the room, giving a nonchalant flap of his hand as the girls gave the full Nazi salute back to him with Germanic vigour. His entourage stood at the door and I noticed he was not in the company of the SA, but black-uniformed SS men. I continued to hide in the filing room, with the door slightly opened, until Becker called on me to come out. I also gave the subservient Nazi salute, almost dislocating my arm in the process. Goebbels flapped his arm at me and I clicked my heels for some reason, which caused him to turn back to me for a moment and smile. He then continued to shake hands with the three secretaries, turning flattery into an art form.

They in turn grinned and curtseyed as though they were being presented to royalty, which he probably thought he was. Even though I was not in uniform, I stood to attention the whole time.

All the while, Becker was explaining the office system like a child trying to please a severe parent. Goebbels made a few comments and seemed pleased with what he was hearing. Becker then directed him towards the filing room, and I stood aside as he entered like a weasel sniffing around a chicken coop. My heart was beating so loud in my chest I was afraid everyone could hear it. Becker followed Goebbels into the room, explaining the card index system and how I had been reorganising it for the last few months.

'Your name?' asked Goebbels when he came back out of the room, wiping his hands on a white handkerchief.

'Franz Schreiber, Herr Doctor.'

'Ah, a good German name. You have done very well here, young Schreiber, and I may be able to use you in my new office … In the meantime you can assist my men in taking all those files downstairs. I will be moving them all today … Herr Becker, you can also give them a hand. It will help you lose some of that weight you have put on since I last saw you.'

'Yes, Herr Doctor.'

My heart was now in my mouth, and I was having difficulty trying to breathe naturally as the SS men began to take out files from the cabinets, casually flicking through some of them before putting them into storage boxes. I managed to swallow hard and tried to take control of the situation, insisting they take them out in order and not mix them up. Goebbels, who was back in the main office flirting with the girls, must have overheard me and ordered his men to follow my instructions. I began to take out the filing in alphabetical order, but my mind was on one thing and one thing only: the notebook.

Becker was already out of breath and soaked in sweat after taking just one box downstairs. I handed him another box as he groaned and shook his head. 'Sometimes less is more, Franz.'

'Hurry up and get those files down,' shouted Goebbels, which made Becker exhale a lung full of resentment.

As the filing cabinets gradually emptied of their files, I worked my way towards the notebook, waiting for my chance to retrieve it. My opportunity came when I handed an extra heavy box to one of the SS men before any of his colleagues got back upstairs. I opened the bottom drawer and took out the notebook, quickly putting it in my pocket.

'What are you doing?' demanded Becker.

'I'm ...'

'Don't be putting so many files in the boxes. They're too bloody heavy.'

'Where is Herr Goebbels?' I whispered, handing him a half empty box, while trying to stop myself from sounding nervous.

'He's downstairs with that chicken-shit Himmler, the sooner we get these down, the sooner we'll be rid of them.'

After another ten minutes or so, all the cabinets were empty, and I took a break. Lighting a cigarette, I blew the smoke and my anxiety out the window. Down in the courtyard Becker was helping to load the last of the boxes onto a lorry. I watched with relief as Goebbels got into a car with Himmler. They drove off, followed by the lorry full of boxes and SS men. Becker gave another exaggerated salute.

With the *Gauleiter* gone, the girls in the office began to say what they really thought of him.

'You wonder what Hitler sees in that little runt,' said Helga. 'He's a cockroach.'

'He gives me the creeps,' said Elise, shaking her body as though he had just crawled all over her. 'His greasy hands felt like they were made of slime.'

'I would be careful what you say,' said Frieda. 'You never know who's listening to us in this place.'

I, of course, said nothing and went back into the filing room, which was now bereft of anything to file. Becker came back upstairs, his braces now off his shoulders and the sweat dripping from his forehead. He was traumatised by the visit.

'They forgot to take the index cards,' I said to him as he slumped himself down on a chair.

'Did you hear me?'

'Leave them there. If they miss them they'll be back for them soon enough.'

'What have I to do now?'

'Don't worry, we'll have those filing cabinets full again in no time. In future, make up two sets of index cards and keep the second lot in my office ... Those bastards want us to do all the dirty work, so they can take all the credit.'

Chapter 23

On the 30th January 1933, Hitler finally became Chancellor. We listened to the radio in the main office in silence as President Hindenburg explained his reasons for appointing Hitler as head of the government. There was utter jubilation all around. Becker opened a bottle of champagne to toast the victory, while the girls set off party streamers and danced around intoxicated with the Führer's triumph. It was a moment of surreal madness as I forced myself to join the celebrations.

Despite my smiles, I felt physically sick and had to excuse myself to go to the toilet. Briskly washing my face to clear my head, I found it hard to believe Hitler was now Chancellor of Germany. The idea only a few years ago was ludicrous, but now it was a reality. With the Nazi Party becoming the new government, passing information to Dieter would now constitute treason. I stared at my pale, frightened face in the mirror and was determined to tell Dieter the game was up and there would be no more spying for him or anyone else. Still feeling nauseous, I went back into the main office.

'Can you really believe it, isn't it just wonderful?'

'It's fantastic,' I said, turning to see Elise standing behind me, teasingly playing with the top button on her blouse.

'Are you going to the parade tonight?'

'What parade?'

'The radio has just announced there's to be a torchlight procession in the city centre to celebrate Hitler's victory. Everyone is going.'

'Who're you going with ... Albert?'

'No, he'll be in one of the bands. I'm going with the girls ... and you, if you want to come along.'

'All right, what time?'

'We're meeting at the Doric around six o'clock.'

'Where's that?'

'It's a bar near to the station on Friedrichstrasse. Don't be late. The parade is due to start at seven.'

'Is Herr Becker going with us?'

'No, he'll be with all the other bosses in the Kaiserhof. He said he might get a chance to meet Hitler again. Can you imagine?'

'Herr Hitler, you mean.'

'All right, Herr Hitler. You're such a fascist, Franz,' she laughed.

The thought of meeting Elise outside work for the first time cheered me up for the rest of the day. However, a Nazi victory march was not the most romantic setting, especially when she would be looking out for her fat boyfriend playing his tuba. I had only seen Albert once, when he came to the office to take Elise out for lunch. He was a buffoon, who only joined the SA a few months earlier when he couldn't find work, and like the millions of others jumped on the Nazi bandwagon once the election results started to turn in Hitler's favour. At least, unlike me, he had backed the winning side. Maybe I was the buffoon.

That evening as I walked to the Doric, the city was buzzing with energy and the triumphant swastika was everywhere. Fireworks exploded in the skies all over the city as people celebrated the hope, which came with every new leader. I joined my three female colleagues, giving each a peck on the cheek, before ordering three glasses of wine and a large schnapps. Elise was looking particularly beautiful, with her red lips looking too good to waste on Albert's tuba-blowing mouth. I lit a cigarette as the drinks arrived. 'Why have you not got your armband on?' demanded Helga, adjusting her own to make the point.

'I have,' I laughed, opening my overcoat to show her the

top of the swastika on my jacket sleeve.

'There's not much point in wearing it under your coat,' said Helga. 'Are you ashamed to be seen with it?'

'No, certainly not. I'm as proud as anyone to wear it.'

'Maybe he's afraid of getting beat up with the communists,' interrupted Elise.

'I'll put it over my coat when we get to the parade. What's the difference?'

'What's the difference? I'll tell you what the …'

'Leave him alone, Helga, you're such a bully,' interrupted Frieda, taking her own armband off and putting it into her handbag. 'I'll wear mine at the parade as well.'

'So, will I,' said Elise, smiling as though she had just joined a game.

'Well, I'm keeping mine on,' snapped Helga.

Elise went to the door as an SA band, playing the usual monotonous music, marched down the street, followed by a crowd carrying swastika flags. People in the bar clapped and cheered, some, including Helga, giving the Nazi salute as the procession passed on its way to the Tiergarten to join up with the main parade. 'It's not his band,' sighed Elise as she came back in, pulling the collar of her coat tightly around her neck and giving an exaggerated shiver as she sat back down. She then delicately sipped her wine, leaving a smudge of red lipstick on the rim of the glass.

'He's probably in the park already,' I said, lighting the cigarette she had lifted to her mouth. She caught me staring at her and smiled.

After another round of drinks, we walked towards the Brandenburger Tor along with the hordes of other excited Berliners. I put my swastika armband on my coat sleeve to tempt a smile back on Helga's sour face and to allay any suspicions she might have about my commitment to the party. It was the first time I had worn the armband in public, something I never thought I would ever do, but it did not seem to have the same stigma now Hitler was in the Chancellery. The nearer we got to the Linden, the greater the crowds and the more swastikas we saw, and the less inhibited I felt about wearing it. On the boulevard the pavements were heaving with overexcited supporters of the new Chancellor, cheering and shouting party slogans. SA Brownshirts were everywhere, but there was no sign of the police on the streets, which I found disquieting.

We pushed our way through the crowds to get as near as possible to Pariser Platz. We could hear military marching music in the distance as we walked by the front of the Hotel Adlon, which had Nazi flags hanging from many of the windows. Elise put her cold hand in my coat pocket, which I held tightly as we watched the parade appear through the portals of the Brandenburger Tor, like a glowing apparition. The bands and columns of SA ranks were soon marching under the illuminated *Quadriga,* like a victorious conquering army back from the vanquished battlefields of Europe. The spectacle was awe-inspiring, even for me. The brass bands played *Deutschland Über Alles*, while the whole boulevard was lit up by the torches carried by the stormtroopers marching in well-rehearsed military formation. Hitler already had his army, I thought as I continued to hold Elise's hand, which was now warm and soft in mine.

By sheer force of will, I managed to get myself and Elise through the throngs of cheering people to Wilhelmstrasse and down towards the Chancellery in the hope Hitler might be watching the parade as it passed below his window. We lost Helga and Frieda in the crowd. I was glad to get rid of them and Elise did not seem to mind. She waved up to the Chancellery balcony, where Hitler was saluting the procession along with Goebbels and Göring. While I watched this Nazi triumph with mixed feelings. Elise suddenly turned around and kissed me. '*Heil Hitler*!'

'*Heil Hitler.*'

After the parade began to disperse and the excitement died down, I went back to my apartment with Elise, where I finally lost my virginity on the day Hitler finally gained power.

A few days later I was instructed, along with the girls, to hand out leaflets to anyone passing by the office. I had no option but to wear the armband and was in a state of high anxiety all morning; wearing it at night was one thing but in broad daylight was a completely different matter. I managed to get rid of my pamphlets before the others by giving them away two and three at a time. Everyone who passed took the leaflets, whether they were Nazis supporters or not. This was not simply another statement by Hitler. It was a proclamation by the Chancellor, which would affect all our lives. I kept one for myself and went back to the office to read what the people had voted for:

PROCLAMATION TO THE GERMAN NATION

MORE than fourteen years have passed since the unhappy day when the German people, blinded by promises from foes at home and abroad, lost touch with honour and freedom, thereby losing all. Since that day of treachery, the Almighty has withheld his blessing from our people. Dissension and hatred descended upon us. With profound distress millions of the best German men and women, from all walks of life, have seen the unity of the nation vanishing away, dissolving in a confusion of political and personal opinions, economic interests, and ideological differences. Since that day, as so often in the past, Germany has presented a picture of heart-breaking disunity. We never received the equality and fraternity we had been promised, and we lost our liberty to boot. For when our nation lost its political place in the world, it soon lost its unity of spirit and will ... Now, people of Germany, give us four years and then pass judgment upon us. In accordance with Field Marshal von Hindenburg's command we shall begin now. May God Almighty give our work His blessing, strengthen our purpose, and endow us with wisdom and the trust of our people, for we are fighting not for ourselves but for Germany.

I was surprised how reasonable most of the proclamation sounded. The proclamation did not seem to be the ravings of a mad man as Dieter had often called Hitler. Maybe the Nazis would behave with more decorum now they were the country's elected government. I put the kettle on and waited for the others to return, reading the proclamation again just in case I missed something.

While I was indexing some new names, Elise came in with a cup of coffee for me and sat on a pile of files opposite. 'Franz, you haven't spoken to me since the other night. Is there anything wrong?'

'No, Elise, but you went out for lunch yesterday with Albert. I thought …'

'You knew Albert was my boyfriend,' she said, looking for somewhere to put the cup down.

'So, what am I?'

'Franz, what happened was a mistake, I had too much to drink and so did you.'

'You only had two glasses of wine!'

'Here, do you want this or not,' she said, getting up and spilling the coffee over the files on the floor.

'Look what you've done, Elise, just leave me alone.'

'You're such a bore, Franz,' she said, kicking the files at me on her way out.

After she had slammed the door, I was left filled with all kinds of emotions. It was not like I was in love with Elise or anything, but I found it hard to cope with her rejecting me so easily. Was I so boring, was that what Rebecca thought of me?

As the morning wore on I found it increasingly difficult to concentrate on the endless filing and convinced myself I would suffocate if I did not open the door for a while. When I did succumb to temptation she was not at her desk, only Helga was still in the office, eating a large piece of *Butterkuchen.* 'If you're looking for Elise, she has gone for lunch with Albert.'

On the 10th of February, the office was in silence while we listened to Hitler's first speech as Chancellor on the radio. His voice was strong, determined and threatening as it sent shivers up and down my spine. ' ... *German People, give us four years, then direct and judge us. German People give us four years and I vow that I will leave this office just as I entered it. I didn't accept the job for salary and reward, but because you wanted me. Indeed, I cannot abandon the faith in my People, cannot abandon my conviction that this nation will rise once again. I cannot distance myself from my love for my People. I am rock solid in my belief that the hour will come when the millions who curse us today will stand behind us. We will all greet our collectively created, painfully fought-for, new German Reich of greatness and honour, of strength and the splendour of righteousness. Amen.'*

'Wonderful ... wonderful,' bellowed Becker, clapping his hands like a happy child.

'He sounds a bit hoarse,' said Helga.

'Why do we need to have more elections now he's Chancellor anyway?' asked Elise, sorting party leaflets for the Hitler Youth to deliver.

'We need a majority in the Reichstag to get anything done,' said Becker. 'Isn't that right, Franz?'

'I guess so, Herr Becker.'

'But what if we lose?' asked Elise, licking each envelope seal with a grimace.

'But we won't,' I said, forgetting to put any enthusiasm

into my voice.

'Here,' said Helga, handing me a batch of new files. 'That will keep you busy for a while.'

The new folders were all marked in accordance with directives from Herman Göring, the new minister for the State of Prussia. The communists, who represented the bulk of the files, were now being stamped in bold red ink: *Enemy of the State*. This A list included all the communist delegates in the Reichstag and would soon include the whole party hierarchy in Berlin. A number of trade union leaders also fell into this category, whether they saw themselves as communist or not. Other organisations and politicians, such as the Christian Democrats, were selected on a case by case basis, before any decision was made on their status. As usual I gave the new files a cursory look before getting down to the job of indexing them. With the ordinary police now under Nazi control, there were new files coming into the office from police stations all over Prussia.

I finally came across Eva's file, and could feel the angst building up in my chest as I studied her police photograph. She looked harsh. Her defiant eyes stared out at the world with bitter contempt. Inside the folder was her history since joining the Communist Party, detailing her rapid rise through the rank and file, before becoming a district commissar in North Berlin at the age of twenty-four. She had a long list of so-called subversive activity detailed against her, but only one minor criminal conviction, for breaking a window during a protest march against the former Weimar Government. I searched through the other files, but still could not find one for Dieter. It was impossible for me to copy the hundreds of names and addresses down into my notebook before the files were removed by Göring's men to the state police headquarters in Prinz-Albrecht-Strasse where, I was told, they would now be permanently kept. Noting endless lists of names and addresses was pointless. All I could do was report to Dieter what the situation was in relation to these different groups under investigation and any other ad hoc information, which might be useful to him. Obviously, I would tell him about Eva's file, and my decision to untangle myself from this dangerous folly.

That evening I tried to contact Dieter, but the line rang out. Had he deserted me, and left the country with the thousands of others who fled when Hitler came to power?

A few weeks later I lay in bed trying to get to sleep when I was startled by the roaring sound of fire engines, their bells ringing like I had never heard before. I went to the window thinking the whole city must be on fire. Just above the rooftops there was a yellow glow in the sky, something big was burning. I put on clothes and went upstairs, deciding to go onto the roof terrace to get a better view. On the landing I met my next-door neighbour, Erich, who was also disturbed by the noise. 'What's going on?' he asked, wiping the sleep from his eyes.

'I think the whole of the city centre is on fire.'

We climbed onto the roof, where we watched in silence as the fire lit up the night sky. The Reichstag was on fire!

We watched the firestorm rise higher as more and more fire engines raced across the city to save our most precious building. I had a deep sense of foreboding as I imagined Hitler, Göring, Goebbels and Himmler, the four horsemen of the apocalypse, riding triumphantly through the crimson Berlin sky. It was a cold night and we stayed there as long as we could bear, before agreeing to go back down. 'There goes our last bastion of democracy,' Erich shouted. I followed him down but said nothing.

As though bonded by our short vigil on the rooftop, and although I hardly knew him, I went with Erich to the Reichstag the following morning. There was already a crowd standing in the freezing cold. A cordon of police vehicles kept the curious back from the burnt-out building, while exhausted firemen continued to douse the smouldering ruins. The smell of charred wood was so strong I could taste it on my tongue.

Then, to my surprise Erich got angry when he saw Göring's motorcade arriving. 'I wouldn't be surprised if he did it,' he shouted, not caring if anyone heard him. As Göring got out of his official car and began to inspect the ruins, one policeman scanned the crowd to see who had shouted. When he turned to look elsewhere, I shook my head at Erich, but he just grinned. 'What are you worried about Franz, he's just a fat Nazi.'

'I better get to work,' I said, desperate to get away from Erich and his reckless comments.

'What is it you do, anyway?'

'I'm an actuary for an insurance company.'

'That sounds boring.'

'It is, but I better go, Erich.'

Before going to work, I decided to try and contact Dieter again and walked briskly towards the public phone boxes outside the main post office. To my relief it was Dieter who answered. He was very anxious about what had happened, and I agreed to meet him at the weekend in a bar on the edge of the red-light area. I put the receiver back down, nervously looking around, before leaving the phone booth.

It did not take long for the Nazi-controlled radio to blame the communists for the destruction of the Reichstag. The police confirmed they had already arrested the alleged arsonist, a Dutch communist, by the name of Marinus Van der Lubbe. With the growing hysteria being whipped up, I decided to wear my swastika armband under my coat. It made me feel more confident just to know it was there as I passed groups of stormtroopers hanging around corners, where they bullied and intimidated anyone they did not like the look of. It was strange just how quickly they had taken over the city, setting up road blocks and carrying out indiscriminate searches at every other street corner. The other paramilitary groups, including the Communist Red Front and the Social Democrat Reichsbanner had simply disappeared. Even the Prussian state police, now under Göring's control, were conspicuous by their absence.

It was after eight when I met Dieter outside the tavern. He looked terrible as though he had not slept for days. Not bothering to shake my hand, he entered the bar with a nervous glance over his shoulder. I was also on edge and we sat in an empty booth at the back of the seedy bar and ordered two beers, checking out the few customers with our intense suspicion. 'The Nazis seem to be looking after you well enough,' he said, lighting a hand-rolled cigarette.

'What do you mean by that?'

'Nothing … It's just that I thought you would have phoned straight after he was made Chancellor. You must have known they were planning to arrest everyone.'

'What are you talking about? I've been phoning the number every day for weeks and no one was bloody answering it until you picked it up the other day. Anyway, I knew as much as you about what they were going to do. I gave you the names of hundreds they had on file. What you and your comrades did about it was up to you.'

'Your comrades … don't you mean our comrades?'

'You know what I meant. Anyway, I thought they would take months to get organised.'

'These bastards are serious. They've been planning this moment for years … even the fire. It's all been planned.'

'The game is over, Dieter. They won, and we lost!' I said, working my way towards telling him I was finished being his informer.

'Is that how simple you see it? They won, and we lost. It's not a game of fucking chess … They arrested Eva yesterday.'

'My God!'

'I've been sleeping in a doss-house the last few weeks,

but Eva thought I was mad and continued to sleep in the flat. I don't know where they've taken her.'

'They must be arresting everyone with links to the Communist Party and anyone else they don't want around in the next few months until they get their elections out of the way.'

'Why are they bothering with more elections? They've got what they want.'

'I heard Becker talking about the plan to have more elections in March. It's all about Hitler needing a majority to bring in the laws he wants.'

'Laws ... They don't even bother with the existing laws.'

'Once they have the majority they need, they'll probably release everyone. What else are they going to do with them?'

'Franz! Are you blind to reality? They have already shot some of our leaders without even the formality of a trial. I'm afraid Eva may already be dead.'

'Would they kill a woman?'

Dieter stared at me with his tired, bloodshot eyes and shook his head. He was about to say something, but thought better of it, taking another sip of beer instead. I nervously lit a cigarette. There was a girl sitting at the bar in a long fur coat and black boots. She uncrossed her legs and smiled over at us. The barman poured her another drink and lit her cigarette. 'Franz! Are you listening?'

'Yes. How do you know they've killed anyone if you don't even know where they are?'

'Do I look like I'm making this up?'

'No, but why do they have to kill anyone? They can just keep them in prison.'

'They want to eradicate us. Don't you listen to what Hitler and his bloodhounds spill from their spleens everyday? You have to try and get more information about their election plans.'

'Dieter, I don't know what you want from me anymore.

I gave you hundreds of names and addresses and you did nothing about it.'

'We didn't have time to do anything.'

'There are thousands of new files, even ones on members of the SA and the Catholic Church, for God's sake. I don't know who they intend to arrest any more than you do, but if anyone is a member of the Communist Party they should change address or leave the country. What else do you need to know ... But they still don't have one on you for some reason.'

'What's that supposed to mean?'

'Nothing, I'm just telling you, they still don't have a file on you.'

'You'll have one in the next few days ... I promise you.'

'How do you know?'

'What do you think happens to those in protective custody? They're tortured for information on their comrades.'

'Shit,' I said as the beer and smoke stuck in my throat. 'Eva will tell them about me.'

'Eva won't. She's too tough and she's the only one who knows you're working for us apart from me. They won't be expecting her to give your name.'

'But if they torture her, she'll talk! I can't go back to the office. They'll shoot me for being a spy.'

'Are you mad? If you don't go back they will know you're a spy for certain. It won't take much to track you down and have you arrested. They have stormtroopers all over the place, in the train stations and even the ports ... Anyway, I need you to find out about Eva.'

'No! I can't do it. Eva may have already told them all about me.'

'If you don't go back, Franz, and get me the information I want, I'll phone them myself and tell them you were working for us.'

'You bastard!'

'And if they don't kill you, I will,' he said, lifting his shirt to show the top of his revolver.

'Shit, Dieter. Even if I find out where they've taken her, what good is that going to do?'

'Let me worry about that. Just find out where she is. If anything happens to Eva …'

He shook his head and got up and left without finishing his sentence. I just sat there for a while contemplating my fate. Dieter was right; if I suddenly gave up working for the Nazis that would make them suspicious and have me arrested and that would almost certainly mean being tortured. I lit another cigarette, wishing I was back in Herr Kolinski's shop cutting some cheap suits and listening to Hannah moaning about her indigestion and gout. I ordered another beer and tried to think of a way of getting out of the situation, but every door seemed closed. I did not even have a passport to get out of the country.

I noticed the girl at the bar had turned on her barstool and was looking towards me, her coat was lying open and the intention could not have been any less clear. After another drink I got up and left. My mind was on other things.

Chapter 24

With no other option, I returned to work in the Potsdamer office as usual, where the only thing that had changed was my fear of being exposed as a spy at any minute. Desperate to get Dieter off my back, I spent hours in the filing room, searching for anything, which would disclose Eva's whereabouts, but there was nothing. Her file was already with the state police.

A few days later my anxiety turned to utter panic when two detectives, wearing swastika armbands, came into the office unannounced. They ordered everyone to stop what they were doing. I put down the files I was working on and felt the blood drain from my body. Eva had betrayed me after all. Expecting to be arrested, I tried to formulate my response. I would deny everything. No, I would tell them everything. What was the point of having them torture it out of me? While I was desperately trying to stop my breathing from becoming audible, the toilet in the hall flushed. A few moments later, Becker entered the main office, still fixing the buttons on his fly. 'What's going on?' he demanded. 'Who are you and what's the meaning of this?'

'My name is Steiger, and this is Detective Gruber.'

'Why are you here?'

'You are Herr Becker, are you not?' demanded Steiger, taking a document from his coat pocket.

'Yes, of course I'm Herr Becker.'

'We have a warrant for your arrest!'

'For my arrest … this is ridiculous!'

'I assure you, Herr Becker, this is far from ridiculous,' said Steiger, handing him the warrant.

Becker took the warrant and read it in silence before

handing it to me. It was from the Prussian Interior Police Office, with Göring's signature at the bottom. It ordered Becker's arrest for treason. There was no mention of me. Relieved, I handed the document back to Steiger as Gruber handcuffed Becker. 'Helga, get a hold of Gregor Strasser and tell him what's happened. He'll sort this nonsense out,' shouted Becker, holding up his handcuffed wrists.

'Put that phone down! I will have you arrested also if you make that call,' ordered Gruber, making his way towards Helga. She banged the receiver back down.

'And you are?' asked Steiger, turning to me.

'Franz ... Franz Schreiber.'

'You will arrange for all the files in this office to be gathered together. They are to be moved today ... Do you understand?'

'Yes. Moved to where?'

'That's not your concern.'

Becker, desperately protesting his innocence, was taken downstairs.

'Why would they arrest Herr Becker?' asked Elise.

'Treason,' I said, shaking my head.

'Treason ... lies ... it's that bastard Goebbels. He's behind this,' said Helga. 'Gregor Strasser will have the little runt shot when he finds out what's happened.'

'That might be too late for Becker,' said Frieda.

'What can Strasser do? He's no longer a member of the party,' I said, still trying to control my erratic breathing.

'He still has friends in high places,' said Helga. 'Are you alright, Franz?'

'I'm fine.'

We watched from the window when they placed Becker in the back of an unmarked police car and drove off at high speed. We began to box all the files as ordered.

SS officers arrived and began removing the storage boxes and anything else of interest. Within a couple of hours all the files had been loaded onto a waiting lorry and we were told to go home: the office was to be closed for good. We looked at each other utterly dumbfounded. Helga made her feelings felt until she was abruptly ordered to keep quiet by one of the senior SS officers. Still tempting fate, she continued to mutter obscenities to herself as she got her coat from behind her desk. Unlike the others, I felt a great sense of relief my life in the office was over; my nerves could not take it much longer. Now I could make a clean break from both the Nazis and the communists at the same time, without suspicion following me. Thank you, God. Thank you, God, I repeated in my head as we collected our belongings, while the SS ransacked Becker's office. They were obviously looking for evidence of some sort to further condemn him.

Downstairs, other SS men were busy destroying the printing rooms; it was clear, now the party had control of the country's media, they no longer needed the expense of a party propaganda office or its staff. The state, and not the party, would be paying for the costly administration of all these secret files and we were now surplus to requirements.

After a few hugs and kisses, I said goodbye to the office secretaries with mixed feelings. I watched them walk away despondently. Elise turned back and waved when they reached the corner.

Feeling like someone who had just been released from a long prison sentence, I greeted the spring sunshine with relief, thankful it was Becker and not me they arrested. Checking first there was no one following me, I went into the nearest phone box to get a message passed to Dieter, to bring an end to our relationship once and for all. The voice on the line was one I was not familiar with. I offered my password and received the usual coded reply. 'Pandora's Box … Who is speaking?'

'Kasper.'

'Kasper … and your second name?'

I hung up ... I had never been asked that question. Had the Nazis seized our secret communications network? After a few minutes, and thinking I might just be getting paranoid, I phoned the number again. 'It's Kasper.'

'Ah, Kasper, our line must have got cut off ... Where are you? I will send a car. We need to meet to discuss things ...'

I hung up for a second time, certain it was someone from the police that answered. I left the phone box and rushed down the street. With no way of contacting Dieter, I felt a great burden had been lifted from my shoulders. If he wanted me, he would have to find me, and with the Potsdamer office now closed, what use could I be to him anymore? If Dieter and Eva were the only ones aware of my communist background, and if Eva had talked, I reasoned I would have been arrested along with Becker. I could only hope if Dieter had been arrested, he was as loyal and brave as Eva.

For the rest of the afternoon I sat at a café on the Linden, smoking and drinking one cup of coffee after another. Once I satisfied myself I was out of the tangled web Dieter had so diligently spun for me, I began to think of Becker's plight. What could he have been doing to get himself arrested? Despite worrying about my own self-preservation, my hopes he would not come to any harm were genuine. I liked him. He was never a bully and I often wondered why he had become a Nazi when he did not seem to like any of them very much, apart from his old boss, Gregor Strasser, and Hitler.

The weeks passed and still there was no contact from Dieter. If he wanted to find me, I was sure he would have done so by now. Maybe he had already left the country, or perhaps he had been arrested and was in one of the labour camps the Nazis were using for the thousands of political prisoners they had arrested since gaining power. Wherever he was, he was now in my past and I was glad to be rid of him. Having never officially joined the Communist Party, I assumed the Nazis would have found no trace of my existence in any of the party's offices they raided. So long as Eva and Dieter kept my secret, I was safe.

Now idle, I registered for work at the labour exchange, and joined the massive ranks of the country's unemployed. In the continuing economic depression work was virtually impossible to find. For a while I considered going back to Herr Kolinski to ask for my old job back, but gave up that idea when Goebbels declared a twenty-four-hour boycott on all Jewish businesses. Not waiting for the official day of the boycott, hordes of storm-troopers took full advantage of this state declaration of random discrimination. They painted shop windows, including some of the city's largest department stores, with the Star of David and the word Juden. The police looked on and did nothing to stop them.

One afternoon I witnessed two middle-aged customers who had defied the ban, along with the Jewish shopkeeper who served them, being paraded in the centre of town with placards around their necks denouncing them. Like most, I did nothing to protest and watched in silence as they were pilloried by a baying mob. In the days that followed the boycott, posters began to appear all over Berlin depicting the Jews as grotesque corruptors of the nation's morals.

Still unable to find work, and with my savings running out, I decided to visit Georgi. It was a pleasant morning and I walked to save the tram fare. On route I passed a soup kitchen. It was besieged with unemployed men. Before they could get their free meal, they had to endure the bullying of stormtroopers, who were handing out propaganda leaflets blaming the Jews for the country's woes. I crossed the road and stopped for a moment to watch an elderly man being pulled from the queue by two SA Brownshirts. One of them suddenly slapped the old man hard on the face, knocking his trilby halfway across the road. Instinctively I ran into the traffic to retrieve the hat before it was crushed by a passing car. I followed the man, who was now hurrying away from the soup kitchen. 'Your hat,' I said, tapping him on the shoulder, but he kept walking, afraid to even look at me. I ran to get in front of him and offered the hat again. He took it without a word. It was then I recognised him, he was a man who I had seen a few times with Herr Kolinski. He turned and hurried down a nearby alley.

The incident was still troubling me when I knocked on Georgi's front door. He took some time to finally answer, nervously asking who was there, before unlocking a plethora of locks and chains.

'Franz! I thought you had forgotten your old friend.'

'Sorry, Georgi, I've been working long hours.' I followed him into the living room. He did not look very well; his hair was wild and his normal exuberance had gone.

'What's wrong, Georgi?'

'Oh, Franz, they closed down the cabaret last week.'

'What? Who closed it down?'

'Those Nazi pigs, they condemned it as anti-German. We're all out of work … and no one is hiring drag acts anymore.'

'That's terrible. What are you going to do?'

'I've some money saved, but not much. It will keep me going for a few months until something better turns up,' he lamented, putting on the kettle.

The apartment had lost its cheerfulness and I was shocked at how cluttered it was. There were clothes everywhere and his kimono was lying in a heap on the floor with his expensive blonde wig. He must have noticed me looking at the mess. 'Oh, don't tell me. I know. I've turned into a lazy slob. I had to bring all my costumes home and there's no where to put them in this place. I'm trying to build up the courage to get rid of some of them … I'll do that when I'm strong enough, but not just now. Do you know anyone who would like to buy some wigs?'

'No, but there must be some clubs still looking for

entertainers ...'

'Artists,' he said, with a hint of annoyance. 'Clowns entertain ... artists perform,' he added, looking in the mirror to reassure himself he wasn't just a clown. 'Oh, look at my hair,' he groaned. 'You should have said something, Franz. I look a mess!'

'You look tired,' I said diplomatically.

'I can't sleep. I lie awake at night worrying myself sick, then the next day I'm totally exhausted ... Sorry I've no milk to give you. I'll have to get to the shops later.'

'That's all right, black is fine. What will you do if you're not allowed to do your act?'

'If I can't get anything before the end of the month I might just go home to Bulgaria, although I don't know what they'll make of me now,' he said as he lit a cigarette and took a long deep draw, exhaling a cloud of grey smoke that caught his throat and started a bout of coughing.

'Are you all right?'

'I'm all right ... I'll have to stop these soon,' he said, taking a sip of tea to regain his composure as the tears and mascara ran down his cheeks. He then stared at the half-smoked cigarette as though it had tried to murder him. 'I won't be able to afford them soon. Anyway, I think they're making my voice too husky.'

'What's happened to everyone else who worked at the club?'

'That bitch Marlon, the one I taught to sing and dance properly. He went off to Paris three weeks ago without even saying goodbye to anyone. He must have known what was going to happen. He'd been seeing one of those fat Nazi pigs for months ... I hope he chokes on a baguette!'

'What about everyone else?'

'I haven't seen anyone, but they'll all be joining those horrendous soup kitchens if things don't start to pick up soon. Enough about me, what have you been up to? Have you popped the question yet?'

'No,' I said, instantly wishing I had not mentioned my feelings for Rebecca to him. Avoiding his inquisitive stare, I could not bring myself to tell him she was already married, and I had just made a fool of myself.

'Never mind, these things take time,' he said, pouring more tea. 'I met that English fellow the other day, what's his name again? You know the one who was always hanging around the cabaret when there are young boys to pick up ... Oh, what's his name?'

'The writer?'

'Yes, anyway, he's said he's had enough of Berlin and the Nazis. He's going back to England to write a book ... and guess what? He asked if he could write about me. Isn't it wonderful?'

'That's great.'

'I gave him my address and asked him to send me a copy when it's published. He promised to send a translation of the chapters I'm featured in ... Yes, featured. That's the exact word he used ... featured.'

'What happens if you go back to Bulgaria? How is he going ... ?'

'Bulgaria! I've no intention of going back there. What would I do there?'

'I thought you said ...'

'Don't listen to me, Franz, I am always threatening to go back, but I never will,' he said, picking up clothes and costumes from the floor, and putting them into neat piles. Each garment had its own history, and he took great pleasure in explaining to me which songs he sang wearing them. He gave those he reluctantly decided had had their day hugs and kisses while he bemoaned he would have to throw them out just because he had no room for them.

'Why don't you sell them?'

'I may act it sometimes, but I'm not stupid. Who would

want to wear, never mind buy these?'

'Maybe you're right,' I agreed, as he held up a ridiculous looking multicolour dress, with its sequins and faux pearls in inappropriate places.

With Georgi in a better mood than I found him, I finished my tea and said goodbye, leaving him surrounded with the remnants of his past performances. When walking downstairs and into the street, I was pretty sure he would eventually convince himself he loved all his costumes equally and would not part with a single dress. I could only hope Georgi, with all his contacts in the nightclubs, would soon find work; even if he had to tone down his act a little. I wasn't so confident about my own prospects. It began to rain as I hurried to catch the tram.

By the time I got off the tram, the rain was torrential and running down the drains in fast flowing streams. The grey sky hung over the city like a shroud of misery. I ran back to my apartment, soaked. I made a fire with the last of the coal and kindling which I had been saving like a miser. I hung up my wet clothes in front of the hearth and rubbed my cold hands over the faltering flames for some heat. Apart from the sporadic sparks coming from the fire, the room was silent.

I took the bedspread off the bed and lay on the sofa to get some sleep. Before my head had even touched the armrest, I heard someone walking up the stairs. I was sure it was the landlord. Erich had told me he had been around the other day looking for his rent. I remained quiet when the footsteps stopped outside my door. Thankfully they began to ascend the next flight of stairs, and I finally let my head rest. I knew it was only a matter of time before he would simply have my things thrown onto the landing. I had no desire to go back to begging on the streets and living under railway bridges. I had to find work, and soon.

Unable to sleep with the worry of being made homeless again, I got up and counted what little money I had left. It did not matter how many times I counted the contents of my pockets, there wasn't enough to pay the rent. The thought made me feel despondent. I began drinking what was left of a bottle of schnapps I found from a previous binge. Being poor and drunk was at least better than being poor and sober. With the bottle soon empty, the daylight gradually faded from the room and I fell into a drunken, melancholic sleep on the sofa.

With nothing in the house to eat, I did not get up until well into the following afternoon. I was so hungry I had decided to pawn all my books. What use were they to me now? They would at least bring in enough money to buy some food. I took them to the nearest pawn shop.

The pawnbroker remarked on my wide range of political literature but declined to buy the communist books. 'I will take the rest. If you're short, maybe you should think about pledging your watch.'

'My watch ... How much?'

'For those books and the watch ... let me see ... I can give you twenty marks.'

'All right,' I said, reluctantly taking the watch off and placing it on top of *Mein Kampf* and other Nazi books mainly on eugenics.

On my way back to my apartment I bought some food and a bottle of schnapps from the kiosk on the corner. While waiting for my change, I noticed a picture of Van Der Lubbe on the front page of one of the newspapers. He was dressed in shabby prison clothes, cowed with his head bowed in utter submission. Even though the trial had not yet started, the article vilified him, and the others arrested as communist scum, blaming them for trying to destroy the country's fragile democracy by burning down the Reichstag. The newspaper, which had once derided the Nazis as thugs, now had a swastika embossed above its title. The communists were finished. I dumped the revolutionary writing of Marx and Engels in a lane nearby, glad to be rid of them.

Chapter 25

It was Erich who eventually woke me that night. Banging on the door like a mad man. The room was in total darkness and it took me a few minutes to regain my senses. I must have been sleeping for hours. I put on my shirt, and let Erich in. He marched past me as if I was not there, ranting and raving, while pacing around the room cursing the Nazis. I lit the oil lamp and washed my face as he continued to berate Goebbels.

It was only when he calmed down I noticed it was almost eleven o'clock. 'We have to do something,' he said, as though I knew what he was talking about.

'About what?'

'Franz, I told you only yesterday about the book burning tonight at the Opernplatz.'

'Oh, that. I don't think I'm up for going out tonight. How can we stop it anyway?'

'I always knew you didn't give a damn about anything.'

'What are you talking about? Who the hell do you think you are?'

'I'm not a coward anyway.'

'Who are you calling a coward?' I was about to punch him on the face when Martina, who frequently shared his bed, came in. We lowered our fists and pretended to be joking around, but I still wanted to punch him.

'What were you two shouting about?'

'Franz is not coming to the book burning. He's chickened out.'

'Shut up, Erich, or I'll knock your head off.'

'I would like to see you try it … chicken.'

'Stop it, Erich. If he doesn't want to go that's up to him. You can't force him.'

'I'll go, but I don't know what you expect to do,' I said, handing Erich a bottle of beer to calm him down.

'There will be other students and masters there trying to do something,' said Martina as she took a drink of Erich's beer.

'Do what? Pray for rain? There'll be hundreds of SA Brownshirts there if Goebbels is making a speech and the police won't do anything to stop them beating people up for protesting,' I said, taking my time getting ready in the hope most of the books would already be burned by the time we got there. 'They'll only burn all the old rubbish that's already falling apart anyway. It's all just a big Nazi propaganda stunt about nothing.'

'Damn you, Franz, I have seen the list posted in the university,' shouted Erich, banging his fist on the table, frustrated by my apparent apathy. 'They are burning books tonight, but as Heine said, *where they burn books, sooner or later they'll be burning people.*'

'No, you're right, Heine was one of my mother's favourite poets,' I said, trying to show some empathy, although the only poem I could remember was *Die Lorelei*. It was not that I was indifferent to the burning of books, even though there were plenty I would like to burn myself, including *Das Kapital* and *Mein Kampf*. No, it was simply that I knew none of us will be able to do anything about it, and to even try was the height of folly. The Nazis were in power and that was that!

'The President should get the police to stop it,' said Martina.

'The President,' laughed Erich. 'What use is he? It was that old fool who made Hitler the Chancellor!'

'You can't blame Hindenburg. It was the people who made him Chancellor,' I said, eventually finishing my beer and putting my boots on. Even though I had no intention of doing anything silly, I furtively put my Nazi Party card in my pocket, just in case I got arrested in some melee. It might keep me out of jail.

There was a chill in the air as we walked down Friedrichstrasse. The streets were busy with people, some carrying books under their arms, making their way to the Opernplatz. It began to drizzle, but I was hoping for a torrential downpour as we reached the Linden and crossed towards the crowds around the Opernplatz. There were stormtroopers and swastikas everywhere. SA bands vigorously played their brass horns, tubas, trumpets and drums, adding to the intimidating mood.

Through the flames, I saw the Minister for Propaganda, Goebbels standing at a podium which was draped in a large swastika, while waves of students carried more and more doomed books to the bonfire in the middle of the square. *'No to decadence and moral corruption!'* Goebbels shouted at the crowd. *'Yes, to decency and morality in the family and the state! I consign to the flames the writings of Heinrich Mann, Ernst Gläser, and Erich Kästner ... '* he ranted as he threw these books into the fire. *'The era of extreme Jewish intellectualism is now at an end. The breakthrough of the German revolution has again cleared the way on the German path ... The future German man will not just be a man of books, but a man of character. It is to this end that we want to educate you. As a young person, to already have the courage to face the pitiless glare, to overcome the fear of death, and to regain respect for death - this is the task of this young generation. And thus, you do well in this midnight hour to commit to the flames the evil spirit of the past. This is a strong, great and symbolic deed - a deed which should document the following for the world to know - Here the intellectual foundation of the November Republic is sinking to the ground, but from this wreckage the phoenix of a new spirit will triumphantly rise.'*

While Goebbels raged on, we watched dozens of

students, even professors, throwing hundreds of books onto the funeral pyre in this Germanic 'bonfire of the vanities'. Others shouted out the names of the condemned authors and their books, including: Sigmund Freud, Thomas Mann, H.G Wells, Ernest Hemingway, Alfred Döblin, Joseph Roth, Franz Kafka and many more. As I watched the flames rise higher in this cultural cleansing, I began to think the only book left in Germany would be *Mein Kampf*, a clever marketing ploy by Hitler. With so many rowdy Brownshirts standing around, drunk on power and beer, Erich was powerless to stop this homage to state censorship. His desolate face expressed his impotent anger.

Then, to my absolute astonishment, I saw Günter Schwartz, only a few feet behind Goebbels, wraith-like in a black SS uniform, his ears almost translucent in the glow of the bonfire. I pulled my hat down and turned up my collar as the SA band began to play the national anthem and the crowd responded in kind to Goebbels' Nazi salute.

Erich had had enough and pulled Martina roughly by the arm as they pushed their way back through the crowds. I shouted on them to wait but did not follow. I turned back to watch the bonfire as the sparks floated into the dark Berlin sky while the SA band made more noise.

His arm outstretched, Günter was singing so loud his voice rose above the tumult. Staring at him in amazement, I recalled the day when I climbed the spiral stairs to his attic room, foolishly thinking he was making magic with the mysterious thing Gretchen had called the alphabet. He was no longer making words, but zealously overseeing their destruction as more books were ridiculed and thrown into the all-consuming fire. In the glow of a full moon, the cathedral bells began to toll, causing the belfry's pigeons to scatter into the sky like bats in a gothic tale. The whole night had an eerie strangeness to it, which I could only describe as demonic. Eventually I decided I had seen enough cultural carnage for one night and turned to go home.

When I got back to the apartment block, the gaslight on the second landing was out. I felt an uneasy chill halfway up the stairs. I stopped and stared into the darkness. Gripping the banister, I could hear someone breathing. The red tip of a cigarette suddenly glowed bright. 'Franz ... you're a hard man to find.'

'Who's there?'

'You've forgotten me already?'

'Dieter, what are you doing here?'

'Give me a hand.'

I heard Dieter groan as the cigarette fell from his mouth and I rushed to stop him falling down the stairs. His body was limp, and his clothes wet and sticky. I held him against the wall and opened the door. He was in obvious pain as I helped him into the apartment and gently laid him down on the bed. I lit the oil lamp and looked at my sticky hands. They were covered in blood. Dieter was now breathing heavily as he tried to sit up and light another cigarette.

'What happened to you?'

'The bastard had a gun under his pillow ... Here, give me a light.'

'Who had a gun?'

'That fat pig, Schultz,' he replied, taking a long draw from his cigarette before coughing up spurts of blood, which he wiped on his sleeve. 'He's lucky ... If my gun had not jammed, he'd be a dead pig now.'

'Schultz? You tried to kill Schultz?'

'Yes. The Nazis murdered Eva ... Have you anything in here to drink?'

'Eva ... Eva's dead?'

'Yes, she was tortured to death by those bastards,' he coughed up more blood onto his torn, dirty shirt as I poured him a glass of schnapps. 'Don't worry, Franz, she never told them anything.'

'I'm sorry,' I said, trying to hide the relief I felt.

'Don't be sorry, Franz, be angry. The meek will not inherit anything in this life,' he preached as he grimaced in pain. 'We were too weak to stand up to those bastards and look at them now. We should have assassinated half of them when we had the chance.'

'How did you know where to find Schultz?'

'I was informed by a comrade he used a hotel in the red-light area where he had his way with a young SA lieutenant at least twice a week. The porter let us know this afternoon that the bastard turned up and demanded his regular room … Franz, give me some more schnapps, my throat's dry … Schultz managed to put a bullet into me when my gun jammed after I shot his boyfriend who Schultz used to hide behind.'

'Maybe you shouldn't drink too much, Dieter.'

'Give me the bottle,' he demanded. 'I need something to stop this pain. Help me sit up.'

'My God, Dieter,' I gasped, opening his raincoat to see his shabby clothes saturated in blood. 'You need to get to a hospital.'

'I can't … every Nazi in the city will be looking for me. I just need to rest for a while … There's a doctor I know in Müllerstrasse … I will go there in the morning.'

'You've lost a lot of blood, Dieter. You need to see a doctor before the morning for God's sake …'

'Don't you understand, Franz? I've just killed an SA lieutenant. The city will be swarming with Brownshirts.'

'How are you going to get there in the morning?'

'There's a comrade who's an ambulance driver at the hospital on Heinz-Galinski-Strasse … ' he coughed again, before taking another drink from the neck of the bottle. 'His name is David Holtz … I phoned the hospital, but he's not on duty until tomorrow morning … I need your help, Franz.'

'Of course, I'll do what I can.'

'Good ... You'll have to be there before six ... and get a hold of him before he starts work. He can take me in the ambulance to Müllerstrasse ... There's no other way.'

'Okay,' I said, looking at the clock. It was already after one. I was about to ask him about Eva, when he passed out. I took the cigarette from his cracked lips and the bottle from his hand. He was still breathing, but his face was sallow. It was then I noticed the drips of blood on the floor, which I followed out to the landing. There was a pool of blood outside Erich's door. I lit a match and followed the trail down the stairs to the street. Rushing back into the flat, I poured water and detergent into a bucket and began to frantically mop up the blood on the stairs.

Once finished, I poured the dirty water down a drain in the courtyard and went back to the front of the building. The street was deserted. I then looked with despair at the trail of blood spots along the pavement. I thought for a moment about mopping it up to the corner, but that idea quickly passed when I saw a police car sitting at the top of the street. I had to do something before it was noticed in the morning. I went back to see how Dieter was holding out.

He was lying quietly on the bed. I checked his breathing again. He was still alive. I took a drink from the bottle of schnapps to settle my nerves. The blood on the pavement outside was preying on my mind. I sat opposite Dieter, listening to his erratic breathing, which every so often stopped, only to begin again with a rasping cough. Believing he was about to die, I made a pot of coffee to keep me awake. I was surprised how little I felt for him as his life ebbed away in front of my eyes. Dieter had stopped being a friend from the time he threatened to give me up to the Nazis if I refused to go back to the Potsdamer office and do his bidding. I did not want him to die, but I could do nothing about it either.

Exhaustion must have overcome me, and I awoke as the morning light began to fill the room. When I gathered my senses, I realised Dieter had stopped breathing. This realisation instantly wiped away any tiredness and I went over to him, putting my hand inside his shirt to feel for a heartbeat. There was none. I closed over his clothes and went through his pockets to make sure he had nothing I had to worry about. I found a piece of paper with Schultz's name, and a hotel address next to it. I immediately threw it onto the cold ashes in the fireplace and set it alight. I looked through the rest of his clothes and found his revolver. I put it back inside his waistband; it was as well being with the body as anywhere else. Once I was sure he had nothing on him, which would lead the police to me, I decided to phone the Jewish hospital to try and get his friend to help me get rid of the body. I put my coat on and left the apartment before the darkness had fully lifted from the room.

The blood stains which had seemed so enormous the night before were only dark spots on the dirty grey pavement that might even go unnoticed. I hurried across the road, suddenly realising I had forgotten Dieter's friend's name. David … yes, David, but I could not for the life of me remember his surname. My mind was tired, and it was impossible to think straight. I reached the telephone booth outside the post office, still unable to remember the surname.

The city centre was very quiet as the first few tramcars began to take to the streets. I did not see any policemen or stormtroopers. They were probably still in their beds, worn out after searching for Dieter all night. How many ambulance men with the name David could there be? I would have to be careful what I said and took a quick look around before nervously dialling the hospital. As the coins dropped, I vaguely asked for David the ambulance driver.

'Which David do you want?' asked the girl on the other end of the line.

'Yes David, he drives the ambulance. His friend Dieter is very ill,' I foolishly said, kicking the booth in annoyance.

Why did I need to mention Dieter?

'Which David … Is it David Rosenberg or Holtz you're looking for?'

'Holtz … Yes, it's David Holtz. Can you bring him to the telephone? It's very serious.'

'I don't know if he's even here now. Hold the line and I will find out.'

I waited anxiously. The pips started, and I fed more coins into the slot, fearing I would run out of money if he did not come to the phone soon. The line went silent, until the demanding pips started again. Hurry up … For God's sake, hurry up.

'Who are you?' inquired a gruff voice. I used the last of my pfennigs to keep the line open.

'I'm a friend of Dieter Jäger. He asked me to call you. He's in trouble.'

'I don't know any Dieter Jäger.'

The phone hung up.

Those few words broke my resolve and before I realised what I was doing, I began to smash the receiver against the booth. Thankfully the madness did not last long, and I stopped when the earpiece flew off. There was nothing else for it. I would have to get rid of Dieter's body myself. It began to rain, not just a drizzle, but a heavy downpour. I hurried back to the apartment.

When I got back, I had a rare moment of triumph; the rain had washed away the blood stains. I ran upstairs feeling less anxious and hurried to get the front door open in case Erich appeared to complicate matters. Once in the apartment I looked back through the spyhole. There was still no light coming from above Erich's door. I would have to wait for him and Martina to leave for university before trying to do anything with the body, but what?

For some reason I felt I had to check Dieter's heart again. His body was already cold to the touch. His face looked at peace and there was the hint of a smile on his lips. I hoped he was with Eva in some communist utopia in the afterlife; a paradox lost on me at that moment. I covered him with a blanket, before lying down on the sofa in a state of physical and mental numbness.

I must have been asleep for less than an hour and awoke feeling sick. I ran to the sink and retched out what little was in my stomach. Once I had stopped convulsing, I washed my face. It was still only quarter to eight. Most mornings Erich did not leave until half past nine, sometimes on his own, sometimes with Martina. Even with them out of the way, I still had no idea what to do with Dieter.

While I waited to hear Erich's door open, I decided to move Dieter's body onto the floor and to get rid of the bloody blankets. I lifted the blanket from his face and stared at him lying there, still smirking as though he was pleased with the trouble he had put me in. I found it hard to believe only a few hours earlier I was speaking to him, and even a little afraid of him.

Having struggled to move Dieter onto the floor, it became clear I would not be able to get rid of the body by myself. Becoming desperate, I took a drink of schnapps and considered asking Erich to help. I didn't know him very well, and although I knew he hated the Nazis, would he want to get mixed up in anything like this? I was just about to take another drink when I heard a screech of wheels outside. I rushed to the window and watched in horror as a canvas covered lorry emptied out a dozen or more uniformed SA men, some with vicious looking dogs, while others had guns or clubs in their hands. I turned back and stared at Dieter lying on the floor.

'Open up!' screamed a frightening voice. The blood drained from my body. I blessed myself and waited for them to spill into the room. There was more shouting, but they were not banging at my door. I ventured along the hall and peered through the spyhole to see the stormtroopers break down Erich's door. I watched the unfortunate Erich, still only wearing pyjama bottoms, being dragged from the flat, his face covered in blood. One of the SA brutes smashed the butt of his rifle down on Erich's bare foot. Erich's screams sent the dogs into a frenzy of barking as he was hauled downstairs. I stopped worrying about Erich when I saw one of the dogs was sniffing at the faint stain where Dieter had shed much of his blood, but his handler did not take any notice and pulled the brute back downstairs.

Almost falling over Dieter's outstretched leg; I rushed to the window just in time to see Erich being thrown into the back of the lorry.

I turned to look at Dieter, who still had an annoying smirk on his face.

Chapter 26

Just in case the SA returned with their dogs, I decided to wash the stairs again. Erich's front door was still lying open. I pulled it over, but the lock was broken. I left the door ajar, still wondering what he had been up to. With a bucket of hot water and using up the last of the detergent, I began washing the evidence of Dieter's presence from the landing. Splashing the soapy water onto the stairs, I was constantly asking myself questions. Why did they arrest Erich? Where was Martina? What did they get up to last night? But the one worrying me the most was how to get rid of Dieter's body? More and more questions without any answers, and the schnapps and lack of sleep were making me light-headed. When I got to the bottom of the stairwell, Frau Keller, who lived on the first floor, appeared with two bags of shopping. She had missed the morning's drama and stared at me as if I had two heads. 'Why are you washing the stairs?' she asked, not sure if she should be grateful or not.

'The SA arrested Herr Vogel. They were a bit rough with him.'

'Is that blood?'

'Yes, I'm afraid so,' I said, wiping the smudged handprint she had noticed on one of the wall tiles, which was too dry to have been Erich's blood.

'What has he been up to? He seemed such a nice young man.'

'I have no idea. I'm sure they'll soon realise he's innocent of whatever it is they're accusing him of,' I said rather doubtfully, continuing to wash out to the front steps as Frau Keller carried on up to her apartment bemoaning the Nazis.

The strain was beginning to take its toll on me. Exhausted,

I sat on the steps outside, with a tune playing in my head. It was a piece Rebecca often played to please her father. The frantic opening score began repeating in my head again and again, until it started to grind on me. It taunted me for being a failure; a failure as a son, as a lover, and a failure as a man. The screech of a passing tramcar mercifully brought the music to an end before it drove me round the bend. I had to stop drinking. I went back upstairs to lie down for a while.

I lay on the sofa, tossing and turning. There was nothing that could be done about Dieter until after dark. My thinking was becoming desperate and more macabre. Cutting up the corpse and dumping it in the river, was the only idea I could come up with. The thought of dismembering the body was too terrifying for me to contemplate and I pushed these ghoulish thoughts from my mind. There had to be a less drastic way to be rid of him. I had to do something soon. There was already a sweet, sickly odour coming from Dieter. Unable to look at him any longer, I pushed the body under the bed until I could decide what to do with him.

Agitated with indecision, I got up and paced around the room, before opening the window to let in some fresh air. A horse-drawn cart passed in the street below, carrying all kinds of junk; old tyres, a copper boiler and lead pipes. If I could get my hands on it for a couple of hours, the corpse would soon be at bottom of the Spree.

I could not stand being confined to the room any longer, and with the first few bars of Chopin's *Ballade* pounding in my head again, I went out to get a packet of cigarettes. The earlier downpour had cleared the air and the sun was now out. The streets were busy with people going about their business in the fine spring weather, and the noise of the passing traffic quickly drowned out the phantom piano. At the corner, stormtroopers were asking people for their papers. I showed my party card and walked on without stopping. '*Heil Hitler.*' Chopin tinkled two defiant notes in my head and then went silent. '*Heil Hitler.*'

At the newspaper stand all the front pages had pictures of Goebbels at the Opernplatz, with deluded students obediently casting the condemned books in to the flames. So much had happened in such a short time. I could hardly believe it was only the previous night I watched the book burning with Erich and Martina. Since then, he had been arrested, and I'd acquired a corpse. I scanned through the Völkischer Beobachter but could not find any mention of the dead SA lieutenant. 'Are you going to buy a paper or not?' moaned the man behind the stand, wearing a dirty-looking swastika armband he probably found in the street.

'Everyone's now a *Gauleiter,*' I said, shaking my head, paying for the newspaper. I stood for a while and looked carefully at each page, taking my time to cover every column, but instead of finding a report about a shooting in a hotel, there was a short article referring to a young female student being arrested for setting fire to a Nazi banner. She was not named, but after seeing what had happened to Erich, I was sure the young woman was Martina.

There was absolutely nothing about the dead SA lieutenant. Was Dieter lying? How did he get a bullet wound? Why would he lie? Were the Nazis even looking for him? I could not believe a dead SA lieutenant was so unimportant to the Nazis that his murder failed to register a ripple of interest in their own newspaper.

In no hurry to go back to the apartment, I went to a nearby café to go through the newspaper again. I sat by the window and ordered a coffee and a pretzel to break my fast. Page after page was devoted to the book burnings, which took place across the country.

After finishing my coffee, I went for a walk to clear my head. The spring weather was at odds with the way I was feeling. I walked for hours until I came to a bar, which served cheap beer to Nazi Party members. Showing my card at the door, I took a stool at the bar and bought a glass of beer. I was still at a loss. How would I get Dieter's body out of the flat on my own and without being noticed?

I was already drunk when I got back to the apartment. Oblivion beckoned. I began to drink what remained of the schnapps I bought the day before. The more I drank the more I cursed Dieter, venting my anger and frustration at the soles of his boots, which were protruding out from under the bed. *So much for your bloody revolution ... The people didn't want you and your comrades running the country. They wanted Hitler ... Adolf Hitler and his silly little moustache ... That's what they wanted ... not a bunch of communists ... I should never have listened to you or Eva ... look at you now ... dead, and for what? The only thing you ever gave me was your corpse to get rid of. You selfish bastard ... Why did you have to come to my door? Where were all your comrades when you needed them? Hiding ... that's where.* I began singing the *Internationale* in a bizarre attempt to mock the corpse further. It was still light outside, but I was exhausted. It was not long before my eyes closed like heavy shutters and the bottle fell from my hands.

The room was cold, and most of the morning was already gone when I awoke. For a moment I thought Dieter's corpse was all just part of a macabre nightmare, but the sickly odour was real. The rigor mortis must have worn off, and the body was now emitting unpleasant gases. I got up and scattered some lavender water around the room to disguise the smell. How long would it be before it became unbearable?

After a strong coffee to wake me up, I went down to the kiosk to buy a newspaper. It was another fine day; even the street peddler had a rare smile on his face. Again, there was nothing about the dead SA lieutenant, which reassured me a little. Maybe Dieter was not as good a shot as he liked to think. Maybe he was just a figment of my imagination. Maybe I was going mad like my mother ...

With the warm sun on my face, I walked back to my apartment block with a sense of purpose taking hold of me. I had to get rid of the body, before it put me in the asylum.

Curiously, Erich's broken door was lying wide open again when I returned. Fearing the SA had come back, I searched for my keys, eager to get into my apartment as quickly as possible. When I finally put the key into the lock, my body froze when Erich's door creaked opened behind me.

'Hello, Franz. I think your neighbours have had their flat broken into.'

I turned to see Georgi standing at Erich's door, wearing his sober brown suit and spats, and looking like a dandy in his fedora hat.

'What are you doing here?'

'Can I not visit an old friend?'

'Of course, but what were you doing in that apartment?'

'When you didn't answer, I knocked your neighbour's door to see if they might know where you had gone. The door almost fell off its hinges. I couldn't resist having a look around, you know me. What a mess … '

'It was those SA bastards who smashed the place up. They arrested the student who lives there.'

'Oh, those brutes. What has he done, failed his exams?'

'It's not funny, Georgi. He's a friend of mine and they beat him up when they arrested him.'

'I'm sorry, Franz. What did he do that was so bad?'

'I'm not sure, but I think he might have set a couple of Nazi banners on fire the other night.'

'Is that all? They should give him a medal … I'm dying for a cup of tea and a chat before I have to go to work.'

'You're working again?'

'Yes, just waiting tables at the Rheingold until I get something better.'

'At least you've got something.'

'It's better than nothing I suppose. Franz, are you going

to open that door? I've not got much time. I have to be at work in a couple of hours.'

'I'm sorry, Georgi,' I said, trying to think of an excuse without hurting his feelings. 'I can't let you in just now ... I've got company ... she'll still be in bed.'

'Ah, no wonder you look flushed ... Rebecca?'

'Yes.'

'Oh, Franz, I'm so ...'

'Georgi, keep your voice down, she'll hear you.'

'All right, I can take a hint, but you both must come over for tea soon. You haven't gone and got yourself married without telling me?'

'No, we haven't, and we'll come and see you soon.'

'Give her my love. Guess I'll just have to settle for a cup of tea some other time. Goodbye, Franz.'

'Goodbye, Georgi.'

Relieved, I listened as he skipped down the stairs, whistling one of his cabaret songs as though he hadn't a care in the world. For a moment I envied him. I turned the key and went into the apartment. I was only in the room for a few seconds before realising letting Georgi go was a mistake. He was one of the few people in the world I could trust. I hurried out of the apartment, jumping down the stairs three at a time, before running into the street. I saw him at the top of the road and called out to him as he turned the corner. By the time I got to the corner he had vanished in the busy main street. Cursing myself, I went back to the apartment to think. After much indecision, I decided to wait a few hours before walking to the restaurant, which I knew to be near to Potsdamer Platz.

With two days growth on my chin and dark bags under my eyes, I must have looked like a down and out. Not wanting to embarrass Georgi in front of his customers, I took a table outside and ordered a coffee and waited for him. Georgi eventually appeared, carrying a tray of goblets. His hair was tied in a ponytail, and there was no hint of make-up on his pale face. He stopped instantly when he saw me gesturing to him. 'I'm going crazy,' he said, approaching my table. 'What are you doing here?'

'Georgi, can you sit down for a minute and keep your voice down.'

'Only for a minute, Franz,' he said, looking around at the prying eyes, now more interested in our conversation than their own.

'I need to meet you after work ... When do you finish?'

'Not until nine o'clock.'

'Can you come to my apartment after you finish? It's very important.'

'Why did you not tell me this important thing when I was at the flat earlier? You're acting very strange, Franz.'

'I know, but I can't explain now. I really need your help, Georgi.'

'All right, if it's that serious I will be over as soon as I get off ... You haven't got Rebecca pregnant?' he said, in one of his asides for the benefit of his audience of eavesdroppers. He had not lost his theatrical desire to shock and entertain.

When I got back to the apartment I could smell Dieter as soon as I opened the front door. There was now a strong, putrid odour coming from under the bed, which would only get worse. I was concerned how Georgi would react when he saw the body. I was going to have to break this to him slowly.

After a few hours the stress and fatigue overwhelmed me, and I fell asleep, only waking again when the room was in darkness. I got up and lit the oil lamps, before making some coffee to clear my head. It was almost half nine, and there was no sign of Georgi. The smell of the body was getting worse and I poured almost a half-bottle of lavender oil over it. The apartment now smelt like a cheap brothel. I waited and waited, becoming more despondent with each passing minute. Just when I was beginning to give up on him there was a knock at the door. I went to answer it, but first looked through the spy hole. He had no idea what horror lay beyond as he preened himself under the glow of the gaslight as though waiting to go on stage. I opened the door.

'Hello, Georgi, come in.'

'I'm so sorry … I didn't get away until quarter past nine. One of the waiters was late and …'

'It's all right, you're here now.'

'I think Rebecca's overdone the lavender, Franz. Where is she? God, Franz, what's that smell?'

'Georgi, take a seat and I'll make some tea. I'm afraid I lied to you, Rebecca wasn't here this morning. She's never been here.'

'Why would you lie to me about something like that?'

'I had to. I didn't know what else to say to you when you turned up this morning. I have a good reason, but you have to promise me you will keep secret what I'm going to tell you tonight.'

'Secrets, Franz, you know I can keep a secret.'

'This is not just some trivial gossip, it's deadly serious.'

'Well, tell me before the suspense kills me, if this smell doesn't do it first.'

'Georgi, I don't know where to begin …'

'Try the beginning, and can you open a window first? I think your drains need cleaning.'

After opening the window, I began to tell him as simply as possible what he had to know. Despite numerous interruptions, it was only when I mentioned the shooting of the SA lieutenant in the hotel that he sat up.

'I heard about that the other day.'

'How did you know about it? It's not in any of the papers.'

'Franz, it happened in a hotel in the red-light area in the middle of the day. Everyone's heard about it. The Nazis have tried to hush it up for obvious reasons. What's all this got to do with you?'

'It was Dieter who killed him … Dieter turned up here the other night with a bullet in him.'

'Where is he now?'

'He's lying under the bed! He's dead.'

'He's dead,' mouthed Georgi, looking towards the bed and then at me in the hope I was playing a joke on him. I lifted the bedcover to show him Dieter's feet. Georgi went into a fit of agitation and acted like he was going to pass out.

'Calm down! It's not like I killed him. I need your help to get rid of the body before it stinks out the apartment and the neighbours get the police involved.'

'Oh my God, Franz, this is terrible. If you didn't do anything wrong, why don't you just tell the police what happened?'

'If I do that, they'll want to know how he ended up under my bed and they'll accuse me as an accomplice in the shooting at the hotel. They only have to look at him to see he's been dead for a while, so they'll want to know why I didn't report this before now. I need to get the body out of here somehow, but I can't do it on my own. Will you help me?'

'Oh my God, Franz … What do you expect me do? I can't bear to look at a dead body never mind touch it.'

'We'll have to wait another few hours until the streets are quiet and take him to the nearest alley and dump him there …'

'What! Carry it through the streets … are you mad?'

'I can't think of any other way. I know it's risky.'

'It's crazy. What if someone sees us?'

'We can carry him upright between us as though he's just drunk. There's a lane between these apartment blocks which is always full of rubbish. We can cover him up and leave him there. The police will think he was killed there.'

'Oh, Franz, please don't ask me to do this.'

'I've got no one else to turn to ... Please, Georgi, I'm desperate.' We sat in silence as he played with his hair like a frightened child. He stared at me and then the bed, before playing with his hair again.

'All right, but if I knew this was why you wanted to see me, I would have never come. You tricked me into this.'

'I'm sorry, Georgi.'

While Georgi, chain-smoked and nervously played with his bangles I went out and walked to the lane to make sure there was no one around. There were plenty of odd bits and pieces of rubbish; it had clearly not been cleaned for months. I noticed some bushes at the far end of the lane where we could leave the body.

Satisfied with its state of neglect, I left the lane and stood for a few minutes at the street corner to collect my thoughts. Estimating it would take no more than ten minutes to get from the flat to the lane and back, I waited for over fifteen minutes to see how many people passed during that time. Apart from a few cars, the streets were quiet. There was no sign of any SA Brownshirts, and thankfully their reputation for brutality was keeping the rest of Berlin indoors after dark. I hurried back to the apartment as it began to rain.

I was surprised to find my front door open and went into the living room to find Georgi gone. In a state of utter distraction, I walked around the flat, cursing him to hell and back. I had been so close to freeing myself from this nightmare, only to be let down at the last minute, by Georgi of all people. I even took my anger out on Dieter's corpse and kicked his feet while passing the bottom of the bed. I sat with my head in my hands; suddenly there was a knock at the front door. It was Georgi. I took a deep breath, trying not to lose my temper.

'Where have you been?'

'You were gone for so long I had to use the toilet downstairs. My stomach's just a flutter of butterflies. What took you so long?'

'I was just making sure there was no one around. Here, give me a hand to get him out.'

After a few moments of hesitation, he put his cigarette out and blessed himself. I grabbed one leg and Georgi the other and we dragged the body from under the bed. Even I baulked at the smell and rapid deterioration in Dieter's face, now translucent and streaked with thin purple veins. I turned to see Georgi standing against the wall, his fingers trembling in front of his mouth. I put the hat over Dieter's face, taking a deep breath before pulling him onto the bed so we could get him into a standing position. I gave Georgi a swig of schnapps to fortify him for the task ahead. After a second mouthful he nodded to me and we both took a hold of Dieter and hoisted him on to his feet, unfortunately the build-up of gas in the stomach caused the corpse to belch loudly. In horror, we both dropped the body back on the bed causing more diabolic noises to emanate from the open mouth. Georgi put his head in the sink and retched violently. I lit a cigarette and took a long hard drink of schnapps to steady my own wrecked nerves.

While Georgi sat with his hands covering his face, I tied a scarf around Dieter's head to keep the jaw up and the mouth closed. Now resigned to getting this over with as quickly as possible, Georgi took one side while I took the other. We finally got Dieter onto his feet and onto the outside landing in one desperate scurry. With little respect for the dead, we soon had him downstairs. The light from the streetlamps gave off a diffused glow in the rain. I fixed Dieter's hat again as we took the belching body between us and staggered along the pavement.

When we reached the lane, we dragged the body to the far end and laid it under the wet bushes. Georgi blessed himself and said a prayer for someone he had only ever met as a corpse. When he was finished, I threw a few bags of rubbish over the body. It was then I noticed the communist books I had dumped there just the other day.

As soon as we left the lane Georgi stared at me with a strange look in his eyes and without saying a word began to walk away. I called after him, but he began to walk faster and eventually disappeared behind the next apartment block. I returned to the apartment and lay shattered on the bed. I could smell Dieter's corpse as though he was still under the bed, but I was too tired to care and gradually fell into a deep sleep.

Chapter 27

The following morning, I awoke cold and feeling nauseous. The wind and rain were lashing against the window. Now rid of Dieter's body, I had no strength left to get up, and I just lay there shivering. In the distance I could hear Church bells ringing, their reassuring sound making me drift back to sleep.

There was a sudden knock at the door which woke me. I sat up on the bed, thinking it must be the landlord looking for his rent arrears. I tried to think of an excuse to give him when the knock came again. 'Police ... open up!' My tiredness immediately disappeared, replaced with panic. I quickly put my clothes on as the door was banged hard. 'Hurry up ... open up, we know you're in there!' My thoughts were all over the place, had they found Dieter's body? How did they connect it with me? Had a neighbour seen us and gone to the police? Maybe I was not careful enough when searching Dieter's clothes. Feeling trapped, I tried frantically to open the bedroom window, but it was jammed tight. Even if it opened, the drop to the pavement would probably kill me. My hands were shaking as I went to answer the door.

The gaslight on the landing cast a halo around two shadowy figures standing in front of me. They were not in uniform and looked more like gangsters than policemen. 'Franz Schreiber?' asked the taller of the two men, while holding out his identification card, which I could barely make out.

'Yes, what is it?'
'You're wanted for questioning at police headquarters.'
'What for?'
'You'll find out when we get there.'

The two men followed me into the room. I sat on the bed and put on my boots. One of the officers handed me my coat. 'What's this?' asked the smaller, more aggressive-looking officer, picking up the silk kippah, lying on the dresser. It was the one Herr Kolinski had given me to wear at Rebecca's wedding. Why had I kept it all this time?

'Are you Jewish?'

'No ... I found it in the street ... Thought I might be able to use it to patch the hole in my trousers.'

'Is that supposed to be funny?'

'No.'

'Hurry up, and make sure you take your papers with you,' ordered the other officer.

There was a strong smell of stale schnapps on my breath as the police car drove through the morning traffic, screeching around corners and ignoring stop signs. I sat in the back, watching with envy the ordinary Berliner going to work. I expected to be taken to the local police station, but we passed it as though it wasn't there, turning towards the city centre. It was now clear to me they were not ordinary detectives and I began to feel ill.

The streets passed by quickly as the police car continued to bully its way through the morning traffic. I noticed the driver's eyes watching me in the rear-view mirror and sat up straight, trying desperately not to look afraid. The car splashed through the streets as the condensation began to cloud over the windows. I was finding it hard enough to control my breathing when the driver lit a cigarette adding clouds of smoke to my growing suffocation. Were they really police officers? Where were they taking me?

When we stopped at the Potsdamer Platz junction, I had an overwhelming urge to open the car door and make a run for it. With one hand on the door handle, I took a deep breath, but a sudden jerk of the car threw me back onto the seat. The moment was gone.

With no other opportunity to escape, the car eventually pulled up in front of a large municipal building draped in long, red swastikas. I began to panic. It was the offices of the secret police, where many of those taken into 'protective custody' were brought for interrogation before they disappeared. My body was shaking as I got out of the car under the shadow of the intimidating building with its neo-classical façade.

Inside, the large foyer was like a Greek temple, with marble columns on either side, leading to a wide, white marble staircase and more swastikas. The building echoed with the sound of numerous voices on the different levels. We stopped outside an office on the second floor, where a secretary, in a white blouse and wearing a swastika armband, sat at a small desk in the corridor. She was busy flicking through a box of index cards with one hand, while speaking to someone abruptly on the telephone. 'Herr Schreiber,' said one of the policemen as the secretary hung up the telephone.

'Take a seat,' she insisted, before lifting the receiver again. 'Herr Schreiber's here, sir.'

'No hard feelings, Schreiber,' said the taller police officer with a laugh in his voice as he slapped me on the back.

'No,' I said, giving him a weak, nervous smile. The other officer just stared at me and grinned before turning away. The two detectives walked back along the corridor as though they had just delivered a child to a kindergarten. I wiped the beads of sweat on my forehead as the secretary looked at me curiously. 'He'll see you in a few minutes.'

Who will see me? I wanted to ask, but instead just sat there dumb as the secretary went back to flicking through the box of indexes on her desk. They were the same as the ones I had compiled while working in the Potsdamer Platz office. I tried to relax.

While waiting, the whole building reverberated with the sounds of doors opening and closing, typewriters frantically typing and telephones ringing. On the opposite wall there was a picture of Göring wearing the *Pour le Mérite* he won in the Great War. Underneath, in gothic script, were the words, *Minister for the Interior*. I jumped a little when the phone rang on the secretary's desk. She picked it up and spoke in short bursts of obedience, before replacing the receiver. 'Herr Schreiber,' she said, tapping the desk with her pencil for a moment.

'Yes.'

'He will see you now, follow me.'

Taking deep breaths, I followed her through a long corridor of polished marble floors, her legs making a monotone swishing sound against her tight-fitting skirt. She stopped outside a door which had a brass plate with the title *Sturmhauptführer* embossed on it. She knocked, immediately opening the door without waiting for an answer. The secretary nodded for me to go in as she held the door open.

'Thank you, Fräulein Holzberg, that will be all,' said the *Sturmhauptführer*, without looking up from the papers in front of him. The secretary smiled at me for the first time and gave a Nazi salute before leaving.

'Come closer and let me have a good look at you. I knew it was you, come closer.'

As I approached the desk he got up to greet me with his outstretched hand. It was none other than Günter Schwartz. His blond hair was short, and he wore round, gold-rimmed glasses and looked like a bank manager. He was impeccably dressed in a grey pin-striped suit and was nothing like the dark wraith figure I saw standing behind Goebbels at the book burning only few days earlier. How could it be?

'Günter,' I said, swallowing hard as he shook my hand vigorously.

'Oh, I'm sorry if my little joke was not as funny as I thought it might have been ... you look rather pale, Franz.'

'I'm fine. I just had a little too much to drink last night. My God, Günter, is it really you?' I asked in a hollow voice as the relief trembled down my spine.

I was beginning to think it was another alcohol-induced dream, until Günter, grinning widely, embraced me, squeezing out any lingering doubts.

'Franz Schreiber ... How are you? Well, I hope?'

'Yes, Günter, and you?'

'As you can see I'm doing all right. It has been a long struggle, but I always had faith in the Führer and knew the day would come when he would deliver what he promised.'

'Why am I here ... is there anything wrong?'

'No, on the contrary, I've been reading your employment file from the Potsdamer Platz office, and it seems you suffered a great deal because of the incompetent Jew-infested governments who have mismanaged the country since the war. Your poor mother ended up in an asylum.'

'Yes, she died there.'

'Those Jews have a lot to answer for, and believe me, they will. Did you know Gretchen married her Jewish postman and had a brood of Hasidic rats of her own to infest the nation?'

'No, I haven't spoken to her for years. How is your mother?'

'Mama is dead.'

'Oh, I'm sorry, Günter. You have my condolences.'

'Thank you, Franz, but she has been dead now for a few years. She had a heart attack while waiting in a damned bread queue.'

'Life is cruel ...'

'Not cruel enough for some ... I'm aware of your present misfortune and the fact you have been unemployed since we closed down the offices in Potsdamer Platz. That is no disgrace. I had to suffer many years on the capitalist scrapheap before National Socialism rose from the ashes of that corrupt republic.'

'You have done well for yourself, Günter.'

'Yes, I have, but not without a struggle. Our Führer will give the German people back their destiny, robbed from us by those traitors who betrayed our nation at Versailles. The Führer has vowed to overturn that criminal betrayal and rid the fatherland of capitalists, Bolsheviks and Jews. We will soon have every German in this country back at work and their honour restored … '

'*Heil Hitler!*' I exclaimed, thinking it a fitting tribute to Günter's rant, while clicking my heels in the way that impressed Goebbels. It had a similar effect on Günter, causing him to lose his chain of thought for a moment as he stared at me approvingly.

'Enough politics for the moment, Franz, I have been going through many of the files you had been organising at the Potsdamer Platz office, and I want you to do the same for me. Himmler has arranged for me to take the offices on this floor in order that we have both SS and state police files in the one building … for security reasons of course. For the time being, this is still under the jurisdiction of Herr Göring, but I'm assured it will not be for much longer. I need a good administrator to oversee this office, and to act as my eyes and ears. We will be friends again, Franz … what do you say?'

'Of course, Günter, I have longed for this day for such a long time.'

'You will receive a salary of fifty marks per month … it's not much, but there will be other perks to this post as time goes on. You must say yes, Franz. I know you will?'

'Yes, Günter, I would be glad to work for you.'

'Good, you can start next Monday morning … You look disappointed?'

'No, I'm very happy and glad to be working for the party again. It's more than I could have hoped for …'

'But you have no money to pay your rent.'

'No.'

'I will give you thirty marks in advance of your salary. Will that tide you over?'

'Yes, thank you, Günter. I don't know what to say.'

'Don't say anything. Remember, we're blood brothers after all,' he smiled, bizarrely lifting his thumb to remind me, the image of him looking through Gretchen's keyhole coming to me at that moment. 'I will look forward to seeing you at seven o'clock next Monday morning. In the meantime, get yourself a decent suit. You look as if you slept in that one.'

'Now I can afford one, I will.'

'Do you drive?'

'No, I've never learned.'

'Never mind, I will have one of my men teach you. I will need you to drive me on official business from time to time … Well, it is good to see you again, Franz. I have a meeting in twenty minutes and must leave soon. Fräulein Holzberg will show you the way out … *Heil Hitler*!'

'*Heil Hitler*!'

Still shaking, I walked out the front door of the building, which had terrified me only a short time before, with thirty marks in my pocket. It had even stopped raining and the sun was shining through the breaks in the clouds. Was I not able to decide what was right and what was wrong anymore? Had I really become a Nazi through my own choice? Did I really care? Fifty marks a month! I hurried along the street as though trying to get away from my own conscience. What about Dieter and Eva? Now both dead for what they believed in; was I so easily bought?

The arguments continued to rage in my head; the forces of good against the forces of evil, conscience against self-interest, while pious ideology was being battered to death with reality. I had no choice … what would have happened if I turned down Günter's offer? The communists were finished, and Dieter and Eva were dead. It was police work after all, government work. The German people had elected Hitler and the Nazi Party to govern, why should I have any guilt about working for them? Why should I turn such a position down and go back to living in poverty? The shirt on my back was still wet with sweat and I began to feel cold as a police car passed with the two detectives who had delivered me to Günter. The driver tipped his hat towards me.

On my way home, I was tempted to buy a bottle of schnapps to celebrate my good fortune, but I was determined not to ruin things by drinking. Instead I went to a café which served a good breakfast, and then spent most of the morning reflecting on what happened. Later I bought two shirts and a pair of shoes and a second-hand double-breasted suit, when cleaned, would look as good as new. My spirits were high for the first time in months. I tried not to think of Dieter lying in the lane covered in rubbish.

On the Monday morning, I arrived at the station just before seven o'clock. Günter was standing at the reception speaking to his secretary, Fräulein Holzberg. He welcomed me with a smile, shaking my hand vigorously, before leading me into the front office. What had been an empty room, only a week before, was now a hive of activity. It was now not unlike the office at Potsdamer Platz, only on a much grander scale. There were over a dozen secretaries, all wearing swastika armbands, busy typing behind five rows of desks. The clatter of keys and ringing of stop bells echoed efficiency and diligence.

Günter raised his hand and ordered them to be quiet. 'This is Herr Schreiber. He is to be my new chief filing clerk. He will oversee the administration and filing of this office from today. If you have any problems, it is Herr Schreiber you speak to. Is that clear?'

Günter asked me to follow him. My surprise at being

appointed chief filing clerk was nothing to my utter astonishment when I entered another office to find Herr Becker sitting behind a cluttered desk smoking a cigar. He jumped to his feet and saluted Günter, who declined to reciprocate. 'I've told you before, Becker, smoking is not permitted in this office!'

'My apologies, Herr Schwartz, it will not happen again,' coughed Becker, while frantically stubbing his cigar out. How was this possible, had Becker not been charged with treason? Nothing seemed to make sense.

'You know Herr Schreiber?'

'Franz, of course, I can do with the help, he's a good worker.'

'He is not here to help you. You are here to assist him.'

'But Herr Schwartz ... '

'Silence, this is not open to discussion. Do you understand?'

'Yes, Herr Schwartz.'

'You will vacate this office immediately and take your filthy ashtray with you. This is now Herr Schreiber's office!'

Things were moving too fast for me. The fact Becker was now my subordinate made me feel uneasy. I watched him clear his papers from the desk with a look of humiliation on his face, making me feel more than a little guilty. At least he was still alive.

'Where is he to go?' I asked, after Günter banged the door closed behind the departing Becker. 'He can go to hell for all I care. He would not even be here if it wasn't for Gregor Strasser insisting the charges against him were dropped. Watch what you say to Becker, he cannot be trusted, and he will report everything back to Strasser. You, on the other hand, shall report back only to me ... Now, Franz, I want you to make sure you keep these files in order. We will soon be getting many more from the police records around the country. We will speak later. *Heil Hitler*!'

'Heil Hitler.'

The office still stank of Becker's cigar smoke and I opened the window to get some fresh air. Nothing felt real, Becker my subordinate? Before I had enough time to get used to the idea, he appeared with a trolley loaded with files.

'Franz, these files are ready for being archived, I thought you might want to go over them before I filed them.'

'Just leave them here and I will have a look at them later. What happened when you were arrested?'

'They accused me of passing information to the communists … Can you believe it … me a communist spy? Thankfully Frieda managed to get a hold of Gregor Strasser and he insisted I be released immediately.'

'Did they do anything to you?'

'A couple of slaps that's all, but they threatened to do all sorts of things, none of them very nice.'

'Well, I'm glad they sorted things out.'

'Thank you, Franz. It will be like old times again.'

'Yes … Like old times.'

The bulk of the files Becker had left for me to check over were of communists, all classified as enemies of the state – many were dead and marked to be destroyed. The others were either in work camps around the country or in exile. I began the laborious process of indexing the files, not bothering to look inside the files of my former comrades. I felt a sudden panic when I came upon Eva's file, her image staring at me from beyond the grave. There were more photographs of her inside her file, bruised and battered. I closed it over quickly. I could not look at them. I sat there staring at the folder for a few minutes; it was marked to be destroyed. Despite my reluctance I had to satisfy my paranoia and find out what was in there. I steadied my resolve, taking a deep breath, I opened the file again. I turned over the photographs and began reading. She had been one of the first to be arrested in the purge, following Hitler's appointment as Chancellor.

She endured three weeks of hideous torture before she finally gave any information. She named Becker as a communist spy, which resulted in his arrest and the closing down of the Potsdamer Office. I read the letter from Gregor Strasser demanding Becker's release. Eva suffered further brutality, leading to her death from asphyxiation. I closed the file. I went back to the files and removed the small photograph of Eva from the cover and put it in my pocket. I then went through the files and noted the details of each victim and how they were killed. Most met their death by SS firing squads; others were hanged or died in work camps from beatings or disease. My hands were shaking, but I was determined not to let these files be destroyed without keeping a record of the victims. I had no idea why I felt the need to record this information. Who could I give it to now Dieter was dead?

When Becker returned I went with him to the cellar where he burned the files in the roaring flames of the furnace. The heat from blaze was intense and I had to shield my face. Within seconds the files were no more. Becker stoked the furnace with a poker to make sure there was nothing left and closed the heavy wrought-iron door. I remembered Erich quoting Heine: *Wherever they burn books they will also, in the end, burn human beings.*

Chapter 28

Two weeks after I started working for Günter, the Gestapo found Dieter's body in the lane. Eventually Dieter's file landed on my desk to be destroyed with dozens of others that contained the details of dead communists. It referred to him as a communist assassin who planned to assassinate Hitler and other high-ranking party officials. I felt my heartbeat racing. There was an itinerary of the Führer's engagements the SS found in his belongings, which were recovered from the doss-house in Alexanderplatz where he had been staying. I wondered if he tried to kill Schultz in his frustration at not being able to get close enough to Hitler, or anyone else of importance. There was little else in the file. I closed it over and remembered him the day I first watched him in the back of the farmer's cart standing defiantly, the doomed aristocrat on his way to the guillotine. Perhaps he always knew he would die someday for his Marxist beliefs. I got up and paced the room with an overwhelming feeling of guilt.

During my first year I organised the filing system to Günter's satisfaction, secretly noting the details of any other files destined for the furnace. I took the evidence of those killed while in 'protective custody' back to my apartment and stored them in boxes under my bed. Over the months my bedroom became a cemetery for the death of German communism. What I was going to do with them I had no idea, but I felt I owed it to Dieter and Eva, and to my conscience.

The number of administration staff increased to deal with the growing caseload the detectives had to deal with. The office secretaries were continuously typing out endless reports on the people Göring was still trying to remove as a threat to Hitler's hold on power. With the communists already eradicated as a political force, the filing cabinets and the prisons were now full of Social Democrats, trade unionists and many others from different political groups who opposed the Nazis' rise to power.

In April 1934, as Günter had predicted, Göring finally ceded control over the state police to Himmler's SS. Günter reverted to wearing the black SS uniform. His manner also changed once Reinhard Heydrich was appointed the new director of the Gestapo. While he was pathetically sycophantic to Heydrich, he became increasingly short-tempered and rude to the staff under his authority. He even stopped addressing me by my Christian name and began calling me Schreiber, even in private.

The week after the change of leadership I was ordered to drive Günter to the Hotel Kaiserhof, where Göring was hosting a reception for foreign dignitaries and the press from around the world. Günter, wearing his SS uniform, revelled in the attention many of the journalists gave him. He handed me his coat; it seemed he needed a valet as much as a chauffeur to impress the media. From the back of the room I watched and listened. When asked by one English Journalist, from *The Times*, why he had the skull and crossbones on his cap like a pirate, Günter was quick to tell him the insignia was in fact an ancient Prussian symbol of military prowess, and, unlike England; Germany did not have a history for piracy. I noticed Himmler smile when he heard this. He took Günter by the arm and they both spent the next fifteen minutes chatting in the corner.

No one took any notice of me. I stood at the back in my dull grey suit, holding Günter's coat. I was beginning to think the only reason Günter wanted me to work for him was to remind him of the change of social order in the country. I, once the bourgeois son of his mother's employer, was now his lackey. I, once the clever student, was now subordinate to him, the class dunce.

There was a briefing area at the far end of the reception room with a table draped in a swastika under a golden eagle insignia. Radio microphones from around the world were perched on, or near to the table. Engineers were busy making last minute checks to the equipment.

Göring finally appeared, flanked by several party officials like ducklings following their waddling mother. The journalists quickly broke off from their conversations and gathered around the table where Göring was now sitting with a grin on his face, shuffling papers and exchanging jokes with Rudolf Hess. Once he was sure the microphones were working, Göring began. 'There are still enemies within this nation, whose single aim is to bring down the elected government by force and return this country to anarchy. The powers conferred on the Führer, under the Enabling Act, are not a threat to democracy, but a bulwark for its continued survival. The communists are, and continue to be the main enemies of this state, but they are not the only ones who threaten the security of our nation … '

After condemning the Jews, Göring went on to try and placate the international media, insisting the rest of the world had nothing to fear from a strong Germany. I wondered if any of the journalists were naive enough to believe him! As he joked in English, he appeared to be nothing more than a happy-go-lucky man of the people who would rather be out hunting than dealing with such weighty matters of state. Unlike the journalists, I had already seen numerous files where he had signed the death warrants of leading communists.

His mood and facial expression changed dramatically when one Dutch reporter suggested the Reichstag fire may have been started by a group of SA men, rather than the feeble-minded Van Der Lubbe, who had been guillotined for the crime a few months earlier. Göring banged the table and ranted at the journalist that Van Der Lubbe was found guilty in a court of law. The journalist made other accusations implying senior members of the Nazi Party were involved, but Göring had had enough and got up and left without answering any more questions. I noticed Günter nodding to two of his men, who positioned themselves near to where the reporter was sitting; making it obvious to him, he was no longer welcome. The press conference was over.

A few days later I met SS-Brigadeführer Reinhard Heydrich for the first time. He was a tall athletic man with a long sharp face, his short blond hair swept back from his forehead. I immediately felt intimidated by his cold stare as Günter introduced him to me along with the other office staff. He declined to shake my hand and turned to Günter and demanded he get everyone back to work. The atmosphere in the building became disturbing.

For the next few months we worked through hundreds of files, which were being passed daily from the various police authorities around the country. Many of the new files contained the details of numerous high-ranking members of the Nazi Party, especially regional *Gauleiters*, SA leaders and activists who were mainly on the left of the party. It was clear Heydrich was creating a dossier of all those in the party he saw as subversive to his own interests.

Günter came into my office one morning with a list of names Heydrich had given him and we went into the filing room where Becker was busy writing out index cards. With his usual abruptness to my old boss, Günter ordered Becker out. He then opened the only filing cabinet in the room locked with a padlock. We both went through the files, all marked Top Secret, looking for the ones on his list. 'Take all those to Heydrich's office,' ordered Günter.

Heydrich was on the phone when I knocked and went in with the files. 'Yes, my Führer … Herr Himmler is here with me … Yes, everything is being taken care of …' shouted Heydrich down the phone. Either Hitler was hard of hearing or the line to Munich was not very good. Himmler touched Heydrich on the arm and nodded in my direction.

'Here are the files you requested, Herr Direktor.'

'Put them on the floor and get out,' ordered Heydrich, after placing the palm of his hand over the receiver. I saluted and made myself scarce.

Shortly after the phone call, both Himmler and Heydrich left for a meeting with Göring at the Reich Chancellery. They were looking agitated and it was clear something was happening that even Günter was being kept in the dark about.

During the rest of the week, various high-ranking SS officers came to the building to spend an hour or so with Himmler and Heydrich before leaving grim faced. Günter spent more and more time running errands for Heydrich, who rarely emerged from his office where he was constantly on the phone to the Chancellery.

One afternoon Günter was called away to a meeting and returned a couple of hours later with half a dozen men, some of whom I recognised as Gestapo officers. I was getting ready to leave for the day with the rest of the staff when he asked me to wait behind. The other men who arrived with him seemed to be on edge. They stood at the window overlooking the courtyard, smoking and talking in whispers. Günter disappeared into his own office. A short time later the phone on my desk rang.

'Franz, will you come into my office at once!' It was Günter. He immediately hung up. It was the first time he had used my Christian name in months and that alone made me feel uneasy. I went to see what he wanted.

He had already removed his SS tunic and shirt. He closed the door behind me before continuing to change out of his uniform. He was breathing heavily and looked worried. I watched him take his revolver from its holster and put it in his coat pocket.

'Franz, what I have to tell must go no further. Do you

understand?'

'Yes, of course, Günter. What's going on?'

'I can't tell you, but you'll know all about it soon enough. I want you to do something for me.'

'Yes, what?'

'Take this letter. I want you to keep it safe … It's my will.'

'Your will? My God, Günter, what's going on?'

'I can't tell you. The name and address on the back of the envelope belongs to the mother of my daughter …'

'Your daughter?'

'Yes, Lena, she's nearly three years old. You must only give it to the mother if I'm killed.'

'Killed, why do you think … ?'

'Never mind, I will hopefully take it back from you on Monday morning. If not, the address is on the back of the envelope. You better go now, and you must not tell anyone about this conversation. I know I can trust you, Franz.'

'Of course,' I said, as he shook my hand as though for the last time.

With Günter's will in my pocket, I was glad to get out of the office and went to the nearest bar for a drink. Becker was already sitting at one of the tables. I ordered a beer and sat beside him. 'What the hell is going on, Franz?'

'I don't know,' I replied, lighting a cigarette and shaking my head.

'You must know something,' he insisted. 'You and Schwartz are as thick as thieves.'

'I don't know anything,' I replied curtly. 'Günter tells me nothing. He's changed.'

'Changed? He's always been a bastard.'

'He's not a bad as Heydrich.'

'Himmler, Heydrich, Schwartz, they're all the same … self-serving bastards.'

'You must not let anyone hear you say such a thing.'

'I don't care anymore, Franz. This is not my party anymore. It's been taken over by gangsters.'

'Here, let me buy you a drink,' I said, looking around to make sure no one was listening to Becker's outburst. He lit a cigar, but he did not look as if he had enough puff in him to smoke it.

'What does Operation Humming Bird mean?' he asked, turning to stare at me.

'I've no idea.'

'It must mean something,' snapped Becker. 'I heard that bastard Heydrich mention it over the phone yesterday and again this morning to Himmler. Something is going on. Why are Heydrich and Himmler constantly on the phone to the Chancellery?' he asked, looking at me for an explanation I could not give him. With Günter asking me to keep his will, I was as sure as Becker that something momentous was about to happen, but what? Were they planning a coup to overthrow Hitler? Did they intend to assassinate him? Had he, like Julius Caesar, seized too much power too soon? These were thoughts I could not speak. So, I said nothing, while wondering if Becker was thinking the same thing.

'Come on, Franz, you must know something?'

'Honest, I don't. It could mean anything, but I don't think you should let anyone hear you talking about it. You might get into trouble if it gets back to Heydrich,' I said, looking at Becker to see if he had anything to say. He just puffed on his cigar and said nothing.

On the Monday morning Becker did not turn up for work and there was no sign of Günter either. I eventually asked one of the secretaries to telephone Becker at home, but she could not get an answer all morning. I was relieved when Günter, still wearing civilian clothes, finally appeared at lunchtime with three Gestapo officers. He ordered me to take them to Heydrich's room where they removed some of the files I had carried up the previous week. They had a list of names and knew which files to take and which ones to leave. The one file that interested them more than the others was thick dossier on Ernst Röhm, and they spent a few minutes ridiculing the SA leader before putting it with the others they intended taking. They eventually filled up two large storage boxes with the relevant files and left. Once they were gone I went down to speak to Günter, who had changed into his SS uniform and regained his wraith-like appearance. I handed him back the envelope containing his will.

He smiled at me. 'It's over.'

'What's over?'

'The SA leadership have been eliminated, all except Röhm who is under arrest in Munich facing charges of high treason. Their plan to usurp the government and take over the country is now in tatters, thanks to our swift action.'

'I don't understand.'

'We had intelligence Röhm was planning a *Putsch* against the Führer. We put an end to his treachery ... You must keep quiet about this, Franz. Herr Göring will be addressing the nation on radio about the necessity of our actions to save the state from these traitors.'

'Why have the Gestapo taken files from Heydrich's office?'

'Herr Goebbels has ordered them to be destroyed ... Schreiber, how long have you been working here?'

'Nearly fifteen months.'

'The identification papers you were issued with when Heydrich became director, have you ever looked at them?'

'Yes.'

'Then you surprise me, Schreiber. Have another look.'

Feeling rather intimidated by Günter's tone, I took out my wallet and removed my papers. My photograph was stamped with the Nazi Eagle standard, which I had obviously seen before, but I had not, until that moment, taken any notice of the tiny printed words underneath: Geheime Staatspolizei -

The Gestapo.

'You may be only a civil servant here, but when you refer to the Gestapo, you should not be under any illusion that since Herr Himmler took over as chief of all police forces in the country, both you and I became members of the intelligence branch of the Gestapo. The officers you see in this building every day are our colleagues, many of whom assisted myself and other SS officers in saving the country from Röhm's treachery. They are now under the authority of the SS, as you are. Do you understand, Schreiber?'

'Yes, Günter ... I understand.'

'Herr Sturmhauptführer,' he shouted, slamming the palm of his hand on the desk.

'Yes, Herr Sturmhauptführer. I understand.'

'Good, now get back to work.'

'Before I go ... Becker has not turned up this morning. I have not been able to get him on the telephone all morning.'

'That's not a great surprise ... He's been shot.'

'Shot!'

'Yes, he was one of Gregor Strasser's men, and another traitor. I had no option but to carry out the order ... in spite of his pitiful pleas. He was always a coward.'

'You killed him?'

'He was executed for treason along with many others, including Strasser. I had to do my duty. You are not to mention this to anyone else ... do you understand?'

'Yes, Herr Sturmhauptführer, I understand.'

'Get back to your work, Schreiber; you're beginning to annoy me with your disapproving tone.'

Over the next few days, details of the number of state sanctioned murders were leaked to the world's press. Both Goebbels and Göring gave their spurious reasons to the country for the necessity to purge the SA leadership before Röhm carried out his alleged plans to overthrow the government. The list of names, many of whom I had created files for, appeared in the few newspapers brave enough to print them. Röhm was now also dead, killed by assassins while in police custody in Munich.

The whole SA leadership was wiped out in a matter of a few days and Günter, like many others in the SS and Gestapo, had played his part with total obedience. I read with some surprise President Hindenburg had written a letter of thanks to Hitler, on behalf of the nation, for saving the country from what he referred to as the Röhm-Putsch. Now even the President was prepared to acquiesce and praise the perpetrators of state sanctioned murder. A couple of weeks later I listened to Hitler's speech on the radio when he personally attempted to justify his actions.

'In this hour, I was responsible for the fate of the German people, and thereby I became the supreme judge of the German people. I gave the order to shoot the ringleaders in this treason, and I further gave the order to cauterize down to the raw flesh the ulcers of this poisoning of the wells in our domestic life. Let the nation know that its existence, which depends on its internal order and security, cannot be threatened with impunity by anyone! And let it be known for all time to come that if anyone raises his hand to strike the State, then certain death is his lot.'

The atmosphere in the office was strained for some time and most of the office staff became subdued when Becker's body was finally found riddled with bullets in woods on the outskirts of the city. The whole world was turning upside down, but I said nothing. What could I say, and to whom? Aneka, one of the secretaries, who was obviously fond of Becker, did react when the news of his murder was whispered around the office that morning. She was the only one to shed a few tears, but even they quickly stopped when Heydrich and Günter appeared in the office. Günter was proudly wearing new epaulettes. He had been promoted to Sturmbannführer for his actions in the purge. In one weekend, Hitler had eliminated the only other major threat to his power in the country. All that stood in his way to absolute power was the old President.

Chapter 29

Despite the fact two army generals, an ex-Chancellor and his wife were murdered along with most of the SA leadership, the initial protest quickly faded. Hitler continued to seduce the German people. They turned up in their thousands to pay homage to him as the country's economy continued to improve and the unemployed were put back to work in their millions. Now the Communist Party and the SA were no longer a danger, the main work of the Gestapo was to gather intelligence on anyone who was identified as a threat to the party's ideology. This process was continually being defined by Goebbels; through directives, office memorandums and press reports. Individuals who failed to embrace National Socialism were now being persecuted and arrested in dawn raids. New camps were built to accommodate the thousands of political prisoners who dared to speak out against the new order.

The last semblance of the Weimar Republic vanished when Hindenburg finally died. Seizing the moment, Hitler abolished the office of President and became the country's absolute dictator. The military were now required to take an oath of unconditional obedience to Hitler, and a few weeks later I, along with all the civil servants in the country, was required to take a similar oath.

Now his authority in the Third Reich was absolute, Hitler was free to turn again to the persecution of the Jews. Within the year the Nuremberg Laws were put on the statute book. I managed to obtain a copy and read it with dismay: *'Entirely convinced that the purity of German blood is essential to the further existence of the German people, and inspired by the uncompromising determination to safeguard the future of the German nation, the Reichstag has unanimously resolved upon the following law, which is promulgated herewith: Marriages between Jews and citizens of German or kindred blood are forbidden. Marriages concluded in defiance of this law are void, even if, for the purpose of evading this law, they were concluded abroad. Proceedings for annulment may be initiated only by the Public Prosecutor. Extramarital sexual intercourse between Jews and subjects of the state of Germany or related blood is forbidden. Jews will not be permitted to employ female citizens under the age of 45, of German or kindred blood, as domestic workers. Jews are forbidden to display the Reich and national flag or the national colours. On the other hand, they are permitted to display the Jewish colours. The exercise of this right is protected by the State. A person who acts contrary to these prohibitions will be punished with imprisonment and hard labour.'*

I was amazed these draconian laws were passed without a national outcry, but with the press now firmly in the hands of Goebbels, any dissent was effectively suppressed. Although my workload had increased over the months, the office on the floor above doubled in size to deal with the deluge of denunciations now flooding into that office from ordinary citizens about Jews, or persons believed to be Jewish, failing to comply with the Nuremburg prohibitions. This department was also under the jurisdiction of Günter, and he began to spend more and more of his time there.

After the Nuremburg Laws were enacted, those Jews who could afford to get out, began leaving the country in increasing numbers. It was around this time I read about Rebecca's planned emigration to America in one of the few foreign magazines still on sale in the city. There was a picture of Benjamin with his uncles outside one of their department stores on Leipzigerstrasse. They had already sold their interests in their department stores, no doubt for a fraction of what they were worth.

It was the first time I had thought of Rebecca in months. I wished her well as I recalled my foolish obsession with her. I was now reconciled I would never see her again. I hoped Herr Kolinski, Leon and Hannah had the sense to leave also. It was clear to me, after listening to Goebbels' frequent outbursts against all things Jewish, life was only going to get worse for those who stayed behind.

With nothing else to do, I buried my head in my work and received my first increase in salary as a reward, which allowed me to move to a nicer apartment nearer to the city centre. The apartment was larger than the tiny rooms I had been living in for the last few years, and my prospects seemed to be good so long as I stayed in favour with Günter.

My department mainly dealt with Aryans violating the country's criminal code. With an ever-growing number of restrictions on the freedom of expression, allegations begat counter allegations. With Goebbels actively encouraging the German people to inform on their fellow citizens, the spiral of incriminations was unstoppable. It was now a serious crime to speak out or even joke about the regime and its policies. Many of the informants were nothing more than vindictive neighbours or spurned lovers and it was often difficult to find a genuine complaint among the bile emanating from so many, mainly anonymous, letters. More disturbing was the number of children, usually members of the Hitler Youth, writing to the office to inform on their parents for making derogatory comments about the Führer or the party. Reading some of these allegations, it was clear the country was now gripped in a vicious circle of distrust and fear. It was a cancer that I was now part of and helping to spread. On the other side of this coin, it could not be disputed that during his first three years, as promised, Hitler had brought the country from the brink of civil war to peace and prosperity. While the rest of the world continued to endure the Great Depression,

Germany had become strong again. German democracy was dead, and few mourned its passing. With most of those who had opposed the Nazis either murdered or in exile, the country entered a period of relative calm. The transformation of the economy had won over many ordinary citizens who had once baulked at the idea of Hitler as Chancellor. Many communists and trade unionists hid their past and gave their full allegiance to the Nazi regime they once hated until it gave them back the dignity of employment. It was with these notions I justified my own twisted morality.

With the country's domestic difficulties behind him, Hitler turned his attention to foreign policy. In defiance of the Versailles Treaty he had surreptitiously rebuilt the country's military power. With rearmament, he had the support of the generals and industrialists, who benefited most from the resurgence of the country's armed forces. Now he felt strong enough to let the world see his boldness.

In March of 1936, I watched the triumphant news reels in a local picture hall glorifying Hitler's newly equipped Wehrmacht as they marched into the Rhineland, which had been a demilitarised zone since the end of the war. Hitler had taken his first military gamble. The French made protests but took no action. The country breathed a sigh of relief and life went back to normal.

In the run up to the 1936 Olympic Games, Günter's SS passed me a list of over six hundred men, women and children of Roma ethnicity living in Berlin. They were to be relocated to a special camp in Marzahn for the duration of the Games. Their papers were placed in a separate filing cabinet; the new Germanic State would not tolerate such people. With the information gathered from a central register by the Gestapo, I was required to dictate the necessary relocation orders from a pro-forma style by simply adding the personal details from the new files. I took the orders to Günter for his signature before they were passed back to the Gestapo.

Within days, all Roma living in the city were rounded up. Although the relocations were temporary orders, the Roma camp soon became permanent.

In contrast to the removal of the Roma, to placate world opinion during the games, the remaining Jewish population was to be given a respite from the increased anti-Semitism that had prevailed since Hitler became Chancellor. The Nazi Press were warned not to print anti-Semitic articles, and the vile graffitti, painted on Jewish premises and synagogues, was removed.

By July, the whole of Berlin was in the grip of Olympic fever as teams from around the world arrived in the city. Günter was on duty at the opening of the games as one of Hitler's many SS bodyguards. I managed to obtain a ticket for the opening celebrations and went on my own.

It was a warm summer's day and I followed the crowds into the spectacular new stadium. All around the arena there were massive banners depicting the ubiquitous swastikas, which had now become the emblem of this new Germany. Then, the moment everyone was waiting for arrived, and, to a tumultuous riot of noise and colour, Hitler and his entourage entered the stadium. Through the forest of raised arms and swastikas I watched Hitler's procession make its way to the VIP box. Protecting his master, Günter marched ahead of a dozen elite SS bodyguards, all watching the crowd fervently and ready to put themselves between their Führer and an assassin's bullet. This may have been Dieter's opportunity had he not tried to kill Schultz out of frustration.

Once the euphoria had finally calmed down, Hitler eventually disappeared into the shadows only to emerge a few minutes later behind a podium where he declared the games open. There were roars of approval and thousands stood with their arms outstretched, singing the national anthem. Hitler took his seat with a clique of high-ranking Nazi Party members and a few sombre looking Olympic dignitaries. Günter was standing on guard like a member of the Praetorian Guard protecting his emperor in the Colosseum. The whole spectacle was quite overwhelming and, like everyone one around me, I found myself singing the national anthem with my arm raised enthusiastically. Hitler had fulfilled his promises and the people where now paying homage to him as the saviour of the nation, and I was beginning to agree with them. No one wanted to return to the chaos of the past, and I was no different from anyone else in wanting a better life.

Chapter 30

1938

There was excitement in the office when Günter tuned into the radio. A few days earlier, after months of negotiation and intimidation, the Wehrmacht marched into Austria. Hitler had secured his *Anschluss* and extended the borders of Germany without a shot being fired. Although it was a further blatant breach of the Treaty of Versailles, the French and British governments merely expressed their condemnation, but did nothing more. The Reich increased its population by almost seven million overnight and Austria was now merely another province of a Greater German Reich. It now seemed Hitler could do no wrong in the eyes of most Germans.

Günter held up his hand for quiet. Then, after a short introduction by Goebbels, the live broadcast from Vienna was transmitted. At first, the only thing we could hear was the roar of the crowds waiting for Hitler to speak. The chanting of *Sieg Heil* suddenly stopped and there was an eerie silence. Then, the Führer's unmistakable voice, breaking with emotion, announced the annexation of Austria into the Reich. The crowds erupted once again with cheers and applause. Günter turned to everyone, with a rare smile on his face. We listened as Hitler explained the reason for uniting Austria with Germany.

Emboldened by the success of the *Anschluss*, within a few months the newspapers began reporting the Führer's intention to further extend the country by annexing the German speaking Sudetenland in Czechoslovakia into the Reich. The Prague government was not prepared to acquiesce to the loss of a large part of its territory and turned to France and Britain for protection. Many, even those who supported him, now feared Hitler had gone too far and there was a real fear the country would be plunged into another war with France and Britain.

On a hot summer's day in mid-August, I recall walking along the central footpath of the Linden under the shade of the boulevard's lime trees. The Nazi banners that draped the buildings fluttered in the pleasant breeze while the cafés were busy with people drinking coffee and enjoying the sun. I stopped for a moment to light a cigarette as two pretty girls on bicycles, wearing light summer frocks and swastika armbands, passed-by ringing their bells and calling out *Heil Hitler*. Now the capital of a Greater Germany, Berlin was prosperous once again and the depression, which had drained the city during the twenties and early thirties, was lifted completely.

There was a sudden roar from above and like everyone else I looked up at the blue, cloudless sky as a squadron of Göring's Luftwaffe flew overhead. They were heading south, no doubt to the Czechoslovakian border to intimidate the beleaguered Prague government into ceding the Sudetenland.

The fear of war was lifted in September when, with the help of Mussolini, Hitler reached agreement with Britain and France. The Czech government had little say in the loss of its territory and the German-speaking people of the Sudetenland became part of the Third Reich with the same enthusiasm as the Austrians. Hitler was now seen as the greatest thing that ever happened to the country and even the doubters were being won over in droves to his way of thinking.

One afternoon in late October, Günter telephoned through to my office.

'Schreiber, I am having a party tonight and would like you to come along.'

'Me?' I replied, unable to hide the surprise in my voice. Günter had hardly said a civil word to me in months.

'Yes, you! There is someone I would like you to meet. You know my address. Be there at eight o'clock.'

'Yes, Herr Sturmbannführer, eight o'clock.'

It may have been an invitation, but it was really an order. I had no option but to attend. I went home after work and got dressed for the party with little enthusiasm.

I arrived at Günter's apartment shortly before eight. A young SS officer took my coat and hat, directing me into the lounge. There were half a dozen or so glamorous looking women in the room chatting to the various business gentlemen and high-ranking officers of the Reich. There were also some extremely pretty waitresses standing around with trays of champagne. I could not see Günter, but saw Himmler and Heydrich standing in a corner with General Keitel and a couple of other senior army officers I did not recognise. I nodded to a few faces that turned to acknowledge me, including two senior Gestapo detectives who worked closely with Günter. Both these men had made their mark during the purge of the SA and were now reaping the rewards.

I began to feel uncomfortable standing on my own sipping champagne, when I felt a tap on my shoulder and turned to see a strikingly beautiful woman standing behind me. 'Can you be a darling and fetch me another glass of champagne,' she said with a smile that showed she was used to getting her way.

I felt angry at her tone of superiority and would have told her to go and get it herself, only I was afraid she might be the wife of one of the senior officers in the room. I took the empty glass from her outstretched hand. While I fetched the champagne, Günter finally appeared from the kitchen, laughing and joking, with two other SS officers who were carrying a large cake. It was only then I realised it was a birthday party. One of the guests began to play the piano. Günter began singing happy birthday as most of the other guests joined in, turning towards the lady for whom I had gone to fetch the champagne. She moved over to the cake and bent down and blew out the candles. The piano player began playing *Lili Marlene* and she began singing with her arm around Günter's neck.

Lili Marlene came to an end to a rapturous applause and the pianist continued to play in the background as the guests returned to their conversations. I just stood around feeling awkward; I had not even brought a birthday present.

'Enjoying yourself?' asked an elderly man, his owl-like eyes looking at me intently through horn-rimmed spectacles. I smiled, hoping he was not looking to engage me in conversation. However, before I could turn away, he introduced himself as the deputy chairman of the Reichsbank and shook my hand.

'Franz Schreiber.'

He smiled as though expecting me to continue. What could I say that would interest such an important man? Should I tell him about the time I helped my mother dispose of her dead baby in a suitcase? Or the time I found myself with a dead communist under the bed? Or maybe he would be interested in the files that were kept in their thousands at Gestapo headquarters. I was sure I could find a file on him if I searched hard enough. However, I merely mentioned the inclement weather before another banker joined the conversation. They began to discuss the social and economic benefits the new autobahns would bring. This led to their concern about the state of the country's growing debt problem, insisting more needed to be done to get the finances in order. They concurred with each other that putting people back to work was good for the country's morale, but building infrastructure had to be paid for by increasing trade with the rest of the world. I smiled and nodded in agreement but offered no ideas of my own as to how that might be done, saying such matters were in the capable hands of the Führer.

I ignored their raised eyebrows.

Günter appeared at my side and interrupted the bankers to tell them this was a party and not a business meeting. They both nodded and moved away.

'Schreiber, why were you talking to those two old bores when there are plenty of pretty girls to chat to?' he said, as the female who had asked me to fetch the champagne appeared at his side and took his arm. 'Oh, this is Sophia,' he said.

'Franz Schreiber,' I said, with a slight bow of the head, handing her the glass of champagne she had asked for. 'Happy Birthday, I'm sorry, I would have brought you a present, but I was not aware this was a going to be a birthday party.'

'Don't be silly, I'm just glad you're here.'

'Franz Schreiber, the bourgeois filing clerk I was telling you about,' said Günter, making an exaggerated laugh.

'Oh, your childhood friend … He's more handsome than you let on,' said Sophia, smiling with a hint of mischief in her eyes.

'You can keep each other company for a while … I have to speak to General Keitel about starting a war,' he laughed again. It was the first time I ever heard Günter sounding drunk or trying to be funny. He winked at me, making no attempt to be discreet, before going to speak to the general.

Sophia took my arm and led me across the room as though I had been given to her as a challenge. 'I'm sure you don't want to spend the whole night talking to bankers and bureaucrats.'

'I was about to die of boredom before you and Günter saved me.'

'Oh, you must not die so easily, Franz. That would be a waste.'

'Are you and Günter … ?'

'What … lovers?'

'I'm sorry, please forgive me.'

'What's there to forgive? We have a six-year-old daughter, but I don't know if you could call us lovers.'

'I should not have been so impertinent to even ask a lady such a question,' I said with as much contrition in my voice as I could muster, but she began to laugh, making me feel even more foolish.

'You're such a gentleman, Herr Schreiber, but you needn't be so gallant on my account. Oh, don't look so embarrassed. Here, let me wipe that,' she insisted, taking a handkerchief from her purse and wiping the trickle of champagne, which had spilled onto my lapel.

In the silence that followed, she continued to sip her drink, nodding to other guests in the room. Despite my obvious unease, I could not help but admire her sophisticated look and attractive smile so many would be only too willing to fall in love with. What did she see in Günter? I began asking her where she came from and what kind of music she liked; more banality. She did not seem to mind triviality as she went to the nearest waitress and returned with two more glasses of champagne. My first impression of her haughtiness quickly changed.

Our tête-à-tête was broken when two SS officers joined us, both of whom I knew from the office. They took turns trying to charm her as she lapped up all the attention with smiles. For a moment I envied their black uniform and knee-length boots, which my double-breasted suit could not compete with. I decided to bow out gracefully, leaving Sophia to enjoy the flattery her two admirers were so well schooled in.

I took a seat in the corner beside an old gentleman, who also looked like he would rather be somewhere else. Thankfully he was not the talkative type and we merely exchanged nods and watched the rest of the guests in stony silence. The only all-male area of the room was the far corner where Himmler and Heydrich were still engaged in aggressive conversation with two cowed-looking generals. I watched Günter join them with a bottle of champagne. They declined his offer to fill their glasses. He stood beside them grinning and laughing like a child enchanted by warlocks.

I stopped sipping champagne and began drinking schnapps, seduced by a bottle within arm's reach. After what sounded like an argument, Himmler and Heydrich made their way to the front door, leaving one of the generals pleading a misunderstanding in their wake. Günter tried his best to placate Heydrich, who was staring at the general with his chilling blue eyes. The tension in the room subsided when he and Himmler finally left.

Once they were gone, Sophia put on the gramophone. More guests, including the berated general, made their excuses and left. I took another glass of schnapps and began to relax a little. I watched Sophia dancing with one of the SS officers, who loosened his embrace on her when he noticed Günter staring at him. With Sophia's encouragement, others began to dance, making me feel nauseous as the schnapps began to take hold. I eventually fell asleep listening to the tedious songs of Zarah Leander.

I awoke at some stage in the early hours of the morning with Günter standing over me with his hand shaking my shoulder. He shook me again as I tried to come out of my stupor. 'Wake up, Franz, there is something I want you to see.' His use of my first name made me instantly suspicious. I immediately apologised for falling asleep as I looked around and saw all the other guests had gone. Even Zarah Leander had stopped wailing. I got up and followed Günter into the hall. He turned and smiled as he stopped outside one of the rooms. It was then I heard a woman's voice. Günter grabbed my arm as he stooped down and peered through the keyhole. I took a step back, flabbergasted. After a few seconds he looked up again and nodded for me to look. It was not a request, but a demand. He stepped aside with the same grin on his face, reminding me of the time he had encouraged me to spy on Gretchen. With his hand now on the back of my shoulders, my heart was thumping as I bent down to take a look. My eyes quickly adjusted to the yellow glow of candlelight. I was dumbfounded. 'Gretchen?' I mouthed. How could it be? I watched the soapy water run down the nape of her back and into the porcelain tub at her feet. She was singing quietly. I pulled away as she turned towards the door. I stood up and stared at Günter in disbelief. It was Sophia.

'Remember, Franz,' he whispered, showing me the small scar on his thumb before opening the door of the bedroom. 'There are some things in life we never forget,' he grinned, before opening the door and going in. Perplexed, I stood in the hall, not sure of what to make of Günter, or Sophia for that matter.

I eventually found my coat and left. It was raining, and it took me nearly an hour to walk back to my own apartment. On my way home, I became increasingly disturbed with what had taken place.

When I awoke in the morning, I was still quite drunk, but got to work just after eight o'clock. Günter was standing outside my office looking at his watch when he saw me approaching. 'You're late, Schreiber.'

'I'm … '

'Never mind, here,' he snapped, handing me a piece of paper with an address on it. 'Take my car and pick up Sophia and Lena. You have to take them to Hamburg. They will be staying with Sophia's parents for a while.'

'To Hamburg?'

'Did Sophia not mention it to you last night?'

'No.'

'Well you know now. Leave immediately. They will be waiting for you … and remember, drive carefully.'

I took the car keys from reception and went down to the backyard. This was a rare occasion when I had access to the car without Günter sitting in the back seat complaining about my poor driving. I sat in the driver's seat and checked the address; 85 Königsallee, which was not far from where I spent the first years of my life. I was a little apprehensive at meeting Sophia after what had happened the night before. I lit a cigarette and turned on the ignition.

Once I reached the outskirts of the Grunewald district I slowed down, looking with a strange detachment at my old house on the corner; it was much smaller than I remembered it. It seemed as if a hundred years had passed since I smashed the glass ball on the nursery floor.

It was another ten minutes before I found Sophia's house, which was only visible from the street now many of the trees in the grounds had begun to shed their leaves. I parked the car on the other side of the avenue, but near enough to the front gate to see the building's grand façade, with its two white vestibule pillars dominating the entrance.

A maid opened the door. She was expecting me, and after taking my hat and coat she showed me into the front parlour. It was a beautiful room with the morning sunshine coming in through the French windows, which led onto a large garden.

'Miss Mayer will be down shortly. May I get you something to drink?'

'No, thank you. I'm fine.' When the maid left, I felt anxious and paced the room. I was tempted to light a cigarette, but there were no ashtrays. I put the cigarette back into the packet.

After a few minutes I went over to her bookcase, which was crammed with a wealth of literature, including many books now banned by the state. I removed a leather-bound copy of Goethe's plays, which was similar to my father's old copy, which I had struggled to read on more than one occasion. I opened it and read the handwritten inscription below the preamble. *Mazel Tov and congratulations Saul on your Bar Mitzvah, we are very proud of you. Love and best wishes, from your Aunty Monika and Uncle Joseph.* This surprised me even more than the banned books. Was Sophia's family Jewish? Was that why Günter was being so secretive about her and his daughter? But who was Saul: her brother perhaps? Before I could consider this any further the door to the parlour opened and I turned to see Sophia standing with a cigarette in one hand and an ashtray in her other.

'Good morning, Franz, I'm sorry for keeping you waiting,' she said, taking a long draw from her cigarette and flicking the ash into her private ashtray.

'That's all right. I'm merely your chauffeur for the day ... I'm in no hurry ... Did you know many of the books in your library are banned?' I asked as I put the volume I was holding back into its place on the shelf.

'They belonged to the previous owners who left them when they emigrated to America. Günter threatened to burn half of them, but I wouldn't let him. It would ruin the look of the room, having a half-filled bookcase, don't you think?' she said with a laugh in her voice ... 'Franz, give me another five minutes. I just must finish getting Lena ready. She's in one of her moods this morning.'

When Sophia disappeared back upstairs, I opened the French doors and stepped into the back garden to smoke. The mystery of the inscription in the book was solved. Of course, Sophia was not Jewish. The thought of Günter having a Jewish mistress now seemed ludicrous.

Before I finished the cigarette, Sophia returned with her daughter. I stubbed out the cigarette and went back into the parlour. 'This must be Lena,' I said, smiling at a curly-headed girl who was not in the least interested in even looking at me. She started complaining she did not want to go to Hamburg, but her mother ignored her. I took the suitcases from the hall and led the way to the car. It was going to be a long journey.

Chapter 31

Apart from the occasional tears of a spoiled child, the journey to Hamburg was uneventful. Sophia was not very talkative. Most of her conversations were with the maid, and mainly about household matters. She only addressed me occasionally, usually to offer directions when I hesitated at junctions or forks in the road.

It was after seven o'clock when I returned to Berlin. The weather had turned bitter cold, and there was an icy wind blowing as I stopped the car half way along Friedrichstrasse and got out to watch a procession of people being marched down the middle of the street towards the train station. I crossed the road to speak to one of the police officers standing on the pavement. I showed him my identification card.

'What's happening here?'

'These Jews are being deported back to Poland.'

'Why?'

'Because that's where they belong.'

I went back to the car and drove passed the silent, desolate faces, young and old, carrying what possessions they could. On the corner a group of onlookers shouted abuse and spat at the departing Jews as if their plight was not bad enough. Others watched in silence, but no one protested against this forced exodus. I looked to see if Herr Kolinski, Leon or Hannah were among the grey mass of hats, coats and suitcases, but saw no one I recognised in this horde of misery. I drove on slowly before turning east down Oranienburgerstrasse.

When I reached Alexanderplatz, a flurry of rain quickly turned to sleet. Not wanting to draw attention to myself, I parked the car in a lane and walked through the bleak streets, putting my armband on when I saw a couple of police officers standing on the corner. I nodded to them as I passed without being stopped.

When I finally turned into my old street, it was with some trepidation that I climbed the stairs past my former apartment to the next landing, half expecting to hear Herr Kolinski playing the violin. There was no music. Instead his front door was ajar and the lock was lying in the hall. I ventured into the living room. It was totally wrecked. The few books which remained from his vast collection were destroyed along with anything not already pillaged by those who wrote the filth on the walls. I noticed Rebecca's photograph lying on the floor with the words 'Jewish Swine' scribbled across her face. I stared at it until I could look at it no more and put it in my coat pocket. The rest of the apartment was in a similar state of destruction; everything not stolen was broken and scattered across the floor.

As I wandered in dismay from one memory to another, a train pulled up outside. I looked down at the ghost-like figures standing on the platform with their suitcases as police officers ushered them onto the train. It was then I saw Herr Kolinski with a suitcase in one hand and his violin case in the other. I tried to open the window, but the catch was encased in hard layers of paint and impossible to force back. I banged on the glass and shouted his name. It was Hannah, who I had not noticed standing beside him, who turned to look up at the window first.

'Look, it's Franz,' she shouted, tugging at Herr Kolinski's arm. He turned to where she was now pointing. I tried again to pull open the window, but it would not budge. I saw Hannah putting her hand to her mouth, but Herr Kolinski remained stoic. He put his arm around her shoulders and they turned to get on the train together. I suddenly realised I was still wearing my armband. I watched as one of the police officers pushed Herr Kolinski hard on the back and ordered him to hurry. I took off the armband and finally managed to get the window open, but it was too late. A piercing whistle sounded, and I watched as the last of the carriage doors were banged closed and the stationmaster signalled to the driver. The train slowly pulled away, belching out smoke and steam which engulfed the station. I was about to turn away when I noticed the old poster board on the gable end now had a poster of Hitler on it with the words, *One People. One Reich. One Führer.* I cursed him for the whole of Berlin to hear, but only the stationmaster turned briefly to look around the empty platform.

The following morning when I arrived in the office, Günter was in high spirits. It was soon clear why he was so ebullient. He had been congratulated by Heydrich that morning for his efficiency in organising the deportations of the Polish Jews from the east of the city. I could see him salivate as he repeated Heydrich's praise.

Only a few weeks later the office came to a standstill one morning when the state radio confirmed that a member of the German embassy in Paris, Ernst vom Rath, had been shot. The person responsible was described as a young Jew named Herschel Grynszpan, who carried out the shooting the previous evening in revenge for his family's deportation to Poland. Günter was incandescent with rage, cursing Grynszpan in a torrent of abuse.

'Schreiber, you see now why these vermin have to be eradicated,' he shouted, banging his fist on his desk as I stood there with the files he had requested earlier that morning.

'This is terrible news. How bad is he?'

'According to Himmler, he will die within hours and the Jews will pay a heavy price for this ... I hope he does die ... He'll be a martyr, who will be the catalyst to rid Germany of the Jew.'

I put the files on his desk and left without saying anything else.

Two days later, I sat in the darkness of my bedroom as the regular radio broadcast was interrupted by a news report confirming the diplomat had died of his wounds. Günter had his martyr. I sat there in a trance, listening to the patriotic music now playing in his memory.

The death of the diplomat gave Günter the opportunity he had been waiting for. On Heydrich's orders, he organised a brutal backlash against the Jewish community in Berlin, which soon spread throughout the country. During the days that followed, synagogues were burned in virtually every city and town in the country. Jewish shops and other business were attacked by vicious mobs spurred on by the bile printed in the newspapers. With reports of Jews being beaten to death in the streets, I was now relieved Herr Kolinski and Hannah were safely out of the country, but I wondered what had become of Leon.

During the repercussion for Rath's assassination, thousands of Jewish men were arrested and taken into 'protective custody', allegedly for their own safety. Only the outcry from around the world helped to bring an end to the worst excesses of the pogrom, but Germany was no longer safe for anyone with Jewish blood, even those born in the country. As the ruins of the city's synagogues continued to smoulder, a degree of normality returned to the streets and the stunned Jewish communities began to emerge from their homes to clean up the carnage and take stock of what had happened.

One evening, on my way home after work, I stopped for a moment and watched a bulldozer demolish what was left of a synagogue. A few onlookers stood and cheered when the large Star of David which hung over the door crashed into the ruins. A ball of dust rushed across the road towards me, stopping at my feet. I looked down as the dust subsided and noticed my shoes were covered in white ash. I was about to bend down and wipe them with my handkerchief but stopped when I suddenly saw Rebecca standing at the junction up ahead, waiting to cross the road.

I wasn't even sure if it was her, but I took off my armband and followed anyway. I pushed through the crowds heading to the nearby underground station and grabbed her by the arm just before she made to go downstairs. She pulled away. 'It's me, Franz,' I said, taking off my hat. She stared at me, the fear in her eyes quickly melting with relief.

'Franz,' she said softly.

'Can we talk?' I asked, letting go of her arm as we walked away from the bustle of the station. 'Have you got time for a coffee?'

'Of course, I'm so glad to see you again, Franz. So much has happened.'

I had never seen her so sad looking before. All the feelings I had so long suppressed began to take hold once again. I took the heavy suitcase she was carrying and put it down on the ground for a moment. 'I know about your father and the deportations. It was awful, but at least he's in Poland. He'll be safe there.'

She nodded and smiled and was about to say something, but our conversation was interrupted when a troupe of boys from the Hitler Youth appeared on the other side of the road, singing and beating drums. We watched them pass. We walked further down the street away from the Nazi banners that made her look uneasy.

'I thought you had gone to America? I read something a few years ago,' I said, as the din from the drums faded into the distance.

'We planned to, but my father would not leave without Leon, who was too ill to travel. I could not leave without Papa. Leon only died a few months ago. We should have gone when we had the chance ... he was going to die anyway.' Rebecca began crying. I embraced her for a moment but was afraid she would feel my heart thumping in my chest and released her.

'You can still go.'

'No, not now ... Benjamin was taken into police custody ... They said it was for his own safety. What's happened in the last few weeks is beyond reason. We have no rights anymore. First, they deported my father, and then they arrest thousands of Jewish men just because of what one misguided boy did in Paris.' She began crying again. 'We were due to leave for England in two weeks' time ... '

'Then, you must get out before it's too late.'

'But I can't leave without Benjamin.'

'No, no, of course not ... But they've already started to release some of the men. They have nowhere to put them,' I said, trying to lift her spirits. 'You can both still go ...'

'Not Benjamin. I went to Gestapo headquarters ... '

My heart began to beat even faster. 'Gestapo headquarters?'

'Yes ... he's been sent to a place called Dachau in Bavaria. It's a work camp for political prisoners. Benjamin a political prisoner, how ridiculous? The man I saw on Friday morning was vile, he began calling Benjamin awful names and told me not to return or I would be arrested. The following day, two of their men came to my house and ordered me to leave within forty-eight hours. The house was confiscated along with everything in it.'

'That's terrible,' I said, while wondering if the person she spoke to was Günter.

'When they arrested him, they found some banned books and are using them as an excuse to confiscate everything we have ... as though they needed an excuse. I must find an apartment, but I don't have much money. The bank won't give me my own money. What am I going to do?'

'You can stay with me until Benjamin is released.'

'The Gestapo have no intention of letting him go, and I can't leave without him.'

'I have a friend ... who may be able to pull some strings ... ' I explained, without any real hope of getting Günter to help. I just wanted her to stop crying.

'You have a friend who can help?'

'Yes, he may be able to help,' I said, slightly qualifying the assertion in her question.

'Who is he?'

'It doesn't matter who he is.'

She stopped walking and turned to stare. 'How do you know him? Can you trust him? I don't know who to trust anymore.'

'Yes, he was the cook's son in my mother's house. We were friends as children.'

'I hope he can help,' she said, smiling through her tears. 'Franz, I am so glad I met you today.'

'Let's have that coffee,' I said, pointing to a café on the opposite corner. As we crossed the road, Rebecca grabbed my arm and pulled me back before we reached the pavement. I turned to look at the notice on the café window she was staring at ... *Juden Verboten.*

'It's all right,' I said taking her arm, 'we'll find somewhere else.'

'No, I will have to look for an apartment before it gets too late.'

'I told you, you can stay with me. Your father was good to me when I was destitute. You must let me repay his kindness.'

'Thank you, Franz,' she smiled.

'We'll get Benjamin released and both of you out of the country,' I promised, not knowing how I could ever keep such a promise.

Chapter 32

We both knew it was a crime, punishable with imprisonment, for an Aryan and a person of Jewish blood to cohabit together. No one would believe that in our case it was purely a platonic relationship. Having read hundreds of the spiteful denunciations against those accused of breaking the Nuremberg Laws, I was under no illusion of the risk we were taking. We had to be careful, especially of my neighbours, who were still strangers to me.

Over the next few days, while Rebecca stayed hidden away in the apartment, I used my position to search through hundreds of documents in the office of births deaths and marriages, looking for a suitable identity to steal. It took some time, but eventually I found the file of Adele Hirsch, who had died a few years earlier from consumption. The file contained a photograph, and although the deceased woman was blonde, she was of a similar age and height as Rebecca. I noted all her details and took the documents confirming Aryan blood and put in my briefcase. They would enable me to obtain the necessary identification papers for Rebecca.

'You look tired,' she said when I returned home with her new papers. 'It's not fair on you having to sleep on the sofa while I take your bed. I should take the sofa.'

'No, I'm fine. You have the bed ... Here, take these and memorise everything in them. We will begin tonight. I bought this for you,' I added, handing her the bottle of hair dye,

'You want me to dye my hair?' she asked, looking at her new identity papers.

'Yes, it will help you become Adele Hirsch.'

'Who is she?'

'No one, she's dead.'

'How did you get these?'

'That doesn't matter. What matters is these documents will protect you.'

'Have you heard anything about Benjamin?'

'All I know for sure, is he is still in Dachau.'

'Can your friend get him released?'

'It's not that simple, he has to speak to someone in the party who has the authority to release him. He will let me know.'

'Hundreds have been released. Why is Benjamin still in Dachau?'

'I don't know.'

'Now they have confiscated everything I can't understand why they just don't let us leave. I thought your friend could help get him released.'

'He will do what he can,' I said, turning away unable to bear her tears and my lies any longer.

That night, we spent hours creating Rebecca's new history. Time and time again we would go over and over the fictional life of Adele Hirsch. I would take the part of her inquisitor, always trying to catch her out in the slightest inconsistency or hesitation.

'No, no ... Your mother died when you were three years old. You were brought up by your aunt. We can't just change the answer every time I ask the question.'

'Sorry, I thought you said it was my father who died when I was three years old. I'm trying my best.'

'All right, what was your first job?'

'Children's nanny.'

'Good, and after that?'

'A primary school teacher in ... Oh, I can't remember ... Saint Benedict's ... '

'No, no, you can't hesitate!'

'I'm tired. Can we stop now?'

'All right, but this is not a game, Rebecca.'

'Adele … my name is Adele, you fool!' We both laughed. It was the first time I heard her laugh in a long time.

After a late supper, she went to the bathroom to dye her hair. I sat in front of the fire and read a book, but I couldn't concentrate as I impatiently waited to see how she looked as Adele Hirsch. I was shocked when she eventually appeared with hair, not only blonde, but cut short.

'You don't like it,' she said as she considered my reaction.

'I do, it's just that you look so different.'

'Is that not what you wanted?'

'Yes, of course. It will just take a bit of getting used to, that's all.'

Over the next few days we went through the same routine until finally I could not catch her out, no matter how devious or contrived my questions became. She had an answer for everything, often embellishing them with some anecdote, making me smile at her ingenuity. She was becoming an even better liar than I. To complete her conversion, I bought a silver crucifix and insisted she wore it whenever she went out; convincing her Jesus was a Jew and therefore who better to protect her. 'There, Adele Hirsch, you will be safe now,' I said, clasping the chain around her neck. She took the crucifix in her hand and stared at it. 'All this hatred because of this,' she said sadly.

The following morning, to encourage her to get out of the apartment on her own, I woke her before leaving for work and gave her some money and a list of groceries to buy. She stared at the list and then at herself in the bedroom mirror. 'I'm frightened,' she said, touching her hair as though it was not her own. 'What if someone recognises me?'

'No one will. From now on you are Adele Hirsch.'

When I returned in the evening, she was in better spirits after spending much of the day in the centre of town. While she made us both something to eat, she began to tell me about her first day on her own as Adele Hirsch. 'Of course, I was nervous at first and had to look twice at myself when I passed my reflection in the shop windows.'

'I told you, you look completely different. Your father probably wouldn't recognise you.'

'Poor Papa,' she sighed. 'I hope he is all right.'

'He'll be fine,' I said, the memory of the last time I saw him coming back to me. 'Did you get everything?'

'Yes, I think so. You can check for yourself. I put everything in the cupboard.'

'That's all right,' I said, unable to remember what was on the list anyway. What mattered was not what she bought, but the fact she was able to go out on her own.

Over the next few weeks, with her letters to Dachau not being answered, Rebecca became more and more anxious about Benjamin. Rarely did a day go by she did not ask me if my friend had found out when he would be released. To put her mind at rest I would insist Benjamin was being treated well and would be freed soon. The problem was I did not have a friend to help or know when Benjamin would be released. Even if I wanted to, I could not get near Benjamin's file, which was kept in the Department of Jewish Affairs. Of course, I could not tell Rebecca this, and had to simply go on lying to her, sure Benjamin would be released eventually.

'When, Franz, when?' she pleaded one evening as the first snows of winter began to fall outside.

'Soon ... '

'Soon ... You've been saying the same thing for weeks, but he's still in prison. When will they let him go?'

'There was an article in one of the papers this morning stating that all Jews still in 'protective custody' will be released if they agree to leave the country. Is there any reason why Benjamin might be refusing to emigrate?'

'No, I told you ... That's what we were intending to do before he was arrested. They've taken everything we have.

Why won't they let him go?'

'It will just be a matter of time. You must be patient. His turn will come.'

'I'm sorry, Franz. I know you're trying your best. You have been so kind to me. I've taken your bed and it's you who has to get up for work in the morning.'

'I told you it's not a problem ... you worry too much.'

'I've got nothing else to do. While you're at work all I do is sit looking out the window until you come back in the evening. I'm a doctor and I should be doing something useful with my time. I am so bored sitting around all day doing nothing.'

'You should try working in an insurance office. Now that's boring.'

'You never talk about your work, Franz. What's it like?'

'Like I said, it's boring. I spend all day working out the premiums for commercial insurance policies. Nothing exciting ... ... I was thinking we should go and see a movie tonight,' I said, to try and cheer her up a little and get off the subject of my work.

'I haven't been to the cinema for years. What's on?'

'There's a new Dietrich film on at the picture house on Leipzigerstrasse.'

'Yes, let's go. I just want to get out of here for a while.'

It was already dark by the time the tram stopped near Potsdamer Platz and we walked the rest of the way. Rebecca turned to me anxiously when she noticed the proclamation on the side of the kiosk banning admission to Jews. I took her hand to reassure her and paid for two tickets.

As the usherette led us to our seats, a newsreel of Hitler's recent meeting with Mussolini was coming to an end and the lights came on as we followed the girl down the centre aisle. Rebecca grabbed my arm tightly. The two seats the girl instructed us to take were flanked on either side by SS officers. I felt trapped as we sat down, but Rebecca must have felt she had entered the heart of darkness.

Before the first feature began, a public information film appeared on the screen: it was titled *The Jewish Plague*. The orchestrated music accompanying the opening captions was manic and had a sinister shrill to it. Rebecca moved uncomfortably in her seat as she watched the vile pictures depicting the Jews as rats infesting Europe and stealing food from Aryan children. I held Rebecca's hand firmly, afraid she might be tempted to get up and leave as some in the audience shouted abuse and laughed at the grotesque caricatures. Rebecca's body was shaking. I could see the tears coming to her eyes as she bravely watched in silence at what her fellow Germans thought of her.

'What's the matter?' asked one of the SS officers, who was sitting next to me and looking at Rebecca.

'Nothing, my wife is asthmatic and is having difficulty breathing with all this cigarette smoke.'

'Yes, I find it infuriating myself,' replied the officer, coughing to make his point, before turning back to watch the beginning of the main feature.

'Let's go,' I whispered to Rebecca as I took her hand and led her along the row of annoyed SS officers. 'Excuse me, my wife is feeling unwell.'

During the short journey back to the apartment, Rebecca was near to tears and I could not find anything to say that would have mattered. She sat with her head stooped. I put my arm around her.

The apartment was cold when we got back, and she went to the bedroom to change as I lit the fire. Just as the flames began to take hold I heard her sobbing and went into the bedroom to find her on her knees. She turned to me in utter distress. 'I don't want to be a Jew ... Why was I born a Jew?' she cried. 'Everyone hates us ... and for what? Because of this?' she shouted, holding the crucifix in the palm of her hand before throwing it across the room.

'Don't say that ... Get up,' I insisted, taking her by the hand.

'Is that how people see us ... as rats?'

'No, that's how Goebbels and Hitler want the people to see you ...'

'You heard them laugh as much as me ... they hate us.'

'I'm not Jewish, and I love you,' I said without being able to stop myself.

She stopped crying and stared at me. 'Please don't say that, Franz. It's not right. I'm married to Benjamin.'

'I'm sorry ... I shouldn't have ...'

Over the next few hours Rebecca became more and more distant and withdrew into herself. I tried to cheer her up but her laconic responses soon left me with nothing to say. We sat through long periods of silence before she turned to me with anger in her voice. 'Franz, why are you lying about Benjamin? I don't think you care if he ever gets released.'

'That's not true ...' I replied, but she just got up and went to the bedroom without another word.

Having spent much of the night unable to sleep, I got up early the next morning. Before leaving I went into Rebecca's room to leave her some money. She stirred for a moment and stared at me, before slowly closing her eyes again. I pulled the cover over her bare shoulders, leaving the crucifix and money on the bedside cabinet. I went into the hall and put on my coat, stopping to straighten my tie in the mirror. I hardly recognised the person looking back at me.

At work, while Günter was out of the office on official business, I requested the file on Benjamin from the administration clerk on the pretext Günter wished to review it. I took it to my office and locked the door. The file was substantial and marked 'Enemy of the State'. I perused the detailed allegations of subversive activities, including conspiring to usurp the government. There was nothing in the file to support these crimes, no witness statements or incriminating documents. The whole thing was clearly a fabrication, which did not surprise me having seen similar distortions of the truth in other files over the years. Benjamin was from a wealthy family and the real reason for his incarceration was clearly to strip him of everything he owned. I read the warrant from Heydrich ordering the arbitrary confiscation of the house and all monies held in his bank account without any recourse to legal process. The whole of Benjamin's assets were detailed and valued down to the last paper clip. The total value was almost half a million marks. My heart began to quicken when I came across a copy letter from Heydrich to Himmler requesting Benjamin be put on trial for treason as a deterrent to others who refused to sign over their overseas banks accounts. It was now clear to me why they were still holding him, unlike the thousands of others who has been released over the last few weeks. Benjamin was refusing to yield to the threats of his persecutors. I removed his passport and the visas he had previously been granted before his arrest.

After taking a few deep breaths, I made my way through the typing pool to one of the secretaries. 'Nina, Herr Schwartz has asked me to dictate this for him; he's rather busy with other matters.'

'One moment,' she said as she finished typing the letter she was already working on.

While I waited for her to finish, I looked around the office, but no one was paying me any attention. I could feel the sweat running down the side of my face as she fixed the ribbon before reloading her typewriter with fresh letter-headed paper. I dictated a brief letter ordering the immediate release of Benjamin Cohen from Dachau. She stopped typing and looked at me. 'Who is authorising this?'

'I told you, Herr Schwartz asked to me dictate this on his behalf.'

'Talk of the devil,' she said, nodding towards the office

door where Günter was exchanging salutes with two Gestapo officers. My heart almost stopped with fright. Once the two detectives left, Günter was about to go back up to his office when he noticed me standing beside Nina. He stood motionless for a moment, his piercing eyes staring in my direction. My heart was now pounding so hard it almost drowned out the clatter of typewriter keys.

'Well,' said Nina. 'I have other work to do. Is this all you want typed?'

'Yes,' I said, turning briefly to see Günter had gone back to his office.

'Do you want me to get him to sign it before he disappears to the Chancellery? He is due to meet Goebbels this afternoon.'

'Thank you, Nina, but I will take it to him. I have other things I need to speak to him about.'

I went back into my office and reread the letter. I then opened Benjamin's file and studied one of the letters Günter had sent to the bank ordering the freeze on Benjamin's bank account. The signature, with its jagged points and troughs, looked impossible to copy. I took a sheet of blank paper from the drawer and made a few attempts to forge it, but my hand was shaking so much it looked nothing like his alpine mountain range of a signature. I clenched the pen in my hand in frustration. It was impossible. I got up and opened the window to get some air to steady my nerve. The cold wind that was swirling in the courtyard raced into the room. It was only then I realised my shirt was soaking with sweat. I closed the window over just as the office door opened. I turned to see Nina standing in front of my desk.

'I thought you might want a coffee, Herr Schreiber,' she said. 'You're looking very tired these days,' she said, holding a cup of coffee in one hand and an envelope in the other.

'I have a bit of a cold, that's all,' I said, desperately aware Benjamin's file was still lying open on my desk with the letter and my failed attempts to forge Günter's signature. I rushed to take the coffee and envelope from her before she had time to put them on the desk. 'Thank you, Nina, just what I need,' I said, gently ushering her back to the door. She looked at me strangely, but said nothing, before returning to her typewriter.

I locked the door and tried again to master Günter's signature. It took another few attempts before I could feel the pen moving with sufficient lucidity to make the signatures begin to look more genuine. Holding my breath, I turned to the letter and put pen to paper in a flurry of anxiety. I stared at my forgery. It was not perfect, but it was not unlike the original. With my hands still shaking, I put it into the envelope that Nina had kindly addresses to the commandant at Dachau.

When I was leaving to go home that evening, Günter called me back from the top of the stairs. I could feel the blood drain from my face. The briefcase in my hand now felt heavy as I turned to meet him coming down the stairs towards me.

'You look as if you are in a hurry to get home,' he said, before taking me by the arm and asking me join to him for a drink. I tried to talk my way out of it, but he insisted.

It was bitter cold outside, but the bar Günter suggested was only a short walk from the office. Günter was in a good mood after spending the afternoon at the Chancellery in the presence of Goebbels, who had praised him for his part in the recent backlash against the Jewish community in the city.

We were on our way to the bar when it began to rain. Günter's long, leather coat and knee length boots were impervious to the downpour, his long strides causing me to almost run to keep up with him. My hat and coat were soaked through by the time we reached the bar. It was only then that I realised my wallet was not where it should have been. I frantically searched my other pockets, but it was gone. Instead of being concerned, I was glad of the excuse to go back to the office and get out of having to endure a drink with Günter.

'No need to go back for it, Stenberg. We are only having a few drinks. Here, take this. You can pay me back tomorrow,' he said, handing me ten marks.

'Thank you, Günter. I only hope I haven't lost it.'

After a few glasses of schnapps, Günter became boisterous and was soon drunk on his own self-importance. Still smitten with Goebbels's praise, he revelled in his part in the pogrom, venting the worst of his bile towards Grynszpan, who was still in a French prison awaiting his fate. 'He must be extradited for what he did and be tried in a German court not a French one. The embassy is on German soil ... Damn Jew, he should get the same as Van Der Lubbe got ... You're not saying much, Schreiber.'

'I'm just a little tired, that's all.'

Günter looked at me in silence for a moment. I was about to say something when he held up his hand to stop me.

'Schreiber, have you been keeping something from me?'

'No, nothing,' I said rather too quickly,

'Don't lie to me.'

'I'm not lying, Günter,' I replied, my mouth becoming dry.

'I have it on good authority you have finally found yourself a woman. Is this true?'

I wasn't sure what to say to him as he waited for an answer. What else did he know?

'Don't look so guilty,' he laughed, slapping me on the back. 'It's not a crime. What's her name?'

In spite of all the hours spent going over Rebecca's new identity and berating her when she got the slightest thing wrong, my mind had gone completely blank.

Günter stared at me impatiently. 'What, the cat got your tongue?'

'No,' I finally said. 'If you have people spying on me, you must know who she is.'

'Spying on you? Why would I have people spying on you? Are you doing something I should know about?'

'No, of course not.'

'Well then, why would I have someone spy on you? You're not that interesting, Schreiber.'

'How did you know about Adele?' Thank God! The name had virtually come out of my mouth of its own accord.

'Now you have accused me of spying on you, I have lost interest,' he sulked.

'I'm sorry. Günter, I apologise.'

'If you must know, you were seen at the picture hall on Leipzigerstrasse last night. But I hear you did not stay very long. Why did you leave before the main film came on?'

'Adele is asthmatic. The smoke in the hall brought on an attack.'

'Smoking ... it's a disgusting habit. It should be banned in all public places. I am surprised the Führer has not decided to do so by now. I hear she is beautiful ... You're such a dark horse, Schreiber. Maybe I should have someone keep an eye on you.'

'Like you said, I am not that interesting.'

'Ah, is that the time? I must go.'

'Are you sure you don't want another drink before you go?' I asked with a forced smile, glad to see him button his coat and put on his gloves.

'No, I have some work to do when I get home. Goodnight, Schreiber. You better get home yourself before this weather gets any worse.'

From the window I watched him flag down a taxi with his usual arrogance. Relieved to see the back of him, I finished my drink and left, quickly making my way back to post the letter. Outside the post office the wind blew into the swastika banners that were hanging from the building, making them look like great sails in a storm. I looked around for a moment, always fearful Günter, despite what he said, was having me followed. I dropped the letter into the post-box and hurried back to catch the tram home.

After shaking the wet from my hat, I ran up the stairs three at a time, excited about giving Rebecca the passport and the two visas and assuring her that Benjamin would be released within days. My elation disappeared when I entered the apartment to find my wallet lying open on the hall floor, my Gestapo identification card lying beside it. I immediately searched the apartment, but Rebecca was gone.

Chapter 33

Exhausted, I watched the dawn break over the rooftops and heard the first trams pass in the streets. My sleepless night waiting for Rebecca to return was in vain. I berated myself for leaving the wallet in the apartment, I had been so careful otherwise. Where would she go?

Time passed slowly, and I sat at the bedroom window and watched the rain wash the dirt from the streets into the gutters. It was only when I heard someone at the door did I stir from my stupor. I rushed to answer it, expecting to find Rebecca standing there but it was only the postman. He handed me the mail. 'Only two this morning, Herr Schreiber,' he said, giving me a rather ridiculous salute before heading up to the next landing. I put the unopened letters on the sideboard and went back to sit at the bedroom window. Where was she? If only I could find her and explain everything. Then, remembering the letter I sent to Dachau, I felt a sudden panic come over me. Even though I was sure it would not have arrived there yet, I could not help myself imagining the camp commandant looking at it with suspicion and comparing the signature with those on letters Günter had sent to him in the past. To put an end to my paranoid thinking, I decided to get ready for work. It was then I found the crucifix and a bottle of dark hair dye in the bathroom. The resurrection of Adele Hirsch was short-lived, and I had been foolish to think it could have been otherwise.

Günter was waiting in my office when I arrived. He had his feet up on the desk, admiring his highly polished boots.

'Late again, Schreiber … You're getting a bit of a reputation for being unpunctual.'

'I'm sorry. I have been working very hard recently.'

'Have you? Doing what, exactly?'

'There have been more and more files coming in from the regional stations and we've had to take over another room to accommodate the additional filing cabinets.'

'You do look exhausted. Are you sure it's not Adele keeping you up all night that's the problem?' he scoffed, getting to his feet. 'Anyway, the reason I wanted to speak to you this morning was to tell you I am going to Hamburg for a week. I promised Sophia I would honour her parents with a visit. Isn't it funny? When I first met Sophia, they would not even let me into their house. Now I honour them with my mere presence. How things have changed, Schreiber ... Don't look so serious. I am not going to ask you to drive me there. Like the Führer, I prefer the train for long journeys. You can drop me off at the station at two.'

In the afternoon, I drove Günter to the station, glad that I would be rid of him for a while. At first his mood was good, and he was singing Hitler's praises when an elderly man walked out in front of the car causing me to brake hard. I apologised to Günter, who was thrown forward abruptly. Günter vented his anger at the old man, who he decided was Jewish and should be in Dachau. I drove on, watching Günter seething in the back seat as he began a tirade about the number of Jewish women who had been writing to him pleading for the release of their husbands from 'Protective Custody'.

He eventually calmed down when we reached the station.

'I will be back on Monday afternoon,' he said, as he got out of the car and handed his case to a porter, before turning back to speak to me. 'Schreiber, get this car cleaned, it's a disgrace,' he demanded, before marching off to the stairs leading to the platform. I watched him go with relief. He had become such an arrogant bastard I pitied Sophia's parents having to endure him for a whole week.

While he was gone I decided to search for Rebecca in

Scheunenviertel. It was the only part of the city I could think of where she might take refuge. It was dark when I took the tram to the terminal in Alexanderplatz, removing my armband before walking the rest of the way.

The Jewish neighbourhood that was once so vibrant was now moribund, with shops boarded up and people too afraid to even look at strangers in the street. I passed Herr Kaufmann's jeweller's which was closed and had an official notice on the door offering the business for sale to Aryans only. Under the notice someone had drawn a caricature of a Jew with a noose around his neck. The marketplace was virtually deserted, and the few people that were there scurried into the shadows before I got anywhere near them to ask about Rebecca. I then reached the place where a Jewish restaurant once stood. It was now a waste ground of rubble and broken glass. I saw what looked like a wallet lying in nearby and I picked it up. It was not a wallet, but a kippah, not unlike the one I wore to Rebecca's wedding. I put it on a nearby railing in case someone came back looking for it.

Turning up my collar, I walked across the road to a tenement block which looked as good as any place to start my search. Unlike some blocks, it had at least some windows with light in them. I soon found out why so many apartments in the area were in darkness, the first one I went to was unoccupied, the door lying open and the inside ransacked. Of the few Jewish people still living there, few opened their door to me, some, who did, closed it back in my face as soon as they saw I was a stranger. Those who were willing to speak to me claimed they had no idea who I was talking about.

By the time I had reached the end of the first street I was no nearer finding Rebecca than I was when I started. Undeterred, I went to the next corner and began knocking on more doors.

It was after midnight, with my hands bruised and my

whole body numb with the cold, that I returned home. Miserable beyond words, I sat in the dark and waited for the morning. I was over an hour late for work, but thankfully Günter was in Hamburg and Heydrich was in Berchtesgarden at a meeting with Hitler and Himmler. No one else took any notice if I was in my office or not.

The following night I continued to look for Rebecca, going deeper into the Jewish neighbourhood until I was lost in the maze of narrow streets and dilapidated buildings. Once again, very few were willing to speak to me. Most just hid behind their doors and waited for me to leave. I began to lose hope of ever finding her.

Then one evening, with little expectation I entered a tenement block that looked like any other in the Scheunenviertel. After having no response from the apartments on the lower floors, I made my way despondently to the top landing. One of the front doors was lying slightly ajar and I assumed it was just another abandoned apartment. I pushed the door open and made myself known. I quickly realised it was not abandoned when I saw a flicker of light coming from under one of the doors further down the hall. I called out again, but there was still no answer. Curious, I edged my way towards the door. It suddenly opened and a young woman holding a child confronted me. 'What are you doing in here? You have no right … '

'I'm sorry, the door was lying open.'

'That doesn't give you the right just to come into my home. Who are you and what do you want?'

'My name is Franz Schreiber. I am looking for someone. I'll leave you in peace,' I said, doffing my hat by way of an apology as I turned to leave.

'Are you the man who has been looking for Doctor Cohen?'

The question made me turn instantly. 'Yes.'

'Are you a policeman?'

'No, I am a friend.'

'Why are you looking for her?'

'Do you know where she might be?'

'If you answer my question first, maybe I will tell you.'

'I want to help her get out of the country.'

The child in her arms began to cry and she hushed her as she studied me, clearly not sure if she could trust me or not. She then turned and went back into the room she had come from. I could hear her speaking to the child before she came back into the hall. 'She is hungry,' she said, 'but I have nothing to give her.'

'I have money, I can give you money for food,' I said, taking my wallet from my coat pocket.

'I cannot take your money. I will only tell you where you can find Frau Cohen if I am satisfied you do not mean to harm her.'

'I promise. I only wish to help her.'

'I have a little tea left, will you join me?' she asked, indicating towards the kitchen. I put my wallet away and followed her into the kitchen. 'There is no milk or sugar. Can you take it black?'

'Yes. Do you mind if I smoke?'

'No, go ahead. My husband smokes.'

'Where is your husband?'

She turned to me. 'I thought it was only the doctor you were looking for? Why do you want to know where my husband is?'

'I don't, I was just making conversation, that's all. Forgive me for prying. It's none of my business.'

'He has gone to his sister's house to see if they have any food they can spare. Her husband is not Jewish and has work.'

I was about to offer her the money again but decided to say nothing in case I offended her. She poured the tea, her dark, searching eyes still wary of me.

'How do you know Doctor Cohen?'

'I worked in her father's shop.'

'You worked for Herr Kolinski … the tailor?'

'Yes, he was like a father to me. He was deported back to Poland.'

'Maybe for the best,' she said. 'Life is becoming unbearable here. There is no work, no food, nothing if you're Jewish.' She then stopped speaking and sipped her tea. Maybe she thought she had said too much.

'It can't last forever. The people will soon turn against the Nazis.'

'Do you think so?'

'I'm sure.'

My answers must have satisfied her suspicions and we were soon having a conversation about the old marketplace and how it was once the hub of Scheunenviertel. 'Yes, you're right,' she smiled. 'If the synagogues are the souls, then the markets are the beating hearts of Jewish life. Without them we have nothing.'

'It's not right what's happening,' I said, stubbing out my cigarette. 'At least the synagogue on Oranienburgerstrasse is still there.'

'Yes, thank God … You look tired and don't look like you have been sleeping very well,' she said, with a hint of sympathy in her voice. 'You must love her very much to be looking for her night after night in this freezing weather.'

I did not answer and turned to light another cigarette to avoid her gaze.

'People are afraid,' she continued, 'they fear everything and trust no one these days. That is why no one has been willing to help you, they don't trust you. You look like a policeman.'

'I'm not, I promise you.'

'I know, I can see it in your eyes that you mean to do her no harm … You will find Doctor Cohen in the Jewish

Hospital; she works there every morning in the children's ward.'

'Thank you, thank you,' I said, getting to my feet, and shaking her hand.

'I only hope and pray you can help her.'

I thanked her again, forcing twenty marks into her hand and insisting it was for the baby. She said something to me in Yiddish, whaever it was I was sure it was not a curse. Once in the street I hurried back towards the main road and took the tram home. With the expectation of seeing Rebecca in the morning, I lay awake for most of the night, my exhaustion kept at bay by the feeling of redemption that overwhelmed me.

The hospital was strangely quiet when I got there the next morning. There was only one young woman sitting behind the reception desk. I gave my details and told her I was there to see Doctor Cohen on a personal matter.

'Take a seat for a moment, Herr Schreiber. I will see if she is on duty.'

I was too nervous to sit, and paced the waiting area, trying to formulate what I was going to say to Rebecca that would make sense.

The receptionist returned a few minutes later. 'I'm afraid Doctor Cohen is too busy to see you.'

'Tell her it's important … I must speak to her.'

'I've told you she is too busy. You should come back another time.'

'Which ward is she in? I must see her,' I insisted.

'She doesn't want to see you,' interrupted a nurse who came into the foyer with a porter by her side. 'I will have to ask you to leave,' she continued, while deliberately barring my way into the corridor leading to the children's wards.

'Okay, can you at least give her these?' I pleaded; taking out a folder of documents from my briefcase that Rebecca and Benjamin would need to get out of the country, including his passport and visas. 'I will leave if you promise to give her these.'

After some hesitation the nurse came forward and took the envelopes from my hands. She then stood and waited until I left the building.

There was a flurry of snow as I walked back through the hospital grounds, not sure how I now felt. Before I reached the gate, I saw two men walking slowly towards me. One was clearly supporting the other, who was very frail although he looked the much younger of the two men. I then realised the frail man was Benjamin. As he passed, he smiled and wished me a good morning. I responded in kind and tipped my hat to him. He walked on with the slow painful walk of a man who had endured great pain. I continued down to the main road without looking back.

I eventually found out from the shipping records in the office, that Rebecca and Benjamin sailed to England within a week of my visit to the hospital.

Life for me returned to some kind of normality, but I found it hard to come home at night to an empty apartment. When I was looking for Rebecca, I had a purpose; now that was gone, I had nothing. I began drinking in the bars around the red-light area, coming home drunk and alone. Rebecca had only shared my apartment for a short time, but it had become unbearable to be there without her. I knew, as I had before, I'd get over her in time, but that did not make my longing for her any less painful.

Then, another one of those days that scars the mind forever arrived. It was a few days before Christmas. I was helping the secretaries put up the decorations around the office. 'That looks good,' I said, holding the ladders straight as one of the secretaries stretched to pin a paper-chain above the window.

'No, I think it needs some tinsel,' she insisted, turning to take what she wanted from the box of decorations I was holding up to her.

'What's wrong?' I asked when she ignored the box and stared straight past me. I put the decorations down and turned to see Günter, flanked by two of his men, coming towards me with a tearful Nina following in their wake. Everyone in the office stopped what they were doing.

'Schreiber, what's the meaning of this!' he shouted, producing the letter that I had sent to Dachau. Before I could think of anything to say he struck me hard across the face. The blow stunned me, but I managed to keep my feet. I wiped the blood from the side of my mouth with the back of my hand. He stared at me, his face contorted with anger. 'Why did you send this letter to get this Jew released,' he continued, with his voice shrill with rage.

'His name is Benjamin Cohen.'

'I know his name, damn you, Schreiber ... I want to know why you had Nina type this letter without my authority!'

'You wouldn't understand, Günter. Where they burn books, they will soon burn people ...'

'What the hell are you talking about? Have you gone mad?'

'No, I am perfectly sane.'

'After all I did for you, Schreiber ... You betray me like this ... You will pay for this ... Get him out of my sight before I have him shot!'

A few days later my fate was sealed when the Gestapo searched my apartment and found the notebooks containing the names and details of all those killed while in 'protective custody'. The next day I boarded a train bound for Dachau, handcuffed to two Gestapo officers.

Postscript

Herr Kolinski and Hannah were sent to the Warsaw ghetto soon after the fall of Poland in 1939. Within the year, Hannah Levi died there of typhoid fever. Following the Warsaw uprising, Herr Kolinski was deported to Treblinka concentration camp where he was gassed and cremated as part of Hitler's final solution.

At the outset of war, Georgi Metrov was arrested for being a homosexual, and was interned at the Buchenwald concentration camp near Weimar, where he was used as forced labour in the nearby armaments factory. He is believed to have died of exhaustion and malnutrition.

Günter Schwartz was captured during the Wehrmacht's retreat from Poland and imprisoned until his trial at the Polish War Crimes Tribunal in Krakow. He was convicted of crimes against humanity, including murder, rape and torture during his time as SS Commander of an Einsatzgruppen that committed countless atrocities on the civilian population of Eastern Europe. His sadistic cruelty earned him the title of Schwartz Herz. He was hanged in 1947.

Franz Schreiber spent two years in Dachau prison before being transferred to a new camp near to what was once the Polish-German border. There he worked as a clerk for the Commandant, which undoubtedly prolonged his life. During this time, he secretly wrote his story in ten notebooks, which were discovered underneath the floorboards of one of the barracks shortly after the camp's liberation by Russian troops. Eyewitness accounts confirmed that Franz Schreiber did not survive captivity and died of typhus in 1942. He is believed to be buried in a mass grave in the forest next to the concentration camp. It was only after the fall of the Soviet Union that the notebooks were rediscovered in the Kremlin's war archives.

Benjamin and Rebecca Cohen spent the war as refugees in England. They moved to Palestine in 1948, only weeks before the creation of the state of Israel. Benjamin later served as a member of the Knesset. He died in 1991. Rebecca dedicated her life to medicine and survived her husband by five years. They left three children and twelve grandchildren. Their eldest son and eldest grandson were both given the middle name of Franz.

Some other books from Ringwood Publishing

Titles are available from the Ringwood website (including first-edition signed copies) and from usual outlets.
e-book also available in Kindle.

www.ringwoodpublishing.com

mail@ringwoodpublishing.com

Dark Loch
Charles P Sharkey

Dark Loch is an epic tale of the effects of the First World War on the lives of the residents of a small Scottish rural community. A crucial central strand is the long-running romance between tenant crofter Callum Macnair and Caitriona Dunbar, the beautiful daughter of the local Laird.

The story is initially set in the fictional village of Glenfay on the banks of Loch Fay on the west coast of Scotland. The main characters are the tenant crofters who work the land leased to them by the laird, Lord Charles Dunbar, and his family. The crofters live a harsh existence in harmony with the land and the changing seasons, unaware of the devastating war that is soon to engulf the continent of Europe.

The book vividly and dramatically explores the impact of that war on all the main characters and how their lives are drastically altered forever

ISBN: 978-1-901514-14-8   £9.99

The Volunteer

Charles P Sharkey

The Volunteer is a powerful and thought-provoking examination of the Troubles that plagued Northern Ireland for almost three decades. It follows the struggles of two Belfast families from opposite sides of the sectarian divide.

This revealing novel will lead the reader to a greater understanding of the events that led from the Civil Rights marches in the late Sixties, through the years of unbridled violence that followed, until the Good Friday Agreement of the late Nineties.

ISBN: 9781901514360   £9.99

Torn Edges

Brian McHugh

When a gold coin very similar to a family heirloom is found at the scene of a Glasgow murder, a search is begun that takes the McKenna family, assisted by their Librarian friend Liam, through their own family history right back to the tumultuous days of the Irish Civil War.

Parallel to this unravelling of the family involvement of this period, Torn Edges author Brian McHugh has interwoven the remarkable story of the actual participation of two of the McKenna family, Charlie and Pat, across both sides of the conflict in the desperate days of 1922 Ireland.

Torn Edges is both entertaining and well-written, and will be of considerable interest to all in both Scottish and Irish communities.

ISBN: 978-1-901514-05-6   £9.99

Between Two Bridges

Brian McHugh

In New York, 1933, Prohibition is coming to an end, but not everyone is celebrating. A few astute businessmen realise that by legally importing liquor before the Volstead Act is repealed, they can net themselves a small fortune. Charlie McKenna, an Irishman who spent time in Glasgow during the Great War, is sent to complete the deal with Denholm Distillers in their St Enoch Square office.

Fast-forward to present-day Glasgow. Still reeling from the murder of their friend, three old friends are once again knocked off-course by the resurfacing of a battered diary. It soon leads them back into their investigation of Julie's grandfather, Charlie McKenna. More troubling tales of war, gold and gangsters soon begin to surface.

Between Two Bridges is a fast-paced adventure with a well-researched historical setting.

ISBN: 978-1-901514-35-3   £9.99

A Gordon For Me

Brian Roberstson

An honest and brave account of National Service in the 1950s. Brian Robertson spares no detail in his story, from simple farmer's son to a Gordon Highlander.

A Gordon For Me is an entertaining and compelling story of one man's experiences of the Armed Forces.

ISBN: 978-1-901514-46-9
£9.99